HIGHEST POINT

HIGHEST POINT

KELS & DENISE STONE

BETWEEN THE SHEETS
PUBLISHING

Published by Between the Sheets Publishing

kelsdenisestone.com

Paperback ISBN: 978-1-964675-06-0

eBook ISBN: 978-1-964675-14-5

Highest Point

Editing & Proofreading:

Caroline Acebo at Brass House LLC

Caroline Knecht

Christine Yates

Cover Design: Chloe Friedlein

For the wild ones who remembered to come home.

Prologue
Alec

I BELONG where the air is thin enough to kill you. One in four die on this mountain, but I climb anyway, because up here in the death zone—where no human should survive—I feel alive.

Finn and I straddle the crown of K2, boots biting into ice that looks more like glass than earth.

"We did it, Alec." His hug knocks what little oxygen I've got left out of my chest. His mask fogs between us, his voice breaking through the hiss of tanks. "Look at us, high enough to touch the stars."

From his jacket, he pulls out a battered Toblerone. A tradition we started at nineteen on the summit of Denali, half-starved and giddy with frostbite. Chocolate is the only thing we can choke down in the altitude of the death zone. The bar's frozen solid, a brick of sugar and ice. Finn smashes it against his axe until a shard snaps off, and he presses it into my glove.

"To the last eight-thousander," I rasp, my mask hanging loose, lips numb.

"The last one."

We gnaw the frozen Toblerone, watching the planet curve

beneath us. The Karakoram Range stretches endlessly between Pakistan and China.

"We need to move," Nadra calls, crouched low against the wind, camera lens trained on Finn. Even now, half dead at 28,000 feet, our cameraman works the shot.

Finn bares his teeth in a grin, lips cracked and bloody, skin raw from the cold. He looks straight into the camera. "Two Men On Top fucking did it," he says, voice shredded by the wind. "Fourteen eight-thousanders. Fourteen of the nastiest sons of bitches in the world. And we finish on K2." He leans into the lens like he's on a talk show instead of standing on the second-highest point on earth.

We've been doing stupid shit together since we were five and jumping off garage roofs with my mom's silk sheets tied to our backs. When we were sixteen, we got our driver's licenses and celebrated by summiting Mount Shasta. At the top, we made a pact. We'd climb the world's fourteen highest mountains, the ones over 8,000 meters. All or nothing. For sixteen years, we've been chasing summits like addicts. Peaks that strip the flesh from your bones, where blood thickens, thoughts slow, and oxygen vanishes. There were failures that hollowed us out, silences that nearly broke us. Still we climbed. Fourteen mountains that reached higher than the gods, and somehow both of us lived to see K2, the monster we swore to finish or die trying.

And we've filmed every climb along the way.

Behind Nadra, the daylight flickers, like it knows it's running out of time.

My watch buzzes—a brutal reminder that the mountain doesn't give a damn about our victory lap. Numbers crawl across the screen, cold facts cutting through the euphoria.

Storm wall ETA: 6h 42m.

Hours awake: 58.

Wind chill: −33°F.

We have to get down to Base Camp Four before night falls and the storm rolls in.

"Wrap it up," I tell Finn. He nods, never missing a beat.

"Huge thanks to our sponsors at The North Face," he says into the lens. "These jackets kept us alive, even when *somebody* stole my sleeping bag." He jerks a thumb at me. I elbow him, not softly. "Anything you want to add, big man?"

"First team to scale the North Face of K2. Couldn't have done it without him." My mouth stretches into a bloody smile.

"That's all, folks!" Finn shouts, and Nadra's already packing up, ropes out, trailing the Sherpas down the safer line.

I allow myself one heartbeat—just one—to turn and look out at the valley below.

There's no sound up here, not really. No birdsong. No engines. No people. Just the hiss of the wind, like the white noise between movements of a Beethoven symphony. My lungs try to catch air that doesn't want to be caught, each breath more borrowed than earned. The sky above is a cathedral, endless and blue enough to hurt.

For a second, I forget I'm human. I forget the throbbing behind my eyes, the pins of altitude digging into my skull, and the exhaustion gnawing at every muscle. I forget that K2 could take me without hesitation, and it would be its right.

That is until my watch buzzes again, reminding me I still have to get to base camp.

We've been standing on the summit for five minutes and twenty-two seconds. That's a minute longer than we're allowed. I've been watching the barometer for days, studying the pressure. The jet stream shifted, cracked open this narrow window for us to summit, and I know it won't stay open long.

There's no getting greedy with K2.

I glance at our gauges. Both tanks quiver around 900 PSI. Enough oxygen to get us back to Base Camp Four if nothing goes wrong. Six hours, maybe more.

I run through the checklist in my head. Harnesses cinched. Anchors doubled. Fixed lines where I set them two days back, still holding. I kneel and tug Finn's left crampon strap one notch tighter.

One more descent.

"Come on," I huff, snapping my mask back into place and scraping the ice from my goggles.

Finn throws me a thumbs-up, shoulders his pack without a word, and heads for the ropes. I fall in behind him, crampons scraping against ice.

Time turns strange on descents. Almost liquid and elastic. You don't want to measure it, but you have to. Every step has its own clock, and every decision its own weight. The ridge is narrow but manageable.

An hour, maybe more, bleeds away before we reach the section that has haunted me for weeks. A five-hour descent over vertical terrain, loose snow, and too many places for the mountain to bite back. Above us, a serac the size of a semitruck looms, a frozen ceiling waiting to collapse. Below, a crevasse yawns open, a wound in the mountain deep enough to consume an entire city. There's no margin for error here. We have to be swift.

My axe buries itself into the frozen hide of the ice face. My body moves on muscle memory. Rappel. Anchor. Shift weight. I've done it a hundred times, *a thousand*. But every creak beneath me, every groan above me, sounds too close.

Two hours in. The wind howls at fifty knots now, and denial is a luxury we can't afford—the storm is early.

Snow slashes sideways, white knives in the dark. My world shrinks to the hiss of wind, the rope in front of me, and the only command that matters. *Don't be hasty.* I recite my family motto, the one I have inked into my skin.

The ground shakes; somewhere in the distance an avalanche roars. K2 is awake, but I'm not afraid. I glance sideways at Finn's shadow, his headlamp flickering along the ridge. We move in rhythm, each step a pact, each breath proof we're still alive.

Don't stop. Don't think. Just move.

I'm so cold, my skin has turned hot and itchy under my clothes. My fingers are wood, my lungs sandpaper. My muscles do the work, but my mind drifts, thin air gnawing holes in my thoughts. I've been dreaming about this day for nearly my entire life, but now that I'm here, clinging onto this wall, I'm wondering why the hell I left my tent this morning.

As if K2 senses my regret, she speaks. A low grumbling comes from under me, like the earth's bones are grinding together. My eyes snap up. But it's too late. There's nothing I can do, because the guillotine's already being released.

The serac tears loose, slides from the slope, and falls with a sound older than language.

Don't let go. Don't you dare let go.

My head whips to Finn. I shout—at least, I think I do—but the wind shreds it. The rope between us jerks. This can't be happening. I reach for it, but it's too late. I grit my teeth and watch as my best friend is ripped from the slope. One second flesh and blood, the next weightless, a scrap of dust flung into the storm.

"Finn!"

No, no, no.

Panic claws at my throat, and it's as if my entire body has been hollowed out, stripped into nothingness. I need to focus. If I don't, they'll find two bodies down there, or none at all. I slam my axe into the ice, anchoring until my arm rattles, and all I can do is shut my eyes and wait for the world to stop ending.

Time stretches until it's purgatory, hell, or just plain fear. Long enough to ask myself the question I swore I'd never ask: *Why the fuck did we ever come here?*

The blizzard assaults me, buries me, and eats the strength from my fingers. I shriek, slipping toward the crevasse, thighs screaming in pain as my crampons scrape for purchase along the slope.

I shouldn't have kept us up on the summit for that extra minute. It was my call to make. If we die today, it'll be my fucking fault.

I feel tiny, foolish, and achingly human.

I do the closest thing I've ever done to praying. Finally, air slashes my back, caressing my neck. A lull in the wind. I'm alive. But as soon as the relief washes over me, dread sets in.

Where is Finn?

I scramble sideways, boots skidding until I'm braced at the lip of the crevasse. "Finn!"

Nothing.

If the wind had pushed five more feet, I would've been—I don't finish the thought. Instead, I clench my jaw hard. *How far did he fall? Did he hit the bottom? Is he still breathing?*

Ice needles into my jacket.

I'm in control. I repeat it over and over. K2 seems to laugh at that. The storm rages harder now, like it's a living thing, howling, smothering, erasing him.

"Finn," I rasp again, throat raw, lungs burning acid. I fling my bag to the ice at my feet, clawing frantically for the excess rope. I only have one choice. I have to go get him.

I suck in one breath, shaking the panic out of my limbs. Fear is death on the ice. If Finn is alive down there, I cannot give up. I'd rather die right here than abandon my best friend.

I scream his name until my voice frays, until my mouth tastes of blood, but the mountain swallows it whole.

Chapter 1
Clementine

I was taught a lot of useful things in my life.

How to twist my hair into a bun so tight it could survive endless fouettés.

How to break in pointe shoes with a needle, an X-ACTO knife, and a tube of glue.

How to tell creditors *Mommy isn't home* in a voice so innocent it almost fooled me too.

And the most important lesson of all: one swipe of a credit card can sand down the edges of almost any disaster.

Today is a disaster.

The kind a normal person might call horrid, or appalling, or just plain bad. But normal people don't spend twenty years drilling their bodies into the shape of a machine. Normal people don't measure their worth by whether their name is bolded on a sheet of paper thumbtacked to a bulletin board at Lincoln Center.

The new season's cast list went up this morning.

I should have been promoted from soloist to principal. I've been waiting for it, training for it, starving for it. Instead, my name remained lost in the middle column, trapped with the workhorses.

Everyone else in Rose Hall was giddy about their promotions. I couldn't even fake a smile. My chest felt like someone had wound ribbons around my ribs and kept pulling.

So, I did what I always do when I can't breathe. I ran. Out of the theater, down the marble steps, straight through the revolving doors of Sephora. The air conditioning hit like salvation, freezing the shame still burning under my skin.

Stores do that. They can change the weather inside your body.

A perfume haze greets me first, sweet enough to smother bile. Foundation samples glitter under fluorescent lights. Paper bags crinkle with promise. There it is, a glittering eyeshadow palette, staring me down like it knows exactly what I came for.

This is the kind of sparkle a principal dancer deserves, it whispers. The kind of beautiful that makes you believe you're worth the price tag.

I run my pointer over the shimmering gold. For one suspended second, the world hushes, muffles as if I've slipped underwater. My pulse slows, and air floats into my lungs again.

"It's a beautiful color, isn't it?" The sales associate appears with a smile so wide it feels rehearsed. "I can make you a sample pot."

I don't need a sample. I know exactly what this eyeshadow will do. It'll fix the ache inside of me.

"I'll take it," I say.

"Would you like to try the new line of ethereal lip gloss?"

"Of course."

She floats around me, plucking items like petals from a stem. A blush to accentuate my cheekbones. Foot masks that promise to soothe my bunions and won't tell anyone that I've been shoving lamb's wool between my toes for ten years.

At the register, she folds each item into tissue paper, tucking my things into a chrysalis of happiness.

Perfume: $319. Eyeshadow palette: $95. Mascara set: $72. Lip gloss: $62. Foot masks: $35.

Total: $583.

I slide the good Visa into the reader—the Sephora card went to collections months ago— picturing myself in Act II of *Giselle*, lips lined with the most glowing pink money can buy.

Beep. Freeze. Flash red.

Declined.

That can't be right.

This card is new. I got it last month. *I think?*

I only put rent, a MetroCard refill, and new tights on it. I do the math in my head. Except math has never been my strong suit.

I swipe again. Maybe I didn't hold it right. Maybe I didn't breathe correctly. Maybe Mercury's in retrograde!

Declined.

"Would you like to try another card?" the salesgirl asks gently.

I laugh brittlely. "Yeah, the chip's just temperamental."

Out comes the other card. The one I swore I'd bury after the collectors started calling. The one I typically keep wedged in my nightstand between athletic tape and unopened envelopes screaming URGENT: PAST DUE.

Declined.

The reality I've been outrunning all day slams into me. My face goes hot and molten.

"Would you like to put these aside and come back—"

"No!" I jerk toward the lip gloss.

The salesgirl freezes, pity already softening her face. *Pity.*

"You don't understand," I blurt. "I've been with the New York City Ballet for eight years. Eight years of auditions, of understudying, of clapping for ovations that weren't mine. I missed birthdays. Summers. Bread." My throat cracks. "God, I miss bread."

A couple behind me stares. I'm unraveling, and all they can do is watch.

"I skipped my prom for a Bolshoi master class in some basement in Hell's Kitchen. Smiled through shin splints, sprained toes, critiques that gutted me. My ribs ache from compression tape, and my hip flexor clicks like a metronome gone rogue. And this was supposed to be my year. Clementine Lennox, Principal."

The associate tries again. "Ma'am—"

"*Ma'am?* Really? Has it come to that?" My laugh splinters into something manic. "Every single lead went to girls who aren't even twenty-one. Twenty-one! I'm twenty-four, which in ballet years is practically spoiled meat. I'm freezer burn with a bun."

I let the lip gloss tube slip from my hand, not bothering to catch it. It clanks pathetically, rolls along the glass counter, and she whisks it away with lips pressed tight.

"I know I can't afford the makeup. *I know.* But it's the only thing that is going to remind me that I still exist. Like if I put it on, maybe someone will look at me and think, *she matters.*"

The salesgirl doesn't blink, her mascara flawless.

"I'm sorry," she says, voice as flat as linoleum. "Store policy."

Security's walkie crackles. Behind me, the couple steps aside. And in that spotlight of rejection, I feel the last thread of my life snap clean through.

I need air.

I need to get out of here.

I sprint out of Sephora. The August heat slaps me across the face. The sidewalk tilts, then blurs. I haven't eaten since a protein bar at six a.m., and my legs wobble.

A storefront mirror snags me mid-flight. I look terrible. Leotard digging into my ribs. NYCB sweats half-slid off one hip, waistband twisted, drawstring dangling. One Croc strap snapped down, laddered tights flashing pale above it.

By the time I crash into the subway, my throat burns like I swallowed a glass of hot water and a pack of matches.

I can't go back to my apartment. Can't go back to the studio. Can't even go back inside my own head.

The air down here reeks of rat piss, brake dust, and wet heat. I press my spine against the filthy tile wall, wishing grout lines could make me disappear. My hands won't stop shaking. Sweat turns my leotard into shrink wrap.

I dig out my second phone, the cracked-screen burner only Gran, Mom, and a few others know about. The one creditors can't touch. My pulse stutters as I thumb open my banking app.

Wrong password.

Another wrong password.

It's been months since I last checked, because if you don't look at the damage, it's not real.

But finally, it loads.

Checking: -$172.

Savings: $0.03.

I swipe through the credit card apps. All five maxed. Late fees multiplying like fruit flies.

Broke would be a relief. Broke is solid ground.

I've slipped past broke and gone straight into free fall.

The tile scrapes my spine as I slide down it. The air won't stretch wide enough. I scroll through my contacts. Roommates who need rent from me, colleagues who just got promoted over me, and Mom, who taught me this self-destructive choreography.

No one can fix this.

My fingertip hovers over Gran. She's the only one who still believes I'm salvageable. For one blistering heartbeat, I consider deleting every banking app, smashing this phone, and vanishing between train tracks. But even escape costs money I don't have.

This is it.

I press call. The ring detonates everything I've been pirouetting toward.

"Clementine?" Gran's voice is warm as always. "Sweetheart? What's going on?"

"I didn't make princi—" The word sticks. "Gran, I didn't get it. It meant more money, enough to stop subletting a pantry in a five-girl crash pad. It meant first pick of roles, private coaching. It meant proof that years of sacrifice led somewhere."

"Oh, my darling girl. What can I do for you?"

"Can you buy me a flight home? I'm so sorry to ask, but I literally have negative dollars to my name."

"To California? To see your mom?"

"No," I whisper. "To you. To Alaska."

A pause, then her voice returns. "There's a seat on a red-eye tonight. Bring your coat. It's already getting cold at night."

"I'm a failure, Gran. I thought I could keep doing this," I choke out, "but I can't. I'm not okay. I'm not okay."

"Oh, honey," she says softly. "You don't have to be. Just get on the plane. I'll make up your old room; it's still just as you left it. I'll bring cocoa and a blanket for the drive. You're not alone, Clem. You hear me?"

I nod like she can see me, tears rolling down my cheeks.

And just like that, I know I have no choice.

I have to do this.

When I get home, I'll pack one suitcase with only the necessities. The rest, the barely worn heels, the hoarded costumes, the unused planners…I'll tell my roommates to sell them, ship them, burn them. I don't care.

For six years I've been whispering the same lie: This will be the season. I've been patient, longing, pouring another year into the hope that someday the cast list would cough up my name. People said it was a pipe dream to be a famous ballerina; I heard them and kept dancing anyway, naive and stubborn. No wonder half the dancers I know are broke and exhausted. The other half are sleeping on studio floors and pretending it's romantic.

My studio is filled with sixty other girls with rosary-thin

wrists and eyes that light up when someone says *maybe this season*. It never is.

Let them promote someone else. Let them find another dancer to bleed into her satin. It won't be me. At least, not this season.

When I land in Alaska, I'll figure out who I am when no one's clapping. When no one's waiting for me to dance myself into dust.

For once, I won't be living for applause.

I'll try living just for me.

Chapter 2
Alec

THE WINDOW finally gives beneath my knife, creaking open just enough to let in a whisper of air. For weeks I've been prying at the damn thing, trying to fight the hospital stench of bleach and recycled air. My lungs yearn for mountain wind, for anything that doesn't smell like disinfectant and stale coffee.

I press my forehead to the frame, close my eyes, and try to breathe.

"You look like shit," a voice wheezes out behind me.

The knife nearly slips from my hand. I spin, heart in my throat. The couch legs screech against the floor. There he is.

"You're awake," I blurt like an idiot.

"Unless I'm dead and this is Hell. In which case, man, you've really dropped the ball by not busting me out." Finn grins his usual crooked grin.

He has always tried to make the world lighter, even when it crushed us. He smiled with his skull cracked open on Denali. Made jokes about frostbite on Lhotse when we could smell the rot in his toes. Laughed when he woke up in Mercy General two weeks ago.

But now that lightness sits wrong, stretched over a pale body wired up with IVs and clamped together with steel.

"I'll get the nurse," I manage.

"No need. They've got me on the good stuff today." He wiggles his taped-up fingers like a magician revealing a trick everyone's seen before. Except this one is morphine.

Thirty years of friendship, and the bastard is still the clown. Stoned, stitched together with screws, lying in a hospital bed, and somehow acting like he just scored front-row seats to the Oakland street fair dunk tank.

I drop into the chair beside him. My skin feels too tight. I wish I could unzip myself and crawl elsewhere.

"Cut it out," he says.

"What?"

"Looking at me like that." He rolls his deep-brown eyes. "They put two more screws in my hip. I'm practically bionic. The next Tin Man. Cheer up."

K2 didn't just break Finn, it obliterated him. His right hip and femur were shattered, bones splintered, the joint crushed, nerves so fucked he still can't feel his leg. The first surgery was just to stop the internal bleeding, save his frostbitten toes, and make sure his body didn't shut down. The second was to bolt him back together.

And it's still not over. In two weeks, they'll cut him open again to rebuild the hip. Only then can he start physical therapy. The doctors warned me—best case, he won't walk for two, maybe three months.

It'll be another month until he's out of the hospital, and then he'll be stuck with a full-time physical therapist. I've already started hunting for the best one I can find. But the truth sits heavy: No one knows when he'll set foot on the ice again. Or if he'll even want to.

"Cheer up?" I echo flatly.

"Yes," he shoots back, his tone sharp despite the haze of drugs. "You're depressing me."

"I thought the Tin Man didn't have feelings."

"There he is." He swats at my shoulder but misses by inches. "My favorite asshole."

I panic, leaning over to push him back before he tears something. He half wrestles me off. Two idiots slap-fighting in a hospital bed. He laughs. And the sound rips me apart. Because it doesn't lift me. Doesn't make me lighter.

"Didn't think I'd get to hear you laugh again," I mutter.

"Oh Christ, not this again." He pushes past the haze for one sharp second and pins me with that look. "I'll say it one more time, and then I never want to hear it again: I chose to climb K2."

He's said that since the evac, since that first night in this ward when the doctors promised he'd make it till morning. But it doesn't land. It can't.

Because I picked the route. I called the weather window. I was the one who took an extra minute at the top. I was supposed to take care of him, the way I always have.

"You don't have to keep feeling guilty—"

"Don't," I cut him off. I can't listen to him forgive me again, like it's that simple.

We sit with only the squeak of the frame clamped around his leg and the steady beeping of the machines between us.

"I'm serious." He waves the TV remote at me. "If you're going to sit here, you can't keep punishing yourself. It's annoying."

I huff out something between a laugh and a *fuck off*, because my guilt doesn't take orders.

"You're right, we don't need to keep talking about it."

"No, man, we fucking do," Finn snaps. "Every other day, apparently, because you're still wearing that tragic boo-hoo face. And you haven't shaved since I got admitted."

I swipe a hand down my beard, which is rough and uneven. "It's not that bad."

"It's gettin' biblical, Alec. Go home. See your parents. Take a real shower. Stop cramping my style with the nurses." He gestures at the couch I've carved a permanent crater into. His usual tan skin looks wrong, his eyes hollow in a way no mountain night ever made them.

He thinks he's here because it was his fate. I know better.

"I'm not leaving you," I say.

I'll never make him understand that I can't shave, can't shower, can't go home until I make this right.

"Then at least take a walk," Finn says, lips slack with morphine. "Put a sock on the door so Nurse Fiona can sneak back in and give me a sponge bath."

"You're disgusting."

"You're jealous." He shifts, groans, then recovers like it's part of the bit. "But maybe I should save my energy for the lady I'm gonna meet in Misthaven."

"Misthaven?"

He blinks like I've sprouted a second head. "Alaska, genius. Don't tell me you forgot everything we swore? We did it. Every fucking peak crossed off our list. We said we'd retire. You said it." His voice drops, serious now. "You and me, growing old in Alaska. End of an era."

You said it.

He thinks that matters.

"We did say that," I mutter, but it tastes like blood in my mouth.

Finn leans forward, IV line tugging. "We didn't just say it. You promised it. You looked me in the eye and said, *No more after this*. You wouldn't make me step foot on another mountain. You said we'd be the lucky bastards who lived."

I would've said anything on K2.

When I lost him in the whiteout, I would've promised God and the Devil both that I'd quit climbing, quit breathing, if only Finn came back.

I spent hours digging. First with a shovel that clinked with every strike, then with my own hands when the metal gave out. My gloves froze stiff, my nails split bloody, and still I clawed. I wouldn't call for a retrieval team; the Sherpas risk their lives every day, and I couldn't bear it if someone died in the storm because of us.

The night sky was collapsing faster than I could move, and when I found him with blue lips, skin the color of ash, half a body already smothered by the mountain, I thought it was over. I thought he was gone.

"That lodge was never a joke, Alec," he presses, leaning back on his pillow. "Did you think I was just fucking around talking about that place at every base camp? I can picture it, man. Long dining room table, a deck to grill on, a fireplace with a bookcase next to it filled with adventure novels. We'll have kids and dogs running across the floorboards. A wife for each of us. A home. Not a tent flapping on some death ridge. Don't tell me you didn't mean it."

His conviction is ridiculous. As if he isn't thirty-two with a hip full of screws, alarms flashing every time his heart rate spikes. But his eyes burn like a summit flare. Hope, alive where it shouldn't be.

"Doubt that place is even standing anymore," I say.

"It is. Margaret Lennox has been looking after it—Bill's wife, you remember. The muffins?" His face softens. "She's kept it going since he passed."

We bought the lodge with our first sponsorship check, drunk on altitude and money after Denali. Finn always said it would be our last stop. A base camp that never moves.

I never paid much attention to that daydream.

We're climbers, not homemakers.

"You really think we're just going to…settle? Fix up an abandoned lodge in the Last Frontier and call that living?"

"Hell yes. That's exactly what I think. We beat the mountains, Alec. You don't get greedy after that. You retire."

Retirement. He says it like it's salvation. Like he hasn't been cut out of the only life we've ever known.

I picture the place, roof probably torn by Alaskan winters, boards warped by rain, windows cracked. And Finn, who won't be lifting a hammer anytime soon. Who may never climb a ladder again.

The thought makes my skin itch. A quiet life in a rotting house. No peaks. No summit fever. No air thinned to glass.

Just a normal life?

But he's watching me, waiting for me to keep my word. And maybe if I get there first, make it whole, safe in a way K2 never was, maybe he won't see me and remember that day.

He lifts his brows. "When have I steered us wrong?"

"Last thing those floors need is your wheels gouging them up," I mutter.

"You're a control freak."

Not enough of one. Not when it mattered.

"Maybe I just know you," I say. "You've never been handy. I've been pitching our tents since we were ten."

He laughs, then winces, metal groaning inside him.

"I'll go up there," I force out. "Get it started."

His eyes widen. "You mean it?"

"What? Now you don't want me gone?"

"By all means. I'd rather not stare at your scraggly mug every day. But..." He swallows, voice softer now. "Don't break this promise, Alec. Don't make me the only one still believing."

So I make the vow, hollow as it feels. I'll put the lodge back together, board by board. Give him the home he dreamed of. A base camp that never moves.

Because I couldn't keep him safe.

But I can do this.

And maybe when it's finished, I'll tell him the truth.

Retirement isn't for me.

Chapter 3
Alec

I'D FORGOTTEN how beautiful Alaska is. I drive the last five hours with the window down, breathing in spruce and the sharp, clean air I can't get in the city. The mountains press close, green valleys and turquoise lakes stretching for miles. Eagles fly overhead, and more than once I spot caribou blurring past my truck windows.

Finally, I pull onto Main Street. Misthaven is louder than I remember, nestled in a valley, surrounded on all sides by the Euspuko Range. The town only has one street—maybe two if I'm being generous—but that one street is crowded, bikes and strollers weaving between café tables, laughter carrying too far. A kid runs past with a balloon tied to his wrist, holding a half-eaten donut the size of his head. Outside Daisy's Diner, an old man in suspenders argues with a teenager about kayak rentals.

Finn loved this place. Blueberry donuts from Yessi's. Jerky from Brown Bear Bags. Waving at strangers until they waved back. He treated towns like collectibles, like each one had to be pocketed and kept.

I keep my hands on the wheel. Heads turn as I roll through in my truck, each one cataloging the outsider.

The houses and cabins branch off from town like ribs from a spine. The five thousand people here all know each other by name or by car.

Ten minutes later, the noise thins, replaced by the fog curling off the lake and the crunch of dirt under my tires. The white-pine lodge finally comes into view after three days of driving from San Francisco. I ease the truck down the dirt road, and a moose standing near the edge of the clearing snorts, raising its head before lumbering off into the trees.

What the hell were we thinking?

The place is massive. Fifteen bedrooms spread out over two stories. The logs are thick and weathered, stretching the width of a football field. It's bigger than I remember, but it's not in terrible shape. The slated roof still holds, though the edges slump in a few spots. The windows could use a wash, and the burgundy trim needs to be retouched. Fresh mulch darkens the flower beds out front, likely Margaret's handiwork. Fireweed blooms tall in the ditch, purple against green. It's almost welcoming, which somehow feels worse.

Behind the lodge is Misthaven Lake. I can almost hear Finn's laughter as he'd plunge into the icy water after our runs. *Will he ever be able to do that again?* At the thought, I bite the inside of my cheek until the tinge of iron fills my mouth.

I sit in the truck longer than I should. There's no way Finn will need all this space. We've always lived out of tents, or backpacks, or any temporary walls we could find. Part of me wants to pitch a tent by the water for the next month while I wait for him to get here and pretend this is just another base camp. Pretend Finn's still climbing behind me.

Lucky for me, I don't have time to waste. The less free time I have, the less time I'll spend reliving the past…or contemplating the future.

I pull out my notebook and start a list.

- *Replace roof*
- *Repaint exterior*
- *Add a wheelchair ramp*

I walk around the back of Finn's Lodge, and in a matter of minutes, the list has quadrupled. I may have underestimated how much work it will take to make this place livable. Not that it matters. I'm not sleeping anyway. Not with the nightmares keeping me company throughout the night.

When I reach the front of the property, a bush by the front-porch steps rustles—whatever it is, it's too big to be a rabbit. I freeze, pulse kicking. I left my damn bear spray in the back of my truck. Day one, and I'm already unprepared.

I slowly back away, not wanting to spook the beast, when a twig snaps under my foot. Immediately, orange hair pops up from the shrubs. Not fur. *Hair.*

A woman straightens, knees scuffed in overalls, one hand still gripping the handle of a tipped-over soil bag. She drops her trowel, grabs the full-length shovel like a sword, and swings it toward me. Stray copper wisps the color of a blood-orange sunset catch the light, wild against the knot of her bun.

"You're not a bear," I blurt.

"And you still couldn't take me if I was!" Her large, expressive blue eyes stare at me, unblinking. Even when dirt crumbles off her blade, those eyes—a color only found on top of glaciers—never leave me. They're too large, too sharp, too expressive. They stream over me, measuring my height, weight, and intent. When they land back on my face, she looks unimpressed.

I clear my throat, wishing for a moment that she was a bear. I don't have the energy to deal with people, especially one so… peculiar. "I'm not here to take you. I just thought I heard one."

"Uh-huh." She scrunches up her nose, waving the shovel around like a wand. "That explains why you look like you're about to wet yourself. Do you always greet women by confusing them with local wildlife, or am I just lucky?"

She looks absurd. And distractingly not absurd. A mix between a garden nymph and a scorned deity. Her face is round, with a soft chin and a button nose, but her limbs are angular and lean.

"Who are you, and what are you doing here?"

She steps forward in her pink flats, the shovel inches from my face. "What are *you* doing here?"

"I asked first."

"I'm looking after the plants. Obviously. This lodge used to belong to me, which means I've got every right to be here."

There's no way she's Margaret Lennox. The age doesn't add up. She looks nearly my sister Frankie's age. Early twenties at most. But maybe I'm misremembering Bill's wife. Or maybe grief does strange things to faces. *Hell, I don't know.* Has to be her.

"You must be Margaret."

The gasp she lets out scares the birds from the canopy above. They flitter around us, and I wish I could take off with them. She lowers the shovel, her gloved hand flying over her glossy lips, smearing dirt across the freckles that line her nose and cheeks. "Excuse me? Did you just say I look eighty-seven?"

"What?"

"I know I may not be at my best right now, all right? I'm a bit out of my element. But I'm twenty-four. Sure, in New York I'm washed up, retired, whatever you want to call it. But here?" She fixes the thin tank top strap on her shoulders and stands an inch straighter. Her posture is impeccable. "I'm a Misthaven ten."

So, she's a city girl? I guess that explains why she's wearing flats and makeup in the garden. I stare at her, too sleep-deprived to even wrap my head around what a Misthaven ten is.

"No, you're not—" I start.

She actually staggers back, one hand to her chest. "That's so rude! Do you make a habit of insulting women you've just met? Guessing ages and—and handing out scores?"

"I didn't guess anything," I growl. "You're obviously—look, I just—" My jaw clicks. Heat creeps up my neck. "Forget it. I own this lodge, and you're the one trespassing."

At that, the shovel clunks to the ground, and her face splits into a smile. Her lips are glossed, her cupid's bow prominent. She smiles like it's her job, like she's practiced this exact smile for cameras. And I don't hate it.

"Oh! Wait, you're Alec Hastings?" She says my name like it's a headline. It's my first time out of the hospital since Finn's accident, and the fucking reporters have already found me.

"If you're here sniffing around for a story, I'm not giving interviews about what happened on K2. Said it a thousand times. Don't care if you're those fuckers from the *Stone Times*, the *Post*, or some blog with a goat in the logo. Not happening." I don't budge from my spot. She's the one who needs to leave.

"Has anyone ever told you you're terrible at first impressions?"

"No," I lie.

"Thought so." She whips around, seemingly over this conversation. "Well, if you don't mind, I just need to finish up here, and then I'll be out of your hair." She grabs the shovel off the ground and jams it into the soil bag. She's not a reporter. Maybe that means she doesn't know my family either.

But it still doesn't explain why the hell she's at Finn's Lodge.

"Then who are you?"

"Oh, now you want to ask questions before making assumptions?" She looks back at me, quirking one of her brows. I don't respond, don't know how. Her entire body deflates in a sigh as she stands back up. "Clementine Lennox. Gran told me you may be moving in."

Did her parents pick her name after seeing that impossibly orange hair, or does fate just have a twisted sense of humor?

She wipes her palms down her overalls, leaving streaks of dirt, and sticks one out. Her fingernails are pink and delicate. I stare at them awkwardly until she lets her hand drop back to her side. Her ears wiggle, just a bit, but recognition sparks within me.

Bill's granddaughter. The tutu stories. The photo in his wallet. That little ballerina can't possibly be this sharp-eyed fox with dirt on her face.

Except she isn't little anymore. She's tall, close to five-nine, with long, slender limbs. Her skin looks soft, though the dark circles under her eyes seem to match mine.

She's nearly eight years younger than me, which is reason enough to stop looking at her. Let alone the fact that I have a list of shit that needed to get done as soon as yesterday.

"Well, you don't need to stop by anymore," I say. "Tell your grandmother the same. I'll be looking after the place from now on."

"If you think you're going to tell my grandmother what to do, I'd pay to watch that crash and burn." She snorts, actually snorts, and I hate that it makes something in my chest twitch.

"I don't need anyone fussing over this place," I snap.

"Clearly." She waves at the peeling paint on the window frames. "Relax, Paul Bunyan. I didn't come here for you." She nods at the flowerpots lined up at the bottom of the steps. "Gran wants these filled with soil and cabbage seeds before breakfast. I'll be out of your hair in a few minutes."

"Cabbage?"

"*Ornamental* cabbage," she corrects, drawing out each syllable. "You know, pretty leaves? Porch décor? Or is that not the aesthetic you're going for?"

I don't answer fast enough. She jerks a bag of soil, and dirt sprays across the steps, my jeans, and my boots.

"Thanks for that," I deadpan. "Now I look like I belong here."

"You're welcome." Her smile is too bright to be kind. She's almost eye level with me, and for some reason that feels more intimate than if she were taller or shorter.

"I told you," I grind out, "I don't need help."

"And I told *you*," she shoots back, "I'm not here to help you."

She rips open the last bag of soil, muscles straining, and upends it into the flowerpot. The dirt erupts across the porch, clouds puffing into the air, grit coating my boots. She doesn't even pause. With one hand, she's already scattering seeds, tossing them in wild, uneven arcs that pepper the soil, the steps, and the boards. Some bounce off my shirt. She moves fast, recklessly, like she's in some speed-planting contest.

Then she dusts off her palms, grips the shovel, and strides right past me without looking back.

"There," she declares. "Enjoy your cabbage." And at the bottom of the steps, she tosses over her shoulder, "Just a warning. The other ladies in town won't be this nice if you mistake them for bears or eighty-seven-year-old women."

"You call this being nice?"

A sly smile paints her face, and she hikes up the path to the house on top of the ridge.

That should be the end of it. But I'm still standing here like an idiot, boots rooted to the porch, watching her stride up the hill. Five minutes. That's all it took for a stranger to crawl under my skin.

I don't wait for her to come back. I slam the door and bury myself in the lodge instead, letting the silence and dust envelop me.

The main living room opens wide, with vaulted ceilings with ash beams and a stone fireplace centered on the far wooden wall. Everything is wood, top to bottom, like the Lincoln Logs I used to play with. The kitchen sits off to the side, cabinets beyond saving and appliances outdated, but the tile floors are salvage-able. From the dining area, a window frames Misthaven Lake. Finn's long dining room table will fit there.

After an hour, I realize the bones are solid. No rot, good foundation, but the rest needs work. Floors are warped, and the pipes cough like old lungs. The lights work, though they buzz and flicker, one breath from going out.

The roof will have to be first. The ceiling over the front hall is bruised with water stains, leaks bleeding through. My pen digs jaggedly across the paper as I scrawl out the list.

- *Seal chimney*
- *Clear attic*
- *Repaint walls*
- *Winterize plumbing*
- *Email Jillian to hire a decorator*

I'm not a carpenter. But I'm a Hastings. I can figure this out, and I need to start with supplies. There was a hardware store on my way in. I grab my keys, the quiet pressing at my back as I head for the truck.

Thirty days to make this place livable. To make it safe enough for Finn.

After that, I can disappear back into the only life I know, the one with no people, no flowerpots, and absolutely no copper-haired women who make me feel like I'm losing an argument I never agreed to have.

Which is exactly what I want.

Chapter 4
Clementine

By day four at Got Wood?, I've cried twice, lied to six customers about screws, and discovered that if I climb the aisle-six ladder and pretend to do inventory, no one questions why I'm sniffling into a box of hammers.

It's not the job that has me weeping in the middle of my shifts. The job's fine, gloriously fine. I wear a green apron with *Do You Need Assistance?* embroidered across the chest, and people hand me money for caulk.

Way better than sitting in Gran's kitchen with the squeaky floor and humming fridge, reminding me I live above her garage rent-free.

It's the quiet that gets me.

At Lincoln Center, silence only existed for about half a second between counts—*one-and-two!*—and then your body was already into the next thing. Here, stillness stretches until my thoughts spill everywhere, and I remember that I gave up my life as a ballerina on a whim.

Cody, the store owner and my gran's longtime co-conspirator, hurries past the counter with a box of hose nozzles balanced on his hip.

"You're doing great, Clem," he calls without slowing.

I hop off the stool behind the register, nearly knocking over a stack of folding camping chairs someone parked too close, and pretend I'm focusing.

"Thank you?"

Cody's known me since I was six, when I showed up to his son's birthday party in a tutu and muddy sneakers. He also knows that I arrived in Misthaven with desperation in my mouth, which is probably why he feels entitled to shout things over his shoulder like we're still in line for cake.

"Is Margaret happy with the soil and seeds for the lodge?"

"Yep. I got the flowerpots filled before breakfast."

He flashes a distracted thumbs-up and disappears down an aisle.

What I don't tell him is that I nearly brained a stranger with a shovel while carrying out those orders.

I slump back onto the stool behind the counter, apron bunching at my waist. If I open my phone, I know I'll be Viggling *How long is too long to take a break from ballet,* even though I know the answer. Or, worse, I'll click through half-filled shopping carts for boots, perfume, or anything to prove I still exist somewhere outside this town.

Both options end with me crying on the aisle-six ladder.

So I don't.

Instead, I pick up my phone, my thumb hesitating, then type in *Alec Hastings.*

Turns out the jerk is famous. Like, actually famous.

There's a Wikipedia page, glossy press shots, and videos with millions of views. His dad is the owner of the largest tech company in the world, which means Alec didn't just come from money—he came from *money* money.

New York is filled with the rich elite who attend galas and after-parties, but this is another tier. I guess I could've guessed from the cashmere sweater he was wearing.

I click on his Instagram and laugh. His handle is @TwoMen-OnTop. What kind of name is that? It's way too sexual for just mountain climbing. But every photo is cliffs and ice and snow. In almost every shot there's a second man, named Finn. He has long hair, a bigger build, and a grin plastered across his face. They look like brothers…or lovers?

I stop on a photo of my new neighbor.

He's shirtless, perched on a boulder, beanie on, an entire mountain range spread out behind him like it was printed there to match his jawline. He's smiling the smile of someone who is exactly where they're meant to be. His hair is a dark chestnut, a little messy, and he's clean-shaven here, unlike the scruff this morning.

I zoom in, which should be a crime, because my cursed thumb double-taps.

"Oh crap, I didn't mean to like your torso!" I squeal, hit unlike, and throw my phone on the counter like it bit me.

The bell above the door jingles. My heart lifts stupidly, but it's just a pair of hikers wearing matching smiles and matching windbreakers.

"Heya!" the guy says. "Do you sell kayaks?"

"Adventure Supply. Two roads down, red trim, smells like patchouli and tuna sandwiches," I say, already inching back toward my phone.

"Told you, Urla," the girl singsongs, swatting him. She grins at me. "We just got in. Starting training today."

"For Denali?" It's the only mountain people train for around here.

"No. For Wild Trails."

"They're still doing that?"

The last time I spent a summer in Misthaven, Wild Trails was just a flyer curling on the bulletin board and my grandpa judging from a lawn chair with a Styrofoam cup of coffee.

"Not only are they doing it, but there's a cash prize this

year!" Urla crows like he's just invented capitalism. "Twenty grand!"

"Twenty *what*?" I choke on air, and also on the past-due credit card bills currently haunting my phone notifications.

"Thousand dollars." His friend slides the yellow flyer across the counter.

I skim it: hiking, kayaking, rappelling. Basically, summer camp activities to the extreme. And you must enter with a partner.

My brain short-circuits. *How on earth did I miss this?* That's not just prize money. That's debt-gets-paid money. That's call-collectors-back-without-hyperventilating money. That's maybe-I-go-back-to-New-York-and-try-dancing-again money.

Impossible? Maybe.

But I've done harder things in pointe shoes.

Somewhere in this five-thousand-person town, there has to be someone reckless or desperate enough to team up with me and win that money.

I'm ticking through the roster in my head—Gran's knees would never allow it, Cody would turn it into a lecture, my old best friend Yura's off in Anchorage wearing scrubs instead of hiking boots—when the bell over the front door splits the air, jerking me back to the present.

This time, my heart doesn't sink back down.

Alec Hastings doesn't stroll or saunter into the store. He enters it like he's trying to outrun his own thoughts.

Same navy sweater as this morning, damp hair pushed back with impatience, sleeves shoved to his elbows. The ink on his skin peeks out in lines. Trees, maybe, or topo maps.

"Welcome to Got Wood?" I chirp.

He stops short, turns fully, and those golden eyes pin me. "It's you."

"Looking younger by the minute!"

Before he can say more, Urla lunges at him. "Oh my god—

are you Alec Hastings? You are, aren't you? Dude, we read the article. That rescue was gnarly. You dragged Finn down with a jacket sled, right?"

Alec doesn't answer.

"Is he here? Are you guys doing Wild Trails?" Urla's friend chimes in. "Man, if you're competing, we should just pack it up and go home."

I know the look of someone white-knuckling their way through a panic spiral in public. I know how it feels to be stared at like you're something to consume, but this is not my problem.

Not my problem!

Alec's lips part, but he seems to shut down, like something heavy dropped through him and buried the sound. "I'm not—"

Ugh, why can't I just stay out of things?

"Hey, Alec!" I cut in like I don't just sell lumber. I *am* lumber, and I dart around the counter to wedge myself between him and the spotlight. "You still want to see the reclaimed wood in the back?"

For a second, he doesn't move. Then his eyes catch mine, and there's relief so sharp it almost hurts.

"Please."

"Nice to meet you!" Urla calls after us. "Hope to see you at this weekend's welcome event!" His buddy elbows him. "What? If he shows up, we're toast anyway."

I steer Alec down the aisle, past shelves that smell like pine and solvent, until we're tucked beside a leaf blower display.

"Thanks for that," he says.

"Got Wood? store policy number one: Always rescue a guy mid-ambush." I lean against a stack of two-by-fours. "Union rules."

"You actually work here?"

"Since this week," I say. I brace for pity. People in Misthaven are fluent in pity since I arrived. But he only tilts his head curiously. Which makes me want to tell him everything while I sob into an oil rag.

He clears his throat. "I drove for three days from San Francisco. Got in this morning. So if I was a dick earlier—"

"You were," I say. "But it's fine. I was too busy being an eighty-seven-year-old bear to notice."

His face softens, and he looks younger. Or maybe I'm just seeing the version from the photo my thumbs accidentally made out with moments ago.

"What I wanted to say is that I'm sorry."

"Apology accepted."

"Great." He shifts, arms crossed, forearms inked and lean. His watch lights up, and he glances at it like he's timing the conversation.

"So, you're from San Francisco?" I prod.

"Marin."

"Fancy! I'm from Concord." I throw in finger guns because Bay Area solidarity. He does not finger-gun back.

"You're not from Misthaven?"

"Technically, no. My mom bolted to the Bay the second she could. I bolted to New York the second I could stand on pointe shoes. We're very good at leaving things."

"And your dad? Siblings?" he asks, like he's running down a checklist.

"No siblings, and my dad was also excellent at leaving." I toss it out like a joke. He doesn't laugh. Doesn't even wince. Just shelves it away like he has a filing cabinet in his chest where he keeps things he doesn't want to talk about. "What about you?" I press. "Family still in Marin?"

"My folks are. Five siblings are scattered." His eyes cut toward me like he's measuring how much I already know.

Clearly, this man has privacy issues.

I tilt my chin toward the front of the store, where the hikers mobbed him earlier. "So…what was that all about?"

"Who knows."

"It seemed like you did."

His jaw twitches. He's so easily irritated it's almost fun to poke.

"I'm a climber," he finally admits. "Guess they were…fans."

"Fans, huh? So basically, I rescued you from a swarm of selfies."

"Guess so."

"So you owe me an apology and a thank-you. Really racking up the IOUs."

"Thanks." He looks like he'd rather chew nails than say it, which only makes me giddy.

"My grandpa was a pretty well-known climber around these parts when I was a kid, but no one ever rushed him like that."

"You didn't take after him?"

"Not really."

He huffs like I'm boring him. "Well, if you don't know who I am, then you've probably heard of my family. My dad owns Viggle."

"*Wow.*"

"My sister Frankie is about to be the first female F1 driver."

"Not big on cars."

"Brooklyn, then. She's a figure skater."

That jolts me. "Wait—*Brooklyn Hastings*? Shut up. I love her. I watch every Winter Olympics. She's unreal on the ice."

"Yep." He shrugs, eyes sliding away like it's nothing, like his sister isn't a national treasure.

"You say that like you just admitted she works at the post office."

His mouth quirks, but his hands are busier, restlessly tugging at the hem of his shirt. His nails are clipped short and neat. Veins track down the backs, into the watch strap and the compass tattoo at his wrist.

Hands that look like they could hang from a cliff by a pinkie, or drag someone to safety, or—God help me—crush me without breaking a sweat. Heat slides traitorously low in my core.

"And you climb mountains." I shake my head, like I can jostle the thought away. "Your poor parents. All their kids out in the world, defying death like that. I'd be terrified."

He pivots. "Do you work in the design department of the store?"

I bark out a laugh. "Department? Please. We're about as corporate as a lemonade stand. It's just me and the owner."

"I assumed since you had so many opinions about the porch this morning."

"Those weren't opinions. That was trauma. Years of immersion in New York City Ballet set notes. You pick up an eye for staging whether you want it or not."

"So naturally you moved on to…"

"Lots of paint and lots of caulk," I say. His gaze flicks to my mouth. "The kind that seals things," I blurt. "Not—" I zip my lips. "Uh, not the kind you were on the porch."

His brows lift. "Did you just say I was being a cock?"

"*Ugh.* I meant, you know, like a big dick. No, wait—" I groan. "Fine, yeah. Cock works. You were being one."

"Am I making you nervous?"

He's disturbingly perceptive. "Being nervous is like ninety percent of my personality."

"*Mm.*" He shrugs and pulls a leather notebook from his pocket, flipping it open.

"What's that?"

"My list."

I lean in, squinting at the page—but really, it's the cedar, road dust, and faint sting of Bengay that makes my stomach cartwheel. "I could help you get started on that."

"Thanks."

He follows me down the first aisle toward roofing. He looks like he wants to do this in silence. Unfortunately for both of us,

I'm the kind of person who fills silence with packing peanuts. "So, are you actually here for Wild Trails?"

"No."

My pulse jumps. That means I still have a shot at that prize money, as long as I find a partner.

"Are you?" He says it like a question, but there's judgment tucked inside.

"Yes," I answer, like I didn't make the call two minutes ago.

"Good luck with that."

"Your first impression is improving." I smile.

"With me, it's usually downhill from here."

"Noted," I say and wave at the shelves. "Well, here's the roof stuff. Roof things, roof screws, roof plans. Basically a roof wonderland."

"Is there someone here who knows what they're talking about?" His tone is mild, but the dig lands.

"You were right," I sigh. "It is all downhill from there."

"Don't take it personally. I don't know much about any of this either."

"Oh good," I say brightly. "We can be the incompetent newbies together!" He remains unamused, which makes me almost feel bad for him. "I'll get Cody," I relent. "He's the owner. He can talk shingles until you beg for mercy."

"Appreciate it."

I start to leave, then pause, looking back at him. "Just put in a good word for me, okay? First week and all. Consider it payback for calling me an old beast."

This time, he almost smiles for real. "Will do."

And that should be the end of it, but my pulse is still sprinting when I round the corner.

Chapter 5
Clementine

"TWENTY-NINE THOUSAND EIGHT hundred sixty-six dollars and forty-two cents," Gran says, peering over the rim of my laptop. She spins it around to reveal the spreadsheet it took her a week to make, the one wrangling up all my debt. A soul-crushing, bright-red grid glares up at me from her kitchen table.

$29,866.42.

It sits there on the screen like a final curtain drop, and all I can think is, *this is what my early twenties bought me*. Not freedom, not a career, not even a pair of working knees.

Just debt.

"I think I'm going to be sick."

"We have to face this head-on." Gran nods sternly. She used to be the bookkeeper for the lodge and a bunch of small businesses around town, and now she's here, calmly confronting the financial apocalypse I dragged into her house.

Meanwhile, I'm hyperventilating into a mug of chamomile tea.

"Are you sure this is the number?"

"Yes, but it's just a number," she says. "And numbers can change."

I let out something between a laugh and a sob. "I'd rather rip the skin off my feet and go en pointe raw than deal with this."

"Paying off debt feels that bad, I'm not going to argue with you."

Gran's always been more like a mom to me than my own mother. Mom's a history teacher at Concord High, and every summer break she'd ship me here while she spent money she didn't have on trips around the world. I love her—I still call, we still talk—but Gran's the one I go to when something really breaks. She's the steady one, the problem-solver. The one who never makes me feel like too much.

Why couldn't I have inherited her accounting brain and not my mom's shopping-to-fill-a-void brain?

"Did you deduct the payment I made last month? I think I put a hundred toward Chase. Or maybe it was Amex. I don't remember." I rifle through the stack of printed bills spread across her homemade quilted tablecloth.

"Clementine." She reaches over, stilling my frantic hands. "I triple-checked it."

Five cards. Five promises to myself that this time would be different.

"It shouldn't even be possible to owe this much when I basically live on Trader Joe's butter chicken and ramen," I choke out. "And it's not even glamorous debt. No Paris vacations, no designer handbags—" I wince. "Okay, maybe two. But they were from The RealReal. Mostly it's just…rent. Groceries. Late-night Ubers when the trains seemed too sketchy. Makeup I couldn't afford. Seamless orders after rehearsals. Physical therapy for my ankle that I had to pay for out-of-pocket."

"That's how it goes," she says.

I press my palms over my eyes, but the number is still seared there.

$29,866.42.

Alaska used to be the only place where I could breathe. Until

I was fifteen and stopped spending summers here because I had to stay near San Francisco to train. Another thing dance took away from me.

I hadn't been back until Grandpa's funeral three years ago. Now I'm here again, a week post-meltdown, calling the old garage apartment my new home.

"The sickest part?" My voice cracks. "Half of this isn't even what I bought. It's interest! Why the hell do they let eighteen-year-olds sign up for credit cards without explaining APR?"

"Because the system's broken," she says.

"'*It's free money!*' the lady at the bank said. Maxed out Chase? Open Amex. Hit the cap on Bank of America? Hello, Sephora card. Fifty bucks off and a birthday gift just for signing up. Of course, I said yes. Who wouldn't want a free mascara that dries up in a week?"

"It's okay. You've got the job at Got Wood?, so you've got some breathing room now."

"Breathing room? Fourteen dollars an hour doesn't feel like breathing room. I'm making less than I did in a single season as a soloist."

"You may have made fifty grand last year, but the city is expensive, darling. Your rent was over half of what you were getting paid. It just isn't manageable."

I look at the math on the spreadsheet. If I live extra frugally, with just groceries, gas, a phone bill, and maybe the occasional blush, maybe I could make it work.

Or I can just pick up another job to pay my debt off faster. Lenni's looking for someone to clean out the dog pens at the sledding center. Five a.m. starts. My debt would thank me. My nostrils might not.

"But look." Gran leans over, tapping a column highlighted in green. "If you pay twelve hundred a month, you could pay this all off in three years and have a little nest egg."

Three years! Three years of handing strangers boxes of nails at Got Wood?, of funneling every single paycheck into a hole I dug swipe by swipe.

I spin my head to face her. "It's Mom's fault, you know."

My mother never passed up an opportunity to swipe her credit card on self-worth, even if it had a 22% APR. I hated it. I hated the cycle of a dopamine rush to guilt-ridden downfall I watched her go through my whole life.

Then, I became her.

Gran raises an eyebrow. "Nice try."

"Okay, maybe it's not entirely her fault. But it would be easier if it was."

She rubs the side of my face. "I do wish your mama hadn't taught you that shopping was how you patch a hole in your life."

I straighten my spine. "It was just how she survived."

And I learned it too well.

After rehearsals, I'd be wrung out and scraped raw. I'd go straight to that little thrift shop near Fifty-Sixth, the one with the creaky floors and the wrap skirts sorted by color. The owner knew me. He'd set things aside—shoes I didn't need, coats I couldn't afford, dresses I'd never wear. I told myself if I could just find the right piece, the perfect version of myself, maybe I'd feel better.

And sometimes, for a little while, I did.

That was the high. That was the hit. A swipe here, a reward there. A hundred became a thousand. Then five thousand. Then ten. Once the debt hits a certain point, it's really easy to keep saying, *What's another couple of charges?*

Now here I am.

"I wish I could take it all back."

"A Lennox never takes the easy route." Gran says it like it's scripture.

I flop into my chair. "My life is over."

Gran slaps her hand on the table, voice firm enough that my shoulders jolt straight. "We are not doing this. You already emailed the company to let them know you're taking the season off. You're going to figure this out."

"I am," I whisper. "Are you sure you don't want to enter Wild Trails with me? Twenty grand sure would be nice."

Last night, I came home from work, slammed the flyer on her table, and announced I was going to win. Since yesterday, I've basically harassed every semi-fit person who's walked into Got Wood?, and they all have partners already. Or they ran away from me.

I even made a sign for the town bulletin board, but I haven't gotten a single call. Just the debt collector, ringing me again.

All I can hear, over and over, is *declined, declined, rejected.*

"I asked my quilting group," Gran says, "but between the arthritis and the hip replacements, I don't think the girls are up for it."

"Damn." I groan, dragging my hands down my face. "Any calls to the house phone? I listed it on my flyer."

"No, but it's only been twelve hours."

I sigh. "What else do you think I can do? Rob a bank? Start an OnlyFans? Sell my left ovary on the black market?"

Her brow lifts.

"I'm joking." *Maybe.* "What I really, really need is a Wild Trails partner! I wish Yura was still here; she'd probably join me."

"Her parents still live down the street. She comes home every Christmas, always asks about you."

Yura was my best friend every summer I spent in Alaska. I saw on Instagram that she's off in Anchorage, working as one of the best sports physical therapists the state has to offer. When we were kids playing pretend, she was always the nurse, the teacher, the mom. I used to envy how sure she seemed of herself, like she was born knowing who she'd be.

Maybe one of these days, when I don't feel like a total embarrassment, I'll drive down there and say hi. It's been nine years since we last saw each other, but every time we did, it was like no time had passed. Hopefully it's still like that.

"Well, I'm glad I'll get to see her in a couple of months. But that still doesn't help with me winning this damn competition. I need that money, Gran."

"The twenty grand isn't even guaranteed. You'd have to win, then split it. And, honey, you haven't hiked since you were half the size you are now. Who even knows if your old boots fit?"

"Don't underestimate me. I have the drive. I just need the right person." I grab my phone. "There has to be some desperate, lonely sad sack in this town who wants a partner."

"Fine. If you're set on this, maybe check Tinder."

I gape. "What do you know about Tinder?"

"A woman can only be in a cold bed for so long, Clementine."

"Gran!"

She just smirks into her tea while I download the top three dating apps. If seducing my way into prize money is what it takes, fine. Desperate girls do desperate things. While the apps load, I glance out the window to catch low clouds pressing down, smoke curling from the lodge chimney like it's judging me too.

The words of the guy who ambushed Alec yesterday ring in my ears: *Man, if you're competing, we should just pack it up and go home.*

"Speaking of desperate, lonely sad sacks..." I sit up straighter. "I might have an idea."

Gran side-eyes me. "More unhinged than telling me you're opening an OnlyFans? Because I do know what that is, darling."

I groan. "I don't want to know how you know that. Anyway," I press on, "what about the man who bought Grandpa's lodge? Alec Hastings. What do you know about him?"

She glances at the photos of Grandpa on the wall. There's the one of him in flannel at their fifty-year vow renewal. Another with me on his shoulders. If losing dance hurts this bad, I can't imagine what losing the love of your life is like.

"Not much. Your grandpa liked him. Said he and his friend reminded him of himself when he was young. Stubborn, hungry, and just reckless enough."

I always knew the lodge would eventually be sold. When I was eight, Grandpa said he was ready to retire, and it still took two years before someone finally bought it. For the five summers after that, I used to sneak in whenever I visited. No one was ever there. By the time I stopped coming at fifteen, most of the furniture had been sold off. Gran still kept up the garden, though. They never knew if the new owners would actually use the place, but I remember Grandpa just being glad he didn't have to clean it anymore.

Now I'm excited to see what it looks like after all these years, to see what he's done with it. It'll be nice to find it fixed up again.

"Well, Alec came into Got Wood? yesterday—"

"Oh, so *that's* the man Cody said was drooling over you."

"That is a textbook HR violation. Please shut down the small-town grapevine immediately."

"I got you that job!" she scolds.

"Doesn't mean you get to use it to spy on me."

"It does when there's romance involved."

"This isn't romance! This would be a strategic alliance," I insist. "Apparently, he's a big deal in the climbing community. Someone even recognized him in the store. If I can get him to partner with me, I might actually have a shot at winning. But there is one teensy, tiny problem." I wince. "He said he wasn't doing the competition."

Gran laughs, full-bodied, like I just told her the sky was green. "When has a Lennox ever taken no for an answer?"

I stroke her weathered hands.

She's right. If I can land Alec, win Wild Trails, and pay down even part of my debt, maybe I could breathe again. Maybe I could save a little. Maybe I could go back to New York with a budget in hand and beg NYCB to take me on for the spring season. People make comebacks all the time. Why not me?

"Right!" I whisper, but the kitchen doesn't answer. So I push back from the table, grab my jacket, and chirp with way more confidence than I feel, "I'm going to march over there right now before work."

Gran arches an eyebrow. "Darling, it's six a.m."

"Then he'll appreciate my determination."

Chapter 6
Alec

SWEAT RUNS INTO MY EYES. I swipe it away with my shirt, which immediately snags on a screw and tears. *Figures.* I sling it around my neck and keep working. The left side of the bed frame is heavier than it looks, and my back protests as I wedge it into place.

Didn't sleep last night. So I spent the dark hours sanding these boards smooth enough that Finn won't even snag a sock on them. I was supposed to be sealing the roof today, but the rain won't let up. Weather doesn't care what's on my list. She never does.

Out the window, three deer nose along the bank of Misthaven Lake. I picture Finn in this room when it's finished. Bed frame cut low so the wheelchair lines up. Dresser edges rounded so he won't split a shin. Table by the window for his coffee. Maybe a photo or two, so it doesn't feel like just another room in just another lodge. It'll be his.

Finn's lodge. His home.

I drive in the last screw, lean back, and the frame holds. It's a small victory, but it's still a victory.

Behind me, the floor creaks, and my grip on the drill tightens.

"Not a threat!"

I spin toward the voice, the drill buzzing like a rattlesnake.

Clementine Lennox bursts into view, arms shot overhead. "It's me! Clem!"

"I know who you are," I growl.

"Then lower the weapon!"

I don't. "You've gone from trespassing to breaking and entering?"

She waves a set of keys like they're proof of innocence. "I know where the back door key is hidden."

"That doesn't make it legal."

She shrugs, bright as a sunrise. "It's six fifteen, Alec. Figured you're an early bird."

I grimace. She grins. Always the opposite.

"You here to take back the cabbage?"

"What?"

"The ornamental cabbage," I remind her.

She laughs. "Seeds don't sprout overnight, genius. I just came to check in. A nice neighborly visit. See how you're settling."

Right. Neighborly. At dawn.

I lower the drill. She stands there and stares, wearing leggings and a pink top knotted at her waist, hair scraped into a bun that means business.

She looks fragile. Framed in my doorway, she doesn't fill the space the way she did outside, when her laughter spilled and her words tumbled over each other. Here she seems almost breakable.

"What do you want?"

"No *good morning, Clementine*? No *thank you for saving me yesterday*?"

I narrow my eyes at her, tilting my head. It's far too early to deal with people, especially people who look like they skip for fun.

She ignores my annoyance and just shoots me a smile that could rival the sun. Then she drifts into the room like she owns it, one foot neatly in front of the other. Ballerina steps. Even committing small-town crime, she has choreography.

She glances around the room. "Are you building that bed frame from scratch?"

"Yes."

"Wow, you must be really good with your hands." She smiles…I do not. "You're going to do something about the bare bulb, though, right?" she asks, pointing up.

I follow her finger to the single light bulb I screwed in this morning. "Huh?"

"You can't leave it like that. It needs a shade. A pendant, maybe bronze. Let it patina over time."

"You broke into my house to talk about light fixtures?"

"Broke in? Aren't we past that?" She shrugs as if she doesn't understand the definition of the word. "The bed frame's really beautiful. From the wood you bought yesterday?"

"Yes."

She drifts along the edge of the room, fingertips trailing over the walls like she owns the grain. Her gaze flicks to my arms, shoulders, and bare chest before jolting back to her shoes. "I mean, I can barely put together IKEA furniture, and you're just here, hammering away."

"Are you flirting with me?" I ask.

Her nervous laugh rolls through the air in jagged waves. She takes a step closer. Morning light slides over her jaw, painting her cheeks a peach flush.

"Flirting? Me? Never!"

That word lands harder than it should. *Never*. Before I can stop it, I bite out, "Never?"

"Well, maybe not *never*. I mean, I didn't come here to flirt."

She's flustered now, hands fidgeting, sentences tripping over themselves. "I definitely wouldn't have shown up like this." She gestures at her leggings and the pink top tied in a bow.

Some reckless part of me wants to ask what she would have shown up in. I kill the thought fast.

"Noted."

"Anyway." She rallies, her smile snapping back into place. "I came with a proposition."

My gut already knows. "No."

"You haven't even—"

"You want a partner for Wild Trails. Answer's no."

Her brows shoot up. "How did you guess?"

"Because it's all anyone in this town wants."

My inbox proves it. Locals, strangers, and even climbers my agent dug up who'd drop their expeditions just to latch on. Money pouring into Wild Trails being the next big thing. Offers I delete without opening.

Because I've never competed without Finn.

Don't break this promise. His voice rings in my head. Even if I wanted to partake in this novice shit, I wouldn't be able to.

She bites her lip and straightens. I've always heard that ballerinas are tough, that they refuse to fold. Guess those rumors are true.

"Look," she says, "I'm not like the other people in this town. I didn't even know who you were until yesterday." Her chin tilts higher, like she's daring me to blink first. "I'd make a good partner. I'm like my grandfather. I'm strong, I don't quit, and I learn fast. I'm not asking for charity." She draws in a breath that shakes but holds. "We can split the prize money. That's ten grand each."

"I don't need the money."

"Maybe not. But you do need help with this place. We could trade. I mean, I could really help you here. Design, organization, whatever you're avoiding. Because this room?" She gestures, graceful even in her irritation. "It doesn't feel like you. It doesn't feel like anything."

The words hit harder than I expect. Shame runs sharply through me, hot in my ears. She doesn't know it, but every nail, every cut of wood, I measured for Finn.

The more she points out what it's not, the less certain I am it'll ever be right.

"This room isn't for me. I'm not staying in Misthaven for long. Just fixing it up for my best friend." The words escape before I can stop them, and the regret is instant.

Don't ask about Finn.

"Is that your climbing partner?"

Of course she knows.

The moment she heard my name at Got Wood?, she probably went home and read every article about us. Every new headline popping up like weeds about the worst day of my life.

The air shifts sharp, cutting through my ribs. My lungs scrape like gravel when I drag in a breath. The walls are closing in, getting closer and closer. I need to get out of here.

I set down the drill, slide past her, and move for the hall. "I'm not doing Wild Trails."

She follows me.

"Why not?" Her voice is soft, fragile as a fault line. "Is it me?"

I make the mistake of looking at her. Those blue eyes fasten me in place harder than any carabiner ever did.

"It's not personal."

The main room opens wide, making the air easier to breathe. It's a relief, until I spot my mat and sleeping bag in the corner. My bed is temporary, small, and for some reason, the idea of her seeing it makes my chest burn with embarrassment.

"But what if—"

"I've got a lead on a designer, so no need to keep offering your help," I lie. "Kitchen's this way." Behind me, silence stretches. She hasn't left yet. I turn, jaw tight. "Leave the keys you found on the table."

Her lips part. A hundred words are stacked behind them, but none come out. She drops the keys, gives me one more desperate look, and finally walks out. The door clicks shut behind her, echoing louder than it should.

I stand there, fists flexing, chest tight.

I've got enough problems.

I don't need another.

Chapter 7
Alec

Trudy's Treasures smells like lemon polish. It's the only place I've ever seen where you can buy a taxidermied beaver, a vintage typewriter, and restored light fixtures.

I'm crouched in a narrow row of metal shelves, scanning for anything to fix a godforsaken bare bulb. Ever since Clementine Lennox pointed it out yesterday, I haven't been able to unsee the problem.

What am I even looking for?

Wedged between a wicker lampshade and a lava lamp, I spot a tarnished pendant light. Under this dim store lighting, brass and copper look the same. The pendant is gritty with dust, but it may work.

"Hey, there you are!"

I don't even need to turn around to recognize the voice rushing toward me. This town is suffocatingly small. Three days in Misthaven, and Clementine seems to be everywhere. I let myself steal a glance.

She parts the cluttered aisles like she owns the shop. Denim jacket, wide-leg pants, and a slick bun that leaves the soft curve of her nape exposed. My shoulders stiffen. She's beautiful—objectively—but today she looks worn thin.

I stare at the pendant in my hands, pretending not to hear her.

Definitely not noticing the reddish-orange freckles dusting the bridge of her nose or the trail of them along her pale collarbones. My mind is used to noticing the small things, that's all this is.

"I've spent the past hour running around town searching for you. Helloooooo," she sings, stopping right beside me. I don't have to look up to know her ice-blue eyes are locked on me.

"You've resorted to following me."

"Aren't you a modern-day Sherlock Holmes?"

From my peripheral, the smile on her face glistens.

"What do you need?"

She shoves a basket toward me. "Thought you could get a taste of my world-class muffins."

Against my better judgment, I glance up. She's standing over me, lit by the shop's dusty front windows, glowing in all her infuriating glory.

Finn always teased me for dating women who were human fog banks in puffer coats. Clementine is a lighthouse beam. Too loud, too sunlit, too everything.

"Appreciate the effort, but I already told you my answer is no," I bite. Finn was always the personable one, especially with women.

"You see, the problem with that is 'no' simply won't work for me." She plucks the towel off the basket, revealing six huge, golden-brown muffins.

My stomach grumbles.

"Gonna have to make it work since that's my final answer."

Her nostrils flare. A small crease forms on the base of her nose before she rolls her neck, widens her grin, and tightens the grip she already has on me.

"Now, you listen to me, sir," she snaps.

"Sir?"

Ignoring me entirely, she barrels on. "I begged my grandmother to make these double chocolate chip muffins for me at the break of dawn this morning—"

"I thought *you* made them?"

"I helped," she fires back. The way she's getting worked up over a basket of muffins almost drags a smile out of me. Almost. "Then I brought them down to the lodge, but your truck wasn't there. So I spent the rest of my morning looking for you."

"Could've left them on the porch."

"For the moose to eat?" She gasps. "Absolutely not."

"You've never shied away from breaking into the place."

"It's not breaking in if I have the key."

What is up with her?

Better question is, what's up with me? Why am I letting a woman with flour smudged on her wrist tie me up in knots? Why am I letting myself get baited by her? God, my sisters would love her. She has that Hastings determination. Neither Brooklyn nor Frankie let me get the final word in. The three of them in the same room together would be a torment.

"One more pitch—" She opens her mouth to start.

"Pass."

"Too late. It's happening."

"With all of your determination, I'm sure you can track down another partner," I mutter, shifting the pendant under my arm. *This will have to do.*

I need to get out of this store.

"But I want you," she says—low, maybe not meaning for me to hear. Except I do. She keeps talking, words tripping over each other. "I got rejected by every semi-athletic person in this town yesterday. Everyone's either partnered up or ignoring me. No one answered my bulletin board notice. Hinge, Tinder, even Base Camp Cuties. Absolutely no one."

My brow lifts. "Are you looking for a date or a Wild Trails partner?"

"I'm being resourceful," she snaps, teeth flashing.

"You're desperate."

"I am! I am desperate. You are the only unattached person in this town, never mind that you might actually help me win Wild Trails. Never mind that I am certain these muffins are basically a gateway drug—you'll taste one, and before you know it, you'll be climbing Gran's porch steps at midnight, hopelessly addicted, begging me for more."

Addicted. Begging. The words wade low in my throat. The only thing I've ever chased like that is a summit. That's the only language I know for hunger. And yet her voice puts the idea in my head of wanting something so bad I'd knock on her door at midnight, powerless against my desire.

My fingers flex tightly around the pendant.

A laugh almost slips out, but I clamp down on it. "On a mountain, desperation gets you killed. And it'll drag your partner with you."

"You wouldn't last a day in ballet," she shoots back. "Desperation is in the job description. You starve, you bleed, you smile prettier than the girl who wants your role. And if you can't, she takes it. That's it."

"Would you drop it? I promise a pretty smile isn't enough to sway me into entering the competition."

Her eyes widen, blush spreading across her cheeks and down her neck. Mine too, damn it. Blushing. For fuck's sake. In the middle of a thrift store? While being steamrolled by a fox in denim?

"You just called my smile pretty."

"You hear what you want to hear." My voice is flat, but my pulse isn't.

"It's called reading between the lines."

"There are no lines to read between with me. I'm direct."

She steps closer, not touching, but close enough I get a waft of something sweet. "I'll remember that when we're on the trail."

"Pass."

"It wasn't a question."

Her hand flares out, the muffins nearly clipping me in the head. "You agree to partner with me. I train myself. You do nothing except show up for the qualifier and the race. And I help you with the lodge, because God knows you need it. You wouldn't be here, cross-eyed over light fixtures, if you didn't."

Her fire licks higher, and the strangest thing is part of me, against all sense, against all the rules I've ever lived by, doesn't want to put it out.

I don't answer. Don't need to. My face probably says it all: not interested.

But my gut won't shut up. She's not wrong. I do need help. Jillian, my agent, emailed me this morning that all the designers she reached out to are booked out for months.

She said she was a ballerina. I believe it. The way she holds herself, even when she's rambling. Straight back. Long neck. Legs angled. Even her hands are deliberate, like she's used to performing down to the fingertips.

"Why does this competition matter so much to you?" I ask.

"Because I need this." Her shoulders twitch, then lock back into perfect alignment. "I'll be completely honest since we're going to be partners—"

"I never said that."

"I spent the last eight years in New York chasing ballet— heck, I spent my whole life chasing it. All it's left me with is debt and a shredded belief in myself. I need the cash. Badly. But I also need to do something I wasn't sculpted into since I was three. I need to figure out who I am without the only thing I've ever been good at."

Her honesty lands like a punch.

I stare at her. The gloss falls away. Her hands tremble. Her thumb rubs the basket's wicker edge in a compulsive loop. Shoes scuffed, bun too tight, sweat brimming around her hairline. Her body's trained into perfect lines, but her edges are fraying. She's still holding my gaze like it's the last rope on the wall.

She wants this.

She's got a chip on her shoulder.

And I know what it's like to move through life with one —lonely.

Thing is, climbing with Finn was the only time I ever learned to move in sync with someone. We didn't even have to talk on the trails. I knew when he was fading. He knew when I needed space. You don't get that with strangers. You earn it one climb at a time.

And it damn near broke me when I lost him.

I glance down at the pendant light in my hand.

Truth is, I miss being out on a trail.

But I don't have the time. Not with the lodge in pieces. Not with Finn arriving next month. And definitely not with a girl I'll be leaving in a month or two. What's the point of making friends when I'm already planning on abandoning this place?

If I say yes, I'd be responsible for her.

"Still no," I decide, even though my throat's tighter than it should be.

"At least take the muffins." She shoves the basket into my hands, decisive to the end, before marching out of the store.

The bell above the door jingles once, then I'm left in silence. Holding her damn muffins.

Subject: Glacial Documentary Climb Pt3 – November in Iceland

From: Jillian@adventurerelations.com

To: alec@twomenontop.com

HEY ALEC,

The film crew for Vatnajökull in November has been booked, and they're asking if you're joining them.

I know things have been heavy since K2, and I completely understand if you're still finding your footing. That said, they'd be thrilled to have you on this ascent if you're open to it, with or without Finn. It would be great to get you back on the wall since you've climbed this path twice before.

I've reattached the brief with the full schedule, safety protocols, and comp details. The footage is slated for release at next year's Climate Film Festival, so timing is tight.

They need an answer by the end of this month.

Also, still no luck on the decorators. Here are a few available in October within your $30k budget, portfolios are attached.

—J

*W*ITH *OR WITHOUT* F*INN.*

The words land like ice in my veins.

FINN

Hip surgery went well! Two more rods. You're gonna have fun walking through tsa with me.

ALEC

did my mom drop off the care package?

FINN

Toblerone already gone!

Hired a PT. Misthaven local. Planning to walk next month.

ALEC

send her info. background check.

FINN

Send pics of the lodge or I wheel myself there.

ALEC

you'll see it when it's finished.

TRUTH IS, his room's nowhere near finished. The roof's sealed, the bed frame holds, the pendant light's up. But there's no paint. No pillows. Nothing soft. Against my will, my mind drifts to someone who is.

FINN

You're a perfectionist.

BTW, saw Jill's email. Iceland doc. You doing it?

The text feels like a test, as if he's checking to see if I'll break the promise I made him. *We beat the mountains, Alec.* His words loop in my head louder than the damn rain.

He says retire, so I retire.

Because if I break that, what do we have left?

ALEC

no time. your room first.

FINN

Work on your own room too. You'll have a lady over soon.

Test passed.

ALEC

no ladies. just people bugging me about wild trails. annoying

FINN

Looked it up. 15-mile rapids? Lol. Remember the rapids on the Russian River? We did that hungover.

ALEC

you puked and lost your oar.

FINN

Good times. Enter it, warm up the locals
for me

I hesitate, thumbs heavy over the keys. Even typing it feels wrong, like I'm cheating on him somehow. Where the fuck is my head? The words burn in my chest. I want to delete them, bury them, pretend they never came. But the lodge needs this, and if I don't tell him, it'll sit in me like rot. So I hit send.

ALEC

Bill's granddaughter asked me to do it.

FINN

Already nailing the wife part.

ALEC

she's 24.

FINN

Perfect, y'all will have the same maturity level.

ALEC

I don't have time for games.

FINN

No, you're doing it.

In fact, bring me back a date too.

ALEC

you want me in the
comp?

FINN

Yeah man, they're our neighbors now. Our
people. Our village. Come on, it'll be great.

The main room hums with how much I haven't done. I drop

down onto the sleeping bag in front of the warm flames. On the stone fireplace sits the wicker basket Clementine hurled at me yesterday. I pull it into my lap. Muffins, big ones, with chocolate chunks bulging at the tops, glossy from the heat. I take a bite.

Fuck. Good enough to make me see her, nose scrunched, sharp brows crooked like she's already winning an argument with me.

I look around the hollow room with bare windows. The bathroom door is still leaning against the wall. Everywhere I look, there are empty corners with too many problems to fix.

Finn's out of the hospital in twenty-six days, and it already feels as if I'm out of time.

Clementine said we could trade services. And Finn, well, he wants me to do Wild Trails. Really, he wants me to find a wife to play out his retirement fantasy, but that part's a lost cause. Still. If I compete, maybe he'll think I'm not stuck. Maybe he won't hate me for saying yes to Iceland, maybe he'll tell me to finish what we started. We climbed the same route on Vatnajökull five years apart to track how much ice had melted. The difference back then was unreal—multiple inches already gone. Now it's been a decade. I want to document it again.

I glance at the eight black lines inked around my forearm. Eight names. Eight people I once thought I'd watch grow old. It would've been nine.

The one thing I've learned to be consistent in life is that people die, especially on the mountains.

I reach for another muffin. Hiding underneath it is the flyer. I smooth it flat on my knee. The competition won't kill me...or her. It's easy.

Day one, kayaking fifteen miles of rapids. Finn's right—I could steer a tandem kayak solo if I had to.

Day two, sixteen miles, five thousand feet of gain up Mt. Euspuko, where most hobbyists will fold.

Day three, a four-mile descent followed by a technical rappel down the mountainside to finish.

Immediately, Finn's shout and the pop of the anchor shifting fill my ear. I shut my eyes and clench my fist, refusing to feel the gutless slack in the rope or the way my palms burned or how my voice shattered against the wind as I fought to get to him.

I press harder on the flyer, like force alone could keep me steady.

Resolution slides over me. I need to do this. Not for Clementine. Not for Finn. But to prove that I can clip into ropes and scale mountains without feeling like the ground is splitting open and dragging me into an endless black void. If I can't, I may as well retire and be stuck here in Misthaven, calling it home because I won't deserve anywhere else.

There are less than eight weeks until the competition. Clementine's a ballerina, so she's at least fit. Work and pain are her daily bread. She's clearly stubborn and irritatingly determined. She can have the prize money in exchange for her design services. It'll be simple and clean.

I reach for my notebook and flip to a blank page.

CLEMENTINE'S TRAINING SCHEDULE

Week One:

- Gear
- Weight training
- Endurance build
- Nutrition

She's a risk, but so am I.

Chapter 8
Clementine

"Okay," I say, "hear me out. I know we decided that OnlyFans was off the table, but maybe some lonely guy out there has a fetish for bruised and battered ballerina feet."

Gran bustles around the kitchen, humming over her kettle, washing blackberries and trimming flower stems. Grandpa used to trail behind her, picking up the fallen leaves and prepping the tea. This house is not the same without him, but the domesticity these days is disarming.

"Only if you charge extra for the bunion."

"You laugh, but someone out there is going to treasure these puppies." I crack my feet and lean into a hamstring stretch, head bent, arms loose.

"You keep telling yourself that, doll."

My body aches to move. I swing my left leg up the wall and settle into a wall split. My lower back protests immediately, but I breathe through it. God, I'm stiff. Alaska is going to murder my turnout.

"The things I would do if I could lift my leg that high."

I glance over to find Gran eyeing me like I'm a piece of art she might put in the foyer.

"Gran!"

She just laughs and tosses a kitchen towel at my head. "What, you get to talk about OnlyFans, but I'm the one who needs a censor?"

"Yes!" I yelp, dodging the cloth missile and switching legs. My hip lifts, then—*crack*, like a glow stick. I fold forward anyway, my forehead pressed to the wall, groaning like a martyr.

There's a knock at the door.

"You expecting anyone?" I ask.

"Maybe Gerri is stopping by to swap zinnias."

Gran disappears down the hall. I keep breathing through the hip stretch-slash-torture, convincing myself that pain is just weakness leaving the body, or whatever those Instagram yoga teachers say.

"Clem, dear? It's for you," Gran calls.

A man clears his throat.

I jolt, almost tipping sideways out of my split, and my hip locks in place with an audible pop. *Ow.*

Alec stands in my grandmother's kitchen.

All he does is look at me. Tall and unsmiling in a Henley, a navy buff holding back too-long brown hair. His pupils widen, then shrink. He doesn't say a word. I am, however, still halfway up the wall in a full split.

His gaze flicks over me—neck to toe, toe to neck—like it can't decide where it's safest to land. Like I've reminded him of a thought he's spent years shoving into a locked box.

"Alec," I breathe, and when I try to move, my hip joint refuses to cooperate. Which means I am stuck. Utterly, humiliatingly stuck. "Uh, did my grandmother's muffins change your mind?" I jut my chin up and cross my arms like standing split in half in front of a man is extremely normal.

His expression barely twitches. "Are you just going to stay like that?"

"Yes." My voice comes out breezy even though my hip

screams for mercy. The stack of papers in his hand crinkles, and I nod toward it. "Do you have a problem with that?"

A flicker of *"Oh god, what am I doing?"* crosses his face before he sighs and holds the papers out to me.

"No."

"Are you planning to sue me?" I eye the perfectly aligned stack of papers in his hand. A vein spasms between his tanned knuckles. I nearly pant at the sight. His hands are absolutely gorgeous.

"What for?"

Reluctantly, I tear my gaze back up to meet his eyes.

"The breaking and entering." I pivot my weight to take them —another *clack*, and my hip finally releases. I drop to the floor, landing on two feet like a normal mortal woman.

"Not today," he says and stretches out the stack to me.

I square my shoulders like I'm at the barre and try to exude confidence. Sure, he's rejected me two times at this point, but now he's here.

My jaw drops open as I scan the top of the first page. CLEMENTINE'S TRAINING SCHEDULE.

My heart kicks. "Does this mean—?"

"I've outlined everything down to the minute."

Not just that, but the thing is color-coded and broken down by week, the kind of obsessive detail that would make a New York City Ballet director salivate. My shifts at Got Wood? are slotted neatly at the top of each day, followed by strength sets, kayak mileage, elevation goals, recovery stretches, meal suggestions, and sleep hours.

He even included the daily sunrise and sunset times down to the minute, which sort of feels cute and tender and sweet all at the same time. A warm feeling ribbons inside my stomach. The same one I had when I walked in on him shirtless drilling that bed frame on Sunday.

I shouldn't be thinking about that at all. I should be celebrating or gloating or twirling into another wall split, because Alec Hastings is going to be my Wild Trails partner.

"I have to ask, how do you know my work schedule?" I narrow my eyes. "Have you been following me?"

"I called the store and asked."

Right. *Duh.*

I gape at him. "You realize that's—what's the word—stalker-adjacent?"

"Guess we're both committing crimes," he says, like he's bored of this conversation.

The stupid warmth inside of me starts to steam. I force my stare back onto the tome of training plans. The more I pore over everything, the more I realize that he's a control freak. But I can work with that. Especially if it means winning.

"As you pointed out, I need help with the lodge." He taps the top page, fingertip resting there like it's casual. I should be looking at what he's pointing to, but—

Ink steals my attention. His left sleeve is a mountain range, all sharp peaks and dark pines, a waterfall spilling into a winding river. A compass hides under his watch. My eyes flick to the other arm—eight black bands circle his forearm, neat and even, like tally marks or warnings. Above them, a coiled rope snakes around his bicep, vanishing under fabric. The itch to roll his sleeve up and see where it ends is immediate and entirely unhelpful.

"We have exactly twenty-five days until the qualifying round." His voice snaps me back.

"Twenty-five," I echo, like I wasn't just mentally undressing him so I could see his tattoos.

"You'll see I've marked the days you'll be at the lodge." He flips the page toward me, all business. "Main rooms done by September second. The rest finished before the race ends. If you can make it feel like a home—something people want to stay in —then when we win, you keep the prize money."

My head jerks up. "Excuse me? *When* we win?"

"That's the deal. Payment for the decorating."

A giddy spark zips through me, I almost laugh. I want to scream. I want to kiss him. Better yet, I want to scream *while* kissing him.

Before I can pick which impulse to follow, Gran's voice blasts down the hall.

"Oh, good! The pair of you finally found your way to each other. Now you can make some strong, healthy babies."

I choke. Alec blinks. The stack of papers wobbles dangerously in my hands.

"What?" she says, utterly unbothered. "Look at him. Those shoulders! You're welcome, Clementine."

And before I can stop her, she continues on. "Even all those years ago, this little one was a looker, just like your grandpa." She turns to Alec. "I told Bill she'd be catching someone's attention someday. Good to see it's yours, young man."

Alec clears his throat and becomes fascinated by his boots, like they might sprout wings if he stares hard enough. Meanwhile, I can feel my face going full heirloom tomato.

"Don't mind her," I whisper, leaning closer. "Eighty-seven years old. No boundaries."

"I heard that!" Gran yells back.

I shut my eyes, mortified. "She has bionic hearing," I mutter.

His mouth twitches like he's fighting a grin.

I flip back to the papers, desperate for cover. "We've got a deal, Hastings. And for the record, I'm a deeply devoted student, and I thrive under criticism," I chirp. "Just ask literally any ballet teacher I've ever had."

"I'll give you my credit card to buy what you'll need for the lodge." He slides a black Amex onto the counter, as casual as tossing a napkin.

My jaw goes slack. My tongue practically hits the floor like a cartoon dog. *A black Amex.*

"Now, get dressed. We're already behind on time."

"Now?" I blink, imagining what sort of limit he has on that thing. "I was going to do barre in the garage first, but—" He gives me *the* look. "But this is obviously more important," I finish brightly.

I flip to today's schedule. We're supposed to hike a trail in under an hour, then do a Fartlek run, whatever that is. My lungs are preemptively filing a complaint.

"You'll need to change," he says, glancing at my leotard and hoodie. "And you need actual hiking boots with ankle support. Trail shoes for the running days."

It's the most words I've ever heard him string together in one sitting.

"Okay. I used to hike with my grandpa. I might still have some of my old gear. Should I bring snacks?"

"Is it on the schedule?"

I flip through the pages, scanning for snack protocol. "No." I frown. "But—"

"I'll see you at the lodge in fifteen."

And just like that, he turns and walks out.

Behind me, Gran slips back into the kitchen, smug as a cat in a birdcage. "You should wear that leotard more often."

"Don't be gross."

"Seemed like he wanted to climb you like Denali."

I groan, glancing back down at the training schedule, my name printed neatly at the top.

"Looks like I'm paying off my debt faster than we thought," I mutter, my heart doing something very, very stupid in my chest.

Gran leans in, eyes glinting. "Better make sure you finish your stretches before your...*training*. Wouldn't want to pull anything."

She winks. I tuck the schedule under my arm and head for

my apartment above the garage. Hiking boots. Trail shoes. Possibly a will. Because if Alec's plan doesn't kill me physically, the way he looked at me in that kitchen just might.

And yet, as I shut my front door, I'm smiling.

Chapter 9
Clementine

ALEC'S TOYOTA TACOMA smells like a worn denim jacket left in the sun after a long day on the trail.

I'm giddy the entire thirty-minute drive to the Euspuko trailhead. Windows down, hair whipping around my face, air sharp enough to make my lungs feel brand new. The sun's out. The pines flash by. It's the kind of crisp green nostalgia that hits you like a creek splash.

Then we pull up to the start of the trail, and my nerves punch me in the gut. I've hiked before, with my grandpa, but it's been nearly nine years since I was on a trail that wasn't in Central Park.

"We'll start here today as a warm-up," Alec says, shifting the truck into park and getting out.

Am I supposed to follow him?

He walks around the hood to my door and opens it. Not in a gentlemanly way, more in a *you're slow, let's go* way. He disappears to the bed of the truck, hauling out two massive slate-gray packs that hit the ground with a heavy thunk.

I jump out, and my boots immediately sink into a muddy puddle. Water seeps into my sock. Guess these boots are no longer waterproof. I want to grimace, but Alec is staring at me, so I just flash a forced smile.

"You're about five nine, so this pack should fit you," he says. I wish for once I could read his mind.

"Have you been checking me out or what?"

He doesn't smile or scowl, just stares like he's attempting to classify me as either a mildly feral forest creature or, more likely, an annoying human female. "It's important for you to have the correct gear."

Uh-huh. Sure. Then he definitely wouldn't want to know I'm tromping around in hiking shoes a size too small and one of Grandpa's jackets, complete with moth-hole ventilation.

"What are you, five-eleven?" I shoot back.

"Spot on." He doesn't even blink. "This pack will be yours for the next eight weeks. In my line of work, sponsors send gear." He kneels to retie his shoelaces, movements quick and sure.

I crouch too, pretending to mirror him but mostly watching the precise crisscross of his knots before double-knotting mine like a kid trying to keep from tripping over her own shoelaces.

"So you're basically...an influencer," I say, grasping at small talk.

"Do I look like I post haul videos?"

I grin. "Depends. Are we talking *Unboxing: Climbing Ropes Edition*? Or *Top Ten Harnesses That Won't Give You Rope Burn*?"

"If that's your pitch, you're not getting a cut."

"Rude," I say, patting the pack. "At least tag me when you post your hashtag sponsored waterfall selfie."

His glare could peel paint. "I'm a climber. Finn and my agent handle the social media crap."

"Oh, right, I should mention that I looked you up. Two Men On Top. With a name like that, I kinda assumed you and Finn were..." I swirl my hand in the air. "You know a thing."

His jaw tightens. "Finn's my best friend," he says, bluntly. "And yeah, the name's dumb. We were teenagers. Give us a break."

"I think it's cute." I ease off, hearing the strain under his words. The accident hovers in my mind, the one every article twisted into a different story. I want to ask, but the instant I move closer, Alec would probably bolt like I'm wildfire.

So, I grab the pack instead and nearly tip over. "Holy hell. What is in this thing, a boulder collection?"

"It's only ten pounds. You'll be carrying thirty for the race." He swings his own pack over one shoulder like it's made of air. "The training packet explains it."

I unzip mine. "The training packet didn't say I'd be carrying literal bricks, Alec."

"Weight is weight." He's annoyingly smug about it. "Now, put the straps on your shoulders, clip the chest buckle, then tighten the hip belt. Most of it should sit on your hips."

I look down. There are straps everywhere, buckles multiplying like rabbits. I yank one and tug another like I'm in a wrestling match with a backpack.

"Not like that," he says flatly.

"The strap's stuck," I lie, still flailing.

"Let me?" He stares, unblinking.

I hold his gaze a beat longer than I should, then shrug like it's no big deal. "Fine, go ahead. Just don't make it weird."

He steps behind me, shadowing me. His fingers brush my shoulders as he tugs the straps into place, and my skin pebbles.

The last man to touch me was a dance partner with soft and practiced hands. Alec's are nothing like that.

But it's not just his touch. It's the smell of him. Nothing like the familiar stench of cologne and avaricious ambition.

Alec smells like sweat, Bengay, and something quietly unshakable.

"Arms up," he says. Not *please*. Not *when you're ready*. Just a command, clipped and final.

I do it on instinct, muscle memory from years of wardrobe fittings and barked orders from ballet masters.

His hands—broad enough to span my rib cage—find the chest strap, and with a clean *click,* he snaps it shut. He pulls the webbing snug with each tug, like he's tuning an instrument.

"This should be tight. Supportive, not restrictive."

Not restrictive? Tell that to my lungs. Every nerve in my body is lighting up like a switchboard, hyperaware of his hands, his nearness, the faint heat rolling off his chest even though we're not touching.

But then his hands drop to the hip belt. My skin, my stomach, the backs of my thighs, all of me jolts awake, and I take a step back.

"Hold still." Another command, with no room for debate. He crouches, close enough that the hem of my jacket brushes his knuckles as he settles the pads against my hips.

Oh my god.

I force my eyes to a tree in the distance, anywhere but him. *No mixing work and play, Clementine.* That's been my rule ever since my first season of *The Nutcracker*, when I made the mistake of losing my virginity to the Cavalier after opening night. A week later, he'd moved on to the Sugar Plum Fairy, and I was in a rat costume prancing across the stage. I swore I'd never let a man make me feel like that again.

And if he abandons me as his partner, it would kill me to see Alec partnered with anyone else. For the competition, of course.

"There," he says, but he doesn't move back immediately. His golden, hawkish eyes travel upward, deliberate, like he's checking out his work. Or me. "How does that feel?"

There are only two other times I've been speechless in my life. The first was when a credit card was declined at a Prada boutique in Midtown after I was cut from *A Midsummer Night's*

Dream. The second was when my gran called me after Grandpa passed. This doesn't feel like either of those times, because I am not the type of woman who gets all hot and bothered by a man doing basic things like fixing a strap.

It's absurd, but I have to remind myself how to answer in English.

"I—uh—" *Clementine, for the love of God, remember feminism. Dignity!* "You're not just good with your hands, huh? You're good with size too." Oh no. *Abort!* "That came out wrong. Forget I said that."

"Too late."

I groan. "Please don't make this—"

"Weird? Because I'm sure that's what *you* told *me.*"

And just like that, the air shifts.

"Well, thanks. It feels better." As good as a backpack full of bricks can feel.

"You're not the first person I've packed for." He tips his head at me and readjusts his own pack. "We're wasting daylight. Keep up."

His boots scuff the ground as he starts toward a little wooden arrow. Strands of dark hair curl at the nape of his neck, and suddenly I'm noticing the way he occupies space.

I can handle hard training. I can handle directors kicking my foot into place and yanking up my chin, but Alec's direction is different. It's precise and commanding, but underneath it, there's a softness, like I exist. My brain circles around the realization as he sets off.

<hr>

THE VIEW on this hike is out of this world. Mountains rise all around us, snowcapped in the distance. Clouds as big and heavy as apartment buildings, skies stretching for miles with no sign of civilization. We pass lakes where moose and other wildlife drink at the shore. The trail winds over rocks, patches of moss, and through a spattering of trees.

The air is so clean it feels like I never really breathed in New York, like it's scrubbing my lungs.

And yet, despite all of that, I spend far too much time staring at Alec.

He's ahead of me, and even as the trail steepens, his stride is maddeningly steady, while mine feels like an uphill sprint through gravy.

I trudge ahead, careful not to wince at the blister burning into my heel. This isn't one of Grandpa's lazy lake loops with peanut-butter-banana sandwiches.

But I keep up. I don't complain. I can't give him a reason to regret partnering with me.

Twenty grand says I can handle this.

He groans softly as he steps onto a rock, then turns to offer me a hand. His palm is warm, and I let him pull me up, suppressing the urge to keep holding on to it even after I'm safely on the ground. I can be attracted to someone I'm training with, right? People get crushes at work all the time. That's all this is.

But then, when the trail flattens, Alec pulls a notebook from the thigh pocket of his army-green cargos and says, "I need to get to know you more intimately."

I nearly trip over my own boots. The word *intimately* lands like a fist to my sternum. Images of his hands tightening my pack straps earlier flash through my brain.

"Need to what?"

His golden eyes flick to me, unreadable. "To prepare for Wild Trails. Your stamina. Endurance. History."

Right. Of course. My cheeks burn hotter. He turns back to the notebook like nothing happened, while I'm still busy pretending I didn't just imagine him whispering the word in a different context.

Over his shoulder, I watch as he flips open pages of clean, block-letter handwriting. The man writes like an architect.

And apparently I'm growing attracted to this level of organization.

I scramble to cover my fluster. I'm poised, cool, and calm, not a babbling woman with a schoolgirl crush. "So, what, you want my medical records? Blood type?"

Nothing. He just writes another note. My stomach knots. *God, why am I like this?*

"Have you been hiking before?"

"You could try not insulting me."

"I wasn't—" He sighs.

"I told you I spent summers here. My grandpa used to take me hiking all the time," I say. "He'd show me the plants, and we'd argue over what the best chocolate was for s'mores. He was a Hershey's man. I was team Dove chocolate."

He doesn't say anything, and the silence grows long like the space between lightning and thunder.

"Okay. Can you tie a bear bag knot?"

"Give me a cherry stem and see what I can tie."

"Can you be serious?" He frowns.

"Can you have fun?"

He doesn't laugh. Just shoots me that signature glare, and it's sharp enough to make me straighten up. "Answer the question."

Part of me wants to see what he'd do if I didn't listen.

"No," I sigh. "That's a no."

"Fire-starting?"

"Not recently."

"Water filtration?"

"Sucking hard through a LifeStraw is pretty self-explanatory."

"Can you pitch a tent?"

"Yes. But it might lean." He makes a note. The pack's weight drags at my shoulders, pressing into my hips, but I keep my face still.

If I stop talking, I'll start limping, and I can't let him see that. Pain is a weakness that someone else could use to take your part. I learned early to bleed in silence.

Right now, my blister is screaming bloody murder inside my boots. I should figure out how to get a pair like Alec's Salomon-looking ones, but with my negative checking account balance, I don't stand a chance of getting new shoes.

Just breathe, step, hip pop, breathe, step…survive.

"What about kayaking?" he asks.

"I've only gone out on Misthaven Lake. Grandpa never let us take the kayaks out on the river because the current didn't care how good of a swimmer you were. Lake water was safe enough. He'd pack sandwiches, and we'd just drift for hours."

"He was right about the current. And drifting, that's where you learn the water. He had the right instincts."

"It's cool that you knew him," I say, my voice softer now.

"Yeah. We talked a few times, and he taught me some things about glacial travel. Didn't talk much about himself, though. Just about his wife, daughter, and you."

"Sounds like him."

Wind rustles the trees above, shaking leaves loose around us.

"I'll teach you how to kayak. I guided whitewater rapids on the Russian River at seventeen." *What hasn't this man done?* "Are you CPR certified?"

"Not since I was a teen."

"I can retrain you." He nods, like it's the simplest thing in the world. "I'm an instructor."

The way he says it shouldn't short out my brain. But I'm picturing his mouth covering mine. Not to save me from drowning, but to keep me under until I forget my own name.

I look away first, scanning the tree line like it holds the

answers. *Is he really this oblivious? Or does he know exactly what he's doing?*

The conversation feels different now. Less like an inventory of my skills and more like something else. Something that edges toward personal.

"Maybe we should just go to the CPR training event next weekend."

"Why would we go to an event when I could just train you myself?"

I reach for a lie. "So we can size up the competition." My smile feels flimsy, and from the way he's staring back at me, it looks flimsy too.

"Fine, but only if it doesn't interfere with our training sched-ule," Alec says, tucking his notebook back into his pocket. "Also, you're favoring your right leg."

"I'm not." *I am.*

"You need to walk with your hips forward. Don't let your knee turn out."

My cheeks flush hot. I don't tell him he reminds me of my ballet teachers—unapologetically blunt, obsessive about form and discipline. The kind of people who expect excellence.

The last thing I expected to keep after my ballet career ended was a degradation kink.

His sigh shouldn't sting, but it does.

"I know. I'm fine," I tell him, keeping my voice light even though it costs me.

"If you were, you wouldn't be favoring your right leg."

It's bossy. Infuriating. And unfairly hot. My first instinct is to snap back, but the last thing I want is for him to think he needs to slow down for me.

"Your people skills are lacking today."

"I'll work on it if you work on your stride."

Stay focused, Clementine. Eye on the twenty thousand dollars.

"Okay."

He turns, and I follow.

"I'm going to put together some mood boards for the lodge and try to figure out what kind of vibe we're going for. I was thinking about the upstairs hallway," I say, forcing my voice steady between breaths. "It's dark. A mirror could pull light from the stairwell."

Nothing.

"Or paint," I push on. "Something warm, earthy. And those ceiling fans in the common room? They hum like angry bees—"

"Clem." My name lands with enough weight to still me mid-step. He moves in front of me, big enough to cut off the sun. "Stay behind me."

That's when I see it. A massive, honey-colored grizzly bear with its beady eyes locked on us. I immediately step backward, boot slick against a tuft of moss.

Alec doesn't hesitate. With bear spray in one hand, his other arm slides back, finding my hip and pulling me in. His body is a wall of heat and muscle, but he doesn't waver, even when a predator is sizing us up.

The bear grunts, taking one slow step forward.

"We gotta be loud," Alec says before roaring out, "Hey bear!"

"Heyyy bear," I mimic with a tremble in my throat. His thumb sweeps along the side of my hand, steadying me, reminding me to breathe. My pulse isn't listening.

Two cubs appear, tumbling out of the trees behind their mom. They stop and stare at us.

"Oh my goodness, they're so cute."

"They could kill us," he cuts in, gaze never leaving the mother.

"Right."

"Hey bear!" he yells again. We shout, retreating step by step until the bear exhales and vanishes back into the trees. The cubs follow.

Only then does Alec lower the spray. His hand leaves mine slowly, like he's making sure my legs won't give out before he lets go.

"You just put yourself between me and a bear," I say, my voice lower than I expect.

"I wasn't going to let it get near you."

Unfortunately for me, I think my crush just became terminal. *No*. I can't be attracted to a man who speaks exclusively in monosyllables and doesn't seem to be even an ounce interested in me. I can't. And yet, this feels like the moment before water turns to a boil, when everything's still but just about to change.

"You thought it might?"

He finally turns around and gives me a once-over, like he's checking to see if I still have all my limbs. His nostrils flare. "You can never predict what happens out in the wild, Clementine. We look out for each other."

"Like camp buddies?"

"No. Not like camp buddies."

"I never went to camp," I offer quickly. "But they use the buddy system, right? Seems smart."

"Let's go," he sighs.

We start moving again, and now my steps match his without effort. I tell myself it's adrenaline from the animal encounter. But it's not. It's the fact that Alec Hastings just faced down a thousand-pound predator with me tucked against him like I was something worth protecting.

And that was very, very hot.

Chapter 10
Alec

My watch buzzes, and Clementine's eyes flick to it. I'd built in enough time between the hike and the Fartleks to fix the damn shutter that's been clattering all night and choke down a kit meal.

"Go grab some lunch," I tell her.

"Do you have something I can cook? As another thank-you for agreeing to this?"

Clementine falls into step behind me as I head from the truck to the porch. Her curls are shoved back, roots damp with sweat, skin flushed. She looks wrecked—but the kind of wrecked you only get when you've actually put in the work.

She worked harder than I expected, honestly. I could hear her breathing, knew she was struggling, but she never complained once. Even with all my training, two months off the trails has dulled my edge. I had to push harder than I wanted to. I'm nowhere near my usual pace.

"I don't have groceries," I admit.

She clucks her tongue. "So no lunch, and no invitation for a quick swim?"

The picture that flashes in my mind—her freckles bright,

water running down her spine—isn't safe. The encounter with the bear has clearly turned my wits to mush. She's egging me on now, I can tell, trying to distract me from how tired she is.

"You could use a shower."

"So could you," she fires back. "We could save water, you know. Take a dip in the lake. Be efficient. Lunch and a swim?"

It sounds like a date. My pulse kicks, but I keep my face flat. "The shower will help with any soreness you're feeling."

"Oh. Right." Her smirk says she's not buying it.

"As long as you're dried off and ready in thirty for Fartleks around the lake." I nod to the spruce tree by the lodge shed.

Her head tilts. "Fart *what*?"

"*Timed sprints*. For speed."

"You're making that up."

"Guess you'll have to show up to find out. See you in thirty."

"See you then." She lingers on the bottom step for a moment that feels heavy, but she doesn't let it last long. She turns, and I watch her head up the path to her grandmother's place.

I couldn't help watching her on the hike either. For safety, obviously. Though I don't have an excuse for all the watching I did when I caught her in splits first thing this morning.

But then I see it.

Step, step…favor.

She hisses under her breath when her weight shifts, quiet enough that most people wouldn't hear.

I'm not most people.

"What's wrong with your foot?"

"Nothing." She flips her gaze back at me, blue eyes wide and guilty.

"You've got a blister."

"I do not."

I glare at her. "We aren't starting this partnership on a lie."

"Fine, I have a blister. But it's not that bad."

"I'm guessing a quarter-sized piece on your right heel?" My gaze sweeps down her legs, catching the faint wrinkle in her sock where the skin's likely rubbed raw.

"You're scary good at that, you know."

I pull my jacket off and toss it on the top step of the porch. "Boot. Off."

"No."

"Yes, let me see it."

"Absolutely not!"

"Why?"

She bites down on her plush lower lip, which is drenched in that pink glossy stuff again. "Have you ever seen a ballerina's feet? The things in these boots are not pretty."

"I don't care about pretty." I hold her stare. Then I nod to my jacket on the top step, and she shuffles forward. "I've seen climbers' feet after frostbite. Fifty hours in boots. Half the nails gone. You can't scare me."

"As gnarly as that sounds, mine are just as bad." She sighs, slumps her shoulders, but finally sits on the damn jacket, stretching her legs out in front of her.

"I'm missing half of one toe," I deadpan.

Her lips curl upward before she tries to mask it. "Seriously?"

"On Cho Oyu," I explain. "Let someone borrow my socks when they had frostbite, only to end up with it myself. Lost half a pinkie."

She stares at my boots as if she's waiting for the leather to turn transparent. "Let me see it."

"Only if you give me that damn foot of yours."

"Fine. Show me yours first, and then you can have mine," she resolves.

I take the compromise and don't hesitate. At least not at first. Boot off, then my sock is halfway down before the weird flush of embarrassment creeps in. *That's new.* Never cared before, but her gaze makes me hyperaware of the gnarled skin, the jagged nail beds, and the fact that these feet have been on more mountains than most people have been on vacations. Still, I peel my sock off.

She leans forward, hair sliding forward to curtain her face as she examines my foot where it rests on the porch step. Coconut from her sunscreen still clings faintly to her skin, sharp against the scent of pine sap and dust.

"Well, color me corrected," she says softly. "Guess I've never met anyone whose feet are more messed up than mine."

I pull my sock and shoe back on. "Glad you're satisfied. Now take that boot off," I call over my shoulder as I grab the medical kit out of the back of the Tacoma and return to kneel in the dirt in front of her.

"Bring it up here." I tap my knee, and she kicks her foot up. My hands close around her ankle, the smooth, warm line of it jolting something low in my gut. I keep my movements brisk, but her mouth curves like she knows exactly how close I am to not keeping this strictly professional.

I slip her sock off and instantly notice it's soaked at the heel.

"Clementine," I mutter, shaking my head as I stare at the crimson fabric. Her foot's a battlefield of split skin, bruised nails, and raw blisters.

"It's not that bad."

"Not that bad?" I echo.

"I've danced on worse. I once had a fracture in my ankle, healed just enough to walk, and I still pushed myself to perform."

"That's not right."

"I'm sure this isn't the first time a partner's pushed themselves around you. I mean, with F—"

His name dies on her tongue, but I've already heard it and am already refusing that I have.

I pour water over the worst of her heel. She flinches, hissing, head tipping back, and I have to drag my gaze away from the long, pale line of her throat. Up close, there's a cluster of freckles on the front of her shoulder blade that reminds me of Ursa Major and another near her neck that forms a question mark. I hadn't noticed them before. I force myself to focus on the task at hand.

"This," I say, reaching for the alcohol, "is going to sting."

Her eyes flick up in a challenge. "Promise?"

Sly little fox. She sucks in a breath as I place an alcohol pad on her skin, and her toes curl into my thigh. I've done this for hundreds of people, probably thousands, but I can't stop thinking about how soft her skin is, how compliant she is when she's not arguing with me.

This whole thing is an arrangement. She didn't ask me to help her train just so I can ogle her like a piece of meat.

"We always stop for blisters," I grit out, steadying my breath. "Always. This'll derail the training plan. You can't hike with open wounds like this, Clem." The words explode out of me before I can catch them, but I need her to understand that I can't let her get hurt. "I can't have you injured week one."

She leans back on her hands, the porch creaking. "I didn't want to stop. And I didn't have to—I did the whole hike. I can do the fart thingies or whatever else you've got."

"That's not the point. You don't have to push through stuff that's preventable."

Something flickers in her face—hurt, maybe—but she looks away, watching a dust mote spin in the air between us.

I sit back on my heels, hands on my thighs. "We need to trust each other out there. And right now? You're making that hard."

Her chin tilts up. "You're acting like this is life or death."

"If you hide injuries, you're a liability. To me. To yourself. I've carried partners out before, it's not happening again."

"You won't need to carry me out."

"That's not your call." It comes out curt, and I feel her flinch before I even register the words.

For a beat, we just listen to the wind through the spruce. She doesn't meet my gaze, and I hate that I put that wall there.

I pull out my notebook, needing something to fix. "Skip the Fartleks. Do tomorrow's weight training instead. Walk to work in something comfortable, wear the weighted vest for an hour, and stretch. River training gets bumped to two days from now. I'll need a day to find us a kayak. Saturday will be the first day with you at the lodge."

She exhales slowly. "Okay. Weight, walk, stretch, vest, kayak on Friday. Helper on Saturday."

"Put your number in." I hand her my flip phone.

She stares at it. "What is this?"

"My phone," I explain. "Most of this place doesn't have service, but this thing can pick up a call or text anywhere. If anything comes up, I want to know. Every blister, rolled ankle, bee sting, weird lung thing. I want to be ready."

Her fingers brush mine when she passes the phone back. "Thanks for not letting me get eaten by the bear. And for…" Her gaze flicks to my hands still resting against her ankle. "Taking care of my feet."

She slides off the porch step, bare soles crunching over dirt. The swing of her hair catches the sun, and I follow the line of her stride until I see it again—that tiny hitch she thinks she's hiding.

Even still. Performing to the very end.

I shouldn't have snapped at her. It's not her fault she's wired to push through pain. I've spent years doing the same thing. But the image of Finn flat on the ice won't shake, and the thought of watching her go down like that because I didn't make her take it seriously hits harder than I expect.

"They're not bad, by the way," I call out to her.

She glances over her shoulder. "What?"

"Your feet. Not by a long shot."

That earns me a real smile, one she tries to smother. "I'll send you a photo of me doing the workout later. And maybe overshare my whole life. But you asked for it, camp buddy."

Buddy.

I hate that word.

Chapter 11
Clementine

LIABILITY.

Alec's word echoes in my head like the thud of a missed landing on stage.

I'm rhinestones and tulle and lemon water with cucumbers. Not the sort of person who scrambles up ridges and yells at bears.

I waddle up the dirt path between the lodge and my garage apartment, my soles collecting grit, my bandages turning a delicate shade of gross. The boots hang from my fingertips, heavy and useless. I'd rather walk barefoot across a lava field than put them back on.

It's day one of training, and I've already failed spectacularly. He thinks I'm a liability, and I was over here batting my eyelashes at him.

My rib cage goes rigid. The crawling, warm, clawed pressure that starts under my sternum and stretches outward until it owns me. My body knows the pattern. The rush of heat in my face, the prickling in my fingertips, the bone-deep itch that says *fix it*.

All I have to do is make sure I never get a blister again. Easy.

I need socks with more padding. Boots that fit better with

just the right ankle support that will make me look like I belong here.

Maybe then Alec wouldn't need to rewrite our training schedule. Maybe he wouldn't look at me like I'm a bad investment. Maybe he won't say *liability* again.

The ache in my feet is nothing compared to the need in my hands. The one that wants my laptop open, a browser tab glowing, the *sort by lowest price* option practically winking at me.

Gear. I just need the right gear.

It's practical. It's for the race.

I unlock my phone, searching for a hit of dopamine, only to find the No Service signal at the top of my screen. There's Wi-Fi in the house, but that would mean going inside where Gran is. And if I go inside, she might ask me what I'm doing. And I would either have to lie or admit that I'm attempting to online shop my way out of yet another shame spiral.

I shouldn't be shopping. I shouldn't want to.

I pace the driveway in slow, stupid circles, holding my phone to the sky like I'm performing some kind of dark little prayer to the algorithm. I just need one bar.

The roof. Of course.

When I was little, I used to sneak up there all the time. Gran would yell that I was going to crack my skull open, and I'd yell back that I'd be careful right before doing something extremely not careful. But up there, the noise of the world didn't reach me. Up there, I could hover.

Barefoot, I tuck my phone into my bra and climb the wobbly lattice behind the garage. The wood groans. Morning glory vines snag my toes. I kick them off like they're trying to shame me.

Halfway up, the clouds part, the heavens open, and Instagram loads.

Sweet, sweet victory.

Within two posts, the targeted ads descend like divine intervention. Trail runners with pink accents. Hiking jackets in colors called "Moss" and "Stone." A jade-green water bottle that promises to make me feel like the kind of person who drinks electrolytes and wakes up with purpose. Anthropologie scarves. Outdoor Voices puffers.

Then a reel. A girl with sun-kissed cheeks and freckles (the good kind, not the I-forgot-SPF kind), laughing on a mountain with gear that's definitely not in my budget.

I want to be her. Or at least look like her long enough for Alec to take me seriously. For him to not need to handle me like I'm made of papier-mâché.

Debt feels safer than this. Debt is numbers, and numbers have rules. But this creeping panic that I'm not enough, that I'm ridiculous and broken, doesn't come with instructions.

I can't click "Check Out" on self-worth.

I can't two-day ship love.

I can't return this crummy feeling of failure.

But I can buy the socks.

And maybe the sweat-wicking zinc panties. And a little keychain to make that gray monstrosity of a pack a little cuter.

Service flickers, so I climb higher. The "Buy Now" button glows like a neon sign. To my joy, my Apple Pay is still hooked up. My thumb presses down on the screen, and relief floods me like an open window after a week of stale air. A three-second chemical high.

Then the service drops.

"No. No, no, no—"

I climb another rung. This time, the lattice lets out a splintering *crack* before the whole thing buckles. My brain has exactly one second to think, *oh, that's bad,* before I'm airborne. Then—*plop*. Straight into Gran's flower bed, in a puff of dirt and marigold petals.

Somewhere in the mess of vines and leaves, my phone chimes. Order confirmed.

A laugh escapes me. I just lie there, vines wrapping my arms, smelling like dirt and desperation.

A bee lands on my elbow.

I don't move.

Let it sting me. At least it wouldn't cost me anything.

Chapter 12
Alec

THE PHOTO'S GRAINY, overexposed, and somehow still beautiful. She's barefoot in a garage, with a pair of pink dumbbells in hand.

JK

I told you, I've had worse, camp buddy.

ALEC

dont push too hard.

cant redo training sched again

CLEM

I won't. Your turn.

ALEC

?

CLEM

Send a picture back. Complete trust and communication, remember?

I stare at the message like it's a ticking time bomb.

I'm not a selfie guy. Finn and Nadra take all our photos. Last time Finn asked me to take one, I almost dropped his phone into a ravine.

I could ignore it. But I did ask her to check in with me after her workout, and it would be unfair if I didn't do the same.

I flip the camera to my face and immediately shut my phone. Fuck, this is embarrassing. I only know one person who could help.

ALEC

how do u take a good selfie

FINN

OH MY GOD

This for the wife?

ALEC

nvm

delete this

FINN

You entered the competition?

If you get married before me, I'm letting you
know now I'm setting the bar very high for
bachelor parties

ALEC

I told you it's Bill Lennox's granddaughter

she needs the prize money

FINN

Should I be jealous you never tried to send any
selfies to me?

photo attached

Guilt knots in my gut at the picture of him in the hospital
bed.

ALEC

she reminds me of you

FINN

so she's devastatingly handsome and
impossible not to love?

ALEC

no. stubborn, loud, ignores instructions

FINN

Ah, if you don't snag her up, I may need to
take her on a date

ALEC

If you wanted to you could.

FINN

Shut up. You're obviously hella obsessed if
you're taking photos for the girl.

A good pic is simple, just be yourself. Smile.

> But if you're sexting her, hold something in front of your junk. Girls don't wanna see that unless specifically asked

ALEC

> shut up

> blocking you

I toss the phone face down on the bed. Immediately, I pick it back up.

What the fuck am I acting like a teenage boy for? I'm a grown man. *This is normal behavior.* I don't need to sit here and debate the moral weight of sending a photo to a beautiful woman.

Attraction is easy. I've never had an issue finding ways to dull an edge or burn off the adrenaline after a summit day. Clem is not some climber in base camp, not a one-night fix to keep the cold out of my sleeping bag.

And even if she were, I'm not that guy. I don't have the energy for a meaningless hookup right now, let alone with someone like her. She's too untouched by the world, too quick-witted, and she reminds me too much of my sisters, the way she pokes at me, testing for cracks.

I stare at her last message until the screen times out.

Complete trust and communication.

Fine.

I flip the camera toward my face. The lighting is bad, my shoulders look weird, and my expression screams *hostage situation.* I adjust. Shift my weight. Try again. The result is worse. My jaw looks like it's trying to flee my face.

This is ridiculous.

I run a hand through my hair, give it one more go in the mirror. I lean against the doorframe. Click. No. Absolutely not.

I exhale, glance over my shoulder, and catch the cluttered

side table in the corner. Half-burned candle, stack of mail, and a lamp that's older than me.

If Clementine's going to boss me around about complete communication, I can at least make our deal useful.

I tilt the phone, frame the table, and snap the photo.

ALEC

needs your decorating expertise.

I hit Send before I can think about it too much.

It's not a mirror selfie.

It's not my face.

It's safe.

And yet…my pulse still ticks a little faster as I wait for her to see it.

CLEM

…That's a lamp.

ALEC

u r my decorator

ur problem now

CLEM

I wanted a selfie.

ALEC

u got pic

CLEM

Of a lamp…

ALEC

ugly. needs fixing.

CLEM

Exactly my type then!

I picture her moving things around in here, her skin brushing against mine as she makes space for something better. Something she picked.

It's just about the lamp.

Still, the thought sticks. Her laugh in the kitchen. The way she bites the inside of her cheek when she's holding back. I let the image drift with me as I set my phone beside the fireplace, roll onto my back, and close my eyes.

For a moment, it's her voice I hear in the quiet.

I PUSH Finn up the ramp, his chair rattling against the wood I measured three times and cut wrong anyway. He teases me for overbuilding, telling me I've made it sturdy enough to hold a truck.

His laugh is oxygen.

For the first time in months, my chest loosens.

I did it. He's here.

The main room glows with firelight. Curtains ripple though the windows are shut. On the coffee table, two tumblers wait, beads of condensation sliding down the glass. Finn stands from his chair, as if he were never injured, and we clink them together.

He's home.

He's whole.

Then the walls move. They inhale, slow and deep, the logs expanding against one another with a groan. Dust drifts down like snow.

Finn frowns up at the ceiling. "That supposed to happen?"

"It's fine."

Another creak, longer this time. The windows bulge outward, flexing like brittle lungs too weak to hold air.

"Alec…you said you fixed this place."

"I did," I start, but a crack slices through the beam above us, splitting wood like bone.

The ceiling sags. A chunk of plaster shears off, exploding against the floor. Finn falls. "You said it was safe. You said you had my back."

"I swear—" I lunge for him, but the lodge lurches sideways, tilting like a slope. The floor heaves under me. Every step pulls me farther away.

Finn claws at the wood, dragging himself forward, but the boards crumble to black beneath his hands.

"Alec!" His voice isn't laced with pain but betrayal. He's slipping backward, vanishing inch by inch.

I sprint. The walls fold like paper. The floor yawns open, inhaling the rug, the floors—him. His screams ricochet off the collapsing beams.

He's right there, with his arms reaching and his fingers spread, but the roof plunges between us. A beam splits the room in half. I dive, shouting his name.

Finn's eyes lock on mine. "Don't let me fall again. Please, Alec. Don't let me fall."

The words gut me. I throw my body against the rubble, heave, claw, and fight like I did on the mountain, every tendon snapping, lungs bursting. But the lodge keeps breaking, keeps falling, keeps burying him deeper.

And then the weight hits. A crushing silence, absolute and heavy.

And through it, I hear him sob.

Finn has never sobbed.

I can't reach him.

I wake so hard I think I've actually fallen.

It takes me a moment to remember where I am.

Misthaven.

Finn's lodge.

Still standing. Still safe. For now.

Chapter 13
Alec

WHEN FINN and I were twelve, we went to summer camp together and decided we could build a boat out of spare lumber we found lying around and zip ties we stole from the counselors' supply shed.

Finn christened it *The Gengar*, after his favorite Pokémon and the game we spent half the summer playing on our Game Boys under the oak tree in my backyard. The boat didn't make it more than ten feet off the shore of Lake Shasta before half of it started to sink, but we didn't care. We climbed aboard anyway and paddled in crooked circles, soaked to the bone, shouting over each other like two pirates mid-mutiny.

When the rest of camp woke up, they found us fifty feet offshore, laughing so hard our ribs ached. We got stuck with kitchen duty for the rest of the week.

Every time Clementine laughs, it reminds me of that day.

Except now, I'm not twelve.

And the girl in front of me isn't Finn.

"We're coming up on a class one," I warn. "Remember, it's small waves, no drop, but keep your center of gravity low."

"Copy that," she answers.

We've been on the river for half an hour. The first fifteen, I drilled her on the basics. Paddle strokes, grip, body posture. I even flipped on purpose so she could practice escaping the spray skirt.

Today's run is light. Class 1 and 2 rapids, ending with a short Class 3. Nothing dangerous, but enough push to punish sloppy paddling.

Tandem kayaking's all about rhythm and trust.

The Class 4 water in the Wild Trails qualifier won't forgive nerves, so Clem needs to find her pace now.

The river threads through steep cliffs and dense spruce, steel-gray water churning around jagged boulders. Mist rises from the surface, softening the edges of trees and rocks, while thick clouds hang overhead, pierced by shards of sunlight that set branches and early autumn leaves ablaze with gold. The current twists and narrows, restless and merciless, beautiful in its power.

The bow dips as the first wave swells beneath us. She squeals but steadies herself before I can bark a correction. *Good girl.* We cut through the next wave, spray slapping sideways, the boat jolting under us.

We hold.

"Alec, did you see me?" She twists around, and her paddle smacks into mine. "This isn't that hard at all."

"Hey! Rule number one?"

"Always look where you're going." She parrots it perfectly. "Forward, I know. I just wanted to see if you were having as much fun as me."

"This isn't for fun."

"Right, I forgot, no fun." She digs her paddle back in. "Even though this is the most fun I've had since I got back to town."

"Pick up the pace," I shout and check my watch.

Air temp: 59. Water temp: 54. Wind: five knots.

Shades of orange in Clementine's hair: nine.

Not that I'm counting.

"Back straight, elbows low," I direct.

"Got it."

"Don't strangle the paddle."

She corrects, and the boat cuts cleaner. I let her set the rhythm. Her wild laughter tears across the water and lodges in my chest. Reluctantly, a part of me answers, betraying itself with a thrill I hadn't expected. Not the kind of reckless fun I had with Finn, racing until our shoulders gave out.

With her, it's different. She's infectious.

It's been a long damn time since I let myself pay this much attention to someone.

Shove it down.

I drove to Anchorage last night for this kayak. Called in a favor through an old sponsor and had it overnighted. Most teams already cleared the shelves of anything decent. Wild Trails has 350 teams registered. Only 100 make it through qualifiers.

We have to be one of them.

"Let's try an eddy turn," I call. "See that pocket behind the boulder? That's an eddy. Calm water. We'll angle in, pivot one-eighty, and stop."

"Stop?"

"In a Class 4, you'll beg for them. They're pit stops."

"Okay. Which way do we rotate?"

"Left."

The rapid surges. Water slaps the hull, drowning half the kayak before spitting us back up. Clementine doesn't flinch. She leans forward, shoulders tight, arms driving. She doesn't cower, she attacks.

"Left!" I bark.

She plants her paddle. On the wrong side.

"Other left!"

"Sorry!" she yells back, scrambling to fix it. Her spine flexes, muscles pulling tight beneath her life jacket, paddle striking the hull before she corrects. The kayak jerks, spins clumsily, then settles as the eddy takes us, bow swinging upstream.

On one side, a cliff leans over the river, a low branch reaching out as if to grab us. On the other side, a smooth boulder rises from the roaring current. My lungs finally let go.

"That wasn't terrible."

"Tell me that was badass!"

It was. *She was.*

"You did good."

"Oh, come on." She groans, dramatic as hell. "Say it. Say I was a badass."

I roll my eyes, but she reaches her paddle back toward me, nearly smacking me in the head.

"Hey!" I bark.

"Praise me or I won't improve," she fires back, like she knows she's winning this argument.

"You were a badass."

We angle back into the river. The current smooths, but we don't. I call, she answers, and our rhythm clicks, like the boat itself finally trusts us.

"Rapids. That's a Class 2, right?"

"Good eye." I'd seen them twenty yards back, but it matters that she did too.

"See?" she says. "You're not just a teacher. You're a student."

I grunt. "I know how to kayak."

"No, a student of the Compliment Clementine course."

If she only knew how fast I'd ace that.

"Be ready. This stretch may turn fast."

We angle into the drop. Whitewater closes in, the world shrinking to froth and roar. Clementine's laugh bursts through it. Silver water catches the sun on her shoulders, glittering like she's made for this.

We round the bend, and my stomach caves. Branches choke

the channel. A fresh beaver dam, stacked high and solid. Shit. I should've scouted this stretch. On Treaddit, some stranger swore the colony was on the east fork. Like an idiot, I trusted them.

With her life.

"Dam ahead!" I roar, scanning for an eddy. "Hard left! Paddle!"

"What?!" Her voice is absorbed by the current.

"We need to stop! Pull out!" I bury my blade. She mirrors me. The river laughs, hauls us into its fists, and drags us straight for the wall.

One thought burns through everything: *Keep her safe.*

"Brace your core! Paddle up!"

The bow smashes a log sideways, and the kayak lurches skyward. The cold air is a razor in my throat. For one impossible heartbeat we're flying, twenty miles an hour, five feet high, Evel Knievel without the guarantee of landing.

The kayak tilts, and the world inverts. I try to flip us back over, but it's useless. The last thing I hear is her scream, and then it's gone as we are engulfed by the rapids moving under us.

The river is all teeth. Whitewater gnashing, the current pulling my body in a dozen directions. The impact knocks the breath from me, the spray skirt holding me in like a trap. My vision is all foam. I kick and twist, but the kayak keeps moving.

I open my eyes.

Where is she?

The bow is empty. My pulse rips through me. She must've gotten free like we practiced, which means she should be at the surface, waiting for me.

I claw out of the spray skirt, exploding upward. Air slams into my lungs, but she isn't here. It's just foam and churn and a hundred places for her to vanish. Her life jacket should have pulled her up. Fear slips through my mind, but I ignore it.

I need to find her.

"Clementine!" I yell and yell until my throat goes raw.

A flash of red hair whips once above the water before the current drags her under. My heart caves as I wrench off my life jacket and dive.

The river claws at me, clamping down like it wants me too, but I fight, arms slamming water aside. Mud and grit cover my teeth. I don't care. All I care about is chasing that streak of red.

There.

Her shoulder bobs upward. Her shirt is snagged on a branch of a fallen tree. Her body thrashes.

Adrenaline courses through me.

I claw at the fabric until it tears under my fists. My hand clamps her waist as I tug us upward, lungs screaming.

We break the surface. She coughs, sputtering.

She's alive.

"Kick." I yell over the river, which seems to rush faster around us, yanking us downstream. I haul her toward me like my arms were built for this one purpose.

I spot the bank and swim like my life isn't mine anymore.

I haul her to shore, stumbling, half dragging, half clutching, until we are standing on the muddy bank. She collapses against me, coughing river water into me. Her braid slaps my jaw, heavy and dripping.

"Jesus, Clem—" My voice comes out shredded. I cradle her face, tilting her chin up, my thumb brushing her throat until I feel her pulse.

Fast. Steady. Alive.

Her lashes flicker. Her eyes open and lock on mine.

"I'm sorry," I rasp.

But instead of fear on her face, she looks…happy? She's smiling, staring at the kayak bobbing on the surface now two hundred meters downriver.

"I got out of the spray skirt on the first try! Like we prac-ticed." She squeezes my forearm, heaving in breaths between laughs.

My skin buzzes with adrenaline—I tell myself it's adrenaline, nothing else. But adrenaline doesn't usually make my temples throb with guilt.

I stare at her. She's okay. More than okay…she's proud of herself?

Meanwhile, I'm still choking on the terror of what almost was.

I should let go.

But I can't.

I crush her against me again and hold on like the river might still steal her if I loosen even an inch. Her heart thunders against mine before she wriggles free, dropping onto the muddy bank.

"I shouldn't have taken us this way."

She tilts her head, still grinning. "Didn't you say nature's unpredictable? That you can't account for everything?"

"You're really okay?"

It's only been two damn days, and I've already put her in danger, first with the bear and now the rapids.

"My ass hurts from that landing, but yeah, I'm good." She winks. "I promise I'll be in perfect working order for painting your kitchen tomorrow."

Her levity is confusing. Maybe I should laugh with her, but I can't manage to move past the tension in my bones.

How the hell am I supposed to manage another six weeks of keeping her safe?

"Are *you* okay?" she asks.

"I need a second." I inhale and press my thumb against the first black band circling my forearm, tracing the ink I've added for people I've lost to the mountains.

If I lost her…

I cinch my eyes together, refusing to finish the thought.

"If it's about the kayak smashing, maybe I can help get us a new one," she says.

"I don't care about the damn kayak." I press harder over the ink, as if I could rewrite what's beneath it.

Her thigh brushes mine, and my insides thrash. My lungs are cracked bells.

Of course she notices. Her hand finds my wrist, her finger skimming the ink. "What are these for?"

Water crashes along the rocks, but her voice cuts through it. I could lie. Should lie. But lies feel heavier than truth.

"They're people," I say. "Everyone I've lost."

Her delicate nails circle the first ring. The heat of her skin brushing mine steadies the storm inside me. "Who is this?"

"This one—" I let my gaze linger on the curve of her damp forearm. "Nikkolo Silva. Cerro Torre, Chile. He used to fold origami out of anything he found. Leaves, scraps of paper, even a Hershey's wrapper once. Laughed so hard in storms the tent rattled." I swallow, the memory still fresh. "He was the first."

She traces another line.

Gael.

Xavier.

Solène. Eight names. Eight silences carved into my skin. The thought pounds so violently I almost say it out loud.

Her palm spreads warm across my back, thumb moving in quiet circles like she's stitching me back together. I hate that it works. Hate that I'm breathing again because of her.

"That's a lot," she whispers.

"It is."

She hesitates, then asks, "Are any of them for Finn?"

Her question is soft.

Harmless to her. To me, it's dynamite.

My whole body seizes. Finn doesn't live in ink. He lives in every ridge we clawed up, in the jokes we yelled across storms, in silence that didn't crush but carried. If I ever had to put him on my skin—*fuck*—I wouldn't stop.

I'd carve him over every inch until I disappeared.

Or I'd climb into the mountain's mouth and not come back down.

Because how do you live without your other half?

You don't.

But I can't say that. Not to her. Maybe not to myself.

"No," I force out.

Her lips part. "If I did anything out there that made you think I was going to hurt myself, I'm sor—"

"Don't." I stand so fast the ground tilts. "You don't have to be sorry."

The river roars loud enough to rattle my ribs, but it's not the water that's making my hands shake. My palms are wet. My vision tunnels. Every part of me is screaming the same thing: She could've been one of them.

It's irrational.

So fucking unlike me.

I don't panic. I don't fear. I don't feel this much.

And now I don't know what to do with it. These messy, overwhelming feelings don't fit inside the man I've built. They don't fit in the pack I carry. They spill over the edges, heavy and unmanageable.

I should've known better. Shouldn't have signed up for this. I pushed her too hard today, and now I have to deal with the fucking consequences.

Why am I reacting like this? Why is she inside my head when I've spent years teaching myself how not to let anyone live there?

So, I do the only thing I know how. I stack the walls higher. Layer them thick. Pretend I'm stone again.

Because if I add another band to my arm, it won't mark me. It will end me.

Chapter 14
Clementine

I WAKE TANGLED in my sheets, the nightmare clinging like smoke. I toss for an hour, counting breaths, bargaining with myself not to reach for my phone.

Because I know what I'll find.

An email notification, glowing smugly on my screen. Confirmation that the clothes I panic-bought on Wednesday are already being wrapped in tissue paper and packed.

Gran still thinks her shredded morning glories were the work of a rogue moose. I haven't told her the truth, that I stress-shopped and the lattice was collateral.

I know. I'll just stash the boxes in my closet when they show up. By the time the credit card statement lands, the qualifying round will be over, and maybe we'll all forget about it.

It's such a cosmic joke. The very thing that calms me down is the thing drowning me.

I kick off my blanket like it's personally responsible for capitalism and lurch out of bed. If I stay in this room one more second, I'll implode.

Outside, the night is ink-black, sticky with the hum of crickets. Bugs fling themselves into the cone of my phone flashlight, kamikaze-thwacking the glass like they're trying to knock it out of my hand.

It's four a.m., which, yes, is technically insane. But Alec strikes me as the kind of person who either never sleeps or wakes up before his dreams are finished. His schedule says I'm not due at the lodge until seven, but maybe showing up earlier will show initiative!

I run across the path between our houses and climb the porch steps, my pulse jittering like it wants out.

The lodge isn't technically ours anymore, but our family's blood is in those beams. Literally. Grandpa sliced his hand installing the front porch banister and bled all over the wood. It's basically still mine.

The key is still where Grandpa hid it, behind warped cedar under the porch elk antlers. The leather tag still says BACK DOOR, his handwriting half faded. *Aha!* Still here. Which means Alec left it here. If he didn't want me to let myself in, he would've moved it.

Duh.

"Alec?" I whisper, nudging open the back door.

Nothing.

I step inside, tote bag sliding off my shoulder, eyes adjusting to the dark. Inside, the hallway is still. I expected it to be a disaster of dust and creaking floorboards, like it was a week ago, but all the floorboards have been replaced with dark wood.

This must have taken hours. What I've gleaned from my first two weeks at Got Wood? is that installing floors is grueling work.

The lodge smells the same as it did years ago. Pine and soap and old smoke. It hits me square in the chest. I used to lie right in this hallway as a kid, listening to Grandpa's climbing buddies through the metal air vent.

Woodsmoke tickles my nostrils and pulls me to the main room. The fire's low, just embers. In front of it, an unrolled sleeping bag lies on the floor with a bunched-up pillow. The zipper's half-open, like someone got too warm sometime in the night. Next to the pack, there are three folded stacks of clothes, a dented metal water bottle, and his notebook.

He's staying here? There are fifteen bedrooms in this place. Fifteen real beds. And he chose to sleep on the floor. Something twists low in my stomach.

I bend down to run my fingers over the plaid sleeping bag. It's cold. He's probably been up for hours or never came to bed at all.

Next, I waddle over to the stone fireplace, hunting along the base. There. Just behind where the firewood basket used to sit. A small dent in the stone.

Clem's Crater.

I must've been six. Maybe seven. Climbed the stone ledge in slippery socks trying to prove I was brave enough to hang with the grown-ups. Slipped and smacked my head so hard I saw stars. Grandpa declared the lodge would remember me forever. Someone made me cocoa with two marshmallows.

Things like that stick.

"Getting your breaking in done early?"

I jerk upright. Alec leans in the kitchen doorway, half shadowed.

"Are you…sleeping here?"

He rakes a hand through his chestnut hair, gaze never leaving me. "Yeah."

"The other rooms not cutting it?"

"I like the view." He tips his chin toward the floor-to-ceiling windows, where the lake sits black and endless.

"Ah, of course. The bleak darkness over a warm mattress."

"I haven't slept on a lot of those."

"Mm."

"You come here to admire my bed, Clementine?" He pushes

off the frame, closing the space between us, work belt hanging low, black tee pulling across his chest like a threat.

"Uh—no." My throat goes dry. Maybe I should've stayed tangled in my own sheets. "Couldn't sleep. Thought I'd get a head start helping you."

"Why aren't you sleeping?" His brows knit. "My schedule has you down for eight hours at minimum." His tone is tight, like it has been since we got back from the river yesterday.

I snort. "Are *you* getting eight hours?"

"Don't worry about me."

Does anyone? The thought sticks in my throat. My eyes snag on the rings inked on his forearm. "I would love eight hours. But nightmares…don't really care about schedules."

"You have nightmares?"

"I think they have me," I joke, but my voice thins at the edges.

"I get them too," he says after a beat, words pulled out like teeth.

"Do yours involve homicidal ribbon and bloodthirsty tulle?"

Something almost like a laugh huffs out of him, but it dies quickly, leaving the space between us restless.

"They're usually about Finn." His gaze holds mine. "I mean, I'm not the one getting hurt in them."

The words feel like a slip, a breadcrumb he didn't mean to drop. I search his face for regret, but there's none, just exhaustion etched into him. The kind of exhaustion that runs bone-deep, like he's been hauling a pack of hundred-pound bricks on his back day after day, without pause. Maybe that is what spooked him after our kayak flipped.

"Right, your partner," I say softly, fumbling for neutral ground. "How did you two meet?" I ask because if I can't crack open his nightmare, maybe I can at least move him somewhere gentler.

"First day of a summer program at a climbing gym. We were

five." His eyes flick away, then back. "He sat down next to me while I was Velcroing my shoes. Introduced himself as my new best friend. And then he just kept showing up."

Buried beneath the exhaustion, his voice carries a flicker of warmth.

"I like him already," I say.

"He's hard not to like. You'll meet him after the qualifiers."

The silence that follows isn't comfortable, but it isn't empty either. It hums, restless, like there's more he could say but won't. I want to press, but the look on his face tells me this is all he has to give today. He didn't flinch when talking about Finn. We're making progress!

"So, how long have you been up?"

"A few hours now."

He tips his head toward the kitchen, and I follow. The space is gutted, stripped bare except for the black-and-white tiles. It's nothing like I remember. The plaid curtain that used to flutter over the sink is gone, replaced by a yellowed pane of glass.

Still, if I close my eyes, I can catch the faint scent of mason jars stuffed with herbs and wildflowers. I can almost see Grandpa leaning on the counter, grinning at me while I splashed in the lake. I miss him so much it hurts. I wish I'd spent more time with him before he passed.

"Let me grab the paint swatches from my bag," I say, already buzzing with nervous energy. "I've been torn between two ideas for this room." Which is mostly code for me scrolling Pinterest between customers at Got Wood? until a Mary Janes ad derailed me.

"I trust you to just order them."

The black Amex hasn't moved off my dresser since I planted it there. I barely trust myself with it, and yet here he is, trusting me as if I'm financially responsible. "I will. Tile samples for the backsplash should be arriving at the store today. I can bring them by tomorrow."

"What exactly is the purpose of a backsplash?"

"It's to make things look cute."

"Cute." He repeats the word like it has no meaning in his vocabulary. "If you say so."

"Don't worry, I have a whole PowerPoint on cute."

"God help me." He exhales through his nose, the barest glimmer of amusement in his eyes.

"I'll grow on you." I wink.

"Help me decide on the stain for the cabinets." He pulls a handful of samples from the drawer like he's been waiting for me to ask. "I want them finished before the sun's up. The faster they dry, the sooner I can install them."

"I'd go darker," I say immediately, holding one up to the light. "Balance the flooring, keep the walls neutral, add texture with curtains and art. There's a guy in town who makes frames out of reclaimed wood, perfect for photos. Do you have anything you'd want to hang? Something special, just for you and Finn?"

"I don't keep anything. Besides the stuff on Instagram."

"Okay, then I'll figure something out. I'll make it special. Something that feels like you two."

"Great." He grabs the darker stain can, clipped and final, then pushes open the back door.

Cold air slaps my cheeks as we step outside. Dew beads the ferns at the base of the lodge. A handful of stars are clinging stubbornly to the horizon.

Floodlights buzz to life, washing the clearing in harsh white. Neat rows of fresh cabinets are lined up like soldiers, and a plywood slab balanced on sawhorses doubles as a workbench, littered with tools. Alec flips on a speaker, and a silver, palm-sized iPod blinks awake. He spins the tiny wheel with his thumb.

"I've literally never seen one of those in person," I laugh, bracing the bench. "I mean, I know they exist, but I thought they were, like, in museums now. Next to dinosaurs and dial-up internet."

"I keep forgetting how young you are."

"I'm not *that* much younger than you."

A crease forms between his brows before he turns back to the iPod, scrolling with that same unhurried thumb. "Well, good things never break."

"Tell that to my fifth iPhone in two years. God forbid a girl wants to watch a movie in a hot, steamy shower. They say it's waterproof—"

"I'm glad you're taking hot showers." His tone is flat. "Are they long?"

"My…showers?"

"Yes."

My brain short-circuits. He's picturing me in the shower.

Nope. I'm picturing *him* in the shower, water sliding down his chest, over that sharp V—

Nope, nope, abort, abort!

"How much time do *you* allot to your showers?" I ask.

"Long enough for my muscles to recover."

I choke on a laugh. "Oh. Right. Muscles. Recovery. Totally normal." I wave my hand like I'm conducting an invisible orchestra. "Yeah, me too. Really focused on muscle recovery lately."

His eyebrow arches, and my face goes nuclear. It probably looks as if I dipped my face in liquid blush.

Mercifully, he taps a button, and music fills the yard. It's a piano playing from the bottom of a lake. Satie. I'd know it anywhere.

"Gnossienne: No. 1?"

He glances at me, surprised. "You know your pieces."

"It's all I listen to when I dance." The melody lilts, a little sad. "You being a Satie guy explains a lot, though."

His forehead creases. "Like what?"

"Like you're the kind of person who could sit alone in his truck for weeks and watch the rain hit the window."

An actual laugh escapes him, so soft I almost miss it. It's only a second, but it hits me like sunlight through clouds, warm and dizzying.

I slap my thigh. "Seriously? That's what gets you? I've been at peak charm level for six days, and you finally crack for *Satie*?"

"No one makes classical music jokes."

I beam. "Look at us, Alec. Agreeing on things. We're becoming best camp buddies. BCBs!"

He doesn't reply, but the left side of his lips twitches, which for him is practically a sonnet.

His laugh, still echoing. The soft way his face shifts when he lets himself smile. He looks younger, lighter, almost breakable. I feel it everywhere. Like the urge to move closer. To touch. To lean in. To do *something*.

Which is absurd. He has his walls, his baggage. I had to beg him into this partnership. He's made it clear: We're a transaction.

So, naturally, I want him. I always want the impossible. The complicated. The just out of reach.

That's my flavor of pain through and through.

He crouches, prying open the can of stain like none of it happened.

I strip off my sweater, purely so it won't get ruined. Not because my skin feels like an oven left on through a summer afternoon. Not because the strap of my overalls slips loose, pink bandeau showing, braid sliding forward over one bare shoulder.

If he notices, he doesn't show it. Which is either comforting or infuriating.

Maybe the mountain froze more than just half his toe.

I risk a glance. Slowly. First at the floor, then at the smear of stain on his forearm, and finally lower. The hem of his shirt rides up as he crouches, gray sweatpants hanging loose on his hips. My stomach flips, traitorous.

No. Definitely not a eunuch.

Chapter 15
Clementine

BY NOON, the lodge smells like sawdust, wet paint, and the faint tang of coffee gone cold. Walnut stain freckles the dining room floor, cans are lined in neat rows against the wall. My brush drags in a steady sweep across the trim while the hollow thunk of Alec's wrench under the kitchen sink keeps time with the music.

Satie faded into Chopin hours ago, now Mozart swells from the tiny speaker. It feels like barre class all over again, with silence that's just music and the work.

The faucet coughs, then clean water spurts out. Alec leans back on his heels, wipes his hands on his jeans, and glances over at me. I look toward the wall like I wasn't just staring at him.

"You hungry?"

"Starving."

He disappears into the pantry. I set my brush down and slide onto a barstool just as he returns and sets down two steaming, vacuum-sealed pouches, a metal spork jutting out of one.

I blink. "What is that?"

"Eggs."

Inside, the yellow mass jiggles like it's daring me to eat it. "No offense, but this looks like space food."

"I usually eat for sustenance, not pleasure."

"But pleasure can be full of sustenance," I counter, already digging into my tote. Out come a couple of apples, a bag of trail mix, and some muffins I'd snatched from Gran on my way out the door. I set them on the counter. "Do you have a knife?"

He slips one from his pocket, thumb pressing the hinge until the brown-handled blade flicks open with a metallic *snap*. He balances it in his palm for a beat, then spins it, offering me the handle without looking away like he's done it a hundred times.

The motion makes my pulse trip. Heat pools low in my belly, my chest tightens, and...*why the hell am I panting?*

"Careful," he says, voice low. "It's sharp."

I take it from him, my fingers brushing his as they curl around the handle, the warmth of the blade lingering from his hand. For a second, I forget what I'm supposed to do with it. *Okay, brain, focus.*

I slice the apples thin, arrange them in a pinwheel on a crumpled copy of *Town Magazine*, scatter trail mix in the center, and set the muffins at the edge. "There. That's a real breakfast."

Alec leans against the counter across from me, muffin in hand. He tears off the top, eyes closing on the first bite, chewing slow, like he's relearning what real food tastes like.

"I used to sneak over here when I was a kid," I say, staring at the apple slice in my hand. "Grandpa was my favorite person in the world. I'd cut through the hedges between our houses and just camp out in the kitchen with him. Once, I decided I was going to make cookies for all the climbers. Didn't bother with a recipe—just pulled things out of the cupboards. Flour, sugar, a fruit cup, and for some reason a Go-Gurt." I laugh. "The guys actually tried to eat them. They were soft and rock-hard at the same time, like a hockey puck made out of a sponge. Grandpa swore they were the best cookies he ever had."

When I glance up, Alec's watching me, nodding. "It's nice

seeing the place come together again," I say. "I'm glad you kept the old kitchen floor. Gran's going to love that."

"He always had a picture of you in his wallet."

I grin, shaking my head. "I know exactly which one you're talking about. He came to watch my first performance in Concord. *Alice's Adventures in Wonderland.* I wasn't even Alice, or the White Rabbit, or anyone memorable. I was one of the queen's cards. Had a pair of red tights, a giant felt heart, the whole deal."

I can still see Grandpa in the front row, his little disposable camera flashing every time I turned my head. "He acted like I was the star of the whole show. Carried that photo around until the corners curled."

"He talked about you a lot."

My heart squeezes. "I'm surprised I didn't see you two around when I was growing up."

"We came in May and only stayed a month."

"That makes sense. I didn't get here until June, after school let out."

"Did your mom come with you?"

I smile. "Look at you, asking questions. Like you're curious about me."

"I am." He says it so plainly I have to look away, down at the apples.

"No," I say after a beat. "She always said she spent her whole life here waiting to leave. She likes the city. Malls are closer there." I laugh softly. "I wish I'd made more time to come back. I missed so much of Grandpa's life." My chest tightens.

"Margaret's probably happy you're here now."

"She is."

Silence settles, easy, with Mozart humming low through the speaker. My shoulders sway, my body loosening the way it always does around music.

"You mentioned you quit dance," he says at last. "Do you miss it?"

"Yes." The word snaps out almost defensively.

"Then why stop?"

I press my thumb into the apple slice until juice seeps out. "It wasn't part of the plan. I was supposed to be promoted this season. Everyone thought I would be. *I* thought I would be. But they gave it to someone who'd barely unpacked her warm-up shoes.

"So I did what I always do." My palms sweat. "I went shopping. Had a breakdown in Sephora over makeup I couldn't afford. That's when I admitted I was miserable, broke, and done sacrificing every part of myself for something that didn't even want me."

The words scrape coming out, but once they're loose, I can breathe. "I don't know if it's permanent. I miss it. And it feels impossible to let go of something you've built your whole life around, but—"

I stop. His stare is fixed on me. Not pitying, not soft. Just steady. Expecting.

"Finish it," he says quietly.

My stomach twists. He doesn't look away, and that alone is enough to drag the rest out of me.

"I didn't move in with my gran because I missed her," I hear myself say. "I moved because I couldn't breathe and didn't know how to tell anyone. Now I'm here, crawling out of debt—desperate for that twenty thousand dollars, yeah—but mostly I just needed to stop. To just…pause."

He nods once. The space between us thickens, pressing in, but it's not letting me off the hook. It wants more. He wants more.

"Part of me thinks I should go back, try again. Part of me thinks I should find something that doesn't make me hate myself. Mostly I just want to stop being the meanest person in my own life." My throat tightens. "I want to feel like I'm enough."

"You are enough," Alec says, like it's the easiest truth in the world.

His hand shifts on the counter, close to but not touching mine. Even that distance feels deliberate, dangerous. I hate how much I want to close the gap. I've chased those words for years, and he just lays them down like they cost nothing.

"Anyway." I clear my throat, pushing for lightness. "Sorry about week one. Total disaster. Maybe I could've tried harder to stop the kayak before we went over a literal dam, or admitted to the blisters, or yelled louder at the bear." I stretch my heels inside my socks; they finally don't ache. "But I'm trying. I'll do better this week."

"None of that was on you." He shakes his head. "I should've known better."

"What were you gonna do, put a camera in my shoe?"

"I should've told you to tell me right away."

"You can't control everything."

His jaw works. "I don't like feeling responsible for your safety."

"I can take care of myself. Even with the blisters, I would've figured it out. And...I actually—" I give him a small smile. "I had fun with the kayak."

"It's not about the kayak."

Of course it isn't. Not about the blister, not about my learning curve. It's about Finn. About the lines inked onto his forearm. About the weight Alec hauls every day, straight-backed, eyes shadowed.

He pulls his notebook from his cargo pocket. "I'm going to be a better partner to you. Because yes, you're not exactly perfect—"

"Ouch."

"Let me finish." His voice deepens, more serious now. "Neither am I. That schedule I gave you? Forget it. Rip it up. Recycle it. Whatever."

"Wait, why?"

"Because I need to be flexible with you. The same way you've been with me. I doubt I'm easy to be around, so the least I can do is figure out how we mesh. Make the most out of this."

My jaw drops. "Oh my god, that might be the nicest thing you've ever said to me."

"I thought it was when I called you an old beast."

"Oh my god—Alec, you made a joke!"

"Don't get used to it."

"Oh, but I might."

He shakes his head, flips open the notebook, and pulls a pen from yet another pocket. "We'll go week by week. That way we can account for changes."

"Deal."

"Tomorrow and Monday, kayak runs. Wednesday and Thursday, long hikes, assuming your feet hold up. After each day, you'll paint the main room so we can finally order furniture."

"Sounds good to me." I nod, biting into an apple slice. "Oh, and Saturday? I signed us up for a CPR class."

"Of course you did." His voice is flat. "I hate group events."

"I can do all the talking."

"I already told you I'm certified."

"But this way we can size up the competition," I argue, waving the apple slice.

He exhales through his nose. "Fine. So, kayaking, hiking, basic training…" He flips a page, scribbling in his neat, militant handwriting. "With the rain and the lack of a climbing gym in Misthaven, I'm not sure how I'll train you for rappelling. Unless we drive to Anchorage."

"I've been rock climbing a couple times. I wasn't horrible." I shrug. "Also, there's a Rappelling 101 course the weekend before the qualifier. Think that's enough time to learn?"

"Depends. How are you with being tied up?"

My brain screeches to a halt. "I—what?"

"If you get tangled in your ropes, I need to know how you'll react."

"Right," I stammer, heat rushing up my neck. "Of course. Safety. Knots. Great."

His brow lifts, a single sharp line. "What did you think I meant?"

"Nothing—ugh—" I cough on apple skin, still flustered, and hop off the barstool for water. The faucet handle squeaks. Something clanks under the sink, then hisses, and a jet of freezing water explodes from the base, hammering the wall, the floor, and me in seconds.

"Oh my god!" I yelp, throwing up my hands. The spray ricochets straight into my face.

Alec is already there. He steps into the torrent, takes it square in the chest, and doesn't even flinch. One arm hooks tight around my waist, lifting me off the slippery floor like I weigh nothing, depositing me on the far side of the kitchen.

"Stay back." His voice is inches from my ear. Then he's gone, crouching under the sink, water blasting over him as he reaches for the shutoff valve.

Adrenaline hammers through me. "Towels! I'll get towels."

"Laundry room," he shouts over the hiss.

I sprint, grab everything I can carry, and skid back. He's braced under the counter now, sleeves shoved up, water streaming down his hair and jaw, hands working fast and sure in the chaos. I drop to my knees beside him, spreading towels, sopping up what I can. A muffin bobs pathetically across the tiles.

He finally twists the valve. The spray sputters, chokes, and dies. Silence, broken only by the drip of water pooling on the floor.

"Where on earth did you learn to fix that?" I gasp, wiping water from my eyes.

"Watched a YouTube video."

"Ah, the universal solution to pretty much anything."

Alec leans back on his heels, shirt clinging to his chest, water still streaming down his jaw. "I'll fix it properly tonight," he says.

I'm on my knees in puddles, clothes plastered to me, hair frizzing. He looks up, and for a second he doesn't look at the mess. He looks at me. My bandeau clings to my skin, wet fabric turning sheer. His gaze catches on the trail of water slipping down between my breasts. For a beat too long, he doesn't look away.

Heat sparks in my stomach. I catch a glint in his gaze. Want, fast and raw, before he reins it in.

He drags in a breath, stands slowly, and grabs a towel from the pile. Turning half away, as if to shield me from his own stare, he steps in close. He drapes the towel across my shoulders, fingers brushing damp skin as he tucks it firm against me.

"I can get you a change of clothes," he offers.

"I'm fine," I manage, though my pulse pounds hard enough to betray me.

He looks like he wants to say something more, then stops. He glances once at the counter, at the mess, then back at me—and this time, he makes himself keep his eyes above my shoulders.

"Okay. You still up for a second coat?"

I nod, forcing a laugh into the towel. "Yes!"

He turns toward the dining room, and I'm left dripping in the kitchen, towel clutched tight, heart racing from more than the burst pipe.

Chapter 16
Alec

I THROW the last branch aside and step onto the Lennox property. Ten minutes uphill, and my hands are caked with mud. I wipe them off on my jeans, clip the shears back to my belt, and pick up the thing I brought.

Not a gift, I remind myself. Just fixing a liability.

Fog clings low across the trees. I cross the garden, quiet as a deer. Then I hear it bleeding from the open garage.

The Carnival of the Animals. "The Swan."

I follow the sound, stopping at the threshold of the garage and staying hidden in the shadow. Fair's fair. Clementine's ambushed me enough times.

Inside, she moves in the center of the garage. The place is cluttered with weights and resistance bands, but she doesn't touch any of it. She dances like the space is hers alone. A single bulb flickers overhead.

Her hair is loose, streaks of pale orange slipping down her back. A green leotard clings to her. She rises en pointe, ankles bending to impossible angles, the kind of thing that makes my joints ache just looking at it.

The cello arcs low.

She leaps, body hanging for a breath before she lands in silence. Then she folds, collapses flat against the concrete before twisting up again, arms slicing the air.

Classical music has always made sense to me. Patterns, form, precision. A well-cut route on a mountain. No wasted steps. No chaos. Just discipline until it looks like freedom. And she is the closest thing I've ever seen to freedom.

I should leave.

The piano follows, and she bends back, ribs flaring like wings. Her hair flies, catching the light like the sun burning off snow. She arcs her leg behind her, and I see the shape of a bird lifting off the water. It's wind reshaping a ridge, or ice breaking free.

My breathing goes ragged, the way it does when the ground slides out from under my boots.

She folds in on herself again, shuddering. And I want to step inside the room, to anchor her against me, to trace the sweat down her spine until I forget my own name.

Instead, I grip the box I'm holding tighter and take one long breath.

Clementine isn't mine to think about like that.

No one is.

No one will be. At least, that's what I always believed. There's never been anyone I wanted to possess. Just summits. Routes. Things I could hold, measure, conquer.

Whatever this is—her jokes, her softness, the way she pulls me into moments I thought I'd aged out of—it's temporary. A transaction. I'll leave Misthaven. She'll pay off her debt. Maybe she'll go back to New York and remind the bastards at NYCB what they lost when they let her slip through their fingers.

I shift back into the fog, box in hand, ready to leave it at her door and stop myself from thinking at all, but my boot clips a rake hidden in the grass. The clang shatters the air, cutting straight through the cello.

She turns. Her eyes catch mine through the mist, wide and bright, her chest rising with the last of the music. Neither of us moves.

"Alec?" she breathes.

And I realize I've been caught in the middle of something that feels holy. But she doesn't look away. She doesn't tell me to go. She just holds me there in her gaze, as if I belong inside the world she was building for herself.

I open my mouth, then close it, then open it again like an idiot. "I—uh—"

"Did I miss training? Did we have something scheduled today?" Panic crosses her face, and I kick myself for breaking the peace she was in. I should've texted her.

"You looked—" I stop, fumbling. *Just tell her she looks beautiful*, but I can't seem to. "That was…you were dancing."

 No shit.

Clementine shrugs, fidgeting with the cap of her water bottle. "A little something for myself. Since we've been training, my body's been aching to move in ways that feel familiar."

I'd pay thousands to see her move like that again.

"It's like that song was made for you."

"Not sure if that's a compliment or not. It's *Le Cygne*," she says, still avoiding my gaze. "Most people call it 'The Dying Swan.' Pavlova made it famous. She thought of the swan as injured and dying, but later dancers, like Plisetskaya, performed it as an old swan refusing to give in. Kind of inspiring, right? Not giving up."

"And the cello?"

"Yo-Yo Ma, obviously. This version's my favorite. I swear, when I see him live, I'll probably cry. He makes the piece."

I shake my head. "I think the dancing was all you."

She waves me off. "I'm serious."

"So am I."

She crosses the garage, looping a soft pink wrap around her

arms, her earlier embarrassment already gone. Stopping in front of me, she taps the shoebox I've been holding.

"Now what do you have here?"

"Oh, it's nothing."

"Please tell me that's not the dead bird from the river yesterday," she says. "Because I was joking about a funeral." I took us on an easier route on the river. Ran it alone first just to make sure it was safe.

"Why would I bring you a dead bird? I'm not a dog."

"But you are such a good boy."

If she asked me to bark right now, I might. But I don't rise to her bait. Instead, I hand her the shoebox. "These are new boots."

Why?"

"Your old boots are a liability."

She jerks back, palms out, like I actually handed her something dead. "Alec, I can't take these."

"You can, and you will. My team needs solid gear. And you need time to break these in before the qualifiers in nineteen days." I add, softer, "I even got you the cute ones."

That makes her hesitate. She edges forward, slowly peeling back the lid, milking the drama like the boots might bite. The tissue crackles, and she gasps. They are the same model as mine, only smaller and far more pink. She looks at boots the way I look at mountains, like she'd climb them if she could.

But then the awe sours. She shuts the lid carefully, like she's putting something fragile back in its box. "I can't. Those are... they're two hundred dollars."

"They're boots."

"They're debt." She shakes her head, fiddling with the ribbon on her wrap, her voice pitching higher. "I already have a pair." She points to the corner, where her old ones with zero traction are left slouching, still dark from last week's rain.

I hear Finn's teenage voice in my head. *Don't buy me things. I haven't earned them.*

"I didn't ask you to pay me back," I tell her, keeping my voice steady. "Call it a bonus. You've already painted most of the main room."

"That wasn't part of our agreement."

"There are no hidden intentions with this, I swear. It's gear. Nothing else."

"In my world, unannounced generosity usually comes with donor dinners and being paraded around. Sitting at tables with people who flash checkbooks and wear clothes straight off the runway. Clothes that make you want them."

I glance around the garage, then down at myself, wet flannel, boots caked in mud. "I don't think these came off a runway."

Her teeth catch her lip. "No, I guess not."

"Okay. If you don't want them—"

"No, I do, I—" She folds her arms tight across her chest, cutting herself off. "I just can't accept them. Not like this."

Her jaw clenches, but I see the panic flicker underneath. Pride and fear all tangled. I recognize it. The same knot I've carried most of my life. The same one Finn carried too, refusing things he needed because he couldn't stomach the feeling of being beholden. But I can't let her keep the old pair. Not when her safety's already been compromised on my watch.

Two strides, and I've got the old boots in my hands before she can move. The leather is soft, worn to death. Dangerous.

"Alec!"

My arm cocks back, and I launch the left boot into the fog. It disappears with a dull thud.

Her mouth drops open. "What the hell are you doing?" She darts after it, pointe shoes smacking the concrete, then the wet grass outside.

I've already got the right one.

"Making sure you wear the new ones."

The second boot sails into the tree line, swallowed by mist.

Her face is flushed when she whirls back toward me, caught between fury and disbelief.

I stand there, soaked in her stare, refusing to apologize. Because even if she hates me for it, at least she'll be safe.

"You're insane!" she shouts, caught between fury and laughter. She jogs back toward me, damp hair clinging to her flushed cheeks, and swats me.

I catch her wrist mid-swing. Her pulse hammers under my thumb.

"And you're stubborn," I growl.

"Pot, meet kettle!" Her blue eyes spark.

"You look like you're seconds away from throwing one of your weights at me."

"Thank you for the idea."

She lunges for the shoebox. I hold it higher. She climbs me like a cat, half wrestling, half laughing, trying to pry it free. Her breath is hot against my neck, her fingers scrabbling at my shoulders.

"Give it back!" she pants.

"Not until you say you'll wear them."

"Over my dead body."

She twists again, momentum pitching her straight into me. The shoebox slips to the floor with a thud as I catch her waist. Suddenly, we're tangled, her wrist in my grip, her body pressed tight to mine, my heartbeat slamming against hers.

If I leaned in, just a fraction, my mouth would be on hers. And she knows it. Her gaze flickers to my lips, then back to my eyes, heat written all over her.

The creak of the porch door cuts the air like an axe.

"Well, holy hell," Margaret crows from the doorway, wrapped in a pink robe, tea steaming in her hand. "Didn't know I'd stumble upon foreplay before breakfast."

Clementine jerks back, nearly tripping over the shoebox. I release her wrist, but she grabs mine again like it's instinct.

"Gran, we were just—" she starts.

Margaret just grins, eyes twinkling. "Don't you 'Gran' me. I may be old, but I wasn't born yesterday. I can see what Alec was just doing." She sips her tea with a wicked smirk. "Though next time, maybe clear the garage floor first. Concrete's murder on the knees."

"Gran!" Clementine squeals, her face flaming red.

"Back to it, darlings. Alec, grab a blueberry muffin when you're done tasting my granddaughter's muffin." Margaret cackles all the way back inside, the screen door slamming behind her.

Clementine groans, covering her face with both hands. "She really needs another hobby."

"Apparently muffin-baking is on the list today," I mutter.

"Stop." She peeks at me through her fingers, then collapses onto the floor, dragging the boots into her lap like a shield. "Jokes aside…thank you. I do like the pink."

"You'll break them in on the hike today. I think you're ready for another brick."

"Exciting," she deadpans, stroking the leather. Her cheeks are still pink. "At least I'll look cute in these."

"And stay dry."

Her eyes cut up to mine, sly. "Right. Because staying dry is very, very important."

Every nerve in me screams to grab her again, to show her exactly how dry I don't want her to be. Instead, I turn toward the trees.

"Where are you going?" she calls.

"I don't litter."

"You're a menace."

"And you've got new boots."

Chapter 17
Alec

THE WHISPERS START the moment we step into Adventure Supply. I know half the faces in here. The other half know me.

Alec Hastings. Here?

Did you hear what happened to Finn?

They were the best.

Only team to summit K2 this year.

Who's the girl?

He's never climbed without Finn.

The words snap through the air like ice cracking underfoot.

I keep moving. I've been buried in avalanches, starved of oxygen on ridges no one had any business crossing. I won't let a store full of gossip take me down.

The Wild Trails CPR training looks exactly how I pictured it: fifteen pairs, Clementine and me included, sitting cross-legged on brown carpet that smells like dust and sweat. Overhead, jaundiced lights wash everyone in a sickly glow. Each team has a CPR dummy on a mat. Ours has a fake septum ring, and within seconds Clementine jammed a beanie on its head and christened it Buttercup.

There are chairs shoved to the walls, backpacks slumped in

corners, and one cracked window trying and failing to bleed out the heat.

The bragging starts immediately.

"Willis Wall, Rainier."

"Rwenzoris, Uganda."

Voices climbing over one another, louder, prouder.

My shoulders knot. The four walls and the bad lighting are too reminiscent of being back at school. I only survived high school because they let me test outside.

Clementine, meanwhile, is electric. She's buzzing in her new pink boots, mud still caked from three hikes this week. No blisters. She leans into me, whispering like we're plotting a heist, eyes ticking from group to group like a Kit-Cat Clock.

For ten days it's been just us, the lodge, the forest, and silence. Now the room crowds in, strangers pressing closer, and it makes me itch. Makes me want to win.

"I heard they're setting the route on the west side of Euspuko," someone mutters behind us.

Clementine elbows my thigh, not subtly, flicking her chin toward the group.

"Are you listening?" she whispers.

"Don't need to," I reply.

Routes are supposed to be secret, but it doesn't matter. Euspuko breaks you no matter where you start.

Another voice cuts in. "No way. Crews were clearing the south side. Straight gravel chute."

Then lime-green hair pipes up. Zak Kwan. Last time I saw him, it was red. "Smartwater's sponsoring. My cousin's putting water stations on the south."

The room shifts, everyone leaning in like wolves scenting blood.

Clementine drops her voice against my shoulder. "So…if it is gravel, do my boots even have enough tread?"

"Yes. We have all the right gear."

She doesn't look convinced. "Okay, but what about them? Don't you want to know what we're up against?"

"We're fine," I murmur. "Don't waste energy listening to climbers brag."

Her nails tap the carpet. "So you don't size up the competition at all?"

I give the room a slow once-over, letting her see me do it. "That group there? They care more about their gear than training. That pair looks like gym climbers. They won't last a day when the trail turns to shale. And Zak…" My gaze snags on the green hair across the room. "Flashy. Always has been. Knows how to make people watch, but he doesn't know how to shut up and do the work."

"Zak?"

"The green hair is Zak Kwan. Climbed Kilimanjaro with me."

She studies him. "He looks badass."

"He tore both rotator cuffs last year," I grunt. "On a trampoline. Idiot."

She stifles a laugh, but she doesn't look away. Zak basks in the attention like always, playing to the crowd. People eat it up. Clementine included. It shouldn't bother me. But watching her stare at him makes me want to drag her attention back to where it belongs.

"They're not competition," I add. "Not for us."

She just smiles like I amuse her, like my irritation is a private joke only she's in on. I don't like the way it makes the corner of my mouth twitch.

A guy in a red polo waddles in, clapping his hands. Short, round-shouldered, gray curls springing out in all directions.

"Alright, folks! Welcome to Wilderness Safety's CPR course. I'm Teddy, and we're going to get started.

"CPR stands for cardiopulmonary resuscitation," he says. "It's what you do when someone's heart stops. First, check if they're breathing. Then call for help. Next: thirty compressions, two breaths. Over and over until help arrives. Your job is to keep blood moving and oxygen flowing. Buy time." He claps again. "Anyone know what song you should do compressions to?"

"'Stayin' Alive,'" I mutter. Finn and I always used "Another One Bites the Dust." Darker, but the rhythm works.

"Alec Hastings knows the answer," Clementine says brightly, pointing at me like a kid.

I click my teeth at her. "You're gonna pay for that."

"Oh, excellent!" Teddy shimmies his shoulders. "Please share with the class, Mr. Hastings."

Clementine beams, batting her lashes. Wicked.

"'Stayin' Alive,'" I bite out.

"A-plus-plus!" Teddy hums the song, swinging his hips. "Come on, class. Mm-mm-mm-mm…"

The whole room joins in, Clementine included, smirking at me as she hums along. I don't. CPR isn't a punchline.

"Now, everyone, hands like this." Teddy interlaces his fingers, pushing down on imaginary ribs. At least he gets the form right. "After thirty compressions, how many breaths?"

"Two," the group repeats in chorus.

"Experts already!" Teddy grins. "Tilt the head back, pinch the nose, seal your mouth, give two breaths. Watch the chest rise."

Beside me, Clementine practices in the air, still humming, swaying closer. Her shoulder brushes mine. I catch it in my lungs before I can stop myself.

"Now…" Teddy scans the room, frowning at the front table. "Looks like I'm a dummy short. And hands-on practice beats theory." His fingers tap together. "I like to show the movements on a real person—don't worry, we never actually practice CPR on someone breathing. It can really hurt them. But for demonstration? Way better than just talking through it. Do I have a volunteer?"

Before I can blink, Clementine's hand shoots up. "I'll do it."

"What are you doing?" I hiss.

"Hands-on practice," she says, already slipping onto the table. Teddy asks her name like he's never been handed a gift before.

She lies back, arms stretched, hair spilling across the wood. She looks—no. I shouldn't even think the word.

Someone mutters behind me, "Lucky instructor gets to touch that one."

No.

My body moves before my brain can stop it. "I'll demonstrate." My pulse slams against my ribs. What the hell am I doing?

"Oooh, enthusiasm!" Teddy crows. "Usually, I have to beg for a volunteer. Looks like we've got a teacher's pet." He punches my shoulder like I'm twelve.

"I'm not a teacher's pet," I grind out.

"That's Alec Hastings!" someone calls from the back.

Murmurs ripple. Teddy beams. "Mr. Hastings, thank you. It's always helpful to show beginners together." He pats my back, steering me over Clementine. She props herself on one elbow, eyes wide, watching me like she's not sure if I'm saving her or losing my mind.

"I'm not a novice," I say flatly. "I'm an instructor too."

"Well, if you're in my class, you're under my instruction. So, follow along. Now—" Teddy launches into a ramble about the origins of CPR.

Clementine tugs on my cargos, jerking her chin down.

"What are you doing?" she whispers.

Truth is, I don't know why I'm up here.

"Just scaring the competition," I tell her, raising a brow.

Her lips open, ready with some smart reply, but Teddy claps his hands again. "Okay, let's get started. Hands stacked, center of the chest, thirty compressions. And don't actually press. Seriously, you could break a rib. Just mimic the motion."

Before I can move, he grabs my wrists and drags my hands into place.

"I know what I'm doing," I snap, shaking him off.

At least, I thought I did—until my palms hover over her sternum. Only a thin layer of cotton separates my skin from hers. Her sweater bunches under my fingers. I lock my elbows, brace my shoulders, and press just enough to show the motion.

One.

Her body freezes under my hands.

Two.

Her breath stutters, lashes flicking down, then up again.

Three.

Four.

Five.

Her eyes catch mine, and for a split second I forget to breathe. I have to remind myself to only use light pressure. No real force. Just thirty seconds. That's all.

In the background, Teddy drones on about depth and pace. I've done this dozens of times, on riverbeds, on rocks high above base camp. But never like this. Never softly. Never with the heat rising off Clementine, never with the scent of her shampoo in my lungs, never with her watching me like she is now.

Ten.

Her lips part on a small gasp.

Fifteen.

Sweat beads down my temple.

Twenty.

My cock shifts in my pants. Fucking hell. CPR is for safety; it is not sexy.

Twenty-five.

But she is. Her cheeks flush deeper. The room's gone balmy.

Thirty.

Teddy whistles. "Good. Nice rhythm. Remember, you're keeping blood flowing, keeping them alive."

Alive.

Clementine is very much alive beneath my hands, and my blood is very much moving.

I don't want to step back. A shiver runs down her spine, pupils blown wide, flecks of pale gray sparking at the edge of her irises.

Teddy's hand claps my shoulder, breaking my trance. I snap my gaze to the crowd. Staring. Waiting.

"Perfect rhythm," Teddy beams. "Now, Hastings—because you're partners, go ahead with the breaths. Two quick ones." He pantomimes. "Show us how it's done."

Heat crawls under my skin. I don't get nervous. But her eyes are on me, wide and unblinking, and it feels like free fall.

I'm about to put my mouth on Clementine Lennox in front of an entire room.

Teddy nudges me forward. "Come, come. Tilt the head back, pinch the nose, seal your mouth. I want to show the class how the chest rises."

I brush her shoulder, fingers sliding to the nape of her neck. Her head fits into my palm like it belongs there.

"This okay, Clementine?" Her name tastes dangerous on my tongue.

She swallows, lips parting. "Go for it."

My pulse slows on purpose. I tell myself this is clinical, mechanical. Except the second my lips brush hers, the lie burns away.

Her skin is warm, like she's swallowed the sun. I savor the cinnamon toothpaste on her breath. Her mouth is soft—so fucking soft that my self-control fractures in an instant. Her lip gloss clings, grapefruit-sweet and tacky, against me, and I can't stop the slip of my tongue as it grazes her lips.

She gasps but doesn't pull back. Instead, she lifts her neck away from my palm, like she's choosing this with me.

It's not CPR anymore. It's not a kiss either.

It's something raw, suspended in the space between.

I want more.

My hands leave the safe place on her chest and trace the line of her jaw, thumb tilting her chin up. Her throat works around a sound that slices through me, soft and wrecking. The class, the carpet, the buzzing lights vanish. There's only the heat of her, the press of her lips under mine, the way every nerve in my body lights up like a storm surge.

"Phones down!" Teddy snaps. His voice cracks through the haze. "This isn't a circus. Respect the training."

I jerk upright, like I've been doused with cold water. My lungs drag in air, rough and uneven. My palms swipe down my thighs, searching for ground.

Did I even get the breaths in? I don't think I breathed at all.

Clementine rolls onto her side, cheeks as pink as a sunburn, eyes catching mine in quick, dangerous flashes. She's flustered but glowing, lit from somewhere inside.

And Christ, she's beautiful.

"Good demo," the instructor says tightly, gaze flicking between me and her, suspicion hanging there. "But let's remember, CPR is about control and focus."

Control. The word slices through me. I had none. Not one damn ounce of it. And I don't know how the hell I'm supposed to keep pretending I don't want her in a way I'm not even ready to try and understand.

I've watched what climbing does to the families left behind. I've been to funerals where partners, wives, and kids are wrecked because some guy thought he was invincible on a mountain. I promised myself a long time ago I wouldn't do that to anyone. That's why it's always just been flings at base camps. No one who'd notice if I didn't come back.

I can't do that to Clem.

When Teddy dismisses us, I move fast.

"I'll see you tomorrow. Something came up," I say. She opens her mouth, but I don't let her respond. I need to get out of here.

The door clangs shut, and I savor the cold rain that hits my face.

Every step across the parking lot reminds me of traversing a narrow ridge. I want to shake off the heat, the taste, the pull of her.

Footsteps scuff behind me.

"Alec—"

I keep walking.

"Alec, wait!"

I stop at the edge of Adventure Supply's gravel parking lot. She skids to my side, purse half slipped off a shoulder, lips— those lips—twisted in confusion. I wrench my eyes away.

"What was that back there?"

"I—" The truth lingers in my pause. "I didn't want Teddy hurting my partner." I'm a coward.

"He's an instructor and, like, ninety years old."

"Why'd you volunteer us anyway? I told you we could've done this at the lodge or before our kayak drills."

"Because I wanted practice."

"Why couldn't you practice with me?"

"Because—" She huffs, snagging her water bottle from her purse and twisting the cap nervously. "I wanted to see someone else's techniques."

"You partnered with me. I have the best techniques," I snap.

"You sound like you have an ego problem."

"The only problem I have is with my *camp buddy* putting herself in danger."

"I could snap Teddy in two." She juts her hip out. "Also, I

haven't been certified in years, but what was that in there? You didn't do the two breaths."

"Yes, I did. You must not have felt them," I lie.

"That felt like—"

"It was training." I interrupt her before she crosses a line. "Like we have tomorrow at five. I'll see you then," I say. I can't stand here any longer, so I pivot and jog. I don't like surprises. I like calculated steps and schedules. I hate that I can't predict a damn thing with her.

"Where are you going?" she calls after me, rain falling harder now.

"Home."

"But your truck."

"I'll get it later," I call over my shoulder, fists shoved deep in my pockets. Then I force air back into my lungs until it burns.

It wasn't a kiss.

It was training.

That's all.

And if I keep repeating it, maybe I'll believe it.

Chapter 18
Alec

Subject: Wild Trails Promo Event
From: Jillian@adventurerelations.com
To: alec@twomenontop.com

HEY ALEC,

Patagonia is asking if you'll speak briefly at next weekend's Wild Trails rappel training event. I know Finn usually does these, but the pictures of you and Clementine at the CPR training have been circulating. Patagonia is offering to amend the canceled magazine spread to feature you at the event, plus add a sponsorship for the Iceland climb. They offered to keep the full payment for the contract.

Let me know soon so I can confirm with them.

—J

From: alec@twomenontop.com
To: Jillian@adventurerelations.com

I WANT Finn to get half if I speak. The rest I need to discuss with him.

From: Jillian@adventurerelations.com
To: alec@twomenontop.com

I'VE SPOKEN WITH HIM, and he's comfortable with the arrangement. He wants you to keep the full check.

From: alec@twomenontop.com
To: Jillian@adventurerelations.com

I CAN TALK to my best friend without your help, Jillian.

Chapter 19
Alec

THE BELL over the door rings when I step into Got Wood?. Clementine is behind the counter, untying her green apron. She hangs it on a peg, hair falling around her face like it knows gravity works differently on her.

"Thanks for picking me up again," she says. "Gran needed the car for her quilting club."

"I needed more nails." I set the box down on the counter. A lie. I've got enough nails to build a church. But excuses come easy when they look like her.

She rings me up, then closes the register with a hip bump, leaning casually against the counter. My eyes follow the curve of her waist, the way her tight pink long-sleeve stretches as she leans forward, just enough to ride up over the top of her jeans. I'm not supposed to be thinking about her like this, but the slight arch of her back makes it impossible to look away.

Her eyes flick to my wrist, oblivious to the pull she has over me. "So, how much time did you give me?"

"What?"

"On your watch. Don't tell me it doesn't say, *Pick up*

Clementine Lennox, five p.m." She drops her voice into a mechanical monotone.

I raise an eyebrow. "Why are you so good at that?"

"The voicemail you are trying to reach has not been set up," she continues in the exact bored voice of every customer service robot I've ever wanted to strangle. She grins. "Mom taught me all the good party tricks. So? How much?"

"Twenty minutes."

She gasps like I just insulted her bloodline. "That's it? Your partner is only worth twenty minutes?" She presses a hand to her chest. "Guess we'd better hurry."

She comes around the counter to join me. There's a faint streak of sawdust across her sleeve, and I have to flex my fingers to stop myself from reaching for her and wiping it off.

"Where are we going?"

"Dinner. I know for a fact you've only been eating that alien sludge of yours." She strides toward the narrow hall that connects the shop to Daisy's Diner.

"The fridge came in yesterday," I remind her, but it's pointless since I haven't bought anything to fill it.

"Yes, but you still have three thousand yellow goop packets left, which means you're not going to buy groceries until you absolutely have to." She glances back, eyes bright. *Damn her.* "Come on, we'll strategize. Eavesdrop on competitors. Poison their drinks. Slip laxatives into their water bottles."

I choke. "What?"

"Ballet school horror stories." She shrugs. "Laxatives were the nice version."

"Remind me to never cross a ballerina."

"Then you should say yes to dinner."

I should say no. It would be easier. Cleaner. But Clementine tilts her head, curls spilling forward, lips pulled into a grin that is half challenge and half promise. Suddenly, "no" isn't an option.

"Strategy's scheduled for Saturday."

"Well," she says, brushing past me, "consider us ahead of schedule."

"That defeats the point of a schedule."

"You said you were going to ease up on all the rigidness." She stops inches from me, batting her lashes, blue eyes sparkling. A loose thread clings to the collar of her shirt, and I press my palms together to stop myself from tugging at it. "You know what? Give me your notebook."

I blink. "What? Why?"

"Because." She digs into her tote and pulls out a pen so violently bright red it could serve as a flare gun. "If I'm dragging you into chaos, your notebook should reflect it."

"No one writes in my book."

She smirks before snagging my notebook out of my back pocket, fingers brushing where they shouldn't. *The audacity.*

"Relax, Hastings. It's paper, not your last will and testament."

Every muscle in me wants to snatch it back. I stand there, rigid, while she flips to the ribbon-marked page. It's vulnerable to see my notebook open in front of her. With a wicked grin, she braces the leather cover against my collarbone like I'm her personal writing desk and starts to scrawl. Her handwriting loops and curls, careless and alive, nothing like my black-ink grids.

"There." She caps the pen with a smug snap.

On the page: *Dinner with Clementine at Daisy's Diner.* Followed by a heart.

It hits me in the ribs like a hammer.

"That's vandalism."

"It's accuracy."

"It's unnecessary."

"It's adorable," she corrects, leaning in until a curl brushes my collar. My eyes snag on a freckle near her jaw, and for a brief, dizzying second, I wonder if it would taste sweet or salty. "Admit it, you like it."

"I don't."

"You do."

I snap the notebook shut and pocket it like I'm locking away something dangerous. "Doodles don't belong in lists."

"Lists beg for doodles. It's like a rule."

"What other rules do you have?"

"Grocery lists always end with chocolate. Packing lists always start with underwear. And my to-do lists always include something I already did, just so I can check it off."

"That's cheating."

"That's human."

I shake my head, but my mouth betrays me with a twitch. She sees it, of course. She always sees it.

"And besides," she adds, twirling the pen between her fingers like it's a knife she knows how to use, "your notebook's too serious. I bet you've got lists for everything."

"That's the point."

"Oh yeah? Weight, calories, miles run, number of times you've blinked today. I bet you even have a list for..." She tilts her head, eyes glinting. "Every time you've had sex."

Heat climbs my neck, but I don't look away. "This notebook doesn't hold a list like that."

Her lips part, surprise flickering before she recovers. "That's tragic."

"That's intentional," I counter.

"Intentional can still be tragic." She leans in, conspiratorial. "Lists don't just have to be about discipline. They can be about pleasure too."

"You think pleasure can be itemized?"

"I think you'd be surprised."

Before I can stop her, she snatches the notebook back out of my pocket, flips to a fresh page, and in bold red strokes sketches the outline of a woman with exaggerated hips, breasts, and curves. She presents it to me with a sly grin. "There. Your first entry."

"And who's that supposed to be?"

Her gaze drags slowly from my shoulders down, then back up. She leans close enough that I catch the faint trace of citrus on her skin. "I'll leave that to your imagination."

She doesn't wait for a response, just heads toward the door, hips swaying with every step.

I snap the notebook shut and tuck it into my pocket. The heart and the sketch burn against my thigh. My hand shifts lower, adjusting myself.

Fucking hell.

Clementine doesn't look back to see if I'll follow. She knows I will.

CLEMENTINE STEPS IN FIRST, and the whole place tilts toward her. The hostess gushes about her earrings. Two old men at the counter salute with their coffee mugs. From the kitchen, someone hollers about rhubarb bars.

She doesn't try, but people notice her anyway.

When I follow her inside, the air changes. Zak Kwan and a couple hikers I've noticed on the trailheads stop mid-bite, voices dropping low. My name rolls through the room like static. I square my shoulders and ignore it, though the truth is I'd rather be back at the lodge choking down one of those protein goop pouches Clementine likes to mock me for.

"I didn't realize I signed up for dinner with the mayor," I say.

"It's called having a personality." She tosses it over her shoulder like a dart, grinning when it lands. "Plus, you've been hiding in that lodge since you got here. You could…I don't know…talk to people."

I won't be here for long. There is no point in meeting anyone in this damn town, but I don't say that. I just glare at her and follow.

We weave through the tables, past a display case full of pies and cakes. The windows are framed by plaid curtains, and the walls are lined with cookie jars and thickly painted portraits of desserts in bright colors. This place serves pancakes at all hours and always smells faintly like syrup and bacon grease.

The hostess leads us to a corner table. I take the seat facing the window. Clementine sits across from me, looking out at the rest of the room. On the table, a pair of tiny ceramic bear salt-and-pepper shakers rest beside the laminated menus.

"You must be Alec, huh?" The hostess leans in, face smiling, burgundy hair bouncing. A crooked name tag on her apron reads *Vallery*.

"Yeah."

"Don't worry, Val, he doesn't talk much." Clem leans back, fiddling with a gold hoop earring.

"Don't blame him, you make most of the men in this town speechless."

I try to focus on the table, but out of the corner of my eye, I see people staring at her.

"You're one to talk, bombshell."

"Stop. After two kids, I'm just glad I can find time to do my makeup in the morning."

"Which reminds me, I have an eyeshadow palette that's not in my season—I can bring it to you tomorrow."

"You're a doll. Also, did you see the picture you hung up? Hasn't moved an inch." Val points to a cake photo hanging above the register.

"Thank Cody. He was the one who taught me how to use a hammer." Clem laughs, and I grunt. I taught her to use a drill to fix the baseboard in the lodge, showed her how to measure, level, hold the bit steady, and now her boss is getting all the credit. Clem smiles at me like she knows exactly what I'm thinking. "Well, Alec over here taught me a bit."

"Well, regardless of who taught you, you did better than Mikey," Val teases. "I've been asking him to hang that damn TV for months, and he never does."

"Seriously?" Clem shakes her head. "I can come over tomorrow after work and help you."

"Would you? I'd love that. I'll pay you in Diet Cokes."

"Oh, now I'll definitely be there," Clem laughs.

They speak like time doesn't exist.

"Excuse me, can I get a beer?" I finally interrupt, or I'll be here all night listening to them talk about who helped whom move a canoe last Thursday.

"Sure, darling," Val says. "You want the sour, the ale, the one Dottie makes in her garage? It's a little soapy, but it supports the locals."

"Don't you just have a Modelo or something?"

"He'll have Dottie's," Clem says, "and I'll have a—"

"Diet Coke, honey." Val laughs and walks away.

Clem glares at me. "I'm rating your people skills a two out of ten tonight."

I can feel it already. This town, its quirks, its endless friendly chatter…it's going to wear me down before my time here is over.

"I was thirsty." I shrug, fingers clipping against the menu.

"Was an allotment of one beer allowed on your schedule today, Hastings?"

"I can be spontaneous too. I'm out to dinner with you, aren't I?"

"Having a watch vibrate every hour gives people the impression that you're always waiting for the next thing."

In one clean motion, I strip off my watch and place it in my pocket. My wrist feels naked, but I swallow away the discomfort. "There."

The waitress slides our drinks in front of us, then waits with her pen poised. I rattle off my order without looking away from Clem. She gets the salmon with a side salad. I get the steak, medium rare, with potatoes.

When the waitress leaves, Clem lifts her Diet Coke, the straw bobbing against the ice. "We need a toast."

"To what?"

"To two whole weeks of training." Her grin sparks like a match. "To not murdering each other. And to the lodge actually looking pretty damn good."

I clink her glass. *Let her have the optimism.*

She tilts her head. "So, how's Finn's bed?"

With Clem painting the main room, I couldn't sleep in the spot I've occupied for the past eighteen days.

"Good," I say, too quickly.

"Better than the ground?" she presses, her grin tucked into the rim of her glass.

"I'm only making sure it's good enough for him." My tone frays, thin and brittle.

"You sleeping better?"

"Are you?" I taunt.

"Maybe once you finish tiling the showers, you can build yourself a bedroom."

Unease creeps beneath my skin. "Maybe." The beer is too bitter, all soap and hops. Nothing like the pitchers Finn and I used to drain until the world went quiet. Nothing like the weight of him across a table, filling the silence with easy noise.

Two more weeks, and he'll be here. Whether I'm ready or not.

When I glance up, Clementine is leaning in, chin propped in her palm, watching me with that look that doesn't let me hide.

"What?"

"You're doing it again," she says.

"Doing what?"

"Disappearing behind your eyes. I swear, you vanish mid-sentence sometimes. So, I'm just waiting to see when you'll come back."

"I do not."

"You do." She points at me with her straw. "All the time. You know you do."

I shake my head. "I'm just—" I exhale. "I have a lot on my mind."

She looks around the diner like she's hunting for someone else, then back at me, mock-serious. "If only there were a willing ear here. *Hmm.* Wonder who might want to listen to you talk about your thoughts…"

"No one."

"You're so annoying!" She kicks me under the table, not hard. My laugh slips out before I can stop it. Strange, laughing in public. Stranger still when I realize I don't hate it.

"Finn and I used to hit a diner after every climb," I say. "Pitcher of beer, burger, fries. We'd stay until we could barely keep our eyes open." My hand curls around the sweating glass, grounding myself in the cold. "So being here…it reminds me of that."

"It's good to remember the good stuff."

"Feels easier to remember the bad now."

Her expression softens. "I get that. I mean, I can't even begin to imagine the bond you guys have or how hard it is being without him. But you've got so many memories, Alec. Good and bad. Don't bury them away just because things changed."

"Did you read that off a pamphlet?"

She smirks. "No. I'm wise beyond my years."

"Sure you are."

"So, tell me the real stuff," she says. "The things your fangirls wouldn't know. What was your first mountain? The one where you knew, *Yep, this is it. This is my life.*"

"Shasta."

"Tell me about it."

I lean back and take a long exhale. "Finn and I had a long weekend off school, so we drove up. Near the summit, there's a lake—Helen."

"I've heard of it."

"Well, we camped there. Snuck beers into our packs. Three days without service, without noise. Just us and the cold. We left saying, *why would we ever do anything else?*"

"And then?" she prompts.

"Then we went back to the Bay. Finn was in Oakland, me north of the bridge. We'd IM trails to each other all week, then disappear every Friday."

She laughs under her breath. "IM? You mean DM."

I roll my eyes. "They were simpler times."

"And that's why you climb?"

I've heard the question a hundred times, from reporters, sponsors, and people who think what I do is something you can dissect cleanly. They want the neat answer: because it's there, because it's conquest, because the mountain doesn't lie.

But Clementine isn't them.

"Nope. I climb 'cause I've always had too much noise in my head," I say. The words grind out, but they're mine. "Couldn't sit still. My parents used to drag us all out on trails—strollers, snacks, the whole crew—and I'd always run ahead, alone. Don't remember the path. Just remember afterward."

"What did it feel like?"

"Like I could finally sit in my own skin." I rub my thumb along the side of the glass. "In school, all I thought about was climbing trees and rooftops. Scaring my mom half to death. Eventually she gave up and dropped me off at a climbing gym. And that—" My throat tightens, but I let the words out. "That was the first time nothing else mattered."

Her lips part. "That's funny because what you're describing, that being-present feeling, that's what ballet was for me. Until it made me want to crawl out of my skin."

She doesn't say more. She doesn't have to. I get it.

For a moment, it's just us, carrying the same ache. Different shapes, same weight.

"Of course, half the reason I loved the climbing gym was because it was hard to find quiet in a house with five siblings."

Her straw pauses mid-sip. "I can't imagine it."

"Someone was always crying, someone else yelling, someone else stealing whatever food you were saving. I used to sprint out the door just to get a few minutes of silence." My mouth quirks. "I love them, but ask any older sibling, they're annoying as hell sometimes."

"Kinda like you," she shoots back.

The last thing I want is her putting me in the sibling category. "Don't push it." I try for stern, but she grins when I fail.

She tips her head. "Did you have a favorite? Someone you're closer to?"

"My sisters, probably. Francesca's the youngest. Her brain is wired like mine, never stops running toward danger. And Brooklyn basically raised half of us."

"Eldest daughters always do that," Clementine says knowingly. "In dance, they were like moms."

"No one asked her to be. She just…carried it anyway."

"What about your brothers?"

"Cameron plays in the Premier League over in the UK, where he lives with his girlfriend. Dante fences and is dating his childhood crush. Ezra swims and is engaged to his high school sweetheart. Has been forever."

"So, you're the last unattached brother."

"Guess so."

"Well…apart from Finn, since he's like an adopted brother. He practically grew up at my house. But unlike my siblings, Finn and I could sit quietly on a ridge for hours."

"Like us."

The words should be nothing, but they hit hard.

"Yeah," I admit. "Like us."

Her grin withers. "I've never had that. Not with friends, not with anyone. Ballet was all pushing, competing. If you weren't speaking, you were already behind. Quiet meant losing."

"For me, quiet meant surviving." My thumb continues to trace the condensation sliding down my glass. "With Finn, it became more than that." I pause, throat tight, then let it out anyway. "With you…it feels different again."

For once, I don't feel like I'm drowning in loss when I talk about the past. I feel like I'm remembering my life. The ridges, the noise of my siblings, Finn. All the parts that made me.

"How different?"

"Good different," I say.

I want to reach across the table, cover her hand with mine, but the waitress arrives, dropping plates that steam and bleed between us. My steak, thick and red at the center, potatoes drowned in gravy, green beans glossy with butter. Clementine's plate is a slab of pale pink fish and an undressed salad.

Her eyes linger on my plate. She tries to play it off by spearing a limp leaf of lettuce, but I see it.

"You don't look too enthused."

"I'm thrilled," she says, gaze locked on my steak.

"You're staring at my meat, Clementine."

She rolls her lips between her teeth. "It just looks so…sinful."

"Then eat it."

Her fork freezes midair. "I don't want to be like one of your siblings, stealing food off your plate."

I grunt. "We're not siblings."

"Right," she says, all fake innocence. "Because we're camp buddies!"

"You've got to stop calling us that."

"Why? Does it make you twitch?" There's a challenge in her voice. Both of us seeing how far we can walk out on the ledge.

You have no idea. "I'm ordering another steak, and I'll eat that and your salmon."

"You don't have to."

"I don't do things I don't want to do." My tone lands rough enough that her fork stills. Before she can argue, I flag the waitress. "Another steak, please." I push mine across the table, the smell of char and salt rushing between us.

Her fingers toy with the edge of the plate. "I haven't had a real meal like this in…" She shakes her head, a rueful smile tugging at her mouth. "In ballet, you're always counting. Calories, ounces, bites. I still slip into that. Especially now, with all this training."

"Fuel's important."

"Spoken like a man who's never been told his worth depends on fitting into a tutu."

"Spoken like a man who knows that starving doesn't make you stronger," I correct.

That gets her to laugh. Full-bodied, head tilting back, the sound cutting through the clatter of the diner. People turn, but I don't care. I'm too busy watching her slice into my steak, juice spilling across the plate like it was meant to be hers all along.

She lifts the bite slowly, and her gaze flicks to me one more time. "Last chance to change your mind."

"Eat," I tell her.

"Bossy."

"Hungry," I correct.

"For food?"

The corner of my mouth tilts. "For now."

Her lips close around the bite, slowly, just to torture me. When her throat works through the swallow, my pulse kicks hard enough that the glass sweats in my grip.

She wipes her mouth with the back of her hand, smirking. "Do you always stare this much at dinner, or am I special?"

"If I say you're special, will you stop talking and keep eating?"

"Maybe." She smiles through another eye-rolling bite.

"You're special, Clementine."

That knocks her off balance for half a second. "Thank you. For this. For sharing all of it with me. I'm enjoying this, Alec."

It should gut me. Instead, it splits something open.

Because I see myself in her, the way she punishes herself for wanting, the way she treats joy like it's a ration, like it's safer to go hungry than to take too much. I know that logic. I've lived by it.

Finn gave me comfort when I needed it most. The kind that made the world less jagged. But Clementine, she gives me hunger again. And the terrifying thing is, it feels like permission.

Maybe this is the point. Maybe living isn't about climbing higher until your lungs collapse. Maybe it's about sitting still long enough to taste what's in front of you.

To admit you want it.

Her hand. Her laugh. My steak.

"Me too," I say.

And for one absurd, ordinary moment, amid syrup-stained tables, the hiss of a griddle, and a jukebox playing something no one's listening to, I let myself believe I could get used to this.

Chapter 20
Alec

I KNEEL in front of Clementine, the straps of the harness clutched in my hands. She's practiced for this all week, but first rappels are when people freeze or, worse, panic. There cannot be another bear or kayak incident.

Not with a crowd this size.

Patagonia banners snap overhead, fraying in the wind. A drone buzzes somewhere above. The air smells like coffee and apple donuts. There are nearly a thousand people here for the Rappelling 101 course, making the outdoors feel crowded.

"Leg straps." I attempt to focus, tapping her calf. "Spread."

"Buy a girl dinner first," she shoots back, laughter threading through her words as she obeys.

"Technically," I grunt, hauling the strap into place, "I already did."

Her eyes glint. "So, this is my repayment?"

"That's not what I said."

"It's what you meant."

"You really have a habit of hearing things I don't say."

"I know." She leans forward like she's sharing a secret. "I just like getting under your skin."

She has no idea how far she's embedded herself into me. Or maybe she does, and that's worse.

I drag the harness up her legs. She's wearing what she calls biker shorts. I call them hell. Black nylon clings to bare skin, my knuckles grazing her thigh as I thread the strap. Her skin smells of sunscreen, sweat, and grapefruit, and it finds its way back into my chest, lodges under my ribs, and stays there.

"You enjoying yourself down there?"

"Checking for safety hazards."

Her smile says she noticed exactly where my eyes lingered. "Remind me again why you're not rappelling too?"

"Because I do this for a living."

"Which is exactly why you should get on that mountain with me and do something incredible. A flip, a spin. Scare the competition."

"We don't need to scare anyone." I tug another strap through to cinch the waist buckle. My knuckles graze her stomach under her thin shirt, and she takes a step back.

"Quit moving," I scold. "I don't want you sliding out halfway up." The harness squeaks as I tighten the buckle. "That tight?"

"Very."

I yank the strap one last time, harder than necessary. She lurches forward. Her hands fly up, bracing the back of my head. The front of her shorts presses into my face.

Every muscle in me locks. My brain says move, but my body? My body doesn't.

"Oh, I see you're enjoying Clem's muffin again," a voice cuts in.

"Hi, Gran," Clementine sighs.

Margaret tips her sunglasses down. "Ever heard of BDSM?"

"Stop," Clementine groans. "Please. Please say nothing else."

"I'm just pointing out," Margaret adds, grinning, "that's a fine-looking harness you've got on there."

Clementine elbows her grandmother, but the affection's there. Margaret's barely five feet tall, hair cropped silver, puffer vest blueberry-blue over flannel. Cheeks flushed from the wind, moving like she's got twice the energy of the rest of us put together.

"Gran, I know you've already met, but let me officially introduce you again." Clementine tugs on Margaret's sleeve like she's corralling a toddler. "This is Alec. Alec, Margaret." Then, lower, she mutters into her ear, "Be normal."

"*Pshh.* Normal's for the boring." Margaret thrusts her hand at me. "Hello, dear. You really are all man, aren't you?"

"Uh—"

"I'm just teasing."

"It's great to see you again," I say, but she wiggles her fingers until I take it. She clearly expects me to kiss her knuckles. So, I do, because what other choice is there?

"My oh my, such a gentleman." Margaret giggles. "I remember you and your friend eating spaghetti Bolognese straight out of the pot like it was the last meal you'd ever get."

"You threatened to use your shears on us if Bill didn't come back in one piece." I let out a laugh.

"Wish I could use those shears to tear up old age. That's the real devil."

"I'm sorry for your loss."

"One loss is another gain." Margaret slings an arm over Clementine's shoulder and plants a kiss on her cheek, leaving behind a smear of lipstick. "Now, sweetheart, give me a hug."

Clementine folds into her, and Margaret squeezes like she'll never let go. "Bill still talked about you," she says to me over Clem's hair. "Wished he could've been around to see you move in. Said you two gave him a run for his money drinking whiskey. We'll have to pour a dram over the first snow in his honor."

"I'm not sticking around for winter."

"Smart. Not many can survive the cold." Margaret tips her head. "Well then, we'll just have a glass when you and my granddaughter win this thing."

"Absolutely."

Margaret's gaze fixes on me. "I still have those shears, you know. One hair out of place on her head—"

"Gran," Clementine scolds.

"She'll be okay," I cut in.

No. Not okay. Better. She has to be. I'll make sure of it.

Margaret glances back toward the crowd. "Oh, Cody just got here. I'll save you both a blueberry donut for when you get down."

"Can't wait!" Clementine forces a smile and watches her grandmother head off.

The horn blows, echoing off the rock face and through the spruce-lined ridge. It's our signal.

"Here, take this." I shove a walkie-talkie into her hand. "I won't be able to hear you up there, so keep it clipped in. If anything looks off, I'll call it."

She clicks the button, and static cracks through the line. "This is so camp buddy coded."

"Never say that again." My hand lands on her shoulder. "You got this."

"*We* got this," she repeats.

Clem starts the hike up while I stay below, the rope coiled at my feet. I already checked her anchor station at the top—twice—but watching her disappear between the trees, I still feel my stomach knot.

In a matter of minutes, the walkie crackles to life.

"Roger, roger. We are officially making our way up the hill. Way easier without the brick pack."

"Focus, Clementine."

"We need code names. That's how this works. You've got to give me one too."

"Clementine—"

"Alec." Her voice sharpens through the line, breath ragged from the climb. I don't like how thin it sounds. I need her focused.

I hesitate, then give her something simple. "Fox."

"Fox!" She laughs, delighted. "Oh, I love it. Fits me, doesn't it? Quick, clever, impossible to catch."

"Sly."

"Perfect." A pause. "So what's yours? Satie?" She's laughing, but she doesn't realize how many nights I've sat in the dark with Satie bleeding through the speakers, holding myself together by a single note.

"Pay attention," I growl.

She hums a bar of the melody through the comms. "Satie and Fox. Has a ring to it."

The ridge crests ahead, wind biting harder. The cliff isn't huge, only sixty feet of granite that is streaked with green lichen. *Controlled wall. Safe wall.* I repeat it until the words sound empty.

The walkie crackles again. "Okay, Jessie's got me all strapped in."

"Jessie, did you double-check redundancies?"

"Yes, I did."

"Check them again."

Clem's voice cuts through, edged with impatience. "We both checked them, Alec."

"Hand the radio to Jessie."

"What? No—"

"*Now.*" My tone leaves no room.

A pause, then Jessie says, "Redundancies checked, Hastings. Twice. Anchor's good. Device loaded."

I exhale through my nose. "Alright."

"There. Satisfied?"

I press the button, but nothing comes out. Because the truth tastes like rust in my mouth. Because if I told her the real answer, that I'm not going to ever be happy when she's dangling from a rope, it would pin me down in ways I can't allow.

"Yes," I manage, finally.

I plant myself at the base, boots dug in, rope tight in my grip. My job as a backup belay is simple. If she slips, if she freezes, if her brake hand lets go, I haul down and lock her in the air.

That's the theory. The reality is that I'm one bad second away from losing my mind.

My hands shouldn't be sweating. I've belayed kids, rookies, clients who couldn't tell a carabiner from a keychain. I've held strangers on walls twice this size. Never flinched. Never once doubted the system.

But this is Clementine, and my body hasn't gotten the memo that she's just another climber on a rope. My throat is sandpaper.

What if her brake hand slips?

What if her knot's wrong?

What if she drops into the void and I'm too slow, too late?

It's not rational. It's not professional. It's not me.

She edges backward over the lip.

Focus, Hastings. Fucking focus.

Her eyes flick down to me between the sixty feet of rope stretched between us, and she steps off.

The system holds. The harness, anchor, and rope are all solid. She lowers herself slowly. Halfway down, her brake hand drifts too high. My pulse spikes, gripping iron on the line. Her descent quickens. Not dangerous—not yet—but the margin shrinks.

"Brake hand low," I bark up at her.

She doesn't correct. My heart claws against my ribs.

"Clemetine," I yell up at her again. "Brake hand."

"I got it," she calls back.

The rope twists near the anchor, and when she pushes off the wall for the last drop, her angle's just a hair off. The entire rappel is less than thirty seconds.

She swings straight into me, hard enough to skid my boots on gravel. I yank the line and lock the belay, arms snapping around her waist. She collides against me with a bright smile.

"Good catch," she beams.

I can't let go. My hands still clamp her waist, holding her there like she might vanish.

"You dropped faster than you should've."

"I'm fine!"

"You twisted the line. Brake hand stays low next time."

"I heard you." She rolls her eyes, and her lips tug between her teeth. "God forbid I ruin your perfect safety record."

The crowd behind us cheers as someone else preps for their rappel, but it's muffled in my ears. The world's narrowed to her heartbeat pressed into me.

"You're not supposed to give me a heart attack," I bite out, still wired, still holding the ghost of her weight against me.

"Guess you'll just have to hold on tighter, then."

So, I do. A moment too long. Until she eases back, hands sliding off my shoulders like it costs her to let go. My pulse hasn't slowed when a slap lands between my shoulder blades.

"Your turn, Hastings?"

Zak Kwan. Green hair brighter than it was at our CPR class, grin cocky enough to split his face in two.

"He's not climbing today," Clementine says, still catching her breath. Her braid slips over her chest.

"And you are?" His voice dips into something meant to be smooth, his eyes dragging over her.

"Clementine."

"Didn't know Alec traded in Finn," he says with a laugh. "Partner upgrade. Lucky guy."

The heat that hits my neck is not from the sun. I take a step closer, my voice flat enough to cut glass. "Get lost, Zak."

Zak flicks his gaze back at me. "Be good to see you on a wall again. What's it been, months?" He smirks and pushes his neon hair back like he's in a shampoo ad. "Scared you won't be able to take on all us younger guys?"

"I could out climb you in my sleep," I grit out.

"Sure you could. And you, Fox?" Zak asks, angling toward Clementine. "First rappel? Looked like fresh meat out there."

Bile burns my throat. That's *my* name for her.

Her face contorts in disgust. "Don't call me that. I don't know you. And weren't you the one whimpering when you went over the edge?"

Zak stumbles, smirk slipping.

I snicker. "Careful, Zak. She'll gut you with a smile if you keep pressing."

He brushes it off. "Competition's fierce this year."

A clipboard appears in my face before I can say anything else.

"Alec Hastings, perfect. We need you in the tent—pictures, quick promo. Short speech before the mayor comes on."

Zak vanishes into the crowd, and a man thrusts a script at me, already walking away like I'm a piece of gear instead of a person. *Right.* Patagonia. The deal.

Clementine's laugh drifts up from my side. "Look at you. Such an influencer."

My eyes stay on her. "You gonna be okay?"

"Are you suggesting I can't handle myself while you're off posing for cameras? Please." She smacks my chest. "Go play model. I'll be fine. Gran owes me a donut anyway."

I don't want to leave her. But the clipboard guy is already waving me over impatiently.

"You did good today, Clem," I call out to her.

"I like 'Fox,' especially when it's coming from you."

"Noted."

Her lips curve, sharp and sweet. "Go strike a pose, Satie."

I let her have the last word, even as the nickname cuts deeper than she knows.

August 24th

From Rope Team to Rift: Alec Hastings Dumps Finn for a New Climbing Partner

August 24th

Betrayal on the Wall? Alec Hastings Climbs Again While Finn Fights to Walk

August 24th

Did @TwoMenOnTop Officially Split?

Chapter 21
Clementine

ALEC

not rly my style

Picture: a pair of panties

CLEMENTINE

OH MY GOD WHY DO YOU HAVE THOSE???

ALEC

got delivered to lodge. thought it was sheets.

CLEMENTINE

No no no no no those are MINE. Don't open the box further.

ALEC

right

CLEMENTINE

I'm coming over right now.

ALEC

weird

CLEMENTINE

> You're judging. I can FEEL it through the phone.

ALEC

> i'm concerned

CLEMENTINE

> I'll be there in two minutes.

"WHERE IS IT?" I hear the panic in my own voice. Alec's eyes flick to the counter.

"What's going on with you?"

"Nothing." I lunge for the box, clutching it behind my back like a raccoon with stolen bread. Heat crawls up my neck.

"What's in the box?" His tone isn't casual; it's that low one he uses when I've screwed up my footwork.

"Nothing! I mean—it's just…stuff. Totally normal."

"Clementine." He says my name like it's a full stop. His eyes are steady, unfairly steady, and my arms are shaking, and my fake grin won't stick.

"I'm embarrassed, okay?" My voice cracks.

He stiffens. "Why?"

"Because I spiraled." The words tumble out. "I bought things I can't afford, I broke my budget, my gran's going to lose her mind when the bill comes next month, and now you know and you'll regret picking me as a partner because—" My throat squeezes. "Because I'm just a shopping addict with no self-control."

He takes the box out of my hands, sets it gently on the counter, and pulls a chair out. "Sit."

"I don't know if I can breathe right now."

"You can sit *and* not breathe. Multitask."

I drop into the chair, arms crossed.

"So, you bought some stuff," he says.

"That's one way to put it." My laugh is humorless. "Right after I screwed up the blister thing. I felt useless, and shopping is the only way I know to shut my brain up. Swipe the card. Boom. Ten seconds of worth. Then shame."

He leans on the counter. "That's a rigged system."

"No kidding. But it's the only one I grew up with. Bad day? Shop. Good day? Shop. Ballet teacher yelling? Shop. Chest feeling hollow? Definitely shop. Then the bill came, and we either dealt with it or we didn't."

"That sounds exhausting."

"It is. And it's embarrassing. And it's mine. Along with the thousands of dollars of debt."

He stares at me for a beat. "I could pay it off," he says simply, like he's offering me a glass of water.

The heat that shoots through me isn't gratitude. It's fury.

"*No.*"

"It wouldn't be a big deal—"

"Alec. No." My voice flares because I need him to hear it.

He exhales hard. "Why make this a thing?"

"Because it is a thing!" My hands fling up. "You grew up with money. I didn't. We see it differently."

"You say that like it's a bad thing."

"It's not. But I don't…I don't do well with generosity."

"I know that, but we don't have to call it generosity. It can be a gift or a loan that you don't need to pay back."

It would be so easy. He'd probably put it all on his fancy Amex and not even blink. My red numbers would disappear overnight. No more late fees. No more letters in the mail. No more pit in my stomach when the phone lights up with an unknown number. I could breathe again.

But if I let him, my debt wouldn't just be gone. It would belong to him. And then so would I.

And if I'm ever going to belong to Alec Hastings, I really don't want it to be like this.

I want it to be real.

Not because of a solution.

"No," I say. "I don't need someone to rescue me. I need to be able to say I did it. That I clawed my way out of this mess. I want to pick up the phone one day and tell the debt collector, 'You've got it wrong, I already paid.'"

He studies me awhile, then nods once. "Okay. I hear you. I'll make sure that in six weeks you'll be saying exactly that." He says it with annoying certainty. His chin tips toward the box pressed to my chest. "But until then? You don't have to do it alone."

Something in me caves because—it's true. I don't want to do it alone. But also, I hate that he's seen me like this. Small. Weak. Pathetic.

He reaches for the keys on the counter. "Come on. We'll go return the stuff."

When I don't move, he just steps in and slides the box out of my arms. Not rough. Just decisive.

"I'll pack it up," he says, already folding the flaps down. "You don't have to stare at it anymore."

I watch him like a bystander in my own disaster. He rustles through the tissue paper, looking for the return slip, and of course his fingers land on the one thing I actually liked. The stupid navy socks with the little mountain range stitched in.

He holds them up. "You should keep these."

"No."

"You need socks. I saw the holes in yours last week."

"It's part of the binge. If I keep even one thing, it's like admitting defeat."

"It's just socks."

"It's a failure."

He blinks at me. The kind of blink that says he's deciding whether or not I'm joking. "They're socks."

"Fine. I guess they are cute."

"They're not just cute. They'll last. The best brand there is."

"Thank you for not judging me."

"Never." He leans back against the counter, casual, like I didn't just peel myself open and hand him the ugliest parts. "Besides, I've got the perfect song for our drive to the post office."

"You're gonna force me through Satie, aren't you?"

"It's not raining, but I can hold the hose over my truck if you want the full effect."

I laugh. A laugh that hits my ribs and probably makes me sound manic. Somehow, for the first time in weeks—maybe months—it doesn't feel suffocating.

For the first time since I left New York, I feel like I can really figure this out.

I'D PLANNED to sit at home tonight, spiraling about Alec seeing the evidence of my shopping binge. Instead, I'm doubled over in his passenger seat, laughing so hard my ribs ache. Satie rattles the speakers, water streaks down the windshield, and he's outside with a hose angled at the glass like it's the most serious job in the world.

When the music cuts, the rain does too. I fling open the door, stumble out into the driveway, and press my hand to my aching stomach.

"My cheeks hurt!" I gasp. "That is the best therapy I've ever had. Your truck is officially nicknamed the Therapy Tacoma."

He stands there on the porch, blue sweater darkened with spray, curls plastered to his forehead, holding the kinked green hose. His mouth curves, and I swear the air tilts.

"You're not naming my truck," he grumbles.

"Already making bumper stickers." I lean against the door, buzzing with leftover laughter. "I'll bill my contractor."

"Do it." His tone is flat, but his eyes flick to mine. "So, I can watch you sprint into another post office like a fugitive."

I groan into my palms, unable to hide the smile glued to my face. "God. I feel ridiculous. Returning things always gave me anxiety. Humans used to be chased by bears, and I was scared of a shipping label."

"You already faced a bear," he says.

"And a wall," I add.

This time, our grins linger. Longer than they should. Then they soften into something else. The night air hums with it. We both watch a flock of birds ripple down to the lake.

"Hey, Clem." My name is softer than I've ever heard it, a fragile thing on his tongue. His fingers knot and unknot the hose. "You wanna come by to try out the new fire pit this Saturday?"

My heart stumbles. Out by the lake, the benches and fire pit he built this morning wait like a promise.

"To talk strategy for the qualifier?"

"No."

"To practice knots?"

"No." His Adam's apple jumps.

"To celebrate the lodge renovations being ahead of schedule?"

"No." His voice roughens. A crackle of electricity zaps between us.

"To just hang out?"

"Yeah."

The smile spreading across my face feels unstoppable. He's asking to see me. Not to train me. Not to fix me.

Just to be with me.

I toy with the hem of my sweater, nerves sparking through my fingers. "Like—"

"I swear to God, Clementine, if you say camp buddies—"
His fake annoyance only makes me grin harder.

"What? Camp bud—"

He unkinks the hose.

A shock of ice arcs into me, stealing my breath.

"Hey!" I shriek, lunging forward. The spray hits us both, soaking my sweater and plastering his blue one to his chest. I grab for the nozzle, slippery with water, my hands tangling with his.

We're too close. Laughing too hard. The hose thrashes like a live wire between us, cold mist on our faces. My hair sticks to my skin, his curls drip, and his breath mingles with mine as we wrestle for control neither of us really wants.

For a beat, I swear the world shrinks to this: the sting of cold, the sound of our laughter, and Alec Hastings looking at me like the fight's already over.

His grin is real this time, unguarded, and it floors me more than the water ever could.

I'm drenched, I'm freezing, but I know exactly what just happened.

Alec Hastings asked me on a date.

Chapter 22
Clementine

ALL WEEK, dinner has become our rhythm.

Monday, a hike followed by steaks at Daisy's.

Tuesday, our fastest kayak run yet, capped off with a box of maple bars from Yessi's that Alec insisted counted as an appetizer.

Wednesday and Thursday, we split one of Gran's chicken pot pies.

Friday, after sprints left me seeing stars, I made peanut butter and jelly sandwiches, and he ruined the romance by chasing it with one of those egg goop packs he swears by.

I've started to like working at Cody's too—choosing pieces for the lodge instead of wasting hours behind the counter.

This morning, I was up at five, hauling treasures from Trudy's, laying down a burgundy rug in the kitchen, swapping out frames for photos I printed for Finn's room and the living room. The lodge is beginning to look like something real. His handcrafted tables and chairs alongside the stuff I picked out. A sectional wrapping around the fireplace. Adventure books scattered on the mantel.

It feels alive now, and so does he.

An hour ago, we finished the final walkthrough downstairs. After the qualifiers, we'll tackle the half-finished bathrooms upstairs. But downstairs looks immaculate. We did it. *We.*

He looks more at ease than he ever has. I feel it too.

He crouches at the new fire pit outside the lodge, right at the edge, where the porch gives way to the lake. Low under his breath, he hums Mozart's Symphony No. 40 in G minor.

The melody drifts through the damp air, threaded with smoke and pine. Behind him, the sun bleeds gold, catching on his shoulders like light can't resist him.

Being out in nature makes me feel feral.

Bare feet on slick rocks, fog sitting heavy over the lake, grass tickling my ankles. I'd never go barefoot in New York, even when my shoes dug craters in the backs of my ankles, but here I used to race puddle to puddle from the lodge to my grandparents' house. I love that feeling.

"Are you happy? Because I think you're happy." I nudge Alec's shoulder with mine.

"Ecstatic." He says it as flat as a stone, face as carved as a gargoyle.

"Uh-huh. Except your eyebrow twitched. Which means you're practically giddy."

The corner of his mouth threatens treason against his stoicism. "And you're grinning so hard I'm worried your face might split."

"Can't help it." I fling my arms toward the water, the lodge, the whole miracle of it. "I feel like it's the night before a recital. There is zero chance I'm sleeping."

"I'm the same before a summit day," he says, stacking kindling.

"I'd toss, stretch, anything to keep my muscles warm. That's how I feel right now. I'm buzzing." I hop onto one of the split logs circling the pit. My legs can't sit still.

"Buzz carefully," he mutters. "I need you in one piece."

That makes me hop down.

"Would you look at that sunset?" I stand in awe. "Before this month, I don't even remember the last time I saw a sunset. Isn't that sad?"

"Last time I checked, the sun still set in New York," he says, pulling a knife and flint from his cargo pocket, bouncing them in his palm.

"Thank you for that piece of science, Einstein." I hip-bump his shoulder. His smirk nearly knocks me straight into the lake— and for a second, I consider taking a dip. Wonder if he'd follow me. Probably not. He'd probably just stand there and tell me to be careful, the infuriating bastard.

"I worked in the mornings," I say instead, eyes on the blood-orange sky splitting open across the lake. "Ballet started after two, sometimes went until midnight. I barely looked up at the sky. I forgot what it felt like to just watch it."

"That's tragic." He looks at me then, not the sunset, though his golden irises are lit with the burn of it. "Do you miss New York?"

"Some days. But I'm happy here. I never thought I'd like kayaking as much as I do." I wrinkle my nose. "Hiking's okay. At least, the parts without elevation."

"Then it's just a walk."

"No. A walk is Grand Central to Central Park. Hiking is dirt and bugs and sweat."

"You get dirtier on the subway."

"Okay, mountain man. Whatever." I throw my hand up in mock surrender, then glance back at the lodge. The siding gleams like it's been photoshopped into real life, trim sharp against the flower beds. "Think Finn will like it? He gets here Tuesday, right?"

"Yeah. Couldn't have done it without you."

It's embarrassing how much that warms me. I smother it with

a grin. "And I couldn't have done twenty push-ups if my life depended on it. Now I throw soil bags like I'm auditioning for World's Strongest Woman. Cody practically knighted me MVP stocker of the year."

"You did good this week," he says, gaze pinning mine. He's still in his hiking gear, a navy beanie pulled low, hair curling out in stubborn tufts.

"Careful." My grin turns sly. "Your compliments might go to my head."

"Then earn another." He nods at the stack of logs beside me.

I make a show of rolling my eyes, so I reach too fast and hiss when bark slices my finger. "Ow. Damn it." The log thuds to the ground as I stick my index finger in my mouth.

"Let me." He's already in front of me, dropping to his knees. I hesitate, then give him my hand. His thumb traces my palm, skin rough against mine, and the touch makes my heart do something it shouldn't.

"It's shallow," he says. And then, without warning, he lifts my hand higher and slips my finger between his lips.

My brain flatlines.

It's hot. Wet. His tongue presses lightly against the sting, and he's so casual about it, like this is the obvious solution, like sucking the pain out of me is first aid.

Heat streaks up my neck.

I can't move, can't breathe, watching him do it with that impossible calm.

And the worst part? The way my body answers before I can even think.

Yes. More of this.

My brain stutters.

What. On. Earth. Is. Happening?

My free hand clamps the log beside me, grounding myself, because the rest of me is tilting toward him like a magnet. Heat coils low in my stomach, spreading everywhere. I'm going to combust.

A treacherous part of me wants to rake my other hand across the bark, fill it with splinters, just to see how his mouth would feel there too. When he pulls back, he spits in the grass, blinking up at me through dark lashes. His pupils have dilated, engulfing the gold in his eyes.

"Got most of it."

"Most?" My voice is a stranger.

"There's still a piece," he says, like it's nothing. "Hold still."

Time stretches. My body feels like a stage, every nerve en pointe, ready to collapse or take flight. His mouth closes over my finger again. Warmth spirals up my arm, teeth grazing lightly, making me jolt.

"You're not holding still," he says against my skin.

My thoughts go dark, tumbling into a place I shouldn't visit. I want to kiss him. Right here. Right now. I'm done pretending. I want to break every no-partner rule I swore by.

"Neither are you," I breathe back.

That earns me the faintest smirk before he goes back to it, infuriatingly thorough, like we're keeping score, and he's determined to win.

Behind us, the stack of kindling slumps into itself, but under my ribs, something else has caught fire.

He drops my hand. "There. Gone."

"You sucked a splinter out of my hand," I say, squinting at him, not knowing how to speak or move or do anything.

"I've done it for other people." His attempt at casualness falls flat, the tension still snapping between us. "Next time, don't grab firewood so carelessly."

"Noted."

"Now wait here. I have a surprise for you." And then he runs —sprints—toward the lodge.

I know he felt it too. Whatever that was.

My heart is still racing, body still tilted toward where he sat. I try to remind myself to think about the debt. About the qualifier. About anything else.

But I can't.

Because I want him.

Chapter 23
Alec

THE TASTE of her blood is still in my mouth.

Not sharp or metallic but faint enough to ghost along my tongue. It replays in my head, over and over, my lips closing around her finger, the heat of her skin, the sound she made when I surprised her.

Now she's next to me on the log, the fire snapping low, a spoon in her hand. Chocolate, banana, and marshmallow melted into a mess. Her tongue flicks out to catch the smear at the corner of her mouth, and she looks right at me as she licks it away.

Sly fox.

Always testing me, and always fucking winning.

"Do you like it?" I hadn't planned to buy the ingredients for the banana boats. I also hadn't planned to ask her to spend her Saturday night with me. But before I knew it, my cart was full, and I wanted to share this with her.

She takes another spoonful from the foil. "This is actually amazing. Where'd you even come up with this?"

"I didn't." I set mine aside, wiping my hands against my

jeans. "Had them on Ouray at fifteen. An instructor made them at the yurts. Exactly like this."

"That's adorable."

"Finn and I ended up smearing it across our sleeping bags. Raccoon unzipped the tent in the middle of the night, tried to steal one."

"No way. Did it really unzip the tent?"

"Hand to God." My voice scrapes with the memory. "Finn screamed so loud the whole camp thought we were under attack. He's never lived it down. Sewed a raccoon patch on his pack like a scarlet letter."

She presses her palm to her mouth, laughter spilling through her fingers. "That's hilarious."

"You really like it?"

"I'd like it more if you weren't watching me eat every bite," she fires back, chin tilting, but her eyes don't leave mine.

"Just making sure you don't get another splinter." It's the worst excuse I've ever made.

"Thank you for your continued commitment to my safety."

She looks at me as if I've given her something holy. And God help me, I wish I had.

My hands itch. My blood snarls. Every nerve screams to drag my fingers down the inside of her wrist, to rest on the curve of her knee, to leave a mark where the world could see.

Instead, I lunge for a leaf at my feet and fold it, my fingers shaking with the lie of distraction.

Her gaze follows every crease. "What are you making there?"

"Not sure yet. What's your favorite flower?"

"A tulip. Can you make one of those?"

"Yeah," I rasp. "Nikkolo taught me all the flowers."

The leaf is too fragile for real folds, but my fingers move anyway, remembering the rhythm. Pinch the stem flat, crease it sharp. Bend the top down, tuck the corners in, twist it once so it doesn't unravel. Crude, uneven, but it takes shape, something that could almost pass for a tulip if you squint hard enough.

I hand her the crooked thing. She takes it like it's worth something anyway.

"I want you to teach me."

I pass her another leaf, guiding her fingers through the folds. My skin brushes hers. It's unbearable. Every graze of my knuckle sparks like a fuse I can't douse.

This isn't origami anymore. She's the sun, and I'm caught in her orbit, powerless to pull away.

"Like this," I grind out, hand covering hers. I'm not teaching her a damn thing. I'm carving myself into her, line by line.

Her eyes go soft, unfocused, drowning in the glow. Mine lock there, refusing to move. The rest of the world blurs until it's only the heat of her knee against mine, her breath teasing the edge of my mouth.

This is where I should scoot over. Give us air. But my body doesn't know that language anymore.

We've been circling for weeks. Pretending.

At some point, a man can no longer deny it. Right?

A low moan gets smothered by her own breath as my touch maps out the line in her palms. I hear it. Fuck, I feel it. My cock jerks, heavy and straining against my zipper, and the leaf nearly tears in my grip.

I can't stop. My thumb drifts down the inside of her wrist. Her skin jumps, shivering under me. I press harder. Her lips part. Her breath stumbles. Another sound slips free, softer, needier, wrecking me clean through.

A shiver rolls down her spine like a wave, visible even in the shadows. I'm already pulling my sweater off, jaw clenched, blood burning.

"I'm not cold," she says, stubborn even now.

"Clementine."

She huffs, rolls her eyes, but takes it. The sweater drops over her frame like it was made for her, sleeves swallowing her hands, hem brushing her thighs. She tucks her chin into the collar, laughter muffled by the wool.

"I look ridiculous."

"You look—" *Mine*. The word claws at my throat. I grit it back. "Warm."

"Guess I'm keeping it."

"Good." It comes out blunt, like I'm scolding. "Don't give it back."

Her gaze lingers at my temple. She lifts her hand and brushes a stray pine needle from my hair. Like it matters. Like I matter. Her fingertips graze my skin, barely there, but it's one of those gentle touches that make me feel like I'm worthy of something so soft.

Her fingers hover, ghosting against my temple, as if she's afraid I'll break if she presses harder.

"You always come back covered in the mountain. It's like it follows you." She smiles like she knows the damage she's done before a yawn cracks out of her, and she fails to stifle it.

"You're dead on your feet," I say. "Go inside. Get some sleep."

Her gaze flicks toward the lodge, then up to her place on the ridge. "I'll be out at four fifty-five sharp."

"Five," I correct. "Not earlier. You need the rest."

She rolls her eyes. "Yes, sir."

"Not a request, Clem."

She smirks, bumping her shoulder against mine. "Okay, Dad."

"Don't call me that."

"You don't like 'camp buddy,' you don't like 'Dad'…" She turns toward the trail, but just when I think she's done, she glances back over her shoulder. The grin she gives me twists with amusement. "What if I say…sweet dreams, Daddy?"

The sound of it punches straight through me. My voice drops

an octave, heavy as stone. "Careful, Clem. That's the kind of thing you can't take back."

"Guess you'll have to dream about me saying it again."

And then she's gone, leaving me with the fire, the mountain, and the ache of blood slamming low, hot, and immediate. I want to drag her back, haul her into my lap, and see what other things I can make her call me. What other lines on her body I can trace with my hands.

I should put the fire out, go inside, and try to sleep. I need to be focused for tomorrow. But I keep staring at where she disappeared to in the trees.

And all I can hear is that one word.

Daddy.

The word loops in my head until it's not a word anymore but a mark.

I imagine her getting home, my sweater hanging off her frame, slipping low enough to bare one shoulder. Maybe she's curled up on her bed right now, fabric bunched at her thighs, biting her lip the way she always does.

My cock swells hard against the denim, every pulse harsher than the last. My thighs lock, teeth clenched so tight my skull aches.

I brace a hand on my knee, knuckles white, seeking to breathe past the ache for her. Trying to leash it…but my body doesn't take orders anymore.

I shove a hand inside my jeans, because there is no fucking way I can stop myself.

The first squeeze of my fist makes her name tear loose, broken, needy, and I hate the sound of it. Like I'm choking on it.

"Clementine."

I see her as clearly as if she were here.

Blue eyes half-lidded, mouth parted, her body shifting into my lap without a word. My breath saws out like she's really there, pressing closer, grinding down until I break.

The fire pops, the cold bites at my skin, but none of it registers.

It's only her. Always her.

Hours. I could spend hours learning what makes her gasp, what makes her shiver, what makes her come apart in my hands. The thought alone is enough to wreck me. My whole body strains with it.

I stroke myself in time with the picture, thumb dragging over my swollen cock.

In my head, she's not shy. She's not hesitant. She's mine.

Moving against me like she's claimed me. Like she owns the ache in my cock, the hunger in my veins, the ruin she's carved out of me.

A growl claws up my throat, and I hurry my pace.

I want her marked. Wrecked. Bent until she doesn't know where I end and she begins. I want her gasps mine, her shivers mine, her moans mine.

Every piece of her, mine.

The thought curdles into obsession. Her voice echoes in my skull, not playful now but raw, reckless, daring—*Daddy.* The word detonates like lightning splitting the sky. My body seizes, muscles snapping taut. I jolt, breath ripped out of me, vision skimming the edges of white.

For a long, brutal moment, I'm nothing but release and ruin, chest locked, pulse hammering until I'm dizzy.

I slump forward, chest heaving, lungs scraping for air. Sweat chills against the night. My thighs ache from the strain. The shame curls black in my gut.

I press both hands over my face, palms rough against my skin.

Months—years—of discipline shattered by a grin, a taunt, a word.

By her.

Worst of all, I want it again. Even in the shame, I want it

again. I want her again. I want the wreckage, the loss of control, the burn, and the breaking.

Because if it's Clementine who undoes me, maybe I don't care what it costs. Maybe I don't want the control back.

Maybe I'd give it all to her.

Gladly.

Chapter 24
Clementine

THE WILD TRAILS qualifier kicks off on the banks of Frog River, just north of Misthaven. By the time Alec and I roll into the lot, it looks like someone dropped an REI catalog from the sky and let it explode. Trucks are jammed in at odd angles, roof racks piled high, kayaks stacked like antlers.

The place hums. Coffee steam curls out of thermoses, half-empty cans of Red Bull abandoned in the gravel.

A guy in neon compression sleeves jogs in place, muttering mile splits under his breath.

Another ties and unties the same knot three times, like the rope might judge him for hesitation.

Someone near us groans, "If I puke, at least it'll be carrying less weight." His partner doesn't even blink.

Alec barely clears the grass before the on-site press converges. Shutters rattle like cicadas.

"How's Finn doing?"

"Is this your new partner?"

"Back for redemption?"

Alec doesn't slow, just keeps his eyes straight ahead. "Not today."

Meanwhile, I'm two-stepping behind him, clutching my paddle. I keep picturing myself lifting it, striking up a downbeat like the whole river's about to break into a marching tune.

My stomach knots and riots, the same rush I used to get in the wings. That breathless moment when it's too late to change my mind.

Gran waves us down for a photo. We line up stiffly, two hundred kayaks crammed on the shore behind us.

"Stand closer, for God's sake. It's not a police lineup."

We shuffle shoulder to shoulder. Alec sighs.

"Gran—" I start.

"Shut up and look happy."

The picture comes out looking like prom night, with life vests in place of corsages, my hair already frizzing from river spray.

"You're going to do great. The race is only a third of the full thing, isn't it?" Gran reminds us, fussing with the camera strap.

She's right. Kayak, climb, rappel. Just enough to weed out the weak.

But out of 350 teams, only 100 will be allowed to compete in Wild Trails.

I frown. "Sampler platter of pain."

"It isn't." Alec shakes his head

"You could at least pretend to be encouraging."

His eyes flick sideways at me, gaze as dry as stone. "If you needed encouragement, you wouldn't be here."

My stomach flips, but I swallow my nerves down.

He's right. There's no going back now.

FOUR HOURS LATER, my shoulders feel like they've been sanded down with rocks, but Alec and I haul our boat to shore and collapse onto the grass for a breathless second. Someone shouts a number from the finish tent—"Ten!"—and it takes me a beat to realize that's us.

Tenth. Out of three hundred and fifty.

"Holy—" I double over, bracing my hands on my knees, stomach lurching from the rapids. "Did we just…?"

Alec doesn't answer. He's already yanking the straps of his pack tight, long strides cutting straight for the trailhead.

"No? Okay. No celebrating. Cool." I stumble after him, legs jelly, lungs clawing for air.

He doesn't look back, just calls, "Keep moving."

Easy for him to say. He runs like gravity owes him money. I run like gravity just called in my debts.

The waterfall to our left bellows, spray clinging to my skin like ice needles. Its roar fills my ears until it feels like we're climbing inside thunder.

Two groups are ahead of us—the brother-sister pair who look like they gargle gravel for breakfast, and Zak with his neon hair, barking at his partner.

"Faster, Marc! You're dragging!" he snaps.

Marc trips on a root, mutters something that sounds a lot like, "Drag this, Zak."

The trail chews at my palms. My ankles and my knees. We've done this route before, but never like this, never with the loudspeakers blaring static. Never with this much pressure pounding through me.

"Status!" Alec shouts over the roar of the falls.

"Status: thighs on fire, lungs plotting homicide!" I yell back, voice half broken.

"That's not a medical update."

"It's relevant!"

"You're fine. Three miles left. Downhill soon. Walk backward if your knee locks."

"Copy." I don't know why I answer like a soldier, but it's easier than admitting I'm dying.

His wrist buzzes. I don't even have to see it.

"Hydrate," he calls, already silencing his watch.

"Already on it." The nozzle is at my mouth before he finishes.

The rhythm finds us before I even realize it's there.

Step, step, breathe. Step, step.

His boots hit rock. Mine follow. When he sidesteps a slick patch, I veer too. When he leans forward to gain speed, my body copies him like some overeager understudy trailing the star of the show. Apparently, in twenty-five days, my muscles have committed Alec Hastings to memory.

We round a bend, and the trail tilts viciously upward. My calves seize, my thighs revolt, and I briefly consider lying down in the dirt and letting nature have me.

"Keep with me."

"I am," I wheeze, though it comes out like a broken accordion.

"Not behind me. With me. That's the difference."

Of course, he says it like that. My legs threaten to collapse, sweat stings my eyes, but his stride and mine fall into line, rope-tight.

"You're holding steady, Fox, you got this," he adds, lower this time, like it's not for anyone else to hear. "Better than half the field. Better than I thought you would."

My chest stutters, not from lack of air but from his words. From him. I know Alec by now. He doesn't say things he doesn't mean.

He turns back to the trail, shoulders cutting up the incline, and I follow, because somehow, unbelievably, I can.

We're a team.

And we may actually win this thing.

Chapter 25
Alec

"We're gaining on them." Clementine tips her chin toward Zak, already crouched low, barking at his partner as he inches toward the wall.

I run my hands over the webbing around her hips again, pulling it snug. "We don't need to beat them," I say, straightening to meet her eyes. "Just qualify."

Up close, her face is flushed tomato-red from the twenty-five hundred feet we've already chewed through. Four hours in, and exhaustion drags at both of us, but she still looks gorgeous, still has energy left. It's exactly how I wanted today to play out.

"You've checked me a million times," she mutters. "Let's go, let's go, let's go."

"Be careful, okay?" I run my fingers over her waist, thighs, that tiny freckle at her neck, confirming, again, that she's all in one piece and that she'll stay that way.

"Steaks and beers at Daisy's after. My treat."

"Sure."

I step back, admiring her one final time. She hesitates before scuffling forward and...*embracing* me? My mind takes a second to catch up. Her arms cinch quickly around my waist, and instantly I'm flooded with her warmth. I feel like a fool not knowing what to do with my hands.

"Hug me back, weirdo." Her pulse jumps against my chest, and I like it so much it terrifies me. Without breaking contact, my strong, fearless fox presses up onto her tiptoes and pecks a kiss to my cheek. My grin breaks free.

She's so close I can smell the peanut butter pretzels she had for breakfast on her breath. I filled my bag today with all her favorite snacks, even though it put my pack three ounces over. I'd do anything to keep her motivated.

I bite down hard against the urge to take her mouth with mine.

"What was that for?" I manage.

There's an endlessness to her eyes, a brightness around the whites, that makes her look lit up from within. "Just—thank you."

For a breath, I let myself imagine days with her. Waking up and pulling her body into mine, learning the shape of how she sleeps, over and over. The shape of a life that isn't just transactions and rope checks. But then reality slams into us when the first team's bell clatters from below, the rush of voices rising up the rock.

"Let's go qualify." I let her go reluctantly, because if it were up to me, I'd say to hell with the race and carry her off this mountain. But this is important to her, so it's important to me.

I peer out at the ridge. It's only two hundred feet, with no obstacles. There are safety people and a first aid tent hidden behind the sponsorship booth. She'll be okay.

She flashes me a thumbs-up. "See you at the bottom, Hastings."

"You got it, Fox." I wink, and the color in her cheeks deepens.

She exhales heavily, nodding her head and whispering a pep talk under her breath. I wonder if this is what she was like backstage before a performance. Except instead of a tutu, she's in a light pink tee and a pair of her grandpa's old hiking pants that she tailored to fit her. She leans into the rope and pushes off the gray slate rock wall, the afternoon sun glancing off her sweat, the forest birds scattering at the movement.

When she's about halfway down, she looks up to me and grins, and it isn't long before her feet land solid on the ground.

"Time to show these noobs how it's done, Satie." Her voice cracks through the walkie, and I finally let out the breath I've been holding. She's safe.

Around the cliff edge, the other teams watch, waiting for me to move, their faces tight, expectant. This is my first time back on a wall, and they all know it. They read the headlines. They know what I did on K2, how I went down for Finn. Their stares press into me, but I shove them off, clip in, check metal, webbing, and anchor over and over—because if I stop moving, I'll hear the cameras clicking, the drones buzzing overhead. I'll feel cold air nipping at me like winter just dropped out of the sky.

I stand facing the section I've been dreading the most. I've been telling myself I didn't need to practice something I've been doing for twenty-six years. Rappelling has been built into these muscles and my hands.

Boots thud on stone, partners call encouragement, carabiners clink against harnesses. Sound after sound piling up and pulling me backward. Back to Finn. Back to when we were kids scrambling up walls, laughing at bloodied knees.

I slam the thought down. Not now.

Control.

I stretch my arms, lock my legs, and the roar of the crowd dims long enough for me to believe I can do this. Of course I can do this. Especially when Clementine's waiting for me at the bottom, counting on me to help her. I made a promise.

I push off the wall and let gravity carry me down. The

harness tightens around my hips, and the rope tenses against the anchor screwed into the stone.

Down.

Down.

I slide down the wall easily, but the closer I get to the bottom, the more the noise swells—voices, shouts, the slap of wind—and my name lifts up into it, split and scattered, echoed. Then a rope pulls taut next to me and snaps.

A flash of Finn's blue lips, his milky white pupils, the emptiness I felt finding his limp, lifeless body. I cling onto my rope.

Get it together! I scream at myself, but my mind glitches, my world tilting sideways. Wind claws up the wall, not steady but ripping, stealing the icy respirator from my mouth.

This isn't happening.

Under my palms, a crack, a slight vibration, and I snap my eyes shut. This isn't real. The camera flashes flicker into snow, white and stinging, needling my cheeks. The air turns to knives in my lungs. The rock crusts slick beneath my boots, and the rope thickens, heavy, wet, and wrong.

I hear a scream down below. *"Alec!"*

It's not Clem's voice. It's deeper, frayed at the edges. I know that voice in my bones.

Finn.

The rock face melts in front of me. The walls vanish, replaced by a glare so bright it swallows the sky. Screaming wind reaches my eardrums, and my breath seizes in my throat. One more blink, and the bottom below becomes a jagged slope of wind-scoured ice.

I'm not in Alaska anymore.

I'm back on K2.

·   ·   ·

THE CROWD below me is gone. I'm back on the mountain, at the hundred-foot drop with a silent best friend dangling from the rope. Breath shreds itself out of me.

He's fine. I'm fine. I repeat it, but it's useless.

"Alec!" Clementine now is cutting through the static, tethering me. "Look at me!"

The roar of the wind eats every sound except words layered over each other until I can't tell which one is real.

"Just let go of the wall. I've got you."

I want to believe her. I want her voice to reach the part of me that's still frozen in that moment, but everything in me is locked tight. Letting go means falling. Letting go means last time.

"I'm here, I'm right here," she calls out.

Her voice threads into the whiteout, warm where everything else is cold. Solid where the rope is not. With my eyes still closed, I bend my knees, press my boots hard into the wall, shift my weight inch by inch. I choose her voice, not the wind, not the crack that won't stop replaying in my mind.

I move, unnatural and slow. *Don't let her down.*

"That's it."

When I hit the dirt, my knees nearly buckle. I catch myself before I fall. I can't get the harness unclipped fast enough. My hands feel like they belong to someone else.

"Alec," she says again, gentle, behind me now.

"Don't," I say tersely. Her face pinches. I hate that. I hate that I made her look like that. "Can you sprint?" I ask her.

"Yes." Her eyes search mine, questions rising, but the race is already surging past us. Who knows how many teams I let pass us. We need to move.

The crowd's roar comes back, but it's muffled like I'm underwater. Clementine's hand catches my sleeve, her voice threads through the static, and we run, sprinting the hundred meters from the rock face to the arched finish line. A red screen hangs overhead, ticking closer to a hundred with each team that crosses the finish line before us.

Ninety-two. The number burns above the finish line, proof of how close I came to screwing this whole thing up. How close I came to letting her down.

Hands slap my shoulders as we push through, strangers yelling congratulations. They don't know what just happened. They didn't hear the crack, the rope, or Finn's voice bleeding into hers until I couldn't tell which one was real.

The air goes thin. Every breath is shallow, greedy, useless. My hands twitch like they're still on the rope.

"Alec?" Clementine's voice cuts through.

"I—" But I can't seem to reach the words.

"What happened up there?" A mic presses under my face. "Where's Finn? Why Alaska?"

The questions batter me harder than the crowd, harder than gravity, and I can't face them.

"I have to go," I mumble.

Clementine doesn't flinch or let me bolt. Instead, her soft hand finds mine, and before I can shake her off, she's pulling me out of the noise, past the questions, toward the dark stretch of the parking lot.

THE STALE AIR from the truck's AC hits full blast. I'm leaning over the steering wheel, head pressed into the leather, pulse still hammering like the climb never ended. Mozart drifts from the speakers, a soft swell against the chaos coursing through me. Clementine sits in the passenger seat, knees folded up, head tilted, eyes catching the light as if she's always known exactly where to be.

"I'm here if you want to talk." Even her voice is soft, and I wish there was a way to escape into it. Escape into her and forget the past hour.

I shake my head, but her hand lands on my arm anyway. Goose bumps flare along its path; her humming threads through the commotion of the qualifier outside. It's not pity in her smile. It's patience, steady, as if she has all the time in the world to sit here with me.

The words have sat inside of me for so long, I'm afraid of letting them out.

I chide myself. When have I ever let fear win?

"I should be over it by now. It's stupid." My hands twist the steering wheel, knuckles aching, trying to wring out the tension that refuses to leave me.

"Your feelings aren't stupid."

A short, dry laugh escapes me. "I've been in avalanches. Climbed unroped on glaciers. I've been to more funerals than most people my age. And Finn didn't even die. He's getting better. But I still find myself on that mountain. I still hear—" My voice splinters.

Her hand slides from my arm to my hand, resting there lightly, grounding me. "Sometimes talking about it helps. I don't get the need to climb," she says. "But I get doing something no one else understands. Doing it anyway because it calls to you. My gran never understood why my grandpa kept going back to Denali, but she understood the way it broke him and healed him too. If you want to tell me, I'll listen."

I swallow hard. "When we were sixteen, Finn and I made a pact—to climb all fourteen eight-thousand-meter peaks. Not just climb them, but take routes no one had ever taken before. Stupid teenage shit. But after Shishapangma, the first one, we realized we could actually do it. So, we kept going. Got sponsors, got paid. One after the other. Years in Nepal, Pakistan, training nonstop. K2…we tried it at twenty-five, had to turn back because of avalanches. K2 isn't the tallest, but she claims more climbers than any other. She doesn't forgive mistakes."

The rest comes out haltingly. The narrow weather window. The minute I kept us there too long. The summit. The serac. Finn falling. Me rappelling into the dark, chipping ice off his leg the size of a washing machine. His pulse under my glove. Hauling him out, dragging him back to Camp Three, praying he'd still be breathing in the helicopter. The weeks in Mercy General, where I stopped shaving, stopped eating, because every second felt like my fault.

And she just sits there, patient, staring at me with those beautiful eyes.

I don't tell her the part that still eats me alive—that Finn wants to retire, and even after today I can't picture myself doing the same. She'd understand. I saw her dance alone in the garage. Ballet lives in her bones the way climbing lives in mine. But after the panic thirty minutes ago, how the hell am I supposed to make it down a wall in Iceland this November when I can't even get down one here?

That's a thought I shove to the back of my mind, a checklist item I'll address later.

When I finish talking, there are tears welling in my eyes. I haven't cried since Bjorn's funeral three years ago. My fingers trace the tattooed rings around my forearm, aiming to ground myself. But then her hand is there. It lands steady over mine, her thumb tracing a scar along my palm. She pushes up the center console and slides close until her thigh presses against mine.

"You went back for him," she says, eyes glassy. "You didn't freeze. You didn't run. You saved him. That's what makes you extraordinary."

I shake my head, guilt clawing up my throat. "But it was my fault we were in that place. Maybe K2 was never meant for us. I shouldn't have let us go up."

"From what you told me about Finn, he seems like the type who would've gone anyway."

"But I was the planner. I chose the window." My hands curl into fists in my lap, nails digging into my palms.

"That first day, you told me nature is unpredictable. I'd bet Finn knew that too. "And you don't know what would've happened if he'd planned the route or if you'd started down sooner."

"He might never climb again."

"Maybe. But he's still here. Have you been blaming yourself this whole time?"

My gaze flits away because I'm afraid she already knows the answer.

"Is that why the lodge is so important? Why you haven't built yourself a room because you don't think you deserve one?" She pulls apart my feelings so easily, like she's felt them before.

"And here I was rambling about being in debt and quitting ballet, and you were just carrying this the whole time?"

"Your problems are—"

"Oh, I know they're valid. But maybe we could've been talking about more than snacks and CPR on these hikes. You could've added to my oversharing! Look at the Therapy Tacoma doing her work today." She strokes the side of the seat, and I let out a small laugh, the first real sound I've made since I left the rock face.

"I thought if I could get the lodge ready for him, I'd get over it."

She scoffs. "I wish forgetting problems was that easy. Trust me, my debt wishes that too." Then her voice softens. "Alec… what happened up there wasn't your fault."

"Yeah—" I try to brush her off, but she tilts my chin back to her.

"What happened to Finn wasn't your fault." She repeats it,

slower this time. "I know we both have issues taking compliments, but this isn't a compliment. This is the truth."

I inhale. "I'm sorry about the competition. I almost made us lose."

"Honestly? It's a relief, because for the last month, I thought *I* was going to make us lose." The corner of her mouth inches up. "Today only made you seem more human. And, like you said, we didn't need to win—just qualify. And we did."

"Thanks to you."

"Thanks to us." Clem gives me a soft smile, fingers still moving absently on my hand, steadying the storm inside of me. "You wanna get out of here?"

"Yeah."

"Let me drive."

"I got it."

"Let me drive. I wanna take you somewhere," she says, firmer this time.

"I don't like surprises," I tease.

"What happened to spontaneity?" She's already flinging open the passenger door, red hair whipping around the front of my truck.

My fingers tighten around the keys before I finally leave them in the ignition. Just metal and plastic, but letting her take them feels like handing over the other end of my line.

Finn gets here in three days. The lodge is ready for him, every corner prepped. And yet the unease clinging to my chest hasn't loosened. I still need to tell him I want to climb again.

I have time, I tell myself. Today, I just want to sit beside the girl who makes the world less heavy to carry.

Chapter 26
Clementine

THE THERAPY TACOMA did her job. I glance over my shoulder to make sure Alec's still behind me. He bats a loose branch out of the way, eyes narrowing when he catches me staring at him.

I'm not used to setting the pace on our hikes. And I'm definitely not used to a man—especially one who's spent weeks pretending ice runs through his veins—opening up the way he did.

Vulnerability looks stupidly attractive on him. He looks lighter now, like he's carrying the same backpack but with all those damn bricks removed. I know that his trauma won't be healed overnight, but I feel lucky he opened up to me. Maybe Wild Trails can be an opportunity for us both to figure out what's next in our lives.

Which is probably why I'm skipping down this trail, unbothered by loose roots or mud.

Or maybe it's because I'm one gigantic step closer to winning twenty thousand dollars and paying off most of my debt.

Or perhaps I'm so giddy because in the month since leaving New York I've started recognizing myself again—stronger, heavier in ways that feel good. Not ballet-thin, but actually muscular. I can carry a pack up a mountain and not feel like I'm about to collapse. I can eat a cookie without hearing the echo of a director's voice telling me to shrink. For so long, my life has been about waiting—waiting to be picked, waiting to be good enough for principal, waiting to claw my way out of debt before I'm allowed to start living.

But here, with him following close behind, something new presses up through my chest, searing and terrifying in its possibility. Maybe I don't have to wait. Maybe I get to want things— messy, dangerous, beautiful things—before I've deemed myself worthy of earning them.

"Are you leading me to a sacrifice?" Alec's voice rumbles behind me.

"You figured it out. My coven's meeting tonight. Lucky you, it's my night to donate an unwilling man."

"You have a coven now?"

"You'll just have to wait and see." I grin, my breath puffing in the cooling air.

The hidden path appears. It's just a thin cut in the brush, marked by a chipped blue painted arrow. I duck down it, careful on the steep slope, until the trees open into my favorite place.

The hot spring looks small and unremarkable at first glance, tucked among mossy stumps and ferns, but steam rises in little ghost curls, catching the lavender twilight. The pool sits high enough that you can see ridge after ridge rolling into the distance, purple shadows stacking like folded fabric.

"Welcome to the Lennoxes' best-kept secret," I tell him, turning back. "My grandparents used to bring me here every summer. Grandpa proposed to Gran on that rock over there."

"It feels like you're inducting me into something."

I smirk. "Welcome to my cult. Perks include free therapy, eternal youth, and skin so soft you'll want to send me a thank-you card in that irritatingly perfect handwriting of yours."

He smirks. "Never met anyone who resents penmanship before."

"What can I say, Hastings? I'm original."

"I'm discovering that." His gaze lingers, steady, and the air thickens with something that has nothing to do with competition adrenaline. "I never got to say you were unbelievable today."

"Really?" I say, obviously fishing for compliments. My eyes flicker down to his mouth before coming back.

"You held your own all day. You fucking scaled those rocks on the hike like they were pebbles."

I laugh. "I appreciate that. It felt good being out there today. Obviously, I miss ballet, but it's nice to finish something and not overthink my performance. I'm just happy we qualified and I did it, you know?"

"Thanks to you. You got some muscles peeking through this shirt, Lennox."

Athletes get called by their last names. It's a small thing, but it sends a ridiculous rush through me. "You have to stop."

"Why?"

"Because I'm already two seconds away from doing something stupid."

His smile curves deliberately. "Like what?"

My fingers move before my brain does. I crouch to untie my boots. "What are you doing?" he asks, staring down at me.

"Scandalizing the local deer." I kick my boots off, peel my socks away, and then tug my shirt over my head, leaving me in a baby-pink sports bra. The evening air bites my skin, but the shiver that runs through me isn't from the cold. It's from the way Alec's jaw tenses, his gaze caught like I've stolen his air. My braid slips forward, brushing over the swell of my breasts. His fists curl at his sides.

As a ballerina, I've always been called cute, and striking, but under Alec's gaze I feel sexy…even wearing clothes I spent all day sweating in.

"You getting in?" I ask, shimmying out of my shorts, silently thanking past-me for wearing my good underwear. "Or are you just going to stand there looking like that?"

"Clementine." My name lands heavy, like a warning sign.

"Alec," I answer, like a dare.

I step barefoot onto a moss-slick rock, the first lick of hot water rushing over my sore feet. It stings, then soothes.

"Careful," he says, already moving closer.

"You can't protect me from way over there." I smile, and that tips him.

In one clean motion, he peels his long-sleeved tee over his head and discards it in the moss. I've seen him shirtless before, but not like this…not for me. His chest is tan, hair spattering over pecs, ink winding up his arm in sharp black curves. There's a slash of an old cut near his ribs, another puckered scar along his side, each one proof of the mountains he's climbed. My eyes drag lower, over the taut line of his abs, down to the V that disappears into black boxers.

My brain screams as I land on his legs. His left leg is completely covered in tattoos—trees, flowers, a family crest, and an ice axe.

Aren't thigh tattoos every woman's weakness? But maybe shin tattoos are climbing their way up there.

"You're the one staring now," he says.

"I am." My grin feels helpless.

"See something you like?"

"Don't act like you don't know you're beautiful," I tease, drifting in deeper, until the hot water kisses my hips. Steam curls up around me, wrapping my skin in heat.

"Don't think I've ever been called that before."

"You must not read your Instagram comments."

"I like it better coming from you." He steps into the water, and my heart jitters. Even half submerged, he's massive, and the steam only makes him seem more solid, more there. "I'm glad you returned the other underwear, because I like these ones a lot more."

The bluntness knocks my breath from me. "These aren't even the best pair in my collection. I've got lace ones, white, with a little tulip embroidered on the hip."

"Clem." He grits his teeth.

"What? Can't a girl tell her camp buddy about her favorite lingerie?"

His pupils swallow the gold in his eyes. "Say that again."

"Camp. Buddy." I grin, and that does it. He lunges, sending a sheet of water crashing toward me. I splash back, laughing, until he corrals me against a moss-slick ledge. The backs of my thighs hit a smooth rock, and I settle on it while Alec wades in the water.

"Why do you hate it so much?" I prod, breathless.

"You know why."

"No, I really don't."

"Because every time you say it"—his voice roughens—"I just want to kiss the word *buddy* out of your mouth."

"Then why don't you?"

"Because of our arrangement."

"But then why spend all these weeks making me flustered?"

His scoff is immediate. "I did not."

"Don't even deny it, it's fun for you."

He slides next to me, his thighs touching mine underwater. Alec's muscles are corded with veins that I crave dragging my tongue over.

"Give me one example," he challenges.

"For one, constantly checking my gear. It's like you're looking for an excuse to get your hands on me."

"That's for safety."

"Sure. And the splinter incident? Who volunteers to suck blood from a paper-thin sliver of wood?"

"That was instinct." He shifts closer, the steam swirling

around him. "You're not making a great case for yourself, Clementine."

The challenge works something up in me, and I allow myself to move in, inch by inch. "So, you're telling me that you get no enjoyment out of knowing that…" I pause and let the courage boil up inside of me. "You're maddening?"

His pupils expand. "I like watching you fight for a comeback. I like the way you bite your lip when you're losing. And I like"—he leans in, his voice barely skimming the surface of the water—"the way you've been staring at my mouth since we got in."

"It's eye level. Where do you expect me to look?" Unintentionally, my gaze drops to his boxers. *Does water distort that much? Because if not…he's huge.* I roll my lips together, eyes widening before shooting back up to his face.

"Naughty, Fox."

The nickname sends a thrill through me.

"Do you expect me to keep my eyes down here?" I reach out under the water, fingers skimming over the ink on his thigh. His gaze bores into me as I move up, higher, until I'm at his bicep. His skin is slick and fever-warm. "Or what about here?"

"Come closer," he says.

"You first," I counter, though my knees are already drifting toward him.

His chuckle sends heat down my spine. "Stubborn."

"Hypocrite."

His hand snakes around my waist under the water, thumb brushing the line of my ribs like he's testing how close he can get before I bolt. I don't bolt.

He's close enough now that I can see a tiny freckle on his bottom lip. I want to taste it.

"Fuck, Clementine. You're making it impossible not to kiss you right now." He drags his free hand over his face, as if he's still clinging to control. When it drops, his gaze shifts, like he wants to consume me. His hand cups my jaw, warm and steady, droplets sliding down his forearm onto my skin.

"You don't have to be careful with me," I whisper.

That undoes him.

The moment his lips claim mine, I'm gone—weeks of wanting, waiting, second-guessing, all collapsing into heat and hunger. He tastes of minerals and salt and something richer, something I've only ever imagined and now finally get to savor. My chest feels too small for the rush of it, like every ounce of self-control I've clung to has been stripped clean. His grip on my waist tightens, hauling me flush until our legs tangle under the water, and it's everything I've wanted and everything I was afraid to want. My fingers clutch his shoulders, greedy for proof that he's real, that this is real.

And for once, I'm not waiting for permission. Not waiting to be picked. I'm choosing this. I'm choosing him. The world dissolves into steam and the pounding of his pulse against mine —Alec Hastings, finally, finally kissing me—and I don't want to come up for air, not yet, not when wanting feels this good.

Chapter 27
Alec

IN LIFE, I have to be organized, controlled, ready for every move. But with Clementine, I want to axe down every wall I've built.

Kissing her is like catching a perfect weather window after weeks of storms. It's the dizzy hit when my boot lands on solid ground after a sketchy climb, knowing I'm lucky to be alive.

She lets out a moan that sounds like a melody, and I growl into her mouth. I've turned ravenous. Feral.

I didn't think you could feel seen while someone's kissing you, but Clementine does it. Like the weeks we spent training together were for this exact moment. She adjusts to me, reads me, yields to my tongue, and then chases me. She nips at my lip unexpectedly, and I pull away, looking down at her.

My sly fox.

My control-freak brain, the one with laminated lists and backup laminated lists, surrenders under the weight of her calm. She's cataloging the small yeses, matching me, holding me.

Leave no person behind. It's a loyalty we vow to each other on the ice, on the mountains, and she did it instinctively. She talked me off that cliff like I've talked so many others down.

Equal. The word rings through my brain. She's spent weeks

trying to prove herself worthy of being my partner, but I should have been on my knees for her.

She's chest-to-chest with me in the steam, breath warm on my lips, body telling me I'm still worth her time. Her mouth opens under mine—citrus and salt, a faint bite of cinnamon—and I want to drink in every inch of her until I forget my own name. My hands thread into her hair, strands clinging to my fingers. Her thighs tighten around my hips, the water sloshing with every press of her body against mine.

She gasps when I grip her ass and yank her on top of me until her underwear drags against the hard line of my cock. I wish the fucking water wasn't here. I want to feel all of this. But as she presses down, moving slowly at first, testing and teasing, I'm glad for the small barrier. My pulse pounds in my ears.

The spring is shallow enough that her chest presses to mine when she rocks forward, her nipples pebbling through the cling of her sports bra. My mouth finds her jaw, the hollow beneath her ear.

"Clementine…" It comes out rough, like I've been holding my breath for hours.

Her fingers hook into my hair, tugging until I have to look at her. Her eyes are molten blue flames. The sky behind us has split open, sunset spilling across the ridges. Oranges in every hue, like her hair. My new favorite color.

I let myself imagine a life where I wasn't running, wasn't always searching for something to chase. A life where I spent my time discovering a new sense of purpose.

"Don't stop," she says, needy and powerful.

I don't. I kiss her harder, teeth grazing her lips. She moans loud, head tipping back into the steam. She's a water nymph come alive to lure me into her depths. And I'd dive headfirst after her every time.

"I hate that I denied myself to you for so long." She rolls her hips again, a dance she's choreographed just for me. I wrap my hand around her nape, nipping at her ear. My fingers grip tighter, pulling her closer to me, inhaling her. She hums, nails dragging down my chest. "God, Clem, you smell fucking divine."

I grip her thigh, then her waist, my hand spanning from her navel to her spine. I leave kisses using her freckles as stepping stones, trailing down her neck and over her collarbone, sucking hard enough to mark her.

"Fuck, baby." She grinds down harder now, sunset casting her in golden light. Her skin is flushed, damp, perfect. And the knot that had been tightening in my chest since the panic earlier is gone. The tension in my shoulders has eased, my breathing's steady. The water, her body, the way she's here with me and not trying to fix me or make me talk…it's like the whole world narrowed into something I can actually hold.

I grit my teeth to control myself and tip my head backward onto the moss.

I let myself enjoy her. This moment. Our sounds intertwine with nature herself.

Until a large, hot, wet tongue drags across my ear. Not Clem's tongue—

My eyes bolt open. "What the fuck?"

Clem freezes, staring at me, dazed, lips swollen. If she's there—

The lick comes again, slower, wetter.

I twist my head and come face-to-face with mismatched irises, one gold, one ice-blue, both staring at me from the edge of the pool.

"A wolf!" I jerk upward, picking up Clem and using my back to shield her from the creature. I scan the mossy ground. *Where the hell is my knife?*

Clem vibrates in my arms, crying? No, wait—she's *laughing*.

I spin around, keeping her wrapped around me as I look at the shore. The beast is a…puppy.

"That's not a wolf," I say, unleashing my grip on Clem. She climbs down and moves toward the animal.

"I think that's a Malamute puppy."

"It looks like a cotton ball with legs." She sloshes toward the rocks. "Be careful. It could have rabies."

She, of course, ignores me, climbing out of the water and scooping him up like he belongs to her. The puppy sprawls across her chest, back legs dangling, and immediately licks every inch of her face with joyful ferocity.

"Clem, he's probably feral." I step forward, joining her on the shore.

"He's clearly a hero," she says, hugging him to her chest. Water runs down her stomach, over her hips, disappearing into the cling of her underwear. "Saved us from whatever that was."

"From *you* making bad decisions."

Her grin turns sly. "Pretty sure *you* were the one making bad decisions." The feral beast keeps licking my girl. "Stop—no— stop that, oh my god—" Unbridled laughter spills through the trees. "It's licking my nostrils—ew! My ears—stop it! Not the neck!"

The neck I was kissing only moments ago.

"Hold on, let me get a look at you." She grips the dog and holds him out. "You're just a puppy, aren't you? And a boy. I think he's a runt," she says, clutching him like a newborn. "He's so, so small. Maybe one of Lenni's got out. Can we keep him?"

"No. He's wild."

She pouts, cradling the fluff demon. "Does he look wild to you? Does this cute little face look like it could hurt you?"

The dog sneezes on her chin and licks her again, fully up the side of her jaw into her ear.

"Yes," I say. "He could be a wolf puppy."

"We're keeping him," she declares.

"We are not keeping him."

"But I already love him."

I glance around, hoping—ridiculously—for the mother or any trace of his litter. But there are only trees and the dark starting to settle in for the night.

I sigh loudly, like it'll make a difference.

"We need to check if anyone's missing a dog," she says. She walks over to our clothes and with one hand retrieves her phone, selects a number, and presses it to her ear. "Hey, Lenni. Are you missing a puppy from Missy's litter?" Grumbles crackle through the phone while the dog stares at me. He's fluffy, mostly white, but he has brown around his eyes like he's wearing a mask. His giant paws are brown as well, as if he's wearing boots. "The runt. I think I found him."

A pause. "Happy to!" Another pause. "Okay. Thanks, Lenni." She clicks off. "He's ours."

"No."

"Lenni was gonna put him up for adoption anyway since he's the runt."

"No," I scold.

"Come on, Alec. I'm taking him to the car," she says over her shoulder, starting up the hill in her sports bra and panties. "Can you get our clothes?"

"You're not going to get dressed?"

"The car is literally five minutes away, and I don't want him running off. He seems cold, and you don't look like you're going to help. Come on, we gotta get supplies."

I'm going to regret this. "Hold on." I throw on my clothes over my wet skin. "Get dressed."

"Are you going to be nice to Mozart?"

"We aren't naming him."

She hands him over to me, and the filthy mutt grumbles at me, narrowing his eyes before whipping his head around to find Clem.

"She's mine," I growl at him.

Clem gets dressed quickly and tries to take the dog. "The hill is steep. If you insist on bringing him, I'll carry him," I say, annoyed.

"You are gonna be such a good daddy."

That fucking word again. "*Clem.*"

She gives me a kiss on my cheek. "Oh, by the way, Gran is allergic to dogs…so is it okay if Mozart stays at your place?"

"We are not keeping the dog."

She hums like she knows she's going to get her way. "Hopefully Dog Days is still open, or else we'll have to drive to Anchorage to get our new boy supplies."

We're absolutely keeping the dog.

Chapter 28
Alec

We had to drive to Anchorage for that thing.

It's nearly ten by the time we arrive at the lodge. I shove open the front door with my shoulder, Clem's laugh still caught in the space between us. Her hair brushes along my shoulder, still smelling of pine and sulfur from the hot spring.

"I still don't understand why we needed three beds," I say as I set down the crate, puppy kibble, and the pile of soft things she insisted on. My keys clatter onto the side table, right beside a new photo of Finn and me in Patagonia. Clem must have just added it.

"Because he needs options." She coos at the half-asleep creature in her arms, kissing the top of his tiny head. Two hours ago, those lips were on me. Blood rushes hot just remembering. Kissing her was like the delirious high of the death zone, and I'd trek miles to taste her again. But for now, I have to figure out how to wash seven pounds of dirt off a dog I didn't ask for.

I glare at the pup.

"I don't understand how you could hate this cute little face and these little toe beans," she whispers as I crouch to unlace her boots.

"I don't hate it. I just…pets are a responsibility. Staying in one place. Finding a sitter."

"Dogs also are routines, and you love routines. You could train him to be your little mini-me."

"I think he likes you better." I rise and catch a faint wisp of smoke. My pulse ticks up. I never forget to put out the fire.

"Did you invite someone over?" I ask, and she shakes her head. I slowly make my way down the hallway, rounding into the main room.

The heat drains from my face. In front of the fire is Finn—three days early. Fuck, I didn't stock the fridge yet or wash his sheets. My mind spirals, flipping through all the unfinished items on my checklist.

He's in a wheelchair, leafing through one of the adventure novels. His face is gaunt, cheekbones pushing at his pale skin. My throat constricts. He's skinnier and paler than I've ever seen him. One of those ragged old T-shirts from some base camp fundraiser we did in 2014 sits crooked on his bony shoulders.

His long brown hair hangs loose, and his beard has doubled in length.

"Finn—"

He looks up, eyes widening, and smiles the only way he knows how—with his entire face. His teeth flash in the firelight. "ALEC!" His voice hits the rafters as he wheels toward me. "Bro, look at you!"

"What are you doing here?"

"Early release. Couldn't stand another day eating Jell-O." His grin tilts. "I caught the tail end of Wild Trails!"

"You saw?"

"Nah, just the last hour. People said you bolted the second you qualified. Nothing's changed, dude."

I scratch my neck, finding myself unable to meet his gaze.

What would he think if he knew the real reason I ran off? Did he show up to see if I was really going to go through with the competition?

If I told him about the panic on the wall, he'd use it as another reason why we should retire.

He slaps my thigh. "Hello? You zoning out already? Lean down here and give me a hug. Pretend you're happy to see me before you introduce me to this lovely lady and puppy you have with you."

"I am happy to see you." It isn't a lie, but unease settles in. I push the thoughts from my mind. Finn's here, and he's alive. That's all that matters. I force a smile and crouch to hug his fragile frame. "Look at you."

"Yeah, I know. Still prettier than you." He smacks my cheeks with affection. "But not prettier than you. Clementine Lennox, I presume. We loved your grandpa. Sorry to hear about his passing," Finn says.

"Thanks. I miss him all the time." Clem sighs before throwing Finn a dazzling smile, the kind that took me a week to earn. "I've heard a lot about you."

"You mean he speaks to you? Wow. Took him three years to warm up to me. So, consider yourself lucky."

"It did not." I roll my eyes.

Clem and Finn exchange a knowing glance, and I hate it already.

"And who's this sleepy boy?" Finn touches the dog's limp paw, and he doesn't stir.

"We just found him today! Alec's keeping him," Clem says.

"He is?" Finn scrunches his face at me.

Before I can respond, a new voice cuts in. "Clementine Lennox, as I live and breathe!"

A woman with long, sleek black hair steps out of the kitchen in turquoise scrubs, a bottle of pills in hand.

"Yura!" Clem lights up, thrusting Mozart into my arms. The

dog jolts awake at the squeals that follow as the two women circle each other, hugging, laughing, and showering each other with compliments.

"Now that's the welcome I expected." Finn chuckles, but the knife twists deeper. I should be happy he's here. He used to be the one person I could spend every single moment with and not get tired, but now all I see is the chair. The chair I put him in.

Why the hell did I stay on that summit one more minute?

"Just tired," I groan.

"That's my nurse, Yura," Finn says, "but you can think of her as my soon-to-be wife." My best friend falls in love like most people change socks. Every summit, every base camp, every iced-over valley, he finds the one. Then she vanishes like snowmelt. I'm sure this one will be the same. "Of course we'd end up with best friends," he adds, chestnut eyes flickering with hope.

Apparently, small-town Alaska doesn't have rules about dating the clientele.

"Yep."

"You really fixed this place up, huh?" He waves his hand in the air. The room looks nothing like the husk it was—new floors, lace curtains softening the windows, a bookcase and a chess-board waiting in the corner; it looks like a home, the kind we've never had. "And you got my adventure books!" He taps the paperback resting on his lap. "When'd you turn into a carpenter?"

"Clementine helped. All the furniture and stuff, she picked out." I stare at the fire.

"I was gonna ask why you never decorated Ghastly this nice." Ghastly was the name of our Mercedes-Benz Sprinter van we drove around the States for two years.

"First of all, that thing was stuffed with our gear," I say. "Second, we barely slept in it."

"Yeah, we did. That hailstorm in Montana."

"Once. In two years."

He grins, and it feels easy, the weight loosening from my chest. "Now you're playing house before me. Got a dog, got a girl—"

"I don't want to keep the dog," I cut in. Clem's still across the room, head bent close to Yura's, her face lit with happiness.

"What about the girl?"

At that, Clem turns, brows lifted. "Are you two talking about us?"

I'm relieved by the interruption. I'm not sure how I feel. Of course I like her, but I don't have a plan.

"Because we are definitely talking about you," Yura says, smiling. She swoops in and hugs me before I can react. "I'm Yura. Finn hasn't shut up about you for the last five days."

"Wait, you've been in Alaska for five days?" I ask, but the real question I want to ask is, why the hell didn't he tell me?

"Stayed in Anchorage for a few days after the flight."

"You flew here?"

"Yeah. Your parents insisted on the jet. Don't worry, I tipped the steward. Dante already scared off the last one."

"Of course he did," I say. My younger brother has always loved giving our family staff a hard time. Not because he's a dick, but because I think he gets a kick out of skirting the line of uncomfortability.

Yura hands Finn a few pills and a glass of water. "Yura's made me a PT schedule you'd drool over. Said I should be walking by your comp next month. Docs said the surgery went well. Still can't feel half my hip, but I can sit up for three hours without popping a painkiller, so hey—progress."

"You should have told me you were here," I grumble.

"You had the competition, and it gave Yura and me time to get to know each other," Finn says, tilting his head up like he can't believe she exists. "You're glowing," he adds.

"And you're full of pain meds," she teases.

They lock eyes for a beat too long.

I clear my throat. "And you two already know each other?"

"Only Misthaven's most notorious girl squad of summers past." Clem sidles up next to me, taking the dog from my arms. I don't want to let him go. I may hate this fur ball, but at least he gave me something to do with my hands.

"Clem made me suffer through hours of dance recitals every summer," Yura teases.

"Hey, that was only fair. You made us all suffer through your sled-dog wilderness phase. Remember? Right up until you realized you had to pee outside."

"Spare me." Yura buries her face in her hands. "I was ten."

"Tell me you've mastered peeing outside?"

"Clem." She elbows her, then slings an arm over her shoulder. "I used to count down the days until Clem visited. Summer was always the best part of the year."

"We basically ran around the lodge pretending it was our castle."

"There's nothing like growing up with someone who gets you, and now we're back together. You have to come over for a sleepover so we can catch up."

"Are you back for good?" Clem asks, petting Mozart's head.

"Yeah. I wanted to move home to be closer to Dad, and then this opportunity with Finn came up, so it kinda worked out. Heavens, it's so good to see you, ClemClem."

At that, Finn yawns, blinking slow.

Shit. My stomach knots. I need to get my stuff out of his room. I've been staying there since none of the other rooms are done.

"Let me show you to your room so you can get some rest," I say, in a rush, like if I move us along quickly enough, he won't notice my cracks.

"Rest? No way. Let's open a bottle of wine. I want to hear

everything—how you two met, how Wild Trails is going, what you've been up to. And Iceland. J said you dropped me off the email chain."

I freeze. Of course he noticed. Of course he's waiting to hear me say it out loud—that I'm backing out on him, breaking the one promise that still ties us together. My chest pulls tight.

"Maybe in a few days," I manage, stiff. "Clem and I have to get to sleep. Early morning tomorrow, first backpacking trip."

Clem frowns. "I thought that was next weekend?"

"Nope. Tomorrow."

"I'm pretty sure the schedule said rest day?"

"No." My voice comes out flat. "We leave tomorrow. Gotta make sure we build the stamina to work hard three days in a row." It's a lie, but I need time to figure out how to be around my best friend without this pang of sadness and contempt sitting like a boulder on my chest.

The silence drags. Clem's mouth parts like she's going to push, but then she presses her lips shut. She doesn't call me out, but I see the flicker in her eyes. She knows something's off.

"But we have Mozart now. We can't just leave him."

"We'll watch him," Finn says.

"You don't—" I start, but Yura's already scooped the dog up, Mozart wagging his tail like the traitor he is.

"We'd love to," she says. "I live right down the street. Since Finn's my only client, I'll be here a lot anyway."

"Good," I say, already edging toward the hall, toward escape. "We'll catch up soon. Your room is the one off the kitchen." My throat feels raw, like if I stand here another second, he'll see everything I'm holding in.

If he pushes again—if he asks me to look him in the eye and admit I'm moving on without him—I don't think I can lie to his face.

I don't know how to stay in Alaska and not feel like I'm betraying the person I became on the side of a mountain.

I don't know how to be Finn's friend and love the mountains he couldn't keep.

I don't know how to let myself want things that might last.

So, like a coward, I abandon him.

Chapter 29
Alec

ALEC

been busy. she's the granddaughter of the guy
we bought the lodge from

CAMERON

Coverage said you froze mid-wall. You good?

ALEC

Rope got stuck. I'm fine

FRANKIE

U sure?

Looked like u were dangling like a muppet!!!

ANYWAY. I wanna come watch the comp.

October 3rd??? I'm booking the jet

ALEC

Don't

CAMERON

we're free that weekend.

DAPHNE

There's some yarn stores there I've had
bookmarked forever!

FRANKIE

DIBS on the biggest room.

Get me a race car bed.

Oooo & also set me up a sim rig.

ALEC

no need to come

FRANKIE

Already booked hehehe

BROOKLYN

Keep ignoring us and we'll come early

ALEC

i go quiet when i train. u know that

BROOKLYN

You're not dangling from a cliff right now. So text more…please

DAPHNE

Send me your new lady friend's measurements

I'll knit us all matching beanies!!

FRANKIE

Found her Insta.

ALEC

i'm turning my phone off

THE GRAVEL PARKING lot of Chugach State Park is empty when we pull in, tucked at the edge of a trailhead that doesn't show up on AllTrails. It's from Bill's old trail journal, dog-eared, water-warped pages circled in red ink and labeled in his sharp, all-caps handwriting: *Best overnight trip with Margaret. 10/10.*

I'm trusting that it'll be a great overnight trip with Clementine too.

It's another overcast day, the September mornings growing chillier by the day. Even with the sun crawling up behind the jagged slate peaks, our breath ghosts white in front of us. Clouds sag low over the ridgeline like bruises, reluctant to clear.

Not everyone loves hiking in this weather, but I can't resist the smell of wet earth, rain-soaked pine, petrichor, and moss.

This trip is to get Clementine used to hiking for multiple days after sleeping on a thin foam pad. There are no showers, no cell service, and hopefully I can put off talking about Finn for another day.

"How's your body after yesterday?" I tighten the straps on

her pack. She could do it herself, but she lets me.

"From the hot spring?" Her beautiful, sleepy eyes blink up at me, pink blooming across her cheeks from the cold. She's fresh-faced today, except for her grapefruit lip gloss. God, I want to taste her again. "What do you think we would've done if Mozart hadn't barged in?"

"Clementine," I scold.

She brushes her fingertips over my jacket zipper. "Admit it, you dragged me out here at dawn for an excuse to spend the night together. If you weren't such an obsessive planner, I might've believed you 'forgot' the tent."

I clench my jaw. Every nerve in me is screaming to forget the damn trail, to pull her in and kiss her until neither of us can breathe. But that's the problem—I want her too damn much, for the wrong reasons. She doesn't deserve to be the distraction that shuts off my brain for a few minutes.

"We *actually* need to sleep tonight," I grit out. "Tomorrow's push will be harder. You gotta get used to three days back-to-back."

"I haven't slept through the night in months. I don't think that'll be an issue." She laughs, but there's a darkness ringing her eyes that I don't find funny. I'd trade an hour of my sleep a dozen times over if it meant she'd wake up rested for once.

"I need to know how you're feeling, Clem, so I know how hard I can push you today."

"I'm sore but manageable. No blisters. Are you sure Finn—"

Thankfully, my watch buzzes, and I turn before she can finish. "Keep up."

We pass a warped wooden trail sign covered in thick moss, *Blu Peak* scrawled in old fading letters. I pat my pockets—map, bear spray, pocketknife.

A few bends later, we pass a pond that spreads out in a clearing. "I like walking behind you," Clementine says.

"Because you don't want to navigate?"

"Because it's the best view on the trail."

I glance over my shoulder. "Are you catcalling me?"

Her grin is unapologetic, bright as the pond water. "Don't act like you don't love it."

"I don't," I lie. We pass over a wooden bridge, and on the other side, large boulders jut out of the ground amid thickets of buckbrush. "Careful up here. The bush is overgrown."

"I didn't think you'd mind overgrown bush."

I click my teeth at her. "Never do." I dig out my axe and cut us a path. There will be no scraped thighs on my watch. When a clear trail opens up, I stop. "You take this stretch. Set the pace, I'll time us. If match day's trail has this much elevation, we'll need to move faster."

She arches her brow. "You're really handing over control?"

"Don't get used to it."

She pecks my cheek before darting ahead, quickening her stride. I inhale once. My control is hanging on by a thread of floss at this point.

Her pace doesn't falter, even as the incline kicks up. Groves of evergreens appear beside us. Geese honk overhead. On the trail I clock moose tracks, caribou, and even a bear pad pressed into the mud. I point things out because it's easier than staying quiet. She stops to inspect a cluster of mushrooms alongside blooms of bellflowers and cow parsnips. Truth is, I'm watching her more than the trail. Clementine looks at the world like it's brand new, like even fungus deserves her full attention.

We cross a river where otters spin in the current, slick rocks bracketing the banks. The mountains rear higher. Not that long ago, Finn and I would've waited for the whole range to ice over, pitched camp for a week, and seen how high we could get. I wish I'd known K2 was our last climb. Maybe I would've savored everything, even the base camp stink, a little more.

Two hours in, blueberries spill across the slope beside a cairn. I call a break, and she immediately eats the berries straight from the bush, juice streaking her chin. My fingers itch to clean the drop of indigo that lingers on the side of her lips. Or, better yet, a quick swipe of my tongue, and she'd be spotless.

I check my watch instead.

"Good job," I tell her. "We're twenty minutes ahead."

She leans against a boulder. Her breaths come out in short, rapid pants. "After dragging me up here, are you finally going to talk about it?"

I freeze. "Talk about what?"

"You got weird last night, and you can't avoid me bringing it up any longer."

"I'm not—"

"Was it seeing Finn?"

I should've told her everything yesterday.

"Part of it," I say. She bites her lip, waiting for more. She's good at waiting. "He wants me to stay here." I pause and stare down at my boots. "And I haven't told him I don't want to."

Her hand brushes my arm, steadying me enough that I push a little further.

"On K2, while I was pulling him down, we promised we'd retire. And I should want that. I almost lost him. But climbing —" My throat closes. "It's my whole life. I don't know how to set it down. And now it's like—" I rake a hand through my hair. "I just…I feel stuck. Like there was life before Finn's accident, and now there's this purgatory, where nothing's moving forward because the person I've done everything with since I was five suddenly can't."

She rubs her thumb along my skin, grounding me.

"It's not just climbing," I say, forcing the words out. "It's everything. We've always been in lockstep. Same trips, same peaks, same risks. We made this unspoken commitment that it would always be both of us or neither. And now…" The sentence collapses in my mouth because there's no good way to end it.

"And now it can't be both," she whispers.

"If I go forward without him, maybe our friendship is over. And then what's left? Just the habit of being friends? Just our history." My voice cracks in a way I hate. "What if that's all we are?"

Instead of answering right away, she squeezes my hand, and I squeeze back. "Yeah. That's hard." She doesn't offer more than that. Instead, she tugs, coaxing me along the trail. Her steps are slow, like she knows I need movement more than I need a solution.

The silence between us is easy, allowing me to focus on my breathing. We keep going up the muddy path until the hill crests and mist shrouds the entire valley, engulfing the trees and blurring the line between forest and trail. It feels like only we exist here. Visibility is nonexistent, but still, we keep walking hand in hand, the only thing clear is the ground under our boots. I keep checking my compass, adjusting us forward, but I never once drop her hand.

"It's like walking blindfolded," Clementine says.

"Yeah. You have to trust the map. Trust the man who drew it. Trust there's something at the end worth finding."

"Maybe that's how it's going to be with Finn." Our gazes connect, and my pulse slows. She's wise beyond her years.

I've spent my life needing to see every route before I took a single step—every hold memorized, every anchor placed twice, every variable accounted for until the margin of error felt almost manageable. Now here I am in the fog, pretending I know where I'm headed when I don't.

This could be what holding more than one thing at once feels like. Not an easy, marked path where the outcome's obvious. Just a strip of earth half-hidden, asking me to believe it'll still be there when the mist lifts.

Avoidance has been my armor for so long. But with Clementine beside me, I can feel the edges giving way, hairline cracks forming where light may eventually get in.

Chapter 30
Clementine

BEING OUTSIDE MAKES my debt feel smaller, like the numbers shrink when the rain hits my skin. It reminds me of being a kid in Alaska, floating on my back in Misthaven Lake, playing mermaids with Yura, or picking strawberries with Gran in the garden. I remember picking out a rainbow tankini at Journeys with my mom that ended up matching the shiny fish scales of a fish Grandpa caught.

Back then, I knew how to be present.

Hiking with Alec pulls me back there. There's no scrolling, no comparing myself to everyone else online. Just the soft grunt of him right beside me, feral, wanting him more than I've ever wanted to swipe a credit card.

The fog cleared a few miles back. Now there are just churning clouds in the gray sky above. The back of Alec's neck is slick with sweat. His deodorant mixes with dirt and pine and wet air. Every time he opens his mouth to point out a plant or bird, I nod silently, hoping he doesn't notice my desire to bite the words off his tongue.

My body, however, is not nearly as romantic. After ten hours of hiking, my back is screaming, my thighs are staging a mutiny.

The last mile, gnarled tree roots spanned the length of the trail. I've kept my eyes glued to my boots, praying not to trip over another boulder or root or bear scat, which Alec pointed out with way too much enthusiasm the first time I stepped in it. Who knew I'd become an expert in identifying animal poop before summer was over?

I'm seconds from collapsing when Alec finally announces, "We're here."

I lift my head, vision blurring until it snaps into focus. The camp sits on a ridge above a celestial-blue lake that stretches out like the edge of the world. Blues, greens, yellows, and browns in every direction. No one else in sight. A river cuts straight through camp, its rush feeding the lake below, fish flashing silver where the sun catches their scales.

I pull my sweaty bun loose and let the wind take my hair.

It's one of the most stunning sights I've ever seen.

I glance at Alec. His jaw is shadowed, eyes scanning the terrain like he's memorizing it. Always studying. When he looks back at me, he smiles like he already knows I'll never forget this.

"You good?" Alec asks.

I'm hunched like Quasimodo, sweat dripping into my sports bra.

"Peachy," I croak, collapsing next to my pack. "My spine's permanently shaped like an S, but otherwise I'm thriving."

He smirks. "You better not tell your gran I gave you scoliosis."

"I'm gonna have to stretch for an hour just to feel human again."

"If you need help with your kinks…"

I shoot him a glare, glad to see the heaviness he carried most of the hike lightening. "Save the dad jokes, old man."

"We've got maybe an hour before the rain really sets in."

"I can do the fire," I say, pushing upright.

"Why, so I can suck more splinters out of your fingers?"

"There's a joke there," I admit, rubbing my temples. "But I'm too tired to find it."

"You can rest. I'll set up."

"No way."

We fall into rhythm, him stacking river rocks into a fire ring, me gathering the least-wet branches I can find and pretending not to ogle his shoulders. His long-sleeved black shirt clings to every muscle as he works steadily and efficiently. When he tosses me his knife and flint, I kneel, strike once, twice, and the flame catches in seconds.

Once the flames are steady, he scuffs his boot across two flat patches of dirt. "Both are good spots for tents."

"I think we should race." I unsnap my bag, grinning like a maniac.

His brow lifts. "You know I've been pitching tents since before you were born, right?"

"That's ageist."

He chuckles again, and something hot twists low in me. "What are the stakes?"

I hesitate, then blurt, "Loser skinny-dips in the lake."

He gives me a slow once-over. "You just want to see me naked."

I press a hand to my chest. "Unlike *some* people here, I would never objectify you with my leering stare."

He gives me a look that says he knows exactly how much I've objectified him already. "And if I win?"

Everything I've been trying not to imagine. You pushing me into a tent wall. Your mouth on every inch of me.

"Same stakes!" I yell, yanking my tent pouch open.

He sprints to his bag. Fabric whips against my arms, nylon snapping in the wind. My breath saws in and out, chest burning. I sneak a glance at Alec. His shoulders flex as he threads his poles, and he's calm, as if we're not in a full-blown tent death match to see each other's skin.

"You're working fast, Clem. Must really want the birthday suit."

"No distractions!" My fingers are numb as I snap my poles into place.

I jam my rain cover into place, clip it down, and fling my arms up. "Ha! Done!"

He gapes, still threading his last pole. "No way."

"You'd better be ready to lose those cargos!" I sing, twirling like a lunatic, hips rolling, hair whipping in the wind. My dance teachers would die at my lack of coordination, but for once I don't care.

"Uh, Clem—" Alec's voice cuts through. I barely register it. "Clem!" he shouts, already sprinting.

I spin, horrified. The universe, petty little bitch that she is, has snatched my tent like a kite. It tumbles once, twice, then lifts straight into the air and sails for the lake.

"Wait!" I lunge after it, but Alec's hand clamps my arm, yanking me back before I go over the ridge.

Together, we watch my tent somersault into the water, poles snapping, nylon ripping, floating off like the saddest birthday balloon.

"Uh, guess I forgot to stake it."

Alec spins me around until we're chest to chest. He's smiling with all his teeth. "Bit dramatic to throw it off the cliff just to share a tent with me."

"I didn't mean—"

"If you wanted to, Clem, all you had to do was ask." He lets go of me and strolls back to camp casually, as if he didn't just nuke my nervous system.

"I can, um—sleep outside?"

"Don't be ridiculous. You're sleeping with me." I blink as he double-checks the stakes in his tent. *Our* tent. The tent we will be sharing tonight. "If you're worried, I don't snore. I once fit four people in here when a storm wrecked half the camp. And they used stakes."

I'm too stunned to answer.

"I do feel bad, though," he adds, glancing over. "Technically, you won. We didn't say the tent had to stay in the camp."

"Next time, we should be more specific about the rules. Looks like I'll have to come up with a new bet to get you in that river," I say, walking toward him and helping him put his rain cover on. Internally, I'm floating into the sky.

"We've got a wet night ahead," he says.

"Wet, huh?"

"From the rain," he deadpans. "Honestly, it makes more sense to carry one tent for the competition. Lighter load for you. That is, if you don't mind sharing after tonight."

I lean into his neck enough to see the sweat gathered behind his ears. "Guess we'll see how generous you are with your body heat."

He looks at me, and I can't look away. His pupils swallow the gold of his eyes, chestnut flakes shimmering like stars. His jaw tightens, five-o'clock shadow darker from two days of not shaving, and my throat goes bone dry. I want to kiss him so badly it almost hurts.

Until the sky cracks open and rain sprinkles down.

Alec steps back. "Fuck, we need to get dinner on."

"You're really killing the mood," I shout over the rain. "I'll get the goop packs," I sigh, wishing there was a better option.

"Don't bother. I'm gonna catch us some food." He kicks off his boots, rolls up his pants, and scans the ground for a stick. His pocketknife flashes; one quick stroke, and he's turned the wood into a spear. Watching him do it—his hands sure, strong—makes my core ache all over again.

I dip a hand into the turquoise river. It's freezing!

Skinny-dipping here would have been torturous, but he wades in like it's a steaming hot bath.

His focus doesn't waver from the river, his brows drawn. Rain slicks down his forearms, veins pulsing under droplets. After a minute, he attacks. In one swift thrust, he shoots the spear into the water and bursts back up with a salmon thrashing wildly.

I leap to my feet. "No way!"

Alec glances over, smug as sin. "Hope you're hungry."

"This explains the entire human race," I shout. "Cavewomen saw this and went, 'Yep. Him. Forever.'"

"Just doing my evolutionary duty."

He laughs, and I want to bottle the sound, drink it until I'm drunk. He lays the fish on a rock and finishes it with quick, clean efficiency.

My stomach growls. And not just for food.

"Eat up," Alec says, sliding a tin plate of salmon toward me. The rain finally let up long enough for him to clean, skewer, and cook the fish over a flat rock, the fire crackling hot enough to chase the damp out of our clothes. Now the sky is black velvet, stars scattered like spilled sugar. I settle on a boulder by the flames, warmth licking up my shins, and he sits beside me, close enough I feel the heat of him even stronger than the fire.

I take a bite and moan into the fork before I can stop myself. "Okay, this is insane. Best fish I've ever had. In the city, this would cost at least sixty bucks."

"Do you always moan into your food?" He side-eyes me, the orange glow sharpening the lines of his cheekbones.

"Only when it doesn't come in a silver packet," I tease, licking a bit of juice from my lip. "I was starting to worry you didn't know how to cook."

"I like cooking over a fire, but I usually don't bother if it's just me."

"Did you learn how to catch fish on YouTube too?"

"No." He takes another bite, the fish on his plate nearly gone. My gran used to scold my grandpa for eating like that. Said he chewed like he was trying to eat the utensils.

"That was Finn's idea. When we were seventeen, we camped near the Russian River during a spawning season. The first time, he nearly speared his foot. After that, we tried to live off what we caught as much as possible."

Alec's pain for his friendship with Finn is nearly palpable. It's clear that he loves him, and although I've only met Finn briefly, the look on his face when he saw Alec was one of adoration. There's no way they'll stop being friends, even if Alec decides to keep climbing. Even after only a month, I can't see Alec as someone you just move on from. Every time he opens up to me, I feel as if I've found a four-leaf clover growing in the subway system.

I smile and take another bite, deeply curious about the man in front of me. "Did you two have any other traditions?"

"We used to share a Toblerone at the top of every peak." He shrugs, but I see a shadow tug at him. "What about you and Yura?"

"We played Fire and Ice," I say. "Kind of like Truth or Dare, except no dares. If you didn't want to answer, you had to pick Fire and tell an embarrassingly personal story instead."

"Well, go ahead then."

"You ask first."

His muscular, tattooed arms are braced on his knees, and I trace the art with my eyes as he thinks. "When's your birthday?"

"May tenth. What about yours?"

"September twenty-second."

"This month!" I smile. "You being a Virgo explains everything."

"A Virgo?"

"Of course you don't follow astrology." I chuckle, knowing I'll check our compatibility the moment we get service.

"Never really liked celebrating my birthday. It's just another day."

I roll my eyes. "You're so predictable, but I love birthdays, so just know I'm going to throw you a party."

"Don't."

"You like pie or cake?"

"I think it's my question."

"Then I'll just have to get you both," I tease.

"Changing the subject now." He pauses. "What was your first job?"

"I drove the carpool for younger dancers at my school in Concord. We choreographed ridiculous routines in the car, and they'd raid my makeup bag. My car was always covered in glitter."

"No glitter in my truck."

"Now that you said it, I'm gonna have to find some." He glares at me, and I can't help but giggle.

"Figures you'd be good at that, though. You have a knack for making things fun."

"Did you just admit I make things fun?" I elbow him.

"You do." Heat blooms across my cheeks at his easy admission.

"What about you?" I ask.

"Guide at the indoor climbing gym."

"Wow. I could have guessed that. My turn?" He shrugs, so I continue, "You go to prom?"

"Took Finn."

"Shut up."

"We went to different schools. He had a date for his, I didn't have one for mine and didn't really want to go. But my mom insisted. It was at the San Francisco aquarium. We ditched after the first two songs to play arcade games on the pier."

"Surprised you didn't try climbing into the fish tanks or something."

"And be ripped to pieces by sharks? No thank you."

"You're no fun," I tease, batting his chest. "I never went to my prom. Booked a session with a Bolshoi master in some basement. So romantic."

"I think I would have preferred that."

"Tell that to the giant bruises I had on my knees for weeks."

"Try wearing a bow tie, it's suffocating."

"You in a suit…now that is something I'd pay to see."

He rolls his eyes, but he's smiling. "Okay, make the next one juicy," I say. I've nearly forgotten this is a game. Now it's just curiosity, peeling each other apart layer by layer.

The fire pops, and the wind picks up around us, blowing my hair straight into my mouth. He tucks it behind my ear before asking, "What's something you're afraid of?"

His voice is soft, and I'm not yet used to a soft Alec, but I like it.

Which probably makes my answer slip out a tad too truthfully. "The future."

He tilts toward me, knees touching mine as he sets his plate on the ground. His full attention is on me.

"I gave up my career on such a silly whim, and I don't know if I'll ever go back. Or how. But there are other options. Teaching. Choreographing. I just don't know what next month or even next week will look like." My shoulders lift helplessly. "I don't know, you know? And I hate that."

"You've got time. You're only twenty-four." His voice is certain. "Whatever you set your mind to, you'll kill it. And if you wanna teach, maybe I'll let you give me a dance lesson."

"I'd like that," I say, imagining being pressed up against him, his hand on the small of my back.

"I imagine you've had other male dance partners?"

"Yep. But if you squeeze into a pair of tights, you might be my favorite."

"Damn right." His hand lands on my thigh, and I bite my lips to hide the smile that wants to creep across my face.

I pretend to think for a moment, chewing on a bite of salmon, then ask the question that's been buzzing in my mind for weeks. "How many tentmates have you had?"

"Over thirty at once, probably."

Probably. Alec doesn't do probably. This is a man who remembers rope brands from climbs that took place a decade ago. He's counted. He's logged.

"A thirty-some? Isn't that practically an orgy?" My jaw drops, and I glance at him, waiting for the smirk.

"No. We were all just sleeping. Big tent for all the river counselors. Though I'm pretty sure Finn was not just...*sleeping.*" He chuckles. "One time Finn hooked up with three people at base camp. We sprinted up the mountain just to avoid the fallout."

"I guess that's why they call you Two Men On Top," I shoot back.

"At base camp, there's not much else to do. Drink or fuck. Unless you're puking your guts out from altitude sickness."

"Sounds romantic."

"Hooking up when you haven't had a proper shower in a month is...anything but romantic."

"Dancers are just as feral, hooking up after hour-long practices. I once walked in on two roommates going at it on a foam roller."

"I don't even want to know the mechanics of that."

"Motion of the ocean." I roll my hips for emphasis, and his nostrils flare.

"Finn and I had a system. Sock on the tentpole."

"Ew." I giggle. "So...you're definitely *tent-experienced.*"

"I'm all about specifics, Clem. If you want to know something, just gotta use that pretty mouth of yours to ask."

"So, you think I'm pretty," I tease, melting into him. He chuckles, and it vibrates down to my core. It really doesn't matter how many people he's had sex with. Sex can just be bodies and flesh, no intimacy, no feelings, no love. Another question burns my lips. "You know what I wanted to ask. So?"

"Sorry, isn't it my turn?" Alec jokes. I reach down and throw a small pebble at him, which he catches. *Damn climber reflexes.* "How many dancers borrowed your foam roller?"

The firelight softens his face, pooling in the hollow of his throat. "A handful," I say, wobbly. "But they didn't always know how to make it *worthwhile.* If you know what I mean."

And I hope he does catch my meaning, because I really don't want to outright admit that I've never had a man-made orgasm. It's embarrassing.

That gets him quiet. The vein in his temple throbs. "Lack of skills or tools?"

"Both. Or maybe it's me—"

"No." The word is clipped, absolute.

"My turn." My cheeks flush, and I drastically want to change the subject. "You ever been in love?"

"No." His answer is immediate, and my chest deflates. "Relationships are hard when you do what I do. They feel like something that could clip my wings."

"Relationships should feel like flying beside someone," I blurt before slapping my hand over my mouth. "God, that was cheesy. Sorry."

"Not cheesy. It's sweet."

"And now?" I ask, discarding my plate on top of his, folding one knee into my thigh so I can face him.

He rakes a hand over his jaw, mouth pressing flat. "Don't know. You've got me rethinking a lot of shit."

I want to grab his shoulder and scream, *What the hell does that mean?* I wonder if Finn has a dictionary to decode these cryptic answers Alec loves to give.

"Alright," he says, shaking it off, "last question before we head in. What's your most memorable part of our training?"

"Besides your stellar personality?"

"That's a given. Okay, let's clean up." He stands, but my hand lands on his forearm, pulling him back down.

"Wait, no…let me think of a serious answer," I say, wanting a real answer from him too.

I sift through memories: his hand on my calf as he patched up my blisters, the adrenaline spike of the kayak, dinners at Daisy's, him picking me up from work with classical music playing, him sucking a literal splinter out of my hand, or giving me the leaf tulip that sits on my dresser. But my brain stops at the hot spring—the kiss. Our skin through wet fabric.

A closeness I don't want to come back from.

"You first," I say, needing to know he feels all of this too.

"It was you," he says, no hesitation. "You've been my favorite part of this."

My breath stumbles. "Me too."

His jaw tightens, like he's holding himself back by sheer will. I look sideways at the tent. Every nerve is alive under my skin, every thought screaming, *Don't touch!* while another part of me wants to press every inch of my body against him, memorize the way his hands feel against me.

The universe seems to answer my pleas, because the rain starts again, harder this time, hissing against the fire.

"We should go to bed."

"We should." Alec breaks first, already moving, dousing our plates in the river and then putting out the flames. "Inside. Now."

There's no room for argument, not with the storm pounding so hard.

Chapter 31
Clementine

ALEC HOLDS the tent flap open, and I hurry inside. It's even smaller than I thought—just two foam pads, sleeping bags, and not nearly enough floor space for two people our size.

He ducks in after me, and the whole tent seems to shrink by half. The lantern hanging in the middle casts his face in warm gold, and suddenly I'm not nervous in the scary way—I'm nervous in the too-good way. The kind where my chest feels tight, my smile won't behave, and the only thing I can think is: *Don't blow this, don't make it weird, just let yourself enjoy it.*

Rain claws heavily above us. Cold bites at my skin as I peel off my jacket and rain pants and hand them to Alec, who places them in a small bag with his outer layers. My leggings and long-sleeved base layer stay put. They're only thin merino wool, but they're better than bare skin in this temperature.

"Uh, which one is mine?" I ask, wrapping my arms around myself. My teeth are chattering, so the words come out uneven.

"Fuck, Clem, you're freezing."

"I'm fine," I lie.

Without a word, he drops to his knees and unzips both the sleeping bags, sliding them together until they make one.

"What are you doing?"

"I can't have you freezing out here." His back is to me, filling the narrow space entirely. He tosses the plaid blanket open like a door only I can walk through. "You gotta use me."

"*Use* you?" I echo.

"Use my body as a tool," he says simply. "You're freezing. I'm wasting heat. That's stupid math. Now get in."

"You sure?" I hesitate, even though my body wants to fling itself inside this huge sleeping bag without any questions.

There is a flicker of something unreadable in his eyes. "I promise, Clem, I will be a perfect gentleman."

I slide into the plaid blanket, instantly feeling warmer. Alec dims the light above until it's only a low nightlight before sliding in beside me. The heat is instant, radiating through the thin layers between us. But he's too far away.

"What if I don't want you to be a perfect gentleman?" I say, confident in the dim light, inching back until my back curves into his chest, and my socks brush his shins.

"Clem."

"What if I'm still freezing?"

His arm comes around my waist, his hand splayed flat over my midsection. He may be only two inches taller than me, but his hands are the size of my head, his fingers the size of two of mine held together.

"Is this better?"

"Yeah," I choke out.

"You're still shivering," he says into my hair.

"I think that might be your fault now."

He laughs, and I feel it in my spine. "Guess you'll have to deal with it."

There's no room for space in here. Every breath brushes the back of my neck. Every shift presses his leg along mine. It feels like we're underwater in our own small and sealed-off world.

I risk turning my head, and then my body, nestling into his

chest. He inhales. His thumb starts tracing slow circles over my side, lazy and sure, and goose bumps race up my arms. The heat spirals through me, tenfold now, impossible to ignore.

"Alec?"

"Tell me," he says.

"Do you want to kiss me again?"

His hand lands on my hip bone like he's fighting with himself. The silence makes me ache until he tilts my chin up to meet his gaze. His golden eyes are molten.

"I've wanted to kiss you every damn day. You think I've been patient? I've been drowning."

My lungs forget what they're supposed to do. The words hit with the force of a confession and a claim all at once, and before I can second-guess myself, I tilt into him.

He meets me halfway, our lips so close together I can feel the heat of him, the stubble of his beard.

The first press of his mouth is slow, almost punishing in its restraint, like he's proving to himself that he can hold back. But when my fingers curl into his shirt, it breaks something open in him. His hand slides from my hip to my jaw, holding me steady as he kisses me harder, deeper, like he's making up for every day we haven't been doing exactly this.

His lower lip is soft and then firmer, drawing mine into the shape he wants, and my body has this ridiculous, traitorous memory from when we kissed the first time. As if I'm humming, *Oh, right, this, this is so right*—and then every nerve lights up.

He tastes like rain and smoke and all the things I've been trying not to admit I wanted.

"You know you scare me, right?" His lips drag over mine.

"I scare you?"

"You don't back down. You don't bite your tongue. You're too much for men who want easy."

He kisses me again, just enough to make my chest seize.

"Too much, huh?"

"Too much for anyone who wants simple. I've been trying to keep things simple." He lets out a humorless huff. "Haven't managed a damn second of it around you."

"What about you? Am I too much for you?"

His gaze locks on mine. "I'm not most men."

He tugs me flush against him as his mouth claims me as his. It's not careful this time, it's hungry and starved and devouring. He kisses me hard, then breaks away just long enough to rasp, "Arms up."

His fingers fist my shirt, stripping it off in one rough pull. He tosses it to the side. Next comes my sports bra. My nipples pebble in the cold.

"Fuck." He looks at me like he's been holding his breath for weeks, and I'm the first gulp of air. "I can't stop looking at you."

"Please don't stop," I moan. The sound feeds him, makes his hand spread over my ribs like he's staking a claim.

"You make me want to take my time," he groans against my mouth, chest rising and falling in uneven waves. "But I'm done pretending I don't want all of you." His teeth catch my bottom lip, hard enough to sting.

"I want you too," I say as his lips trail along my neck and my brain liquefies.

"You're stubborn." Kiss. "You're a fighter." He nips my ear, and I buck. "I want you so fucking bad, baby."

The word *baby* makes heat flood to my core.

I close my eyes. "You have me," I whisper, desperate.

"Not yet." His smile is wicked. "But I will."

"I want this off." I yank at his clothes. He strips his shirt off. I've seen him shirtless countless times over the last month, but it never gets old. There's nothing better than running my hand over his washboard abs and the V that leads to his pants. I trace the black-ink tattoos that snake around his biceps and down his sculpted chest.

It's like he was carved out of the rock and ice he climbs. I prop up on my elbows and yank him toward me until we are skin to skin. I delight in the weight of him on top of me.

"You tell me. Say stop, and I stop. Say slow, and I slow. Say my name and—" He cuts himself off with a low rumble that vibrates against me. "I'll give you whatever the hell you want."

"Alec." My voice collapses, and his groan answers like I just gave him permission to unravel.

His mouth drags down my collarbone, teeth scraping, tongue soothing. His hand grips my thigh, firm, possessive, sliding higher until I'm trembling.

There is a steadiness in his arms. I realize, briskly, that there's a difference between being held and being handled.

I've had partners who were careful because they thought I'd break. Alec holds me like he'd fight gravity to keep me in his arms. My core tightens. My tights drag across his forearms. His exhale brushes the curve of my ribs. This man could carry me over ice and fire, but somehow his touch is both soft and caring.

"Mine," he hums against my skin. "My girl."

The words hit harder than the kiss, harder than the storm that's hammering the tent.

"Alec," I pant.

His hand slides lower, finding the waistband of my leggings. "Lift." The command vibrates against my mouth.

I arch into him, balancing my weight on his chest as he tugs the fabric down over my hips. His knuckles brush my thighs, his forearm grazing the inside of my knee. I bend my knees, and he strips the leggings off completely, tossing them aside with the same growling impatience.

By the time he looks down at me again, I'm breathless, stripped to my underwear in the low lantern glow. His hand spreads wide over my stomach, sliding up to my ribs. I've never been touched like this. Never felt so wanted.

"Christ," he mutters, voice wrecked. "Look at you."

"I could say the same to you." I grin up at him. His shaggy, damp hair drips water onto my chest, and he follows the droplets along my sternum, over my breast. I bite my lip and squeeze my thighs together. My eyes drop to his pants, to his erection pressing up against the fabric. I reach for him, but he bats my hand away.

"Not yet, sweet girl." I want to protest, but when his fingers slip lower, my thoughts slip from my mind. "Christ, you are so wet. Spread for me," he pants, nudging my knee open. He trails his hand along my inner thigh, teasing me.

I obey, head falling back into the small pillow behind me. I thought I'd feel embarrassed or nervous, but Alec makes me feel safe.

"You're so fucking beautiful it hurts."

Our gazes are locked. One of his strong fingers finds my clit, and I gasp, pressing into him. I've drooled over his hands for weeks, wondering if he's gentle or rough. Somehow, he's both. He circles my clit softly, then fast, sliding down lower, slowly opening me up before his finger is inside of me. The stretch is sharper than I expected, my muscles clamping down so hard around him it almost hurts.

"Easy," he growls. "Breathe. Take me."

My chest heaves like I've just sprinted a mile. I let out a jagged gasp, and that's all it takes for him to slide deeper.

Nothing has ever felt so right.

The pressure is shocking—burning, aching, overwhelming. My body doesn't know whether to close up or pull him in tighter. Tremors run through my muscles.

He sets a rhythm, slow and devastating, pulling nearly all the way out before pushing back in. I feel every stroke, every drag, like my body's being rewired from the inside out.

"That feels so good." I rock into him, and he presses on my lower abdomen.

"You take what I give you." He crooks his finger inside me, and my whole body bows upward.

"God," I moan.

A gasp tears out of me, high and broken, echoing in the dark tent. My chest arches, and my nails rake against the sleeping bag. He does it again, slower this time, dragging deliberately against that spot, and I moan. My eyes drift closed.

A tinge runs up my spine, so electric I almost don't recognize it.

"No—no, wait—" I gasp, panic flashing hot through me. No one has ever made me come. "It's too much—"

"Do you want me to stop?"

"No. It's just a lot."

"Shhh." His forehead presses to mine. "That's it. That's the place. Don't fight it."

"I can't—Alec, I—"

"Yes, you can." He pushes deeper, adds another finger, stretching me fuller. The pressure is unbearable, electric. "You can take it. You're built for this. Open for me, Clementine."

I shake my head, as if that will stop the flood building inside me. "I don't—oh god—I don't know—"

His thumb finds my clit again, circles lazily, cruelly patient. "Don't hold it back," he mutters against my ear, his breath wrecked but sure. "Let it happen. Let go for me."

I'm gasping, panting, nails digging into his shoulders. Every sound that rips from me is humiliatingly raw. The pressure builds, unbearable, until I can't keep it down anymore.

"Come for me, baby." He drops his mouth to my nipple, sucking hard.

The climax rips through me, violent and hot. My body clenches around his fingers, spasming uncontrollably. My thighs shake, and I'm kicking.

"Alec!" I scream his name again and again.

He holds me through it, fingers never faltering. My heart thunders.

"That's it," he groans, his forehead pressed to mine, voice shredded but proud. "That's my girl. Give me all of it."

When I finally collapse back, limp and shuddering, he drags his hand free. It's slick with me, and he places his fingers in his mouth, licking me off of him.

"Fuck, you taste like mine." I smile up at him, wrapping my legs around his waist. He kisses my temple. "That's one," he hisses. "And we're nowhere near done."

Chapter 32
Alec

"You should know by now, Clementine, there's no lack of skills or tools here."

The tent is too damn small, but I don't give a damn. I strip off my pants, discarding them to the side. Every shift forces her closer, and that's exactly where I want her. She's still catching her breath when I roll her gently onto her side. The nylon walls brush my shoulders, but there's just enough space to work.

"Mmm."

"Easy," I whisper, fitting myself behind her, my chest to her back. My arm hooks under her top leg, dragging it high over my hip. The move opens her up, making room for me where the tent doesn't. "You're fucking gorgeous."

Clem's hair is damp against my jaw. I shove it aside and drag my mouth down her neck, teeth catching her shoulder. She's soft everywhere I'm hard. And she lets me hold her like this, lets me cage her completely inside my arms.

One hand grips her ribs, palm spread wide across her breast. The other clamps her thigh over mine. She's locked in my frame, nowhere to go, nowhere I won't follow.

"Right here," I growl into her ear. "Stay open for me."

I press forward, inching her panties to the side. My erection springs from my boxers, and I slide my cock along her wet cunt. She's soaked and ready, as if she's been wanting this as bad as I have.

And I have. Weeks of thinking about her. Her mouth, her smartass comebacks, how tight she'd feel around me. Now she's here, and I've got to pace myself, make it count.

But all I want is to bury myself deep and not come up for air.

"Protection." The word scrapes out of me. My forehead presses to the back of her head. "I've got some in my pack."

She turns her face, close enough that I catch the corner of her mouth. "I'm on the pill. I'm clear. I want you."

My jaw locks. I search her eyes. "You sure? Because if I push inside you now, Clementine, I'm not holding back."

Her lips part. "Certain."

I tilt her face to mine, capturing her lips and savoring her taste. "Right answer," I growl, lining up, pressing forward until the head of me pushes into her. She moans a sweet, soft melody, and I damn near lose it. I pause. The angle's brutal, her soft ass curving around me as her tight pussy strangles me inch by inch. My lungs tear open on a curse against her neck.

"Clem." I bite her shoulder just to steady myself. "You feel unreal."

"You too." She gasps, nails digging into my thigh, her body clamping like she's not sure she can take it. She squirms, and I lock an arm around her ribs, keeping her flush against me.

"Patient," I grind out, my breath rough in her ear.

"Alec," she whimpers as I slide in deeper, savoring how wet she is.

"There you are, brave girl." She turns until her gaze is latched on to mine. Her lashes flutter, but she doesn't look away.

I set a rhythm, thrusting in short, deep strokes—there is no room in this tent for long ones. Doesn't matter. Having her so willing and needy like this is enough to make me see stars. She writhes in my hold, every twitch squeezing me tighter.

"Stay with me." My voice is hoarse. "That's it. Take it. Good girl."

Her hips roll back, desperate, and I grunt, clamping her soft leg higher as my cock buries deeper into her. The angle nearly knocks me out. She cries out, and my whole body answers.

"Fuck, you're so hot," I sigh.

Her body trembles, clenching hard; she's on the edge again. I strain to hold back, because if I give in now, it's over too soon. And I'm not letting her go with just one.

Her breath fractures into panicked little gasps, like she doesn't know what's happening to her own body.

"Don't fight it, Fox. Let it happen."

"Kiss my neck," she moans, and I oblige, taking one of her perfect pink nipples in between my thumb and palm.

Her cunt convulses around me, and I have to bite my cheek until the tinge of iron fills my mouth. I'm not ready to come yet. I want this night to never end.

"Alec, please."

"Good, baby, ride it out." I grind into her, and she spasms around me.

Pride and hunger slam through me, and I hook her leg higher, driving deeper, grinding her into the sleeping bag so she can't escape a second of my cock making her come.

"Take it, Clem. Take every fucking inch. You're mine."

"I'm yours."

At that, she finally breaks. Gasps rip out of her throat, her body convulsing helplessly around me. It feels like she's tearing me open from the inside out. I hold her through every shudder, every quake, not letting go, not easing up until she's slumping, boneless, against my chest.

And even then, I stay buried deep.

"That's two." I nip at her earlobe as the aftershocks run

through her. "And I'm still not fucking done."

The storm outside hasn't let up. Rain pounds the nylon, wind pushes at the walls. Inside, it's heat and breath and Clementine all flushed, wrecked by me but still looking like she wants more.

"Alec," she says with a dry throat.

"You want more?" I ask against her mouth. "Say it."

I roll onto my back, stripping her panties off. Next come my boxers, and soon we are both completely naked. I drag her on top of me, guiding her thighs around my hips. She's so gorgeous above me, her copper hair falling down her back, her breasts so perfect. Her cheeks and lips are flushed.

"I want more." She leans down, biting my lip. My little fox comes alive.

"Take it. Take what you want."

She rakes her nails along my chest, and I delight in the pain. She looks like a dream and a dare in one.

"You don't fucking know what you do to me. Sitting over me like this, flushed and so perfect." She could break me apart with one more roll of her hips.

"Do I drive you wild?" Her blue eyes flash with fire.

I slowly drag a thumb over her swollen pink clit as she grabs my dick, and I tip my head back. *Control.* I don't want to look away. She bites her lip as she lines herself up over my cock and then lowers, torturously slow.

"Yes. You're killing me, Clem." She smiles wickedly, like she knows how much power she has over me. "Tell me you've thought about me?" I beg. She keeps riding me. I prop up onto my arm, sucking her nipple, biting it until she gasps louder. "Tell me."

"I picture you every night," she admits.

She rolls her hips, slow, deliberate, and my breath tears out ragged. Too tight. Too good. Christ, I can't hold on like this forever.

"You think I don't notice?" I growl, eyes burning into hers.

"Every bratty comment. Every look. Had me hard for weeks. Yeah, you did it. You wrecked me before I even touched you." I buck into her. "You like this, baby."

"God…yes." She drops her head back, the light casting her in an otherworldly glow. Then her eyes connect with mine again. "Admit it. Me calling you Daddy did it for you."

That word.

"My brat, fuck—" My voice shatters on a curse. "Don't say shit like that unless you wanna finish me right here. 'Cause one look at you like this, one word, and I'm gone."

"Daddy."

The word detonates in me. I've turned feral. My vision turns white at the edges.

"Fuck—" My grip clamps on her hips like a vise, dragging her down harder onto my cock, deeper. My rhythm shatters. I'm thrusting up into her now, hips jerking rough, no control left. "Ride me," I growl, voice breaking. My hands lock her down, forcing her pace to match mine. "Come on, sweetheart. Grind that pretty body on me."

She's laughing now, her body tossing around the tent as I fuck her hard enough her eyes roll back. Her rhythm shifts, short bounces now, just enough to make her breasts brush my chest, just enough to slam me deeper every time she drops. My hips jerk up to meet her, helpless. Her pussy squeezes around me. I love the sound our bodies make together.

She's close—so close—her thighs shake.

"Fuck me, baby. Take it. Harder."

"Yes, daddy…please…" Her hair falls wild around her face.

"Don't stop. Don't you fucking stop."

Her face twists, she gasps, and I know she's about to break. I drive her down hard, hips surging up to meet her, every thrust deep and brutal.

"Come with me," I growl against her throat, my breath shredded. "Right now. Give it to me."

She jerks once, twice, and then she breaks.

Her whole body convulses around me, walls clenching in hard, erratic pulses that nearly drag me under with her. Fuck—she's strangling me.

"That's it. Ride it out. Good girl." My hips jerk up into hers, helpless against the way she's milking me. "Fuck—you feel that? You're wrecking me. Never had anyone do this to me. Never."

When it's done, we collapse, tangled together, my chest heaving under her weight. My hands still clamp her hips, like I can't let go, not yet.

I drag the sleeping bag over us, wrapping her up, sealing us in heat. My chest rises and falls under her cheek, her heartbeat pressed right against mine. One hand tangles in her hair, stroking damp strands back from her temple. The other clamps her waist, holding her against me like if I let go, I'll wake up alone.

Christ. I've never let anyone this close. Never needed anyone this bad. She's turned me inside out, and I don't even care.

"Hey," I whisper into her hair. "You okay?"

"Yeah. You?"

"Not sure I've ever been this good."

She lifts her head, eyes hazy, cheeks flushed, lips swollen.

"I swear I've never seen anything so goddamn perfect."

"For someone who doesn't talk much, you're awfully chatty now." Her nose scrunches, teasing.

"Hush up, my perfect, perfect girl." She rests her head on my chest, and I stroke her hair.

The tent creaks under the wind, rain still hammering outside, but in here it's steady. Her breathing slows as she slips into sleep. I stay awake, arms locked around her, memorizing every inch of her against me.

I've stared down storms, avalanches, nights when the mountain tried to break me. None of it ever touched me like this woman did just now.

Nothing ever will.

Chapter 33
Alec

Every morning since I can remember, I rushed to get out of bed. Rushed to my to-do list to keep my mind quiet. But today, my mind is only on one person.

Clementine sleeps peacefully on top of me. Her copper hair is draped along my chest, legs wrapped in between mine. She never once stirred in the night, like I wore her out as much as she did me. Even on the thin foam padding and with the storm raging all night, I slept better than I had in months, finally not visited by nightmares.

Outside the tent, the sun rises, birds chirp, but I stay still, worshiping her warmth. I kiss the top of her head, inhaling her sweet smell, treasuring the weight of her in my arms.

She stirs awake, tilting her head up and kissing my lips.

"You just been staring at me, you creep?" Her laugh vibrates against my chest.

"Yeah," I admit.

"You've been awake long?" She blinks up at me, beautiful as morning dew.

"No. Did you sleep okay?"

"Better than okay."

"It's the first time I slept through the night in months," I admit.

"Me too." She kisses me again, soft and gentle, before pulling back. Her hair is sticking up in a few places, her lips are swollen, and I spot a few marks I left on her neck last night. I adore seeing her covered in me. "Who would've thought? You're a certified cuddler. Your gruff mountain man reputation's ruined."

I break into a smile. "Oh well."

"But you kinda look like a sheepdog." She tugs an elastic off her wrist. "Hold still."

"What are you doing?"

She gathers my hair and ties it into what I can only imagine is a crooked knot. "Now your exterior matches that cute interior."

"Christ." I roll my eyes but don't fix it. I'd do anything to hear her happy. "Now it's your turn." I roll on top of her, and she shrieks.

She tries to shove me off, but I drag her back into me. We roll around on the foam, me tugging at her hair, her yanking my ear. The tent shakes with our happiness. The world outside ceases to matter.

I pull her close, press my mouth to her temple. Goose bumps pebble her naked body. "We're not hiking today."

"What do you mean?"

"Day off." I grab my clean, long-sleeved shirt and tug it over her.

"Day off? Who are you, and what have you done with Alec Hastings?"

"You heard me," I say. "I have no interest in moving when I've got you right here."

We drift back to sleep until her stomach growls like thunder in the tent. She groans, stretching against me, and I laugh, pushing us up and outside into the thin mountain morning.

She wrinkles her nose at the goop packets I pull from my bag, batting them away like flies. "Absolutely not."

Breakfast turns into the blueberries we picked yesterday and a granola bar, heated up over a fire. I watch her eat. She looks outrageously good—hair tangled, my shirt crooked on her shoulder, knees drawn up like she belongs out here in the wild with me.

Like she's always belonged.

"Hmm," she hums around a bite, finger tapping theatrically against her chin. "What are we going to do all day?"

Before I can answer, she bolts. "Race you!"

"To what?"

"The bottom!"

And then she's throwing herself sideways down the grassy hill that leads to the lake, limbs flying, laughter spilling out like she can't contain it.

I stand there dumbstruck. *Ah, the hell with it.* I dive after her. The grass smacks my arms, mud streaks my back, the world flips over and over—sky, earth, sky, earth.

For a second, I'm twelve again, reckless, weightless, and alive.

When I finally land beside her, I'm dizzy and grinning, and I can't remember the last time I let myself be this stupid.

"You did it!" she gasps, shoving my shoulder. "Mr. Mountain actually rolled down a hill."

I snort, eyes closed against the sun. "You're lucky we didn't break our necks."

She sprawls beside me, hair plastered to her forehead, chest heaving. She threads her fingers through mine. "You loved it."

"Yeah," I admit. "Guess I did."

She gasps. "Alert the press!"

I turn my head and watch the sunlight catching her lashes. "You make me feel young again."

"Good. Though, for the record, I love this little gray hair you're starting to get." She tugs at my hair, which has already fallen from the elastic she put around it.

We lie there awhile, damp clothes sticking, grass seeping cool against my back. The hill presses into my shoulder blades, her leg thrown half over mine, heavy and warm, like she forgot to untangle herself.

"I got hill stains on your shirt."

I grunt. "Grass stains build character."

"You know I've never done this." She runs her fingers over my chest.

"Rolled down a hill?"

"Woken up with someone. Played. Been…like this." Her thumb brushes over my knuckles where our hands are still linked. "It feels *easy*."

Something in my throat locks up. Because I've never done this either. Not like this. Not with laughter still echoing in my bones.

"You call tumbling down a wet slope easy?"

"Don't dodge the compliment."

Her hand is small in mine, but it fits like I've been carrying the space for it without realizing it. "Fine. Easy."

"You still owe me a skinny-dip, since you did say I technically won."

She's joking, but she's right, and before I can second-guess myself, I jolt upright and bolt to the lake.

"Where are you going?" she yells behind me.

I glance back over my shoulder, grinning, already tugging my shirt over my head. "Coming?"

"What are you doing?" she calls

"Like you said, I owe you a skinny-dip." I kick off my boots.

By the time she shouts, "I lost the tent!" I'm already waist-deep in freezing water, diving under with a yelp.

"You should join me."

On the shore, she kicks off her boots, toes sinking into dark gravel slick with river silt, then peels my shirt off. She doesn't hesitate. She never does. Her body flashes pale, and my chest caves at the sight.

"You're insane!" she shouts as the icy water hits her ankles. Her hair is wild against the blue sky, droplets already catching on her skin.

"Jesus, Clem."

"What?"

"You're fucking beautiful."

"Wow. Keep the compliments coming." She splashes toward me, nipples perked up against the cold, skin pebbling. "This was a terrible idea!" she shrieks.

"It was your idea!" The current presses hard against my legs, numbing them, but she's still grinning, wild and alive.

She moves closer, and suddenly she's in my arms, legs wrapping around me like she can't stand any space between us.

"Trying to steal my warmth, I see." My gaze drags lower—to her throat, her collarbone, the faint shiver that runs through her body. The river swirls around us, cold and merciless, but none of it touches the fire cracking open inside me.

"I'm going to kiss you again," I say.

"You never have to ask."

I cup her face, brushing back a wet strand of hair. I read the shape of her mouth like it's the only map I've ever needed. Our teeth chatter against each other, but neither of us cares. Nothing matters but this—her, me, us.

Her thighs tighten around me. Her nails dig into my shoulders. My hand fists in her hair, dragging her closer, as if I could ever get close enough.

"My fox."

Out in nature. Out in the wild. With fog curling over the mountains and river rocks slick between our toes, I don't feel like I'm counting steps or summits. I don't feel like I'm carrying the weight of anything.

I just feel *here*.

It terrifies me, and it frees me.

Chapter 34
Alec

THERE'S an itching under my skin as I walk Clementine home, like something's trying to climb out of me. Like my body knows what my brain's still trying to argue against. I don't want to leave her side. Not now. Not after a night with her pressed into me like she was built to fit there.

I want to carry her back to the lodge, lay her down in a real bed, and have her stay. Not just the night. All of it.

That thought is a red flag waving in my chest.

It's too soon. Reckless. I know better than this. I promised myself I wouldn't be that guy. The one who strings a woman along while he's still chasing mountains that might kill him. I met too many of them. Husbands who never came home. Kids left behind. I swore I'd be the one who didn't do that.

But then she reaches for my hand like it's the easiest thing in the world, and I feel the ground shift under me.

A worry for another day.

"Maybe we can do our weight workout together tomorrow before you go into work?" I ask, slowing our steps near her garage. "Then walk Mozart around the lake after."

"MoMo," she corrects, grinning. "Or Mo, Modoodle, Malicious, or even Sir Mo, Duke of Snacks. Depends on the mood."

"He's never going to learn his name if you keep calling him a hundred different things."

"That's what Dad is for, huh?" she says. "I had a lot of fun, Alec."

"Me too," I say. And I mean it more than I want to admit.

"I have inventory at Cody's for the next two days. Twelve-hour shifts, but I can come in the mornings to take Mozart for a walk."

"Don't worry about it. I can take him." I give in. I'd rather Clem get a few more minutes of sleep. "We'll take it easy on training and pick it back up later this week."

"Are you gonna miss me?"

"Every second."

"Stop being cute." She leans in and kisses my cheek. "I'll see you soon." She walks backward into the garage, slowly dropping my hands like she doesn't want to go, and disappears behind her door.

I stand there long after it shuts, staring like it might swing back open if I wait her out. It doesn't. The air is cool enough to sting the inside of my nose.

I turn toward the lodge. The trail crunches under me, and the world opens wider with each step.

Mist clings low to Misthaven Lake, curling around the shoreline like it doesn't want to let go. The water itself is black glass, rippling only where a loon cuts across the surface, her wings trailing like ink.

I breathe deep. It hurts my lungs in the best way.

My chest is full of something I don't have a name for yet.

But I know it's hers.

Chapter 35
Clementine

CLEMENTINE

> Thank you for the coffee and the ride this morning.

ALEC

> didn't want u to scrape ice off ur car alone

CLEMENTINE

> Last I checked, there's no ice in the forecast.

ALEC

> free tonight to pick you up.

CLEMENTINE

> I get off at two.

ALEC

> ik. see u then

ALEC'S TRUCK rumbles down the gravel drive, headlights shrinking into the dark. The crickets pick up where the engine leaves off, the air sharp enough to sting my lungs. I press my fingers to my lips. They're still swollen, still humming from the last thirty minutes tangled up with him in the cab. For a man so rugged, his lips are pillowy soft.

I should go to bed. That would be the sane thing to do. I'm exhausted after twelve hours of inventory. But I'm buzzing, like someone poured espresso into my veins. Or maybe like someone kissed me until I forgot my own name. Same difference.

I deserve one of Gran's almond muffins and a cup of tea before snuggling up in bed. I actually slept well last night, although I did wish Alec was next to me.

I'm still smiling when I tug open the side door and—

"Jesus Christ!" I clap my hands over my eyes. "I'm sorry!"

Gran shrieks, Cody groans, and I sprint back out into the night before I can process the full extent of what I just saw. The garage keypad blurs as I jab in the code.

Of course, my grandmother is allowed to date. She is not, however, allowed to do whatever *that* was on the kitchen table where I eat my scrambled eggs.

The garage door scrolls upward, and—because apparently tonight is a parade of emotional ambushes—there it is. A fortress of cardboard boxes stacked wall to wall. My name scrawled across every side.

I peel off an envelope stuck to the box closest to me and unfold the note.

Clementine,

We hope you're happy, whatever you're doing. We miss you in rehearsals and in the dressing room. Your things have been in the storage closet since you left, but the building's changing hands, and we have to vacate. We thought you'd want them.

We wish you the best—always.

Love,

The Ladies

· · ·

MY THROAT TIGHTENS as I skim it again. It's all here. The life I left on a subway platform. Tutus, leotards, maybe even the dumb lavender candle we kept burning in the living room. My ghosts, mailed to me in bulk.

The garage door swings open. Gran shuffles out in her robe, cheeks pink, hair sticking up at every angle like she wrestled with the sheets and lost. For half a second, I think maybe I hallucinated the whole thing.

"Thought you'd be with Alec," Gran says, laughing softly, like this isn't the single most surreal ambush of my life.

"When did this show up?"

"This morning. Delivery men were very efficient."

My chest feels crowded—by Alec, by Gran's sex life, by this avalanche of past selves. And suddenly, the one thing I've been hiding gnaws too loudly to keep quiet. "Gran, I—I have to tell you something. Last month, I had a bit of a spiral and bought some stuff on Apple Pay. Socks and a couple of other things. I returned it all except the socks. I should've told you."

Her brows lift, kind but not surprised. "Clem, I have online banking. You think I wouldn't notice a few charges to your account?" The words hit like a dunk in ice water. "I figured maybe you needed something for Wild Trails," she continues, tying her robe tighter. "I wanted to see if you'd come to me on your own. But honestly? You don't have to hide things like that from me. You returned what you didn't need, which was smart. I trust you to figure these things out."

The breath leaves me in a rush. I'd been flogging myself over socks. *Socks!*

"You mean I've been spiraling for a month, and you were just sitting there watching?"

"Hard to keep anything from me."

"Apparently." I sigh, but then I narrow my eyes. "The dining room table, Gran? With my boss?"

She presses her lips together in a rosy smile. "I didn't want you to think it meant I stopped loving your grandpa. But it does get lonely here. And Cody, well, he makes me laugh."

I cross my arms, leaning against a box labeled GALA DRESSES. "Does he make you happy?"

Her eyes soften. "Yeah."

"Well then," I sigh, the corner of my mouth tugging upward, "I'm happy for you. Even if I now need to bleach my retinas."

That earns me a grin. "And what about you? Heard Alec's truck pulling away a little while ago."

My cheeks go hot. I play it casual, like my insides aren't doing cartwheels. "I like him. Don't really know what we are, but I like being with him."

"Sometimes that's all you can do. Enjoy it while you have it. Everything else works itself out."

She pulls me into a warm hug before her gaze flicks to the towers of cardboard. "Goodness, how did all this fit in your old apartment?"

"It didn't. We had to climb over piles just to get to the fridge. Pretty sure one roommate slept on top of her costume trunk."

"What will you do with it all?"

The answer presses against my ribs, formed the second I opened the letter. I run my hand over the edge of a box. "I think I want to sell most of it. I don't need half this stuff, and I'm not going back to New York anytime soon."

"You're not?"

I shake my head, a laugh slipping out because I almost can't believe I'm saying it. "I think I want to stay here a while longer."

The words unlock something tight in me.

"I miss dancing. I probably always will. But I don't miss everything else—the casting, the competition, the waking up every day already behind. My whole life was a checklist of how close I was to something I never actually got. I don't want to live like that again.

"Since I've been here, life has slowed down. I notice things. Like the way the trees smell after rain, or how quiet it is on the trail when the deer are still out. I actually drink tea in the mornings with you instead of chugging coffee and sprinting to the subway. I didn't even know I liked mornings until now."

Gran's eyes crinkle with a smile.

"And yeah, maybe being a cashier at Got Wood? isn't my forever job," I add. "But maybe I can try a few other things around town. Or something in Anchorage eventually. At least I'd still be close to you."

My voice croaks. "I missed so much with Grandpa. I don't want to make the same mistake with you. I don't want to spend my life rushing past what actually matters."

Her blue eyes shine. "I love you, darling."

"Love you too."

She swipes at her cheeks. "A garage sale, then."

"I doubt anyone in this town wants my old costumes."

"Don't underestimate my quilting club. Half of them keep saying they want to get more active. Leotards could be their gateway drug. Shawls on top, spandex underneath."

"Okay. We'll try it, and I can sell the rest online. I'll put up a flyer at Got Wood? tomorrow."

She pats my arm like she's already building a spreadsheet in her head. "Perfect. We'll talk through numbers on Sunday."

The boxes don't loom like gravestones like I thought they would. They're just things. Clothes, shoes, relics of a girl who thought her worth lived and died in casting calls. They don't define me anymore. If anything, they're proof I can pack up a version of myself, ship her away, and still find another—one who sleeps better, laughs harder, notices the air after rain. One who might actually belong here.

CLEMENTINE

I caught Gran and Cody doing it on the kitchen table.

You think you could build us a new one? lol

I STARE AT THE MESSAGES. Nothing. One hour turns into three, then into twelve. Not that I should care—he warned me he's terrible with his phone, but still. A little bubble back wouldn't kill him.

CLEMENTINE

Did my arm workout today. Tell me why I'm already walking like a T-Rex.

selfie in barre leotard, mid-stretch

Don't worry, I'm using my 60 second rest to text you. Unlike some people.

ALEC

phone was lost

gran + cody??

CLEMENTINE

Yeah. Retinas ruined forever.

Also, told Gran about my sock spiral last night. She already knew.

And all my New York stuff showed up. Might need a day off training for a garage sale.

ALEC

OK with me

I bite the inside of my cheek. The man can build a deck in one afternoon, but stringing words together apparently takes days.

CLEMENTINE

Anyway—double date tomorrow? Me and Yura will cook.

ALEC

might be weird

CLEMENTINE

You and Finn need a first step. Why not with real food?

ALEC

pushy

CLEMENTINE

You like it ;)

So?

ALEC

ok

just bc u asked

CLEMENTINE

Knew I'd wear you down.

Chapter 36
Alec

Subject: Iceland

From: Jillian@adventurerelations.com

To: alec@twomenontop.com

Alec,

I need a response about the Iceland climb. ASAP!

—J

FINN'S BEEN HOME for four days, and I've managed to dodge him like a coward. I blame the remodel upstairs or tell myself I need to train. Slip out before he wakes, come back after he's down for the night. It's pathetic. I know it. But every time I think about sitting across from him, the words knot up in my throat. I kept hoping a six-mile run would shake them loose, or the hours I spent laying flooring upstairs for the last two days. Busy hands, empty head. That was the plan. Except my head's never quiet where he's concerned.

And now, with Jillian breathing down my neck about Iceland, I'm running out of excuses. Finn and I need to talk. Soon.

I've dreaded this double date all damn day.

Downstairs, Clementine and Yura turned the kitchen into something warm and alive—Mozart barking for scraps, venison sizzling in the cast iron, potatoes roasting until the whole lodge smelled like salt and rosemary. I hid upstairs until the last possible second, listening to their laughter and music filter up through the floorboards, pretending I had one more thing to sand, one more nail to set.

But here I am, at the table. The food's steaming in front of me, and all I can think about is how my clothes feel too small. Clementine sits beside me, her oversized pink sweater swallowing her frame, her cheeks flushed from cooking and wine. I want to be anywhere else with her—back at the lake, where it was just us.

Across the table, Yura traded her scrubs for a navy dress that makes Finn stare like he's seeing the moon for the first time in months. He gushed for ten minutes about the oak table I built in the yard, every board hand-planed until my arms ached. I grunted something that passed for thanks, and now he's holding court, all grin and hand gestures.

"It really happened by mistake," Finn continues, puffing up with that look he gets when he's about to cast himself as Bear Grylls with better hair. "The usual route was closed from an avalanche, but we'd already quit our jobs. No way was I about to cancel our first international climb."

I keep my jaw tight while he spins the story. He always did love being the mouthpiece.

"We extended the trip," he says, running his hand through his beard. "And Alec, being Alec, went full *Beautiful Mind* with alternate routes. He's got these notebooks—one for each mountain—covered in topographies and equations that only he understands."

Clem perks up, polishing off her venison. She doesn't even notice the half slice of cornbread she shoves in with it, crumbs scattering. She's listening—really listening.

That tug in my chest tightens.

"I reached out to sponsors," Finn goes on. "Told them we were gonna climb a new ice face, some sidewall that hadn't been summited. They said if we could document it, they'd consider funding the next one."

"Wait, this was Patagonia, right?" Clem straightens in her chair. "What was the route called?"

Her eyes are on Finn, but then they flick to me. Like I'm the one who really holds the answer.

"The locals called that side 'Chucao Tapaculo,'" I say. "It's a bird with a red chest. When the sun hits, the ice catches the color. Whole wall looks like it's bleeding."

"Jesus," she breathes. "That's badass."

I've missed this—Finn sharing stories, captivating everyone's attention the way he used to at base camps. But the hit of happiness curdles fast, shadowed by the fact that maybe he'll never have a new story of ours to share. I knock back a swallow of whiskey, forcing myself to stay in the moment.

"So, we set out. Hooks in, ropes set," Finn continues. "Then a block of ice the size of a damn bus comes loose and takes out all our anchors. Could've bailed, *should've* bailed. But we were eighteen and dumb, and we looked at each other and said, 'Guess we're going up.'"

"And you did it?" Clem's eyes are wide, her voice threaded with awe and disbelief.

"Fifteen-hour climb," Finn says. "Sun started melting the ice. But then—" He pulls out his phone and shoves it toward her. "This is the shot that got us our sponsorship."

She gasps. "No way. Look at you. Baby Finn. And Alec— your hair!"

I groan.

"It's practically to your ass!"

"When we got back, his brother Dante sat him down and hacked it off immediately," Finn crows. "Said he looked like a deranged surf monk." He leans back, red hoodie bunched to his elbows, the same one he's worn since our Tahoe ski-instructor days—sleeves chewed with holes, logo faded to nothing. I used to think he'd outgrow it, but he never did.

Clem laughs, eyes still on the photo. "You look so happy here."

"We were," I admit. My throat's tight. I want to get back to that guy—to who I was before pain rewrote everything. "Surprised you didn't see that pic when you were stalking me."

"I didn't stalk. I was researching." Her smirk dares me to argue, and I want to kiss it clean off her face.

Mozart whines, pawing at her thigh until she drops him a cube of venison. He scarfs it down, licking her palm like she's the only person in the world. "You're perfect."

"Don't feed him from the table," I tell her, but of course she ignores me, kicking me under the table with a smug grin.

"Thanks for letting Mozart sleep in my room," Finn says, scratching his ears. "I like the company."

"I told you a service dog would be helpful for your PT," Yura says, leaning into Finn. The two of them fit together like they've been practicing this for years. They seem so comfortable after barely a week. Sometimes I wish I were more like Finn. I watch the three of them click into their own orbit and feel, not for the first time, the pull of a gravity I didn't know I wanted.

"Our little community dog," Finn says, raking a hand through his hair, some of the gauntness already gone from his face.

"See you brushed your hair." I tip my glass toward him.

"Nah, this one did." He pats Yura's arm. "But I see those dark circles under your eyes are gone? Guess the overnight trip was good?"

"Alec rolled down a hill!" Clem giggles, proud of herself.

"With or without clothes on?" Finn arches one bushy eyebrow, and Clem rubs the back of her neck, already blushing. "See? I said you'd love settling down."

The words scrape bone. Clem must feel it, because her hand brushes my arm, steadying me. She has no idea how close I am to bolting.

"Honestly, I'm relieved you're not going to embark on any more death wishes," Yura says, bracelets chiming as she waves her hand. "I can't imagine how many heart attacks the partners of climbers must have. At least now his idea of risky is acting like a stubborn idiot in physical therapy."

"Hey," Finn protests, squeezing her hand with that soft look —the kind that says he knows he put her through hell, and he's damn grateful she stayed. "I'm a *reformed* idiot."

"Jury's still out," she teases, brushing her long black hair behind her back.

I press my fork into the last bite of venison, holding back a grimace and hoping someone will change the conversation.

Clem leans forward, lip caught in her teeth. "I guess I didn't realize how dangerous things could really be. Grandpa climbed Denali almost every year, and he always came back with nothing worse than a sprained ankle."

"Clem, have you seen their documentaries?" Yura scoffs. "They're hanging on to walls with nothing but a flimsy rope and a screw jammed into moving ice."

I bristle. "It's not more dangerous than base jumpers, or MMA fighters, or F1 drivers."

"Yes, but MMA fighters don't deal with crevasses that can swallow half a mountain." Finn says it as a joke, but when he rubs his leg under the table, I shudder.

The dining room shrinks, meat lodging itself in my throat. Outside, the trees edge forward under the wind. I want to get up and go—anywhere. Be anywhere but sitting at my own damn table while everyone debates which way the mountain will take you.

"I'm so glad you're done with that," Yura says, kissing his cheek.

It's exactly the scene I feared: Clem's eyes on me already, imagining all the ways I could die. I hate that she's worried.

I feel like I'm split down the middle—half of me wanting to leave, half of me wanting to stay. I remember the fog that covered us on our hike. *Just one foot in front of the other.*

"Not done completely," Finn says, staring at me. "Jillian wants me to make an appearance at Wild Trails. With Alec."

"She does?" My voice scrapes out flat.

"I've been trying to tell you, but you've been *busy.*" Finn drags his tongue along his teeth, the way he always does when he's annoyed.

"You've also been busy."

"I have." His thumb drags slowly over Yura's knuckles. "But *I* haven't been avoiding you. We really need to sit down, Alec. Catch up. Talk about contracts. Iceland. Everything."

I've been through fucking avalanches, and I'm sitting here scared to talk to my best friend. Enough. I'm here for at least the next month, and I'm tired of things being strange between us.

Clementine's hand brushes mine under the table, a small reminder that I'm not alone.

I tip back my glass, whiskey burning. "Let's go out on the porch."

"Now?

I shove my chair back, the legs scraping too loud on the floor. "Yes, now. Just you and me."

Chapter 37
Alec

"You done hiding behind chores?" Finn asks the moment the back door closes and the motion lights flicker on. His wheels thump across the floorboards as he follows me to the railing.

"I wasn't—" The lie tastes sour before I even finish it. "I wasn't hiding."

He scoffs. "Please. I've been here four days, and you've spent more time hiding upstairs than looking me in the eye. You're acting like I'm some rookie at base camp you don't trust with your gear."

"I've had stuff to do." I stare at the inky black lake, wishing for a moment I could sink beneath its depths and avoid this conversation.

"Sure," he says. "Because God forbid Alec sits still long enough to use actual words."

My thumb rubs along the porch rail. The ornamental cabbages Clem planted by the steps catch my eye—stubborn little things, frosted at the edges and still hanging on. She told me once they don't know the difference between dying and surviving. They just keep pushing. She'd tell me to stop stalling.

An owl calls from somewhere in the trees. The silence it leaves behind is worse.

"You want words?"

"Would be hella nice right about now."

"You remember Patagonia?" I ask. My voice comes out rough, safer in old stories.

"You mean the story I just told at dinner? Yeah. I was there."

"You looked…happy."

"So did you. We were eighteen. Didn't even know how to be unhappy yet. We just kept moving." Finn sighs. "Man, will you look at me?"

My blood runs cold, but I turn to him. His hands are in his lap, and he's staring up at me. Gone is his usual grin, replaced by dismay.

"I—" I open my mouth, but the words don't come. I've had weeks to think about this conversation, and still, I don't know how to start it.

"Come on. I know I'm the talkative one, but fuck, dude, you did not just pull us away from our women to not talk. So, move those lips."

I start with the truth. "I—I can't look at you without seeing K2."

"Not this again. I'm doing fine. Got custom wheels." He runs a hand over the prayer flags strapped to the back of his chair. The same ones we carried up every mountain.

"Your lips were blue," I whisper, needing him to understand that this wasn't like every other climb. Not like any other accident. "I didn't know if you were breathing. I keep seeing it— your body under the ice, me yanking you out of the crevasse, not knowing if you were alive and—" My voice cracks. My chest burns. I bite it back, but it doesn't stop the shaking.

Finn's brow furrows. "You're still blaming yourself."

"I pushed us too far."

"There it is," he groans. "Alec the martyr. Starring in his own guilt opera."

"I'm not—" My hand fists the railing until the wood bites my palm.

"Alec. We never pitied each other. Don't start now. Every second you pity me, it's like we should've died on that mountain. And I'm not dead. Neither are you." His words burst out of him. "When you told me about Wild Trails, I thought—finally. He's moving on. And then Clem. Man, I was happy for you. But you're still here spiraling. So, what's the real problem?"

"Finn."

"Stop dragging your damn feet. Say it."

My mouth's as dry as dust. But I force it out. "I'm not done climbing."

He doesn't answer right away. Just lets it hang. The pause is worse than shouting.

"Okay. So climb."

"What?"

"Don't stop fucking climbing, dude."

"But you said we were done." The words rip out, loud and ugly. "In that hospital bed—where I sat beside you for weeks— you said you were done. *We* were done. And you made me promise." The words grind up my throat, jagged. "I sat there watching tubes run into you, watching machines breathe for you, and you made me swear I wouldn't drag us up a mountain again. I said yes because I thought you were dying."

Finn almost laughs. "I was higher than a kite on morphine, man. I barely remembered my own name. What I meant was, we're done with eight-thousand-meter suicide missions. That chapter's closed." His eyes find mine, steady. "But climbing? No. Not ever. Yura thinks I'll walk again. Soon. And when I do, I'll be back. Not Everest. Not K2. But Denali. Rainier. Something sane. Because I still fucking love the mountains."

"You're serious."

"As a heart attack." Finn shrugs, but there's steel under it. "I don't need glory anymore. Don't need sponsors or summit photos. I want a home. But I don't want to be done."

"So, you won't be mad if I say yes to Iceland?"

He shakes his head. "I'd be mad if you didn't."

"We always did climbs like that together."

"And now you'll do one without me," he says simply.

"I don't want to."

"I know. But you will."

I look at him—scar above his brow, tremor in his hand—and I hate it. "I hate the idea of getting to the top and not seeing you."

"You'll hate it more if you never get there," he says.

"So you're good with me climbing Vatnajökull."

"You were always gonna say yes."

My teeth grit together. "Feels like saying yes to Iceland means leaving you behind."

Finn slams a hand on my back. "Alec. You were my best friend when we were five. You'll be my best friend when we're eighty. You can't leave me behind. Even if I'm not on the rope, I'm still in your corner. Always. And maybe, if this hip ends up doing what Yura swears it can, I'll be back next to you again. But you don't need my permission."

I shake my head, the words burning. "It's not about permission. It's about…" My chest locks. But I force it. "I thought I'd lose you. If we weren't doing the big climbs, if we weren't planning the next summit. That's who we were. It's what we did. And if we weren't doing that together, then what were we? I thought—" My voice breaks. "I thought I'd lose my best friend."

Finn stares at me. Really stares. "Jesus, man. You've been carrying that around? For weeks? Months? You could've just talked to me."

"I don't know how to. Not about this. I'm learning. Right now."

"Looks to me like you're doing a damn good job. Saying it. Finally. But you've got to hear me to—you don't have to climb for us to be us. You don't have to bleed on a mountain to keep me as your friend. I don't care if you never strap on crampons again—you'd still be like a brother to me. Always. I told you at five that you'll never get rid of me."

I scrub a hand over my face. "I didn't know how to separate it. Climbing, us. It's all I've ever known."

"Then learn," he says. "Because I'll tell you something. I've got friends. I've got Yura. I've got my dad and your family. But I'll never have another you. You're my big buffoon of a best friend. Nothing changes that."

I stare at him. Twenty-seven years of jokes, stupid dares, and shared flasks of whiskey at three a.m. when we couldn't sleep. I've held back his hair when he was sick from altitude, and he made me laugh when my head felt like exploding.

"You won't resent me?"

"Resentment doesn't stick. Not with us." His voice roughens. "Now hug me, you big idiot."

A broken, wet laugh spills out before I can stop it. I press my hand to my face because I don't want him to see my eyes glass over. "I missed you."

"I never left," he says quietly. "You just stopped letting me in."

No blame in it. Just the truth folded plainly between two people who've climbed and crashed and kept climbing anyway. It cracks me open in a way that's both awful and the only kind of salvage.

"I love you, man."

"Wow…I think that's, like, the third time you've ever said that to me." He punches my leg.

"No, it's not." It probably is. Saying *I love you* got harder over the years, like each death stripped the words from my chest. It's easier to say goodbye to people that way.

"Alec Hastings is capable of love!" he screams out to the lake, cackling.

"You're scaring the bats, dude." I roll my eyes.

"Love you too, man." Finn tilts his goofy grin up to the sky. "Look at us. Still touching the stars out here."

Something shifts in me. A weight rolling off. An ice block finally breaking free after years jammed tight in my ribs.

For the first time since K2, I can breathe.

Chapter 38
Clementine

By midafternoon, it seems like the entire town of Misthaven showed up for my garage sale.

Between training with Alec and shifts at Got Wood?, I managed to dig through every box in the garage, keeping only a few talismans: my first pointe shoes with their frayed ribbons, the softest sweaters, and the seventy-five-dollar bergamot Malin + Goetz candle I'd been saving three years for a *perfect occasion*. Turns out the perfect occasion was last night, baking muffins with Gran while *Sixteen Candles* played for the hundredth time.

Gran, Yura, Finn, and Alec all showed up at six a.m. to help. Alec and Yura argued over whether sales are tracked better in a notebook or on a tally sheet. Gran declared herself CFO of Clementine's Old Life, settling into her chair behind Grandpa's old metal tackle box.

My little life, piece by piece, hour by hour, has been vanishing into other people's arms: the leather jacket I bought in Hoboken, the self-heating mug I swore would make me get to practice more awake, the pair of Louboutins I wore once before realizing New York sidewalks would eat them alive.

It's harder than I thought, watching the things I collected slip into someone else's story. I trail my fingers over the sequins of an untouched costume rack. Hopefully someone online will take all of this.

"Deary, look at you, all grown up." Gerri, one of Gran's friends, sidles up next to me. She's in a striped sweater with the sleeves shoved up. Her gray hair is streaked with pink, and a spray of flower tattoos winds down her arms.

"Hey, Gerri." I wipe my hands on my jeans, watching her pluck sequins from the rack, her mouth hanging open like a gull down at the docks about to steal someone's french fries.

"Your gran said you had old costumes," she coos, already elbow-deep, tugging at a leopard leotard, a tie-dye wrap, a tutu I wore in *Coppélia*. "Mercy, these are as gorgeous as that man over there. Cody said he's been picking you up from work a lot."

I groan. "Small-town news travels with all the grace and subtlety of a moose crossing Main Street."

"What else is there to gossip about if not the youth?" Gerri snorts, giving the leopard print a good shake. "You think I could wear this with some hot-pink knitted leg warmers? Janice could crochet me a pair by next Thursday. She's been on a tear since her husband brought home a fifty-pound king salmon; she swears she works faster when he smokes fish."

"You'd kill it."

"Oh, and Dottie would love this tie-dye thing," Gerri adds, piling it over her arm. "Though, she'll say it's too loud, then wear it to the church potluck just to stir up Mrs. Barker. You know Mrs. Barker—she's been side-eyeing everyone since the quilting club voted against her rhubarb pie for the bake sale."

"I'm sure she'll look beautiful in this."

"Let's hope so." Gerri leans in, eyes glittering under frosted blue eyeshadow. "Your gran's been saying you might be sticking around longer. So, what do you think about teaching us old gals a class or two? Doctors say dancing keeps the creaks away. And between you and me, we'd rather learn from you than from YouTube. Half the time we can't get the Wi-Fi at the community center to hold unless Kenny's kid parks his truck in the lot and leaves his hotspot running."

The idea blooms warm and ridiculous in my chest. "Gran mentioned that too. I don't have much experience teaching, but if you'd like to be my guinea pigs…"

"Guinea pigs?" Gerri barks a laugh. "We're more like hyenas. We'd love to do something daily. We'll pay, of course. There are eleven of us, including Margaret."

I curl my toes into the wet grass and take it all in.

Eleven women. Maybe twenty dollars a class. Once or twice a week. That's a few hundred a month right there. Between my Got Wood? paycheck, the lessons, and a garage sale here and there, it starts to stack up. I could always offer my decorating services to locals, especially with how beautiful the lodge looks now. Add in the balance transfer card Gran keeps nudging me toward, the costumes going to good homes, maybe even a kids' class or two…

It doesn't feel like drowning anymore. It feels doable.

"I have Wild Trails training until next month, but after that I'd love to set something up," I promise. "I think the community center has a room we could use."

Maybe I don't even need Wild Trails to save me. Though it'd be nice, I can do this on my own.

Her eyes crinkle as she claps. "Perfect. In that case, I'll buy the whole rack. We'll keep the costumes at the center, swap pieces, maybe even put on a little performance for next year's Wild Trails."

"Really?" The idea of a little troupe of older women in sequins makes the inside of my chest feel like the sun has moved an inch closer.

"Now," she grins, "your gran said you can put your leg over your head. Think there's a chance I could do that?"

"Maybe!" I laugh, waving Alec over to help Gerri roll the rack to the pay station. She squeezes his bicep and asks him how much weight he can lift. He shoots me a look that screams, *help me*, and I just chuckle.

I walk over to Mozart, who's sprawled on the grass like an indulgent toddler, tongue lolling, belly on display. Earlier, Finn set out a mason jar beside him labeled *Tips for Rubs*. It's already full.

I curl my toes into the wet grass and take it all in.

"Thank you for helping out," I say to Finn beside me. He's absolutely demolishing one of the pumpkin muffins we made last night. There are crumbs stuck to his thick brown beard.

I've been learning that Finn's got the eager vibe of a golden retriever. Alec is more of a hound, steady and watchful.

"I'd work for muffins any day," Finn groans, the sound muffled around another bite.

"Wait until Gran breaks out the tomato jam. Used to smuggle jars back to California in my carry-on."

"This muffin with a piece of aged gouda on the top of Makalu would have made the descent a thousand times better."

"Cheese and pumpkin?" I stare at him.

"My taste buds are all fucked up," he cackles. He's in a pair of cargos that match Alec's and a baggy red sweatshirt, and a matching knitted beanie is pulled over his long hair.

"Where is Makalu?"

"We climbed the Nepal side. Spent almost five years bouncing around the Himalayas." Where Alec held his stories back like rationed water, Finn hands them out like candy.

"What did your parents think about you being away so long?" I ask.

"It was just me and Dad. My mom died when I was three."

"I'm sorry," I say.

"It's okay. I don't really remember her. I only remember that one day she wasn't there anymore."

"My dad left before I was born. It's always been me and my mom. Well, and my grandparents every summer."

Finn flicks a crumb to the bird pecking under the table leg. "Single parents are superheroes. I used to be pissed at my dad for never being home. Especially when I compared it to Alec's family. They took me in as one of their own sons. I probably spent more nights there than I did at my own house. Not that my dad wasn't a good dad. He worked all the time. But now, I get it. He worked nights. Slept in his car between shifts. Dropped me at the climbing gym after school so I wouldn't come home to an empty house. That's where I met Alec."

"Sounds like his hard work rubbed off on you."

"It did. And you and your mom? You guys close?"

"I call her once a week, but Gran's always been the one I go to for help. I love Mom, but she thinks a new jacket, a vacation, and a spa will fix all her problems." I force a laugh.

"Sometimes that works." Finn shrugs. "But I get what you mean. I can call Selene, Alec's mom, about anything, and she'd answer no matter what she was doing. Dad takes a few days to respond."

"That's sweet of Selene." I smile, picturing Alec's family and hoping that I get to meet them one day. "You guys seem better after the other night," I say, jutting my chin across the lawn. Alec's been lighter since the double date.

Finn's grin creases his eyes. "Dude's a stone wall, but once he lets you in? You're in. Just don't expect much conversation."

"You don't say," I joke, sarcastically.

"He likes you, Clem. I've never seen him look at anyone the way he looks at you. At base camp, people always thought he hated them. He doesn't hate anyone. Just never quite figured out small talk. Or medium talk. Or really any kind of talk. We've lost a lot, and it wears on you, you know? But Alec's good. Always has been. Most people would've left me up there," Finn says. His gaze drifts across the lawn to Yura, who's standing toe-to-toe with Alec, finger jabbed at his chest, her braids swinging. "God, isn't she gorgeous?"

"When should I expect the wedding invitation?"

"It's been two weeks, but it feels like forever. She's smarter than me. Makes me laugh. Makes me feel safe." His eyes are dazed. "But what do I know? My longest partnership was with Alec, and we never even made it to first base," he jokes.

"Not *once* in all those years sharing a tent?"

"It's tragic, I know." Finn winks.

"Did you know he's sleeping on the floor in one of the bedrooms?"

"Yeah, next to my room, so he can take Mozart out in the middle of the night."

"I knew he liked the dog." I chuckle. "Do you think Alec would mind if I set up a room for him? We're gonna be wrapping up the upstairs renovations this month, and I think the corner room would be perfect for him."

"He'd like it. Just won't ask. Never was good at setting down roots."

"You two talking about me?" Alec calls, striding across the lawn in a navy sweater that makes his eyes glow like coins.

"Yes," Finn and I chorus.

"Figured." Alec pulls a coppery leaf from his pocket, tip curled like ribbon, and presses it into my palm. "Thought you might want another tulip." He bends to kiss my forehead like it's nothing, though it feels like everything.

Finn whoops. "A leaf! That's basically a proposal in Alecese."

"Shut up," Alec mutters, grinning anyway.

I twirl the leaf between my fingers, pretending not to notice Gran and Yura snickering. "At this rate, I'll have a whole bouquet of leaf tulips."

"That's the plan." Alec glances at Finn's crumb-covered beard. "See you found Margaret's muffins."

"Can you learn how to bake, man?" Finn swats his leg.

"Don't tell me he's still living on goop packets," I cut in.

"Hell no. Bread and peanut butter." Finn laughs as Mozart rolls belly-up in the dew. "The dog loves it too."

"Yura wants you, said something about your afternoon stretches," Alec says.

"Perfect excuse to get out of cleanup duty." Finn smirks, already rolling across the lawn.

"Yeah, yeah." Alec rolls his eyes and bends to scratch Mozart's head. "You did good today, nearly three thousand dollars. And whatever else is in this tip jar."

It's probably not even a quarter of what I paid for all this stuff, but it doesn't matter. It feels good. A clean slate for this next chapter of my life.

"Wow, maybe we can celebrate over steaks tonight. My treat." I drag my fingers over the weave of his sweater, dizzy with exhaustion and happiness.

"We can go after we clean up. Looks like things are wrapping up here anyway."

"Thank you for helping."

"Anytime, but you better not be too sore for training tomorrow. We can do the weights together."

"Just admit it, you saw all my sports-bra selfies on Instagram, and now you want the live version."

"Or..." His hand glides along my collarbone, goosebumps chasing after it. "I want to take you out of them." My breath catches. He grins smugly. "Thinking about another backpacking trip this weekend. Maybe bring this guy." He nods toward Mozart.

"Yeah, I have the weekend off. But maybe we can do another kayak run tomorrow? I need to practice not tipping on those class fours." I bite my lip, then remember. "Though Cody might need me to stay later."

"I can just pick you up from work."

"I'll text when I'm about to get off." I shove his chest with mock annoyance. "Though you're horrible over text."

"Someone once told me I have horrible people skills. Guess that expands to the digital world too." I raise my hand to swat him again, but he catches my wrist. "I'd much prefer to leave notes at your door."

"What you're telling me is that you're basically a pigeon."

"Never been called that before." Alec squeezes my wrist once before letting go.

Inside my sweater, my phone vibrates. I fish it out. The screen flashes the same words it always has: DO NOT ANSWER.

For months I turned these calls face down, shoved them under pillows, fantasized about hurling the phone onto the subway tracks.

"Who is it?" Alec asks.

"The creditors," I sigh, knowing what I need to do. "I'm gonna put all the money I made today toward my debt."

"You want backup?"

I shake my head. "No. I need to do this."

"Proud of you, Fox."

I kiss him once, thumb hovering over the screen before I click open the call.

Chapter 39
Clementine

OUR TRAINING SCHEDULE doesn't feel like training anymore. It feels like dating.

With Alec, the stopwatch always ends up forgotten. Hikes spill into banana boats by the fire with Mozart. Kayak sessions end with us plunging into the river. Breakfast at Daisy's Diner before my shifts at Got Wood?, where Alec loiters in the aisles pretending he needs screws we already have. Evenings with Yura and Finn at the table, Monopoly somehow always stacked in Alec's favor.

"How was work today?" Alec says when he parks in front of my place.

"The mayor came in to buy supplies to start building the Wild Trails stage," I say. "The river's packed. With twenty grand on the line, every outdoorsy person within a hundred miles is showing up to train. Cody's thrilled—we're selling out of everything."

"I'm sure that has less to do with need and more to do with the woman selling them stuff." He cocks his brow at me.

"Someone sounds jealous!"

"I don't get jealous."

"Sureeee," I tease, not ready to say good night. "You wanna come upstairs?"

He doesn't answer or hesitate. Just shuts off the truck and opens my door.

By the time we're climbing the steps above the garage, I babble, "I've never had a boy over before."

"Should I go ask Margaret for permission?"

"Oh, please don't. Cody's bike is outside, which is basically the backwoods version of a sock on the tentpole."

"Good thing. I was going to put a sock on your door, but I guess I get to keep it."

"So presumptuous."

"Bold sentiment from someone who made me perform minor surgery on her ass last weekend."

Our training usually ends with us finding some excuse to touch each other again. A "stretch" that turns into me straddling him in the grass. A "warm-down" that turns into sex against a tree, hence the splinter. We've had sex in a tent, in the woods, even in the damn river. But never in a bed. If he isn't making a bed for himself at the lodge, then I can give him one here, at least for tonight.

"Oh my god." I nearly drop the keys. "You're not seriously bringing up the splinter."

"Hard to forget." He leans closer. "Not every man would rise to the occasion."

"You sucked one splinter out of my butt cheek, you don't get a medal."

"I think I deserve at least a patch."

"Well, good news for you, no bark up here."

"Too bad." He grins, and I'm already warm all over.

The truth is, I never really invited guys over when I lived in New York, either. Not after the disaster of my second year, when one roommate snuck in a guy who just never left. He ate our groceries, hogged the bathroom, and basically became our sixth roommate until someone staged an intervention. After that, no boys were allowed, and I didn't complain.

But now? Now I want Alec here. In my space. In a bed with me, even if the mattress is older than I am, and the futon's stains are hidden under three thrifted blankets.

"Thought we could watch one of your documentaries tonight," I say, fumbling with the lock. "And I could cook you my specialty."

"Oh yeah? What's that?"

"Butter noodles."

"How could I possibly say no to that?"

When the door finally swings open, nerves flutter in my chest like I'm introducing him to a secret version of myself. The apartment is tiny, with a galley kitchen, a bathroom with a sink barely big enough for a toothbrush, and my room in the back, with a queen bed squeezed beside a chipped dresser.

"It's small, but—"

He steps in, hand brushing the futon. "It's very you."

And for the first time in forever, I don't feel embarrassed about that. I like being me.

THE TV SCREEN glows icy blue, the only light in the room. An Icelandic glacier sprawls across it, ridges glittering like knives. Alec is there too, not just beside me on the futon but on the screen, five years younger, leaner, sharper, moving across an aluminum ladder bridge so flimsy it makes my stomach pitch.

"How on earth are you walking on that?" I ask, twirling my fork but not taking a bite.

"Yeah, you gotta to summit Hvannadalshnúkur." He's in a black crewneck and sweats, and his posture is maddeningly relaxed given what's going on in this documentary. "We used it as a warm-up before Vatnajökull. God, I don't miss those bridges." He flicks his fork toward the image of him moving across the horizontal death contraption. "Step wrong, you're gone. Straight into a chasm."

"That's horrifying."

"Look," he says, leaning forward, pointing again with his fork. "You're clipped on leashes with the carabiners. Finn's right behind me, and he's always got me." The camera pans to Finn, who's smiling in the snow. They have helmets on, but what is a helmet to do with a drop into a hole that seems to have no bottom? When Alec told me about K2, I couldn't imagine it, but seeing it here, I can picture the drop that wrecked Finn. They move like they are walking at Disneyland, not over a thin metal bridge that creaks with every step. The boots on their feet are massive, jarring metal spikes biting into the ground and over the rung of the ladder.

A shiver zips down my spine. "So, if you'd fallen—"

"Finn would've caught me, obviously."

But my chest feels tight. Because it's *not* obvious. Because on-screen, all I can see is him moving over nothingness, the void ready to eat him alive. And he looks so young—careless in a way the Alec beside me isn't anymore.

He finally turns, catches me watching him. I straighten, force my expression smooth.

"You'd maybe like climbing," he says. "You've got good balance."

"I'll take the compliment, but I'll stick with butter pasta."

We finish the bowls, and I lick my fork clean just to keep from screaming out how insane all of this is, how insane he is. Alec washes our dishes immediately, stacking them neatly on the drying rack. A man who can dangle from glaciers like they're jungle gyms but can't leave a dirty plate in the sink.

What a man.

The fear presses under my ribs, hot and insistent. I can't sit in it, can't keep staring at the screen where he's dangling over a void.

The documentary cuts to a wide shot of the ridge, wind tearing across the glacier, and I can't breathe. This is what he does for fun. The man I've been straddling in the grass and laughing with over banana boats…he treats staring down death like a casual hobby. Yura was right. This is nothing like my grandpa did. No way.

The camera jolts as Alec falls from the ladder. My heart lurches, but he catches himself, hanging from the lip of the metal by nothing but two gloved fingers. Just two. His whole body dangles before he hikes himself up in one smooth motion.

My brain doesn't know what to do with the information. 'Cause, yeah, he could've died…but the way he just pulled himself up with two fingers.

Fingers that have been inside of me. That grip. That strength.

"You did that? With just your fingers?"

Alec doesn't even blink. "Yeah."

"Can you still?"

"Definitely."

"What are you waiting for? Show me!" I shove him off my futon.

"What do I get for it?"

"Bragging rights?"

His mouth twitches. "Pathetic."

"*Fine*. The satisfaction of proving me wrong."

"Tempting," he says flatly. "But no. Try again. I wanna see what you can do."

My jaw tightens. Of course he won't just take the win. He wants to drag it out, wants me squirming, wants me to offer.

It shouldn't thrill me, but it does.

What do I even have? A thirty-two fouetté sequence. A penché so deep my nose hits the floor? I could arabesque across the futon or snap into a triple pirouette. All the things I've trained my whole life to perfect, and none of them feel like enough against the way he just hauled his whole body up on two fingers.

Which leaves me with exactly one trick worth throwing on the table. The kind of move that isn't in any ballet manual but might just knock that smug look off his face.

"Best I can offer is a standing split, leg over my head, and you already saw that in my gran's kitchen. Not sure it tops your finger trick, but it's flexible in…*other ways*."

"That's your bargaining chip?" He strolls toward the doorway that leads to my bedroom.

The way he fills the frame makes the whole apartment feel smaller.

"It's a good one."

"Think of something better." His eyes flick down my body like he's already imagined ten things I could offer.

He lifts his hand, two fingers, pointer and middle, pressed together, and my stomach doesn't just drop, it plummets straight through the floor. Then he grips the doorframe, and with the kind of terrifying ease that makes no sense in the human world, he pulls his entire body upward. His whole five-eleven frame suspended on nothing but tendon and bone and willpower.

Muscles coil, forearms as tight as rope, veins snaking to the surface like lightning. His shirt rucks up, flashing a hard line of abs and the curve of his hips.

Every rational thought I have short-circuits. My inner ballerina catalogs the mechanics—lats firing, scapula pinned, knuckles white around the doorframe—but my cavewoman brain? She's already dropped her club and is fanning herself in the corner.

My thighs squeeze together on instinct. Heat slams through me so fast it almost feels unfair. Because there's strong, and then there's this.

I gape, words scrambled. "That was so hot."

"For that, you're going to have to offer me something better than a wall split."

"You're getting what I've offered, and that's final," I fire back, even though my throat is tight, and my pulse won't quit sprinting.

He smirks, still hanging there, shoulders broad, body taut as a bowstring. "I can do the splits too, you know."

"Absolutely not. You're way too bulky."

"Clementine." He finally drops down, light as air. "Did you not just spend an hour watching me cross a glacier with these legs?"

He's right. Objectively, painfully right. But still.

"I'll show you mine if you show me yours," I say.

"Go on, then."

Challenge accepted.

My toes flex against the rug before I stand, rolling through my spine the way I've done in warm-ups a thousand times. Only this time it's not for an audience, it's for him.

One step forward, and I'm close enough to feel his body heat. I lift my hand, press it flat against the opposite doorjamb, steadying myself. My palm squeaks faintly against the paint, my wrist bending back, every line of me elongating as if I'm about to start a variation.

I let my weight tip, hips canting just so, and drag one leg upward. My thigh brushes the frame, pajama shorts sliding higher with each inch of skin revealed.

Higher.

His eyes follow the climb, every muscle in his body locked tight. But his eyes drink me in like he's starving.

Higher.

My hamstring protests, the stretch sweet and biting, but I keep pushing because I can. Because I know what this looks like.

My heel arcs up until it points skyward, calf tight, toes like a compass needle stabbing the ceiling. My free hand smooths down my thigh, as if to show off how far I've gotten, how easy I make it look.

I glance down at him through the split, upside down, my chest heaving. His eyes are black, unreadable, but the hunger in them makes my stomach flip.

"Ta-da!" I raise a mocking brow at him.

His hand comes up, his knuckles skimming my shin as if he's testing how high I've taken it. Then his palm slides up along the inside of my stretched thigh. Calluses catch faintly against my skin, rough dragging over soft.

He doesn't rush. No. Alec doesn't know the meaning of the word.

He lingers, thumb pressing just enough to remind me how little my pajama shorts still cover.

"Fuck." It falls from his mouth like he hadn't meant to let it out. I'm pinned in the most vulnerable position I know, part dancer's pose and part offering.

"Now say it," I coo.

His thumb strokes the bare edge of skin by my upper thigh. "Say what?"

"That you were wrong. That you should've been impressed."

"I was wrong."

He presses closer, chest brushing mine, and I feel him. All of him. Hard, thick, and impossible to ignore as he drags himself along my thigh through the barrier of his cargos. The grind is punishing, like he wants me to know exactly what I'm not getting. My knees tremble in the stretch, not from the pose but from the sheer pressure of him. He looks at me like he's one second from sinking his teeth into my throat.

"Uh-uh, mister. Your turn."

A dark laugh rumbles from his chest. "Really? Now?"

"I take competition very seriously. Trained by the best."

Reluctantly, he peels back, then lowers himself into a perfect split, smug as sin. "You gonna try to top that?"

"Easy." I push higher into the wall split, toes brushing the doorframe, and, just to show off, I pivot out of it. My hand slides up for balance as I swing my right leg wide and lift it vertically into a standing split. My heel points toward the ceiling, my body split in half.

The shorts rise higher with every breath, leaving me stretched and very exposed. My chest heaves as I lock into the pose, grinning even as sweat beads at my temple.

Alec's eyes go black. "Jesus Christ."

"Impressed?"

"More than impressed." He smiles. "Can't help but think about what we could do with your flexibility and my strength."

"Bold of you to assume I'd let you do anything," I shoot back.

"Oh, sweetheart." He prowls closer, shadows stretching long across the wall. "You're already pinned."

My eyes flick to the heavy outline straining his pants. "I'd say I'm the one who's got you pinned."

His laugh is guttural. "Yeah, maybe you do."

His hands go to his drawstring. His sweats hit the floor, and then his boxers follow.

I suck in a breath. His cock is hard and already dripping at the tip. Just raw want, right there in front of me.

"See that?"

I swallow. "Yeah. Confirms it—I've got you under my control."

"What are you gonna do about it?"

I don't get a chance to answer. My right leg is in the air, stretched to the limit, when Alec moves. One arm grabs under my thigh, locking me open against the doorframe. His other hand slams to the wall beside my head, pinning me there. I gasp as his thumb drags over my clit before his fingers slide lower, into the wet mess he's already made of me.

I'm utterly exposed to him, braced only by his strength and the wall at my back. Who would have thought a month ago, when he walked in on me doing the wall split, that we'd be here…except now he's the wall.

"You just gonna hold me here until I tap out?" I pant.

"Not planning on letting you tap out."

"That's cheating."

"That smart mouth of yours isn't gonna negotiate you out of this now, Fox."

He shifts his stance, sliding my right leg onto his shoulder. My left is still firmly on the ground. I gasp as his hips pin my back harder into the wall. He yanks my shorts to the side, his other hand wrapped around my right thigh. He's a perfect height, so he only has to slightly bend his knees to press the tip of his cock right at my entrance.

"Going straight for it?" I manage.

"You wanted proof that I don't play fair. Nothing about you standing like this is fair, Clementine."

My head tips back against the wood. "God, you're insane."

"Take this fucking cock, Clemetine, and shut the fuck up already."

The kiss that follows is teeth and heat, his strength holding me suspended as he thrusts into me hard enough to rattle the doorframe. My nails claw into his shoulders, his body scorches against mine. Every slam of his hips sends sparks ricocheting through me, pleasure so intense it's nearly pain.

"Oh my god—" The cry claws its way out of my throat, and he hushes me with his mouth against my cheek.

"Shhh."

I can't seem to manage it.

My nails claw into his shoulders, his shirt riding up as he drives into me, each thrust slamming me against the frame. My legs lock tighter around him, spreading wider, giving him leverage. The scrape of the wall against my back, the creak of the doorframe, the ragged sound of our breathing.

He grabs my jaw, thumb and fingers framing my face, pulling me so close I can taste his breath.

"Quiet, Clementine," he growls.

"I can't," I gasp.

His mouth twists, feral. "Then I'll make you."

"You wish," I shoot back, biting his lip, dragging my tongue along the sting.

His thrusts drive deeper, harder, knocking moans out of me I can't hold back. He slaps his palm over my mouth, pushing in brutally until my cry is swallowed against his skin.

"You like this, don't you? Acting up just to make me put you in your place. My pretty little brat."

"Please—" I sob into his hand. "Please, Alec. Don't stop."

"That's better," he moans, forehead pressed to mine, sweat dripping between us. His hips grind deeper, relentlessly, like he's set on breaking me wide open. "Beg me right, and I'll ruin you. Beg me right, and I'll fuck you so full you'll be dripping me tomorrow."

"Alec—" My cry cracks. Pleasure burns heavy through me, and the sting of an orgasm trembles my veins.

"Come on, sweetheart. Say it again. Beg for it. Beg for me like you mean it."

"Please," I choke out, my body shuddering against his. "Please, Alec—harder, don't stop—please—"

"Say it again." His voice is guttural, his hips bruising deep. "Say my name when you come. Let everyone know who's got you."

"Alec," I cry. White heat tears through me without a warning. Every nerve flares as I clamp around him, crying into his hand. I feel myself gush, slick running down my thighs, and he groans like the feeling is dragging him under too.

"Jesus, Clem—fuck—" He slams into me once, twice, then shudders hard. His cock pulses deep inside, heat filling me, his groan rough in my ear. His grip tightens on my hip, grounding me through the aftershocks as I convulse around him.

We cling to each other, breath ragged, bodies trembling against the wall. He finally pulls out, slow enough that I feel every inch drag, and I whimper at the loss. His cum spills hot down my thighs, and before I can even think about being embarrassed, he murmurs, "Stay put," like it's an order.

My legs are jelly anyway, so I sag against the wall as he tugs his boxers back on, then crouches to grab a clean dish towel off the counter. He wets it quickly under the tap, wrings it out, and comes back to me.

"Lift," he says gently, sliding his arm under me to pick me up against his chest. I don't even try to argue. My head falls to his shoulder as he carries me to the bed.

On the edge of the mattress, he sets me down with care, one big hand braced at the back of my head like he's afraid I might break. Then he kneels in front of me, spreads my legs softly over his thighs, and runs the warm cloth between them.

I shiver at the sensation. "Alec…"

"Shh," he mutters, focused. "Just cleaning you up."

The casual way he says it nearly undoes me more than the sex did. His brows furrow in concentration, knuckles grazing my skin as he wipes me carefully until I'm clean. Then he presses a kiss to the inside of my knee, as if he's sealing the gesture.

When he finally climbs into bed, it's with his chest pressed to my back, one arm banded around my waist, the other tugging the blanket high. His lips graze my temple. "You did so fucking good," he whispers, raw and quiet, meant only for me.

I smile into the pillow, body sore, heart full. There's nothing left in me but warmth, and when his fingers find mine under the covers, lacing tight, I let myself drift, held completely.

Chapter 40
Clementine

ALEC HASTINGS IS MY SUNDAYS. The slow mornings, the warmth I swore I'd never need. I used to think happiness came in shopping bags and routines—new heels, perfect serums, a color-coded calendar. But nothing has ever touched the kind of ecstasy that comes from waking up to Alec's kiss.

"Hey, baby, we gotta get going." His voice is rough with sleep, low enough to curl around me like the last thread of a dream.

Baby. I'm somebody's *baby.*

I blink against the dim light, and there it is, an outfit already waiting on the chair. Jeans, a thick sweater, wool socks. Alec's quiet kind of care, practical and protective. I pull them on, still drowsy, and ten minutes later we're in his truck. Mozart is hanging out with his Uncle Finn today.

The heater hums against the early morning chill, Chopin trickling softly from the speakers. We rattle past houses that look like they were built with whatever lumber was lying around, porches stacked with moose racks, rocking chairs, and split firewood.

The road winds along the edge of a lake, water shivering

with wind. Spruce trees shoulder the road on both sides, tall and black and endless.

We pass a hand-painted sign nailed crooked to a fence post: ELK MEAT FOR SALE. RING BELL. Next door, someone's strung up Christmas lights they never bothered to take down, blinking half-heartedly against the dawn. A mailbox is plastered with bumper stickers: SAVE THE SALMON, COEXIST, like the whole town's worldview has been condensed onto one metal flap.

When the truck slows, it's still dark out. Alaska-dark, which is to say the sky is more bruised purple than black, the kind of half-light that makes you think the sun is just running late.

"We're here," Alec murmurs.

"This isn't the trailhead I pictured."

A small airstrip stretches ahead, hangars silhouetted against a paling sky. My pulse spikes. I've never been on one of the small planes Alaskans treat like taxis.

"No, I promise I'm more than just a catalog of trails," he says.

"Are you flying?"

"My buddy Rob owns a plane. He's taking us up."

"You…wait—you have a buddy?"

"Get your ass out here," he says, leaning over me and opening the door from the driver's seat.

The horizon yawns open, dusky blue bleeding into pink, the crescent moon still stubborn in the sky.

Alec calls out into the hangar, "Rob!"

A man in his late thirties pops up from behind a striped plane, beanie pulled low, Carhartt jacket battered by a dozen winters.

"Alec, how the hell are you, man?"

I barely have a second to marvel at it—the way his eyes actually light up as stoic, solitary Alec folds another man into a hug, arms wrapping tight like it's muscle memory. I blink hard. Maybe I'm still dreaming.

Alec Hastings just hugged. An entire human being.

My mouth opens, ready to tease him, but one brisk glance snaps it shut.

"When you said you were bringing someone, I figured it was your other half," Rob says, tipping his head toward me.

"Not today." Alec shakes his head. "Today I have Clementine here with me. My Clem."

The words land like a flare in the dark. My body reacts before my brain does. It's too much. Too much to be claimed so easily, so carelessly, by him.

"Hiya!" I blurt, way too bright, like that'll distract everyone from the fact that my insides are melting.

"Alec Hastings with a girlfriend. Never thought I'd see the day."

And my emotionally allergic Alec doesn't even twitch. He doesn't laugh it off or roll his eyes. He just waves a hand like, *Obviously. She's mine. Next question.* "How's Betty?"

My heart stumbles so hard it nearly face-plants. He let someone call me his girlfriend. In public. With zero hesitation.

I just stand here, pretending the entire axis of the earth hasn't tilted.

No correction. No retreat. No escape from the fact that my brain is screaming, *Holy hell, you have big feelings for him, like capital-F feelings. Maybe even L-word feelings.*

And, God help me, I'm not even sorry.

"Betty's good. Another rascal on the way." Rob pats his stomach like he's the one carrying the baby.

"You'll make up half the population soon," Alec teases.

"Nothing else to do in the winters," Rob shoots back. "Spent the summer adding two more rooms. Figured I'd better get ahead of it."

Alec huffs, amused. "Practical as ever."

"Hey, someone's gotta keep this town running." Rob grins,

then tips his chin at Alec. "What about you? Still wandering, or finally settling down?"

"Alec's been fixing up his lodge in Misthaven," I jump in, proud, before he can dodge.

Rob's brows lift. "*Your* lodge? Thought you were just here to scout climbs. You moving in, man?"

"Fixing it for Finn."

"He's here?"

"Yeah, you gotta come over some night for dinner."

"I'll be there." Rob smiles. "Now, let's get in the air before sunrise."

I hover back a step, eyeing the plane like it's equal parts thrill ride and death trap. My stomach flips, a sour-sweet lurch that tightens my throat. "So, how long have you been a licensed pilot?"

"Licensed?" Rob says with a bark of laughter. "This is Alaska, The Last Frontier, sweetheart. Rules are for outsiders."

My breath stalls.

"He's kidding," Alec cuts in quickly. An arm slides around my waist, drawing me closer until my shoulder presses into his chest. His hand settles at the small of my back.

"Is he?"

"He's flown since I was nineteen," he explains. "Safer than anyone I know. I'd never let anything happen to you."

"You better keep that promise."

"I will."

We climb in, and Rob lifts us off the ground. My breath stutters as the runway shrinks and the earth tilts away.

Alec's hand finds mine. Fingers threaded, grip unshakable, like he knew I'd reach for something. His palm is rough, grounding. I clutch back, and he only squeezes tighter, like it pleases him.

"Look."

I do, and the world steals my lungs. Glaciers glow as if lit from the inside. Rivers flash silver between forests. Mountains punch through clouds. It's like someone remade the world while I wasn't looking.

Alec is watching me instead of the view. Sunlight carves his profile into something intense, almost holy. His eyes move over mine, and I can't tell what's stealing my breath: the altitude or him.

"You like it," he murmurs. Not a question. I nod. "Wanted you to see it. My place. My glaciers."

The plane dips. I laugh without meaning to, high and bright, and he leans in, lips brushing my ear as both hands steady me. "Got you, Fox. I got you."

It comes fast, terrifying in its clarity. *I'm safer hanging above a glacier in a machine I don't understand than I have ever been standing on solid ground without him.*

Chapter 41
Alec

The word rings in my head long after Rob says it. *Girlfriend.*

I didn't correct him, but it sits wrong in my gut. I haven't had a girlfriend since middle school, and that barely counted. She only liked me because she could hang out with Finn, and all I wanted was to climb the cypress tree in her yard.

That's the truth. I don't do relationships. I don't know how.

But Clementine's here. And, for reasons I can't explain, I wanted her here. Wanted to take her somewhere I love, show her something that's mine, that's real.

Maybe that makes her my girlfriend. Maybe it makes her more.

I don't fucking know.

The engine roars under my boots. The plane is cramped, four seats that might as well be three. We're close enough that our shoulders stay welded together. Every creak causes Clementine to clamp down on my arm.

I don't mind it. Not one bit.

"I wanted you to see a glacier in person," I tell her. "See what life with me really looks like."

Her voice cracks through the headset. "How are you not terrified up here?"

"I've flown into the Tenzing–Hillary Airport in Nepal eight times. Most dangerous in the world. This is nothing."

I grin. She squeezes tighter anyway.

The clouds peel back, and the world breaks open. Peaks rip out of the earth like bones.

"Oh my god," she gasps as Rob banks us toward the ice.

"That's the Matanuska Glacier," I say. "First one I ever climbed."

It's sprawled out like a beast, scarred and cracked, blue as deep water. The kind of blue that swallows you whole.

She squints at me. "I'm pretty sure that exact shape is tattooed on your leg."

"Surprised you could tell."

"Spent a lot of time staring at those legs," she says, winking. "What can I say? Thigh tattoos do something to me."

I huff a laugh, but my eyes stay on the glacier. "It used to be bigger. A lot's melted."

Rob twists to look over his shoulder. "Losing about a foot a year. You wouldn't believe how far it's receded in ten."

"One of the climbs Finn and I did was to raise awareness," I tell her. "Vatnajökull in Iceland. That's the one in the documentary."

Her breath fogs the window. "Would you climb this one again?"

"Actually, that's part of why I booked this flight. I wanted to scope it out."

Rob glances back. "Too hot the last couple weeks. Probably won't be good to climb until October. Though if a window opens up before then, you're gonna want to take it."

October. That's after Wild Trails. I cringe. I'd hoped to climb sooner.

There's a small, ugly worry riding me—if I don't stand on

real ice before Wild Trails, will my hands hesitate on a rappel? The nightmares have been quiet most nights, but they're only quiet; they're not gone. A gym session isn't the same. I need the wall, the real bite of crampons, and the clean math of axes and screws to prove that part of me still works.

I don't want to let Clementine down again.

Clem swivels toward me, eyes darting between the ice wall and my face. I catch the edge of nerves in her eyes. "You're really going to get back on the wall."

"Not just this." My voice drops lower. "Told my agent I'd climb Vatnajökull in November."

"You'll have people with you, right?"

"Yeah. They're bringing in some new climbers. And Herald. I've climbed with him before. Not as quick as Finn, but smart. He can spot an avalanche risk a mile off."

"And how do you feel about climbing this one?"

"I think I need to prove I can do it without Finn. I need to prove to myself that I still have it in me."

"Right." Her voice is low.

"You okay?"

"Just one thing to see it on TV and another to see it up close. I don't want you to get hurt."

I keep my gaze locked on the glacier. I can't handle the fear in her eyes, because it cuts deeper than anything I'd prepared for.

I don't know how to hold what I feel for her and what I feel for the mountain without one ripping the other to pieces.

The mountain was my first love, and Clementine is—she's important too.

"That's why I brought you out here." My voice comes out rough. "If you're with me, you're going to worry. Every climb, every storm, every time I step onto ice like that." I nod toward the glacier swelling larger in the window, the blue of it cutting into the sky. "That's what you'd be signing up for. It's part of what I do. Part of who I am."

The plane tips sideways, and her nails dig into my arm.

"I know." Her voice trembles, but she doesn't let go. "And I don't want to miss out on this just because I was scared of what might happen."

I glance at her. She's scared and still here, pressed into my side.

"I don't have this figured out," I admit, low, only for her. "How to let someone in and still climb the way I need to. Because I do need it, Clem. The ice. The burn in my lungs. The pull in my arms. It's how I breathe right. I can't lose that."

"I don't want you to lose it," she says softly. "I just…I just don't want to lose you."

Something twists in my chest. Two truths, both immovable. I'll always need the mountains. And right now, I want her too.

"I like having you here," I tell her.

"Good. Because I like being here."

"We'll talk about it after Wild Trails. Like Rob said, I probably can't climb until October anyway," I say. My fingers fumble in my jacket pocket. "For now, I have something for you."

"More than a plane ride?"

I pull out the small origami box I made for her, the edges damp from my grip. I wasn't supposed to give it to her yet, not like this. But I need to replace the look on her face with something else.

"You know I'm not great at saying things, and maybe this explains it better." Her brows lift, and I hand it over. "And don't start with the whole I-can't-accept-this thing. This one's nonnegotiable."

She works the flap open with clumsy gloved fingers.

"Who knew a man so rough could make such cute little boxes?" she teases. But when she sees what's inside, her whole face changes as a smile as wide as a crevasse stretches on her face.

"Alec," she breathes, laughter spilling into the word.

"You like it?"

She presses the two tickets against her chest. "I've never even been to Paris."

"You've also never seen Yo-Yo Ma."

She stamps her feet with excitement, reading the tickets again and again. "I can't believe this!"

"Booked the family jet. We leave next week for the night. Hopefully one of those gala dresses survived the garage sale."

"I have three to choose from."

"Then maybe try them on for me first. Let me pick which one I want to take off."

Rob's voice crackles through the headset. "Want me to switch channels for this?"

Clementine buries her face in my chest, giggling. The sound vibrates through me, shaking loose knots I didn't even know I'd tied.

"Thank you," she whispers.

I hold her closer, eyes on the glacier stretching endlessly beneath us. The climb will always be there. But this, her warmth pressed against me, her laugh still in my chest, is hard to replace.

Chapter 42
Alec

Two weeks to Wild Trails, and somehow Clementine has me on a schedule I don't want to break.

This morning, she pushed my pace on the trail until my lungs burned, grinning back at me like it was nothing. Now I'm upstairs, brush in hand, the tang of wood stain clinging to the air.

Mozart follows at my heels, nails clicking on the floorboards. He always waits for me, by the door, at the bottom of the stairs, outside the bathroom, like if he keeps watch long enough, I'll let him in on the secret of where I'm going.

When I pause to shift the ladder, he sits back on his haunches, staring at me with those heavy-lidded eyes. I drag my hand over his head, scratching behind his ears.

"Alright, beast," I say. "Let's go find your mom."

The word slips out too easily. *Mom*. Fucking hell. I shake my head, muttering under my breath, "Pathetic, Hastings." But the dog thumps his tail like he agrees with me.

Down the hall, Clem's singing cuts through the music she's blasting in whatever room she's working on. It gets under my skin in a way I don't mind.

I've built base camps, bivouacs, whole damn shelters on the side of ice walls. None of them ever felt like this. These walls, with the sound of her joy bouncing off them, feel closer to a home than anything I've managed on my own.

The gear room downstairs is still empty. Every time I walk past, I see it in my head: a dance studio for her. Mirrors on one wall, a barre under the window where she can watch the deer in the morning. She shouldn't have to trek to the community center in winter to teach her new classes when there's a perfectly good space here she can walk to. Haven't told her I think about it. Not yet.

Nights fall into their own rhythm. I pick her up from work, and she pulls me straight into her world. She grins like she's pulling one over on me when she cues up *Barbie in the Nutcracker.* I lasted two whole princess films before threatening to call Brooklyn and have her body-double me through the rest. Clem laughed so hard she cried, and I sat through another one just to hear it again.

Other nights, we head the opposite way, out into the trees. Pitch a tent by the lake. Wake up with dew in our hair and the water so still it looks like the sky dropped down to meet us.

"Hey, Clem," I call out, searching for her upstairs, Mozart on my heels. "Room next to the bathroom's ready for paint. That yellow you showed me would look good."

I push open the door to one of the corner rooms.

And stop.

The room isn't empty anymore. It's furnished.

My stomach drops. I just stand there, hand still on the doorknob, every part of me telling me this is wrong. This room should be bare, dust and boxes, maybe a new coat of paint. Nothing more.

"What is all this?"

Clem turns, caught mid-movement, like I'd just walked in on her stealing cookies. She tucks a strand of hair behind her ear, smiling guiltily. "You keep spending the night at my place. I figured maybe you could have a space here too." She gestures at the window. "Picked this room because it faces mine. "

I can't answer. My eyes move over every detail.

Slate-blue walls, the same shade as glacial ice. An oatmeal rug under a bed frame I thought I was building for a guest room. A plaid blanket that matches the inside of my sleeping bag. Photos of me with Finn. Photos of me with her. On the sill, a smooth river stone, a compass, and a neat row of carabiners. Maps of the peaks Finn and I climbed, pulled straight from my binders.

It's me. My life, pinned down inside four walls.

It rattles me. Hard. My chest goes tight. It's the same pressure I feel at the base of a climb, staring up at a wall of ice. That split second before I move, when the only choice is up or back.

She's still watching, reading too much in my silence.

"You hate it, don't you?" She frowns. "Oh no, I'm sorry. I know you said you've never really had a room, but this one just seemed right."

"I don't hate it."

"I just thought we could use the walkie-talkies again. Wave to each other across the hill." Her smile turns tentative. "And maybe you wouldn't have to sleep on the floor anymore."

"It's a mat and a sleeping bag," I remind her.

"Now it's—well, a bed. A slightly more comfortable bed." She tilts her head. "It's too much, isn't it?"

"No." I force a smile and walk over to her. "No, it's not too much."

"Even when you're gone...on climbs...you'd have somewhere to come back to." She says it lightly, but her eyes flick away, then back again, and I catch the truth under her words.

She's been building me a tether. Something to hold me when she can't.

Anxiety knots low in my chest, tangled with something else.

Want, maybe, or just the ache of knowing I don't want to let this go. This room means I've already stayed longer than I ever meant to.

For once, I don't move.

I stay.

Chapter 43
Clementine

THE FIRST THING I do is open the bathroom drawer. Not because I need anything, but because I want to see if the hand cream is the kind that costs more than I've ever paid in rent.

It is. Of course it is.

Two months ago, I was queuing for a single shower in a drafty apartment, tugging clumps of hair the size of tennis balls from the drain. Now I'm standing in marble and gilt, pretending this is my life.

Alec booked us the Belle Étoile Penthouse Suite—the kind of place that is more urban legend than hotel room. A rooftop terrace that looks out on the Tuileries, the Eiffel Tower shimmering in the distance, Montmartre rising like a postcard I'd stared at too long. Every Paris landmark I'd memorized from watching *Amélie*, suddenly on the other side of the glass.

"You know, you've ruined flying economy for me forever," I call, dragging a finger through the hand cream sample like it's frosting. "And hotels too. Did you stay in places like this a lot growing up?" I ask, brushing blush over my cheeks, eyes darting to the chandelier above me, the terrace beyond it, the velvet armchairs no one will actually sit in.

"Once or twice." Alec's voice drifts in from the other room. I hear the hiss of steam from the iron and picture him smoothing out a tux.

"Once or twice what? A year? A month? Did you have birthday parties in hotel ballrooms like this? Did you just…take off to Paris when the other kids went up to Stinson Beach?"

"Clementine." His voice carries that low warning, the one that means he's smiling even if I can't see it.

"I deserve answers!" I grin at my reflection, refusing to let him off that easily. "What about room service? Did you order ice cream sundaes at two a.m. just because you could? Did you ever get lost in a place this big?"

"You almost ready?" He cuts me off right on cue.

"Are you?" I shoot back, but silence answers. Typical Alec. He'll drop twenty-four thousand on a hotel room without blinking, but ask him to explain it, and he forgets to speak.

I take one step back.

The mirror throws me a version of myself I almost don't recognize. A column of red silk clings close, a slit teasing up my leg, cutting straight down before spilling loose at my ankles.

The dress came with a matching scarf of sheer fabric, draped at my neck and trailing down my back.

I bought it last year after *Giselle*, a stubborn, shining protest against all that heartbreak. I never thought I'd have the occasion to wear it. And now here I am. In Paris. With him. Going to see Yo-Yo Ma in person. Like I've slipped sideways into somebody else's story.

The door clicks behind me, followed by his voice. "Fucking hell, Clementine."

I spin, and my jaw nearly smacks the marble floor.

Alec, who basically rotates between one pair of cargos, one pair of jeans, and the same five T-shirts he scrubs clean with the precision of a surgeon. Alec, whose idea of dressing up is swapping his fleece for a flannel or the one sweater he actually owns.

That Alec has vanished.

In his place is some impossible version conjured by Paris itself. His dark hair is slicked back, beard trimmed, and the tuxedo is molded to every hard line of his body like it was tailored for sin. On his lapel sits a tulip boutonniere, almost absurd against the breadth of him.

He looks devastating.

The sight knocks the breath out of me, because it's so unmistakably him and not him all at once. I grip the gilded frame behind me because my knees have apparently decided to stage a coup.

"Fucking hell yourself," I manage, though it comes out more prayer than joke. He looks so good I don't know whether to laugh, cry, or drop to my knees and lick him. "Did you—" I swallow, heat clawing up my throat. "Did you put mousse in your hair?"

"A bit." His mouth twitches, but his eyes don't leave me. They run their slow marathon over my body, equal parts savoring and suffering. "You sure you don't want to skip the orchestra?"

"Give me a spin," I blurt, because if I don't toss levity into the silence, I'll combust.

"No."

"Please. *For me.*" I tilt my chin, lashes lowered, pulse galloping so hard I'm surprised he can't hear it.

"Did Mozart teach you those puppy-dog eyes?"

"I'm waiting." I tap my heel against the ground, and he groans, but he turns anyway. I whistle. Paris could keep her landmarks. I'd still say this was a view worth crossing an ocean for. "I think I have a thing for your ass in those pants."

"Yeah?" His brow kicks up, mouth tugging at one corner. "You don't miss my cargos?"

"Actually, I do. Every time I hear a Velcro wallet at Got Wood?, I half expect you to appear."

"Gotta Velcro kink, Fox?"

"Maybe."

He huffs out a laugh, and his eyes drag down me again, slow enough that I feel it. "You look stunning. Just so fucking beautiful." He pauses, head tilting. "But something's missing."

My hands fly to my face. "Did I forget mascara?"

"Nope." His answer is clipped and sure, like he's been waiting for this. He crosses the suite, heads straight toward the second mini-fridge—because of course this place has more than one—and pulls out a small plastic box. Inside, nestled like treasure, is a corsage. "You mentioned you never went to prom."

"*Alec.*"

"Put out your wrist." His voice leaves no room for hesitation, so I obey. He smells expensive tonight—cedar, spice—but beneath it is that deep earthiness that's just Alec. He fastens the corsage carefully, the flowers cool against my skin: tulips, baby's breath, and a tiny blue blossom we'd seen clinging to a rock face on one of our hikes.

My fingers brush the petals as heat pricks my eyes. "Nobody's ever done anything like this for me."

"You deserve the fucking sun, Clementine."

Then his mouth is on mine, and it steals whatever words I might've had. By the time he pulls back, I'm swaying into him, breathless, lips tingling.

"We should get going, or we'll be…" He pulls his wrist between us, glancing down. That's when I see it. A heavy gold watch glinting in the low light. Nothing like the battered mechanical one I'm used to. He adds, almost distracted, "…very late."

"What on earth is that?"

"My watch?"

"What happened to the ugly analog one?"

"Hey." His smirk is defensive. "That ugly watch tracked you kicking ass on hill runs yesterday." Then he notices my gaze still lingering and flexes his wrist, like he's only just remembered it's there. "This one's different."

"Different how?"

"I buy one after every big climb. Not for show. Just…markers, you know? Something to keep time by."

I blink. "Wait—you? Collecting shiny things? I thought you were strictly tattoos and scar tissue as souvenirs."

"Ink for the climbs. Watch for the summit."

I gape at him. "You're telling me you've been out here quietly building a watch collection? What even is this one?"

"Rolex Explorer II."

"Rolex." My jaw drops. "As in a house payment on your wrist?"

"Not quite."

"Not quite?" I throw up my hands. "Do you know how insane that sounds? Do you just have a vault somewhere? Do you keep them in little glass cases? Do you polish them yourself? Do you—"

"Don't start."

I gawk. "For a guy who lives on goop packets, you're wearing this way too casually."

"Smartass."

"Smart aleck…wait, was that insult named after you?" I rub my finger over his wrist. "No, seriously, how many are we talking? Five? Ten? A hundred?"

"*Fox.*" He cuts me off, threading his fingers through mine, tugging me toward the door with that infuriating calm. "You're going to interrogate me all night if I let you, and we'll miss the orchestra."

I stumble after him, still gaping. "Oh my god. You're secretly a watch guy. A bougie, shiny-wrist, horology-nerd watch guy!"

He glances back at me, golden eyes amused, lips curving just enough. "Full of surprises, remember?"

"Maybe you can set that little watch of yours to remind you

to take this dress off of me…on the terrace tonight, when the Eiffel Tower lights up." His erection is instant, pressing up against his black pants.

"Baby, if you keep talking like that, we aren't going to leave this hotel room."

Heat slams through me, my face flaming so fast I have to glance away, but I'm smiling, giddy, caught between laughter and wanting to drag him outside.

"How bad is my makeup?" I whisper, dabbing under my eyes with the corner of my program. I'm still buzzing, heart jackhammering after watching my favorite composer in person. My mascara is probably halfway to my chin.

Alec leans forward in his velvet seat, swiping a thumb under my eye. "You look beautiful. A little raccoony, maybe. But beautiful."

"Shut up." I laugh, pressing the program to my chest like it's the only thing keeping me upright. "Oh my god, did you hear the way Yo-Yo Ma played 'The Swan'? Like the cello was alive. I swear I felt it in my teeth."

"That one was good. But the Bach was my favorite."

"You're only saying that because it was the saddest." I nudge his knee with mine. "Leave it to you to love the piece that sounds like someone bleeding into wood."

"Maybe," he says, a little smile ghosting across his mouth. "But he made silence feel heavy."

I know exactly what he means. The pause before the bow dragged again, the hush that spread through the hall, like everyone had stopped breathing at once.

I flip open my program, scanning the list even though I've memorized every line. "I can't wait for the Dvořák concerto.

That's when he gets unruly, makes you think the cello's about to split in half under his bow."

"Unruly, huh?"

"You'll see." I grin, tapping the page. "It's like the mountain version of cello repertoire. All cliffs and avalanches and air so thin you can't breathe."

"Then I'll probably like it."

The Palais Garnier is too much and not enough all at once. Marble staircases curling like ribbons, arches carved so delicately they look spun, gold spilling over every edge. Above us, a painted ceiling swirls in impossible colors, anchored by a chandelier so massive and glittering it's as if Alec plucked the stars out of the sky and hung them here just to watch me gape.

Our private box tilts the stage toward us like a jewel case, every instrument catching the light. Crimson velvet muffles the sound of shifting bodies, leaving the music to glow brighter. I thought I'd ache watching other people onstage, remembering what it felt like to belong there.

But the moment Yo-Yo Ma walked out, bow in hand, the ache dissolved into awe.

The curtain behind us stirs, and a waiter slips in, soundless on the velvet carpet, two flutes of champagne balanced perfectly on a silver tray.

Alec straightens in his seat, shoulders squared. *"Oh non, nous n'avons rien commandé."*

"You speak French?"

He shrugs, maddeningly casual. *"Un peu.* From high school."

Obviously, everyone remembers the subjunctive a decade later.

The waiter politely inclines his head. *"Non, c'est bien pour vous. J'ai une commande pour deux verres de champagne."* He sets the flutes down on the small lacquered table between us, then vanishes back behind the curtain with the same effortless grace.

"They must've gotten the wrong box," Alec says, still frowning.

"Actually, this is all me. Thought the least I could do to thank you for all of this is get us a little intermission treat."

"You never have to treat me."

"I want to. Besides, I saved for it, and I'm enjoying myself, and that's a massive success."

The chandelier above us dims, gold and crystal dissolving into shadow, signaling that intermission is almost over.

I reach for my glass, brushing his fingers on purpose as I hand him his. A shiver shoots up my arm. The champagne is crisp, effervescent, almost too tart, and I sip it too slowly, drawing it out, like maybe it can anchor me here. In this city. This music. This man.

He doesn't touch his glass. Doesn't even glance at it. His eyes stay fixed on me, like the whole damn Garnier could collapse around us, and he wouldn't notice.

"I need to find a way to thank you. *Je veux te remercier, mon focx.*"

My pulse is thunder, and for a moment I can't tell if the orchestra has started again or if the music vibrating through me is only him.

"Alec—" I begin, but the rest catches in my throat as he shifts, tuxedo lines folding as he sinks down onto his knees in front of me.

"What the hell are you doing?"

"Showing gratitude." His voice is maddeningly calm, like this is a perfectly reasonable thing to do in a place where royalty used to sit.

"You can't," I hiss, though my body is trembling as his hand runs under my dress, along my thigh. "We're in a concert hall!"

"That we are." His mouth curves in a dangerous tilt. He tugs his bow tie loose with a practiced flick, the silk whispering free like a promise.

Heat spikes low in my belly. "Alec," I warn, though it comes out more like a plea.

"You have no idea what you do to me," he murmurs, eyes dragging over me like he can't believe I'm real. He takes my wrist and knots his bow tie around it, anchoring me gently to the armrest while he pins my other hand to the chair.

"You're mad," I whisper through my teeth.

"For you, always," he says simply, leaning close, hawkish eyes searching mine. "But you can tell me no, Clementine."

"Someone will see us."

"Never stopped us before," he whispers into my neck. He parts my thighs, slipping his hand into the slit of my gown. My nipples tighten, unaware we're in a room with hundreds of people.

"Alec—" I whisper, scandal and want tangling. Across the hall, balconies glitter in the dark. For one dizzy second, I'm sure they can see us, the velvet shadows not nearly deep enough to hide. "We're going to get in so much trouble."

"Guess you'll have to perform, Fox." He bites the inside of my thigh. "Make sure they don't notice."

The chandelier above us dims completely now, the hush before the music thickening. I wet my lips, tilt my chin higher, and whisper, "Fine. But at least enjoy the symphony while you're down there."

His mouth curves wickedly, awe burning through the hunger in his gaze. "Oh, I plan to."

Then his shoulders press between my knees, his head vanishing beneath the red silk. In one motion, he slides my panties down with his mouth, fabric whispering against my skin.

As the strings rise, his tongue lands on my clit, and I bite my palm to stop my moan. The shock of it rips through me like lightning. Hot, wet, dizzying.

Alec's tongue moves across me like he's trying to unspool me in time with the violins.

My hips betray me, lifting toward him even as I try to wriggle back. The velvet seat creaks with my struggle.

He only hums against me. The vibration ricochets through me, and I choke on another sound. I swear the couple across the room is staring at us. My wrist tugs against his bow tie. I shoot my free hand to his shoulder, pushing, clawing. "Alec—" My whisper frays, brimming with panic and want. "We can't. Someone will see—"

He catches my hand easily, pins it to the armrest with his own, his grip firm but unhurried, as if this struggle is part of the performance.

I twist against him, fighting the thrill of exposure, the dizzy terror of it. My thighs clamp shut, then tremble open again when another hum reverberates low against me. The sound ricochets through my core, stealing the strength from my resistance.

The orchestra surges, strings winding tighter, my pulse louder than the timpani.

Until his teeth lock around my clit. Not cruel, not breaking, but enough. Teeth biting, a sting that burns into pleasure. Heat blooms hard and fast. My hips arch into him instead of away. My wrists strain, not to stop him now but to keep from falling apart too quickly.

"Good girl," he murmurs toward me. "Behave."

Every flick of his tongue, every press of his hands, feels like a command. My body is no longer mine. It's his instrument, played mercilessly, every movement pulling me closer to the edge.

The crescendo climbs, and I'm no longer a dancer or audience or woman at all, but sound, vibration, sensation. When my orgasm tears through me, piercing, the words slip out before I even recognize them. "You—I—oh god—I think I'm in love with—"

Silence slams into me after, like the air's been punched from my lungs. The orchestra thunders on, mercifully swallowing my cry, but the echo of it still rings in my ears.

God, I didn't mean to say it.

I blink down at him, bleary and starry-eyed, chest heaving, mind a jumble of heat and light. He retreats from my dress and looks up at me, lips slick, eyes molten, and I can't tell if he heard.

Panic sparks, hot and wild, and I lunge forward, almost desperate, pulling his mouth to mine. The kiss tastes of champagne, salt, and relief. His hands cradle my face like I'm fragile, like I didn't just come apart in his arms, and I try to bury the words there, to pretend they never slipped free.

For one suspended second, it works. There is only him, his mouth, his hands, this impossible secret we're holding.

When he finally pulls back, I feel good. Better than good. I feel like Paris belongs to us, even if only for one night.

Chapter 44
Clementine

"Thanks for doing this with me," I murmur, leaning close to swipe blush onto Yura's cheek.

She narrows her eyes at me in the mirror. "Never in my life would I have guessed that the hyper-focused ballerina I spent summers with would turn into a horny little rascal."

I snort. "What can I say? Apparently a grizzly mountain man does it for me."

She smirks, tugging at her too-loose tutu strap. "Did he do it for you on your hike this afternoon?"

"No, that was all PG," I shoot back, though the memory makes me smile anyway. Alec tried to play it cool while I unpacked a picnic of Toblerone, muffins, and Daisy's steak sandwiches on the summit, like he wasn't practically swooning over the chocolate.

Yura bites down on her lip. "Well, after that, he's definitely going to ravish you later."

"I hope so." I grin, and when our reflections catch, two grown women in neon tutus and tinsel crowns, Mozart in drag between us, I dissolve into laughter until my cheeks ache.

The whole day has been like this, stitched together with

ridiculousness and breathless moments. Alec swears he doesn't celebrate his birthday, but he didn't exactly complain when I slid into his bed this morning, pressing my cold toes to his calves just to hear him groan. We tangled in the sheets until the alarm dragged us onto the trail. Later, back home, Finn and Yura joined us for too much pasta and a cutthroat round of Trouble, though somehow Alec "won." Now he's downstairs by the fire, smug and unsuspecting, convinced we're sneaking off to grab his cake. He has no idea what's coming.

Yura digs another macaron out of the white box on Finn's dresser, her tutu puffed around her like a turquoise cloud. "Okay, one last bite of these, and then we're going out there and giving those two mountain men the best show of their lives."

"Your tongue is going to look like Skittles vomited on it," I tell her, brushing glitter across my collarbone.

She mumbles through crumbs, "Thanks again for these. I didn't even think I liked macarons."

"Trust me, nobody does until they've had the real ones. Try the orange, it'll ruin you for life."

She licks powdered sugar from her lip. Her green eyes shimmer from the bronze pendant light above, the one Alec picked out nearly two months ago. "I still can't believe Alec whisked you off to Paris for a single night."

"Best concert I've ever seen," I admit. "It felt too quick, though. I'm already dying to go back. He had a late dinner catered on the terrace so we could watch the Eiffel Tower light up at midnight."

"Who else was lit up?"

"Me." I wink, leaning back like I'm not about to confess I downed half a bottle of champagne by myself. "I was so tipsy I cried during the light show. Told Alec I'd never seen anything so beautiful. He thought I meant him."

"He is *nice* to look at. They both are."

"Also very nice to touch."

She squeals and pitches a pillow at me. I dodge it, nearly knocking over the blush palette, and collapse onto the rug, laughing until my stomach cramps.

It's exactly like being kids again—knees skinned, fingers sticky with glitter, choreographing routines in the lodge lobby while our grandmothers pretended not to notice. Back then, we used to bet on how many cartwheels it would take before one of us smacked into the moose head on the wall. I'd forgotten how easy friendship could be when nothing's at stake. Ballet friends had always been rivals in disguise. Yura just feels like home.

"Okay," I tease, catching my breath, "this from the girl whose grunting I heard in this room the other day. That did *not* sound like physical therapy."

She gasps, diving into Finn's pillow like she's twelve again and hiding from Gran. "You're evil."

"And you missed me," I singsong.

She peeks over the pillow, cheeks flushed. "Nine years was way too long."

"I think so too." My throat tightens. "Now we've got two boys and a dog waiting for us."

"The best little Monoodle Malamute muffin in the entire world," I say, pointing at Mozart, who's gnawing the lavender tutu tied around his belly.

"Isn't he the sweetest, most—hey! No! Not the ribbons!" Yura lunges.

"Mozart!" we shriek together as he tears around the room, ribbons streaming behind him like parade streamers. It takes both of us to pin him down, and we giggle helplessly as he wriggles, tail thumping, while we smother him in belly rubs.

"Co-parenting is going great," Yura says, breathless.

We collapse onto the rug, Mozart sprawled between us, tail still wagging like he's in on the joke. And I think again how easy it is to love people who don't ask me to earn it—people who clap for me whether I'm en pointe or flat on my face.

For a week, I scrolled gift guides, fingers itching for the quick fix of buying my way into the perfect present. That's always been my reflex—shop until I find something shiny enough to say what I can't. But Alec isn't like that. He doesn't need me to prove I'm clever with gifts or good at getting deals. He doesn't want *things*. He wants moments. And tonight, I have the perfect one in mind.

Yura flops back dramatically on the rug, glitter smeared across her cheek. "Okay. For real. If I forget the steps—what then?"

"Then we do the Macarena," I tell her, offering a hand. "It'll still be a perfect gift."

She grips my fingers, letting me tug her upright. "You're right. They're obsessed with us. There's no way we can screw this up."

"Obsessed," I confirm, and she grins so hard I swear her face will split.

We shuffle toward the door, Mozart clicking along at our heels, and for the first time in years I swear I've never felt sillier —or freer.

The stereo clicks, bass thrumming, and "Think Pink" from Barbie blasts through the speakers. I throw my arms wide, glitter already shedding from my tutu as we walk into the main room.

"Presenting Clementine, Yura, and Mozart!"

Alec and Finn glance up from the fire, both trying—and failing—to keep straight faces. They're sprawled on the huge beige sectional that fits perfectly in front of the stone fireplace, flames licking warmth across the room until my calves sting from standing too close. A deep burgundy area rug sprawls across the main room, soft against my toes when I bounce off the wood floor.

A half-empty popcorn bowl and the Trouble board sit on the coffee table, buttery salt hanging in the air. Mozart sprints in, heading straight for the popcorn, and Alec snatches up the bowl just in time.

Yura grabs my hands and pulls me onto the floor, eyes—hell, everything—sparkling. "Five, six," she hisses.

I grin, counting us off. "Five, six, seven, eight!"

The second Yura launches into our old opening move—those giant, jerky jazz hands we choreographed when we were nine—they lose it. Finn doubles over on the couch, Alec's laugh cracks wide open, and I swear that sound alone is worth the humiliation.

And then we're in it: the twirls that always made us dizzy, the leaps that clear half the area rug, the spins that crash us shoulder-first into each other because Yura never remembers which way to turn. We're shrieking before we even finish the first eight count, and Mozart weaves between our legs like a manic stagehand, tail wagging so hard his lavender tutu slips sideways.

The boys whistle, clap, and stomp on the floor.

I don't care that my fingers aren't pointed to perfection with every jump or that my turnout is nowhere near where it was two months ago. Because this isn't about perfect pirouettes or clean lines.

I'm not performing for an audience.

I'm performing for home.

I spring upright, hair wild, sweat prickling my temples. "Now for the big finale!" I declare. I sprint to Alec, dragging him toward the makeshift dance floor.

"No, no," he protests, palms up, grinning. "I could never top that."

"Come on, Satie," I tease, using the old nickname I've only recently resurrected. "Just because it's Barbie doesn't mean you have to act allergic to it."

"I might actually be allergic," he deadpans.

"I saw your foot tapping!" I shoot back.

Yura collapses next to Finn on the couch. He nods at me like *do it.*

"You just stand there," I tell Alec, planting him in the middle of the rug.

"And then what?"

"I'm going to run," I say, skipping backward, "and you're going to catch me."

"Catch you? How—"

Before he can protest, I take off, leaping into a tour jeté, legs slicing the air in a clean split, the old ballerina muscle memory flooding my body. I dive straight into his arms.

He catches me like he's been waiting his whole life for this exact moment. I hook one leg around his waist, flinging an arm out in a dramatic pose as the music hits its last chord. He doesn't set me down right away, just holds me. Then he lowers me slowly, as if he's reluctant to let go.

My body skims down his, breath ragged. There's glitter clinging to his stubble, and from the heat in his eyes, I know the performance has been a success in more ways than one.

"How was that?" I ask.

"Very impressive," he whispers.

At that, Yura uncorks a bottle of champagne, the cork ricocheting off the rafters, and pours it into mismatched enamel mugs. We clink haphazardly, bubbles spilling like it's New Year's Eve.

We fall onto the couch, and I tilt my mouth to Alec's ear. "Be honest. Wasn't that worth turning another year older?"

His hand tightens on my thigh. "Definitely." His kiss is slow, champagne-sweet.

I breathe it all in—the warmth, the chaos, the love that doesn't ask for anything in return. I haven't let myself dwell on the *I love you* at the concert. I've spent two days praying he didn't hear it, because if he did and chose not to say it back, it might undo us, and I don't want to ruin this.

"I think you're going to have an issue untying all these ribbons, Hastings." I laugh into his neck.

"Clementine, I grew up learning how to knot and tie things," he teases. "If I can't get them off...I'll tear them off with my teeth."

Chapter 45
Alec

I WAKE to a buzz on my nightstand and flip the phone open to see a message from Rob.

I shoot up before I can second-guess myself. This may be my only window before Wild Trails. I've been carrying a doubt for weeks that if I don't stand on real ice before the competition, I'll freeze on the rappel again and let Clem down.

If I can stand on Matanuska without Finn beside me, I'll prove something to myself: that I'm still a climber, still a man who knows his body, still someone worthy enough to push off the shore next to Clementine.

I need that proof.

Three hours up, one hour down.

I can be back before Clem's afternoon stretches. Back before the steak dinner we have at Daisy's tonight to fuel up for tomorrow's race.

ALEC

b there in 2 hrs

I type out a message for Clem, but my screen dims and then flips black. It's dead. *Fuck.* I search my room for a charger but can't find one.

I'll write a note instead.

I pull my notebook from the drawer; there's still glitter stuck in the spine from Clementine's birthday performance last week. I brush it off, flip open a page, and scrawl:

Sorry to miss the walk. Back before dinner. Promise.

I stare at it until the letters blur. It feels too impersonal. I tear the page out and start again.

Don't worry. Just a quick climb. Training before Wild Trails. I'll be back soon. Save me a smile for when I get in.

Still sounds like I'm trying too hard. Like I'm begging her not to worry when I already know she will. I rip out the page and try again.

Weather looks good on Matanuska. Couldn't waste it. I'll be back before dinner. I want to earn that steak. Trust me.

I let the words sit on the page. They feel plain, like something she can hold. The way I want her to hold me when I walk back through her door. This note, I keep. I fold it slowly, crease by crease, until the sheet turns into a tulip.

Then I move, quietly grabbing my pack and boots and heading out the door.

Finn and Yura will be tied up in Anchorage with Mozart's checkup, so no one will ask where I've gone.

Clementine's house rises out of the dark in front of me. I crouch, slide the tulip under the welcome mat, and let my palm rest there. This is proof that I can do two things at once: leave but not disappear.

Because maybe healing isn't a single summit. Maybe it's a string of these small ascents. Writing the words instead of saying nothing. Folding them into a tulip instead of crumpling them up. Letting someone worry about me.

The real climb is waiting, but this was the first ascent of the day.

EACH SWING of my hooks is a test, like pressing two fingers to the glacier's throat. Alive or hollow, solid or about to give.

Ice never lies.

The silence on Matanuska is meditative. I drive the front points of my crampons into the brittle blue, two at a time, feeling each tooth find purchase. My breath fogs in front of me, like smoke curling into the late morning air. The pick of my axe lands with a perfect, swallowed *thunk*—no dinner-plating, no splintering. Just honest placement.

I'm not naive. Matanuska is no K2, but she is not gentle. Every few seconds she creaks with the rising sun. A hundred meters away, an entire ridge collapses.

I'm 3,500 feet up, alone. Solo roped. Just me and the wall.

There's no Finn yelling below me. No Clementine beside me. No one to save me if I screw up. That's the point. This is where I prove I still have it. That K2 didn't strip this out of me.

That I can climb clean, methodically, unbroken.

That I'm still worth a damn.

I screw another anchor in, hand steady, run a sling, and clip in. The carabiner is a promise, and I treat it like one: deliberate placements, redundancy where I can build it, eyes always scanning the next ten moves. I don't romanticize it; I count it. Pick, step, torso close to the wall, so my center of gravity stays neat. Good stance, good balance, keep the load on the tools.

Clementine lingers in my thoughts the entire climb. A flicker at the edge of my vision, a flash of orange hair like a fox darting through snow. For a beat, I almost turn my head, almost call her name into the wind.

I miss her. I do.

But the ache is different here. This ache feels stronger, cleaner, something I can carry. It's not a weight pulling me down, it's something to climb toward.

That's the difference. I'm not clawing at the wall to prove I can still cling to life. I'm climbing because I want to go home to her. Because I finally know what it feels like to want more than the summit.

God, this is where I belong. Climbing through the silence now so I can go back to the life awaiting me. I belong here because it reminds me of who I am. And I belong there because she reminded me of who I could still be.

Glacier climbing is a different muscle than alpine climbs or rock. There's a logic to moving up a vertical sheet of ice: the axes are variables, my feet are coefficients. I read the ice better than I've ever read people's faces. A ripple of meltwater means softness; a shadow may hide a hollow. Every decision is small and exact, which is exactly what I need right now. Tiny certainties in a world that has given me too many big, ugly unknowns.

I move higher. Flick my wrist and secure my axe before driving another screw into the glacier, making sure it has hold before clipping in.

I have a lifetime of ice under my boots. A thousand climbs etched into my bones.

My watch chirps a storm warning, and I feel the hair rise along my neck. I'm moving slower than I want. Rob warned me a front was coming; if I stay efficient, I can top out this line and be tucked back into lower snow before a storm folds over the ridge.

I haven't felt this free since the accident. Not since guilt sank into me like frostbite.

Trust the gear. Trust your body.

The last push is steeper. My quads fire, lungs pulling cold air. Snow crystals against my jacket.

I reach the top and mantle the lip. Fifteen years on ice taught me how to pull with my whole body instead of letting one muscle fight the rest. I drag my weight up and roll until I'm standing, both axes buried in the hardpack, and the world opens.

The sky is a hard blue dome. My chest is heaving, and the urge to howl up at that wide sky comes from somewhere ancient. I howl and cheer and scream and let go of everything I have been holding on to since Finn's accident. My voice scours itself against the valley, echoing back to me. The sun strikes the ice, and a thousand little flecks wink.

In that dizzying blue, I see her everywhere. Freckles scattered like specks of dirt locked in the ice. The curve of her laugh traced in a ridge where the sun carves light into shadow. And her hair—god, her copper hair—is the horizon itself.

The thought hits me like an avalanche in my chest, tearing through every layer of armor I've built.

I love her.

It rips out of me raw. The mountain doesn't need to hear it. She does.

I wanted to shield her from my storms, keep her from worrying every time I clipped in. But maybe this is the point: the blessing is having someone who will worry. Someone who waits. Someone who loves me back.

Suddenly, all the instincts that have kept me climbing for years—the hunger for summits, the drive to stay on the wall longer than anyone else—flip inside out. For the first time in my life, I want off the mountain more than I want up it.

This time, the summit isn't the goal. The goal is down. Home. Her.

I've never wanted to get off a mountain faster.

"Rob, I'm coming down. See you at the bottom," I say into the radio.

"Alec wa—" The walkie cracks, then goes to static.

"Repeat. You're cutting out."

"Behind you."

I turn around and see a blizzard speeding toward me. *Fuck.* The horizon dissolves into white. A wall of snow tumbles down faster than I can move. I need to hurry.

I settle into the harness, crampons locking into the frozen wall, and descend. Each motion is exact, practiced, and for a moment the edge of fear fades—I am present, the nightmares held at bay. I unscrew my first anchor and pick up the pace.

Anchor. Unclip. Kick. Drop.

A cold current sweeps down. The chill that hits my right cheek is so harsh it's like a dragon exhaling ice along my face. A gust tears at my rope. I hear a pop, and then I'm falling.

I feel nothing and everything all at once. The harness cinched hard across my hips, the rope biting into my hands like a living thing, my crampons scrabbling uselessly against nothing.

I slam into the ice. The pain is instant, spread across my back, and knocking the air clean out of me. My ribs compress, and the breath tears from my lungs in one hot, animal gasp. Snow and ice explode into my face, needles that sting like a dozen thrown pins. My head throbs as I hang there. The harness is a godawful snugness across my pelvis, but I'm alive.

I spit out blood and realize that I'm dangling from an anchor that has held.

Adrenaline detonates. My body shakes wildly with it.

Every vision of my girl hits harder than the fall. And I know —I know—I cannot die on this wall. Not with her humming "The Swan" through my head. Not with Finn's grin, Mozart's stink. Not with Wild Trails tomorrow. Not with my whole life ahead of me.

It takes everything—strength I didn't know I had—but I right myself, crampons finding ice, axes digging in above me.

I'm raw, cut, and burning where rope sliced my skin, but I am moving. Down.

Beneath every placement, every strike: her. The race. The life waiting below.

I will not vanish into this wall. I will not leave her wondering.

If I make it down, I'll never climb solo again.

If I make it down, I'll tell her I love her.

If I make it down—no, *when* I make it down.

Chapter 46
Clementine

I WAKE with a kind of happiness I've never known before.

Wild Trails is tomorrow.

Weeks of training have carried me here. Hauling bricks up hills until my lungs were on fire, paddling across the lake until my arms felt like they might fall off, squatting seventy pounds while sweat burned my eyes. The old me, the one who used to sit in front of a mirror the night before a cast list went up, tallying every flaw, wouldn't recognize this girl.

But I do.

And I'm proud of her.

My hair's longer. My thighs are solid. My biceps curve strong beneath my skin. I look at myself and think not of what's missing but of what's been built.

I am strong.

I tug on a pair of leggings Alec likes and the sweater he left at my place, grab a muffin, and settle on the porch steps. The morning air is cold enough to bite, but I'm sparkling with warmth. Today we'll take one last walk around Misthaven Lake, keeping our muscles loose for tomorrow.

I watch the path between our houses, already picturing Mozart bounding ahead with Alec laughing behind him.

Any second now, they'll both be here.

But no one comes.

By the time I've eaten a second muffin, the first flicker of unease skims across my chest. In two months of training, Alec has never once been late. I'm not even sure he knows what being late actually means.

I pull out my phone. Dial his number. Straight to voicemail.

Maybe he doesn't have service. Maybe he stopped in town for supplies. Maybe he's planning some last-minute surprise before the race. I keep stacking reasons in my head, but none of them settle the knot in my stomach. Then it lands, sharp and sickening.

The glacier.

Rob had said something about a weather window, about a possible climb that wasn't meant to happen until after Wild Trails. What if a window opened, and Alec—being Alec—went? What if he's up there right now, ice axe in hand, alone against the wall?

The thought freezes me. My chest goes hollow. Would he really risk it now, right before Wild Trails? Even if he decided to go, he would've sent a text, or called, or something. Right?

He's a mountaineer. The mountain calls to him the way the barre calls to me. How angry can I be at the truth of who he is? I know this about him. I've always known it. Loving him was never going to mean keeping him on the ground.

Still, the ache is there. Because love doesn't cancel out fear, and understanding doesn't erase hurt.

The fear is alive and gnawing, and I can't shake it.

So, I lace up my shoes and head out. Routine is better than waiting. The trail around Misthaven Lake is familiar now, every turn woven with memories of him. I catch myself noticing details he would have pointed out. The way a scatter of leaves makes a crooked tulip, the flat stones perfect for skipping, the flash of deer disappearing into the trees.

With every step, the thought stalks me. *Please, God, don't let him be on that ice.*

I keep walking, pretending it's just another training day, even though the silence presses in heavier without him beside me.

When I get back, there's still no sign of him.

I help Gran weed the garden, stretch on the living room floor, even put on music and dance in place to burn off nerves. My body follows the checklist of the day, but my eyes keep darting to my phone.

By the time the sky fades to indigo, the bright stories I've been telling myself all day collapse under their own weight.

My screen stays blank. The longer I stare, the heavier my chest feels, like I've swallowed a stone.

I call Yura. She answers on the third ring, her voice crisp above the noise of muffled announcements and footsteps. "Hey, we're at the clinic. Finn's getting looked at. What's up?"

"Have you heard from Alec?" My voice comes out tight. "Or Mozart? Did he have him with him today?"

A pause, then a quick inhale. "No, Mozart's here with us. He's fine. Why? Did something happen?"

I hear someone call her name in the background. She lowers her voice. "I have to go. Text me, okay?"

The line clicks dead.

The silence in my ear feels worse than the silence on my screen.

I grab a jacket and step onto the path between our houses, the one worn smooth from two months of footsteps. The night air is cool, but sweat prickles at my neck. When I reach the driveway, the empty patch where his truck should be stops me cold.

I don't even have to crouch by the steps to fish out the spare key from under the stone planter anymore. I keep it on my key ring, like it was always supposed to be there. My hand shakes as I slide the key into the lock.

I move fast. Up the stairs two at a time. The room I made for him is too neat, untouched. His pack, always by the door, gone. The boots that lived in his closet, gone.

My stomach twists. It's like he was never here.

My chest burns as I claw my phone from my pocket, scrolling through our thread. His last message was days ago, my unanswered texts stacked below.

I hit call. Ring, then voicemail.

Again.

Voicemail.

Again.

I drop onto the edge of his bed, gripping the frame so tight my knuckles scream. Anger spikes through me, hot and clean, but it only half covers the hollow underneath.

He left.

He knew what this race meant. What we'd built together. He promised me we'd stand at that starting line side by side, and I believed him. Not just believed—I counted on it. I let myself think it wasn't just training anymore, but a vow. And now it feels broken.

The memory hits like a punch: Paris, music swelling, my mouth betraying me. *I think I'm in love with you.* I laughed it off, kissed him too fast, convinced he hadn't heard. Relieved he hadn't.

What if he isn't climbing? What if he left Alaska?

The embarrassment burns, and I hate it. Two months. That's all it's been. Two months of dizzying closeness, of pretending tomorrow was implied, of never actually saying it out loud. Maybe my heart sprinted ahead while his stayed cautious.

But the part that guts me isn't the possibility that I scared him. It's that he didn't tell me. That he just…went. Let me sit here inventing reasons.

I press my palms to my thighs and force myself to breathe. If he comes back, he's going to hear me. All of it. The fear. The hurt. The love. Because I can't do this halfway. If he wants me in his life, he doesn't just get the easy pieces. He gets the truth.

The silence presses heavier.

Hot tears streak down my cheeks. I swipe them away, but my chest keeps tightening, memories collapsing onto me. The subway in New York, the panic clawing through me as I bolted, leaving everything behind. That same dizzy, gasping fear swells now, like I might unravel if I let it take over.

But I've grown since then. I'm not her anymore.

I push myself to my feet and leave the lodge. The air outside is harsh. By the time I step back into my own apartment, resolve steadies me. I pull my backpack from the closet, setting it open on the bed.

I pack with steady hands. Trail shoes, rain jacket, granola bars, wool socks.

Because tomorrow, I'm doing Wild Trails.

Even if I have to do it without him.

Even if it means I won't win the twenty-thousand-dollar prize.

I put in the work. I earned my place.

I can carry myself.

I smooth the zipper shut, the sound like a period at the end of a sentence. My chest still aches, but the ache no longer decides for me.

Tomorrow, I'll walk to that starting line, not as the girl waiting for someone to choose her. As the woman who has already chosen herself.

When I glance at the window, I imagine headlights sweeping into his drive, a truck door slamming, his boots on the path. My chest clenches before I can stop it.

For one reckless second, I almost believe he'll come back.

Chapter 47
Clementine

A HUNDRED KAYAKS gleam in the early morning sun along the bank of Frog River, numbers stenciled bold on their sides. The air smells like wet cedar and camp coffee, like someone split a log just for the occasion. Racers swarm in pairs, all elbows and nerves, cinching vests, shoving shoulders, jittery with adrenaline. The whole shoreline hums, paddles clattering against plastic hulls, names shouted across the current.

Behind the crowd, the town shows up in layers. Trucks parked crooked in the dirt lot, coolers swung open on tailgates, kids in puffy coats weaving through legs with dogs chasing behind them. People wave their cowbells like they're personally responsible for morale.

I stand still beside the yellow kayak Alec and I checked in two days ago, ninety-three painted on the side, Lennox and Hastings scrawled beneath it. It looks ordinary, just another bright shell lined up with the rest. Except it isn't. Because there is no Hastings. Not today. Not standing here with me.

Across the river, mountains shoulder into the sky, jagged and unapologetic. Snow clings to their crowns even though it's only early fall, streaks of white like warning signs.

I tug the zipper on my life vest until my ribs ache and stretch my arms, my legs. The motions are steady, automatic, a shield against the fact that I'm the only one without a partner. I avoided Gran this morning, told her to just show up with Cody before the race starts. I didn't want to explain why I'd be racing alone.

Whatever Alec couldn't carry, that's his burden. Not mine.

"Clem, is Alec grabbing snacks or something?" Finn's voice cuts in as he wheels up beside me on the shore, Yura close behind.

"You tell me," I say.

"We just got here."

I plant a hand on my hip, heat rising in my chest. "I thought we were building a friendship. You could've at least warned me he was going to bolt."

"Alec's not here?"

"I don't have time for this right now," I say. It's not an answer, but it's all I can give them right now.

Finn frowns, pulling out his phone, panic already creasing his forehead. Yura's mouth opens, but the loudspeaker cuts her off.

"Racers, sixty seconds until start. Get your life jackets on and your paddles ready. Your bags will be waiting fifteen miles downstream at checkpoint two."

That's my cue.

I bend, grip the kayak's edge, and haul it into the water. I wish I'd had time to at least get a single kayak. I'll need to sit in the back and steer the boat. In Alec's spot. The river snaps cold against my ankles. The boat wobbles under me as I get in, then steadies. I plant my paddle, jaw tight, back straight.

The bell clangs, and the shoreline explodes into motion. Paddles slam against the river in a syncopated thunder, fiberglass boats scraping and knocking as racers shove for space. Cold spray hits my cheeks, the taste of brackish river water on my lips. My kayak cuts its own crooked path through the churn, steadier with every pull.

I don't let myself look at the empty seat in front of me, at the pairs moving in perfect tandem. I will not break here.

Through the roar, one sound cuts clean.

"Clementine!"

It rips across the river. For an instant I think it's a trick of sound, my mind filling the absence with what it wants to hear. My paddle dips wrong, skidding over the surface instead of slicing through. My pulse is frantic against my rib cage. My arms are moving, but I can't feel them, the current dragging me forward whether I'm ready or not.

Again, louder this time, undeniable.

"Clementine!"

I know that voice. I would know it anywhere.

I don't turn. Not yet.

Chapter 48
Alec

THE LAST TIME I prayed like this, I had Finn's blood on my hands, and I was dragging him off K2 in a whiteout.

Now I'm praying because I'm late. My watch has been buzzing for hours, a tiny, relentless jury reminding me that I'm failing the one person I can't afford to fail. My girl. She's probably seething and hurt, and I hate that I'm the reason for both.

The storm broke just long enough for me to rappel off the glacier, and Rob flew his rust-bucket plane back to Misthaven on fumes. He dropped me a mile out from Frog River, and my boots were on dirt before the plane skidded to a stop.

Seven minutes of running like hell. Seven minutes of lungs burning, legs screaming, the world tilting with every stride. Still, when I broke through the tree line, the kayaks were already in the water.

I spot the shade of orange in the middle of the pack. I'd know that color anywhere, the same way I can pick one blaze of leaves from a forest in autumn.

Clementine's in the stern of our kayak, rushing forward. Every stroke says the same thing: She doesn't need me. She'll run this race on her own, and she won't look back.

"Clementine!" My throat shreds raw around her name. The sound comes out with everything I've held in since the storm broke.

She doesn't falter. Doesn't even turn her head.

The crowd catches me then, hundreds of onlookers swiveling toward the man screaming his lungs out on the riverbank. My pulse slams harder. There's no hiding now, no waiting, no begging for a better moment.

She's already out there, and I'm losing her with every yard of the current.

"Where the hell were you?" Finn's voice snaps, cutting through the roar. He wheels toward me, Yura close behind, her face tight with confusion.

"Make sure my pack's at checkpoint two!" I bark, shoving past them. It doesn't matter. I don't have time to explain. Every second is another stroke of her paddle pulling her farther away.

The river greets me like a fist, slamming against my legs, freezing and merciless. October water in Alaska isn't just cold, it's violent. It cuts straight through fabric and skin, latches on to bone, clamping down on my lungs like a vise.

My breath seizes, but I dive anyway.

Cold swallows me whole. It's teeth on every nerve, fire and ice ripping through my chest. My ribs feel crushed, lungs screaming for air. Hulls slice past like blades, the current throwing me under, spitting me up, dragging me under again. I choke on river water, spit, claw forward, my arms burning, my body howling to stop. The current doesn't just want to sweep me; it wants to keep me.

But none of it matters.

Because she's out there. And if I don't reach her now, I may never get another chance.

Under. Up. Under again. Eventually, I manage to break the surface beside her hull, gasping.

Her mouth is a flat line, all the hurt I put there hidden behind it, and it's more than I can stand.

"You left," she hisses, eyes hot enough to boil water. "I thought you left me. I thought—" She breaks off, swallowing it, like the words themselves burn.

"I'm sorry, Clem." The apology feels flimsy. "There was a storm—on the glacier—I couldn't—"

Her paddle jerks, the boat angling away, but her eyes never leave mine. Blue fire. Fury, betrayal, a thousand questions stacked between us.

"What glacier?"

"I left you a note," I choke out. "Under your door."

"There was no note."

The thought makes me sick. She thought I just walked away. Vanished. No word. No reason.

A paddle smacks the side of my skull as another boat cuts past. White sparks explode in my vision. I spit water, cough, and push closer to her hull.

"Clem," I rasp, teeth chattering, lips already numb, "you have to let me in the boat. I won't make it the next ten minutes like this."

I see the fight in her, the part of her that wants me to stay right where I am, to feel every ounce of what she's felt.

Another wave slams me sideways.

She curses under her breath, then jerks her paddle toward the stern. "Fine. Front seat. Now."

I hook an arm over the side, haul myself in clumsily and half-drowned, water pouring off me in sheets. My hands barely work. She doesn't look at me, doesn't ask if I'm okay. Just keeps rowing, shoulders set, back rigid with anger and adrenaline.

"Clem, I—"

"Tonight." Her voice is stern, but there's something trembling underneath. "We'll talk tonight. Right now, we've got a race to win."

I hunch low, grab the spare paddle from the side of the boat with fingers stiff as wood, but I fall into rhythm with her.

And God help me, I've never loved her more.

BY THE TIME we drag our kayak up the bank, my back is on fire, mud is sucking at my boots, and my shoulders are shredded from two hours and forty-three minutes of paddling. Our fastest run yet. One of the first five boats to land.

We should be celebrating.

But Clementine hasn't spoken to me since I pulled myself out of the river, and her silence feels worse than drowning.

Fuck, what if she's already done? What if I lost her before I even had the chance to say everything that's been clawing through me?

"We'll set up here." She shoulders her pack and drags it a few feet from the waterline, dropping it with a heavy thud. "Get the tent out."

The sun is still high, tents popping up around us, and I just stand there. "Clem," I rasp. "I fucked up. I know I did. I'm sorry."

"You don't have to spin some storm story," she sighs, grabbing the tent from my pack and dumping the contents on the ground. "Rob said you weren't cleared to climb that glacier until late October. Just admit it—you panicked. I almost said I loved you in Paris. I made you a room. I brought Mozart into your life. I pushed too hard. And you never wanted that, so you ran."

She doesn't give me her eyes. She just grabs a stake and hammers it into the mud.

And that kills me more than if she'd screamed.

"That's not true. Rob called. Said there was a window. I thought I could be back before Wild Trails. Then the storm hit. I was stuck. I was a fucking fool."

Her head snaps up. "You could've texted. Called. Anything."

"You're right." My chest heaves like I just took a punch. "Fuck, you're right. I don't know what the hell I was thinking. I left a note 'cause my phone died, and I didn't want to wake you or worry you." I shake my head. "I don't know how to try and do this, Clem. I've never known."

"Communication isn't something you *try*, Alec. It's the bare minimum. You were supposed to be my partner."

"I know." My hands curl into fists. "But I had to do that climb."

"Why?"

"Because I didn't want to face this race, or my life, as half a man." I tear the words from my chest. "I owed you more than that. I thought if I could climb, if I could take the glacier alone, then maybe I could take you too."

"So, what—you thought nearly dying on a glacier would make you *worthy* of me?"

"No. Because the mountain wasn't the fear. It's you. Not you —fuck—not you. I feel for you, Clem. And I didn't know what to do with that." My voice breaks, a jagged sound, close to a sob. "This whole time, I thought if I kept you at arm's length, I couldn't ruin you when I didn't come home."

"That's not your decision to make. It's mine." Her breath comes out clipped. "But you do scare me, Alec. Not just the mountains. *You*. I don't know how any of this is meant to work when I may be waiting for a call that might never come."

I step closer, every nerve on fire. "And I don't know if I can live without you. So, tell me—what the fuck do we do about that?"

Her eyes flash. "You tell me."

"Christ, Clementine." I drag a hand over my face. "You're the reason I want to survive all of it. I've never felt more alive than I do when I'm watching you laugh, or listening to you argue with me, or paddling that damn lake with you. You think I want to throw myself off mountains now? I don't."

She stares at me, chest rising fast. Then she rips her sleeping bag out of her pack and hurls it at me. The weight thuds against my ribs. Around us, people are staring, but I don't give a damn.

"Fuck you." Tears streak her face, but her hands don't stop moving as she clicks the tentpoles into place, sliding them through the loops. "You don't get to disappear, leave me to worry all night, and then show up with the most you've ever said to me."

"Then don't believe the words. Believe what I do. Believe I'll be here tomorrow, and the day after, and the day after that if you'll let me. Believe that I'll choose you every goddamn day."

"You're maddening, Alec!"

"I am."

"Ugh," she groans. "Everything I've ever teased you about, it's all true." Her voice cracks, but she keeps going. "You scared me so badly. Do you understand that?"

"I know. I do understand. I am every joke you make of me, every poke and prod and tease. I'm not great at this, I'm not." I swallow, trying to figure out my words. "Clementine, you are the home I spent my entire life searching for on peaks." I close the space between us, and she doesn't step away. "And I don't want to throw my life away for a summit anymore. I don't need the death-defying climbs, the solo risks. I need you. It's you. Not the mountain. You."

"I thought I lost you. I was so sure. And I didn't know how I'd survive that."

Her hand jerks upward in exasperation, but I catch it mid-swing, steady, my fingers firm around hers. She doesn't fight me. Her eyes shine, glassy with fear.

"You quiet my head," I whisper, swiping a tear from her rosy cheek. "You make me feel like a kid again, before all the years of pain." She's trembling, furious. I cup her jaw with my other hand

and tilt her face to mine. "I love you, Clementine," I say. "And I will spend every day proving it to you."

Her whole body jolts, like the words knock something loose inside her. She shakes her head once, twice, tears spilling unchecked. Finally, she crumples into me, fists balled, pressing against my chest like she wants to shove me away and hold on at the same time.

I wrap my arms around her, bury my face in her hair, and breathe her in like air after almost drowning.

She sobs, "You're such an asshole."

"I know," I murmur, holding her tighter. "But I'm your asshole, and I fucking love you."

"I fucking love you too," she says into my chest.

Chapter 49
Clementine

His words loop in my mind like a melody I can't get out of my head.

It's you. Not the mountain.

You.

I wanted to roll my eyes, tell him it was too easy, too neat. He doesn't get to vanish on me and then patch it up with an I love you. But when I look at him, when I see the way his jaw softens and his whole body leans into the quiet, a different part of me hears that promise and wants to believe. That's the part that scares me the most. Because he did leave. He could do it again. Note or no note.

We move through the motions of setting up camp and making dinner. He notices I'm cold and hands me his fleece without question; it guts me, because that's exactly who he is when he's not running—competent, careful, offering. We don't talk. The day has emptied us. When the sun drops, we crawl into the tent and slide into our sleeping bags.

Alec lies just far enough away to give me air, deliberate in his distance. There's a split in his right eyebrow, dried blood clinging to it. His sleeves are pushed up, and I spot black and blue bruises along his tattoos. His lips are chapped and bloody too, charred from the cold. It makes my chest ache to know what happened on that glacier. But he doesn't complain or wipe away the blood, like a part of him thinks he deserves it.

For once, he isn't pacing, isn't solving. He is still. I don't know how to be with that stillness.

The fleece smells like him. I twist it in my hands until the fabric is warm and say the thing I've been circling forever. "I don't know how you expect me to believe a promise like 'every day.' Do you even get what that means?"

He props onto one elbow and looks at me in the low lantern light, and for a second, the man I've been learning to trust is fragile and very human.

"It means I stay," he says. "That's it. I stay."

"You say it like you haven't built your whole life around leaving."

His mouth opens, then shuts again. "You're right. Leaving is what I know. It's what I've always done. But I don't want to keep being that man with you."

"When you were gone, I told myself a hundred stories. Why you left. Where you were. Every one of them hurt. And every single one ended with me not being enough."

"You're the only thing I've never doubted. It's me I don't trust. I know how I move in the mountains. I calculate wrong, the weather shifts, one anchor fails—and that's it. Game over. I can live with that risk for myself. But loving you..." His throat works. "It felt like tying you into my rope system knowing damn well I might fall and drag you with me. What if I didn't come home? What if I left you carrying that weight?"

"That's not your call, Alec. You don't get to untie me because you're afraid of the fall. Climbing with you means I know the risk too, and I still choose the rope or trail or whatever analogy you need to get it through that thick head of yours. I don't need you to promise you'll never slip. I just need to know you won't cut the line when it gets hard. I need you to keep me harnessed in."

He nods, scooting closer to me. "I'm scared now. More scared than I've ever been. And I'm still here. That's the promise I can make."

The air feels like the silence itself is listening.

"Then stay," I tell him. "Not just for tonight. Not just for this race. If you're mine, you stay. And if you want to climb, I'll support you, but you can't keep things from me."

"I'm yours, baby."

His hand rests between us, palm open—an offer.

I stare at it until my vision blurs, then lay mine inside his. His hand closes over mine, warm and rough. And that's it. No grand gesture, no sweeping declaration. Just the two of us lying side by side.

I let myself picture a future with him. This feels like a beginning.

It feels like love.

WE WOKE before the rest of camp, crawling out of our tents while the mountains were still purple with dawn. The air bit cold, tin bowls clattering as we scarfed down oatmeal before packing our camp. We were the first at the race line, our shadows long on the dirt. When the gun cracked at seven, we lunged forward like the trail had been coiled under our feet, waiting to spring.

Euspuko's east side is no one's friend. Slate breaks loose with every step. Alec's only a foot ahead, navy buff pulled high, calves flexing with each push, and I can't stop the grin tugging at my face.

We rehearsed this for months, and we're doing it.

Despite every challenge along the way, we're doing it.

We've got about five miles to the top. A few hikers are behind us—I can hear their boots crunching—but we don't glance back. The trail thins into a knife edge, cliff dropping away on one side. My pulse spikes, ears roaring, but his arm stretches back without looking, fingers brushing mine. A tether. I step into it, match his pace, trust his body more than my own balance.

Alec rounds a corner; his pack scrapes against a jagged outcrop. The fabric tears with a sudden, harsh snap. A tin cup bursts free, clattering down the slope.

"Fuck." He jerks sideways, trying to grab for it, the whole pack shifting wrong on his shoulders.

"I got it!" My knees crack hard against stone as I lunge, palms raw, fingers snagging the cup before it tips into the ravine. Adrenaline spikes, swift enough to taste. I shove the cup up toward him like it's proof I can keep up. "There. Saved. We need to take care of this rip."

He exhales through his teeth. "Leave it. We don't have time."

"We do if you don't want your whole pack exploding." I'm already crouching, shrugging off my bag. My breath is ragged, but I dig fast. "One minute, tops."

"Clem—"

"Do you want to lose our stove next? Or our headlamp?" I pull the tiny sewing kit free, thread between my fingers, before he can argue again.

He groans, running a tight circle on the gravel, hands fisted at his hips. His chest heaves. He hates stopping, I can feel it vibrating off him. But he listens, and I get to work.

"Relax." My fingers are already working, needle sliding through torn fabric. "I once sewed ribbons onto pointe shoes while a stage manager was literally shoving me toward the curtain."

"You terrify me."

"Good." I laugh and bite the thread clean, knotting quickly

before the mountain can eat more of our time. His shadow looms over me, jittering with impatience, but he doesn't move.

"There." I tuck the cup back inside and shove the pack at his chest.

"You really didn't have to do that."

"You cover me, I keep your gear from self-destructing. That's the deal."

"You're right, we're a team," he agrees. "But next time, we're using duct tape."

"Hot pink duct tape. So it matches the stitches."

His mouth tips up, and he shrugs on the pack. "Thank you. You're wonderful."

"And indispensable." I bump his shoulder with mine, then hitch my pack up, lungs already clawing for the next breath. "Now quit stalling. Zak's hair is practically flagging us from the ridge."

We fall back into step, shale grinding under our boots.

One more night in a tent. Four miles down tomorrow, and then the rappel.

We don't talk, couldn't if we tried. Still, I hear him in every movement. The scrape of his boot warns me where the slate's about to betray us. His hand flicks quickly when the trail marker hides in shadow.

When I spot the next arrow first—green paint flashing in the rocks—I bark us uphill before we follow another team into nowhere. His nod is barely there, but it lands heavy, like someone pinning a medal straight through my chest.

The pack is mended. The stitches hold. And so do we.

Chapter 50
Alec

It's only seventy meters down. A piece of cake compared to the storm I was stuck in on Thursday.

Seventy meters. I repeat it under my breath as we reach the granite base, early sunlight warming the back of my neck. A few teams are already set up, helmets clipped, ropes threaded, anchors checked twice. One of the safety leads marks arrivals on a clipboard.

Clem and I are next.

Her hand squeezes mine when I slow. "We've got this."

My stomach is tight, but she's right.

We'd practiced enough that my body knew the rhythm before my brain could catch up. Knots by the fire until my fingers cramped. This isn't the unknown. It's muscle memory.

I shrug off my pack and line everything up the way I always do: harness, rope coils, helmets, gloves. Clem hums some half song under her breath as she steps into her harness, tugging the waist belt snug. She doesn't need me to check, but I do anyway, tightening a strap and tugging the buckle. That's the thing about us, we know when to let the other fuss.

"Good," I mutter, more to myself than her.

She grins. "Didn't doubt it."

When an anchor frees up, we move forward together. I thread the belay device, clip the carabiner, say the steps out loud even though she already knows them. Saying it steadies me.

The safety tech checks our systems and tugs the ropes. "You're good to go."

"I'll be down there waiting for you. Remember, knees bent, feet shoulder-width, don't choke your brake hand."

"I know," she says with a smile.

I clip in, pinch the rope, back toward the edge until my heels hang in the air. My pulse quickens, but the system holds. It always does.

"On rappel," I call.

"Hastings, you're clear," the tech shouts back.

I lean back into the rope, weight shifting until the wall takes me. Trust the anchor. Trust the system. Push off. The rope feeds smoothly through the device, brake hand steady at my hip. My eyes scan the rock for edges that could cut, my feet finding solid holds on the granite.

The ground comes up faster than I expect, even though I keep the pace controlled. My boots touch down firmly. I ease the rope through, lock it off, then unclip quickly, swinging clear so she'll have space at the bottom. Walkie in hand, I call up, "Off rappel. Your turn, Fox."

Her reply crackles back almost immediately, "On rappel!"

I tilt my head, eyes locked upward, every nerve strung tight until I see her clear the lip. Exactly the way we drilled it. I don't breathe until her boots hit dirt.

She pops off the wall at the last meter, landing lightly, and before she can steady herself, I'm there. I catch her around the waist, hauling her in against me.

"Talk about falling for a guy," she jokes, and I kiss her. "Okay, we'll have time for this later. Let's go fucking win this thing." I nod, grab her hand, and we take off.

Without another word, we sprint toward the two wooden poles that have a Wild Trails banner bridged between them. For a heartbeat, it's just us, no crowd, only our lungs burning in sync, her hand hot in mine.

We cross the finish line hand in hand.

For months, I've lived with the weight of what I couldn't fix, every mistake, every silence, every summit I chased instead of showing up. Guilt made a home in my chest and whispered that I wasn't worthy of anything steady. I thought the mountain was penance, proof that I could carry pain alone.

But she's here. Still here.

And her hand hasn't let go of mine once.

And when I look at her, I see the same fight written across her. The girl who thought she had to buy her way out of emptiness, who thought shopping could fill the ache inside. She's here too, stripped bare by this climb, and her eyes say it clearer than words—she's not running anymore.

We made it this far.

Not by outrunning what hurt, but by turning toward it together.

I feel something uncoil in me, something I've been holding too tight. I'm not afraid of what comes next. Because it isn't about conquering the mountain or outracing ghosts. It's about choosing her. Every time.

"We did it," I whisper as I haul her into my arms. My fleece on her smells like river and sun and her.

She presses her face into my neck, breath hot and shaking, and when she looks up, her smile is wet and certain.

"We did," she says.

The officials are shouting, the scoreboard flickering, but none of it matters anymore.

I kiss her again. "Let's go find everyone."

And together, we do.

Chapter 51
Clementine

"Hey, son," Alec's dad says as he approaches us, wrapping his arms around him. They are nearly identical, with the same jawline and stiff posture. But Alec got his dark curls and golden eyes from the gorgeous woman joining the hug.

"All of you are here?" Alec says, confused.

"Finn and your siblings invited us. Although we would have loved to get the call from *you*," Selene says in a tone only a mother could master.

"He doesn't know how to use a phone," I say. Leo's laugh is deep and hearty. It's hard to believe he's the owner of the largest tech company in the world. He's dressed in a gray cotton sweater, jeans, and a Giants ball cap. But as I scan around us, I notice security guards flanking a journalist who's snapping pictures from a distance.

"Alec, I'm so happy to see you," his mom says.

The shock on Alec's face dissipates. "This is my girlfriend, Clementine Lennox." He extends an arm out to me, offering me a place in the fold. Despite the casualness of his movements and words, it feels like a standing ovation. I'm a girlfriend! "These are my parents, Leo and Selene."

"Hi!" I don't bite back my giddy laugh as they both embrace me like I've always been part of their family. My face rubs on the shoulder of Selene's cashmere sweater, and I inhale vetiver and wood and…my BO. "Sorry if we smell. This is the longest I've ever not showered, and this one wouldn't let me bring my lavender body wipes," I tease.

"Stop, you smell delicious." Alec wraps his arm around me and buries his nose in my sweaty hair, inhaling.

His mom shields her grin with one hand, the other squeezing my forearm. "It is so lovely to meet you. And trust me, as the mom of six kids, I've smelled some things. You smell like morning dew." I shiver under the compliment. She shifts to her son, running the back of her hand along his cheek, as if she can't contain her happiness at seeing him alive. I wonder how many nights she lay awake wondering if he'd come home. "It's so nice to see you smiling." Alec glares at her, then kisses her on the cheek. "You looked breathtaking on that wall up there," Selene says.

"She means literally breathtaking, because I swear she didn't take a single breath for the last hour." Leo wraps his arm around Selene's shoulder. "Come on. Your siblings saved us a table with some beers and reindeer hot dogs—which, I'm not sure how they differ from regular hot dogs, but I'll try anything once."

"Trust me, I thought the same thing, but they're actually really good," I say, following them into a blocked-off area toward the edge of the event.

"I'll take your word for it."

I knew Alec had a large family, but seeing them all next to each other is intimidating. Gran is there under a tree, with a blanket over her lap and a paper plate on her knees. Yura and Finn are next to her, foam sticking to Finn's mustache.

You can pick out the Hastings siblings instantly. Same dark hair, olive skin, and golden eyes. Except Ezra, whom I only recognize from pictures.

The youngest Hastings sister spots us first. Frankie explodes up from the grass, grass stains streaked across her jeans, Mozart yipping after her like a partner in crime. She charges straight into Alec with a squeal that rattles my eardrums.

"Holy shit, you two were insane out there!" she yells, clutching my hand with both of hers and shaking it so hard I nearly lose my footing. "I thought my heart was gonna burst watching you rappel. Do you have any idea how sick that looked? God, I'm so jealous—" She drops into a squat mid-sentence and starts wrestling Mozart, like her adrenaline has nowhere else to go.

"Frankie," Alec warns, though his mouth twitches like he's fighting a smile.

"Thank you," I beam, cheeks aching from how wide my smile has gotten. "It's so nice to meet you!"

"Meet me?" Frankie barks out a laugh, throwing her arm around my shoulders like we've known each other for years. "You're about to be inducted into the Hastings Hall of Chaos. No more handshakes, only blood, sweat, and probably beer."

"That sounds terrifyingly fun."

"Good answer," she says. "You'll survive here just fine."

Alec groans. "Frankie, stop hazing her."

Before I can answer, a low chuckle cuts through the noise. Ezra leans against the table, beer bottle dangling from long fingers, blond buzzcut catching the light. He's the only one without the family's dark hair, sunny where the rest are night. He's broad-shouldered and easygoing, an Olympic swimmer carved into every line of him.

"You both did so well," he says warmly, golden eyes crinkling at the corners.

Frankie crows, throwing her arms out. "If Ezra says it, it's gospel. He never says anything he doesn't mean."

"But I also don't think I've ever heard him say anything rude either," Alec says.

"Hey, I've said mean things," Ezra protests.

"No, you haven't." The woman tucked snug against his side gives him a look over her glasses. Her curls are pulled into a messy knot, tattoos peeking along her forearm where she grips his bicep. "Don't let him fool you. He's the family golden retriever. I'm Hazel." She raises her ring finger.

"My fiancée," Ezra adds.

"They've been attached at the hip since they were, like, twelve," Frankie adds. "Though bro's still afraid to tie the knot. They've been engaged for years."

"We aren't in a rush." Hazel's smile wavers, not quite reaching her eyes, but her nails dig in to Ezra's arm. She's clearly uncomfortable.

"Alright, knock it off, Frankie," Alec cuts in. "Leave them alone."

Frankie groans but backs down. Ezra just shrugs, still smiling, as if he's used to it. Hazel presses closer to his side, her tattoos shifting with the motion.

"You're Clementine, right?" A woman in a lavender sweater dress approaches, tucking a stray black hair behind her ear. "We're so glad to welcome you to the family. I'm Brooklyn."

"I know who you are," I blurt, because I'd recognize that face anywhere. My cheeks heat, but I push on. "Sorry, I just— wow. I've watched all your programs. You were my absolute favorite at the last Winter Olympics."

"Thank you, love. Hold on one second." Brooklyn squeezes my hand, her eyebrow piercing glinting in the sun. She looks so badass. "Did you hear that, Dante and Ezra? Clem's *favorite* event." Brooklyn laughs, prodding at her brothers.

A man—who I assume is Dante—rolls his eyes.

"I'll introduce you to a proper sport when we get back to the lodge," Dante says to me. He oozes confidence in a James Dean sort of way. His girlfriend, Reese Sinclair, stands beside him, wearing oversized glasses and a baseball cap with her new short bob tucked underneath, looking like she's trying not to be recognized.

I tear my eyes away from her. Every girl in my elementary school cut their hair into the famous Sinclair. I begged my mom to take me to Claire's to get her peach lip gloss collection.

"I'm always trying to one-up my brothers." Brooklyn shoots me a toothy grin.

"You're making me wish I wasn't an only child."

"Ugh, the only one who ever got to enjoy that was this one." She nudges Alec.

"It was the best year of my life."

"Whatever. You love me." They roll their nearly identical eyes at each other. "You're a dancer, right? We should go out on the ice sometime. Maybe you can give me some pointers on my choreography for this season."

"I would love to! But you have to promise you won't make fun of me, 'cause I kinda look like Bambi on ice."

"Don't worry, everyone thinks Ezra is the sweetheart, but I'm the nice one out of all of us. I have to be good this season. My coach is already telling me I'm at risk of aging out."

"Felt." I sigh. "Sucks being a woman sometimes."

"Yep. I'm aging out, and my little sister is about to be at the height of her career," Brooklyn says.

Frankie pokes her head up. "Fuck yeah! Come work for me, Brooklyn. I'll teach you how to change a tire."

"I know how to change a tire, thank you very much." She spins toward me and mouths, "I absolutely cannot."

"Me neither." I scrunch my nose.

"You kids are always giving me a heart attack. Why couldn't you all have picked a sport like golf or something?" Selene sighs from the wooden table, finishing her second hot dog.

"'Cause you're our mom," Alec says.

"Basketball isn't dangerous."

"Tell that to your torn ACL, and how many fingers have you broken?" Ezra chimes in.

"Beside the point." Selene waves him off, eyeing a third dog.

It's easy, effortless, like we've skipped the awkward introductions and gone straight to the late-night-gossip-over-wine stage.

Alec leans in close enough that only I can hear. "See? They're not all feral."

I elbow him lightly, though my smile won't fade.

"We're not all quite so dramatic," Dante drawls, flashing me a grin so practiced it borders on illegal. "In fact, some of us prefer to make people feel welcome, not traumatized. I'm Dante, this is Reese."

Reese swats him lightly but offers me a conspiratorial smile. "Ignore his dramatics. We're really glad you're here."

"Same," I manage, trying not to gawk at Reese Sinclair in real life.

"I absolutely loved watching you rappel!" Reese gushes.

"Thank you. I loved your *Robyn Hood* movie! I saw it in theaters."

"Appreciate that," she says genuinely. "I'd love to pick your brain about climbing. My production company is looking at a project about the first woman to summit Everest."

"Oh, Alec is probably going to be better at that."

"Yes, but not the woman stuff. Like, where do you go to the bathroom on these overnight trips?"

"Oh, I can show you my shovel."

Reese's face goes pale.

"Don't worry, fighter, I'll fly you out your own bathroom." Dante drapes his arm around her waist and pulls her in close.

"Oh my god, some of these little booths are so cute!" a bright voice says behind us. A girl with lilac hair appears carrying a tote stuffed with booth finds. This must be Daphne. Her boyfriend, Cameron, looks at her. He has a quiet presence that reminds me of Alec. "Look at these tiny little jars of jam!" She holds the glass jar in her palm.

"If you like jam, you have to try my gran's gooseberry jam," I say.

"Gooseberry! Oh my god, that is perfect for you, Cameron!" She shakes his shoulders. It must be an inside joke. "Sorry, I'm all over the place. I'm Daphne Quinn." She sticks out her hand. She's wearing a beautiful plum fisherman's sweater with a striped scarf.

"I'm Clem."

"I made you something." Without hesitation, she presses a knitted bundle into my hand.

"Made me something?" She doesn't even know me.

"It's kind of her thing," Alec whispers. "She's a knitter."

Nestled in my palm is a tiny knitted charm, a ballet pointe shoe, the palest shade of blush pink. A little loop of silver thread is stitched through the back so it could hang on a tree or dangle from a keychain.

My throat closes. "Oh my god. This is…you made this?"

"Of course," she says. "I like to knit things that remind me of people. You're a ballerina, so pointe shoes felt right."

I blink fast, but my eyes still sting.

Beside her, Cameron folds his arms, but his voice is warm when he finally speaks. "She's underselling it. She's brilliant. Knit me a pair of socks last season with tiny stars. Haven't let in a penalty since." His mouth barely tips up at the corner, but it's there. Pride. "She never gives herself enough credit."

Daphne swats at him. "Cameron."

"What? It's true," he says simply.

The affection between them is so easy, so obvious, it makes my chest ache.

"You all…you make it look so easy. Loving each other like

this. It's just—" My voice cracks, embarrassingly vulnerable. "I've never been around a family like this before."

"You're here now," Daphne says simply, pulling me into a hug.

Behind her, I spot Gran. She's waving her hot dog in the air like it's a conductor's baton, ketchup dripping onto her blanket. Her long gray hair is loose today, held back with a floral silk bandana that makes her look like a gorgeous woodland witch in the best way possible.

"There she is! My girl!" she crows. She kisses both my cheeks, smearing mustard across one. "Look at you, string bean, scaling cliffs like my Bill! Nearly gave me a coronary."

"Made Grandpa proud today," I say.

"You sure did! You should have heard the crowd when this one jumped into the water after you." She elbows Alec.

"Sorry about that." Alec's fingers squeeze my shoulder.

"It's fine. You showed up, and that's all that matters."

"You two did so well!" Yura says, hugging me tightly.

Mozart leans back on his haunches, pawing at me, and I bend down to let him kiss—more like devour—my face.

"Thank you for coming!" I get out between licks and nips of sharp little puppy teeth.

"Mozart, heel," Finn commands, and immediately Mozart sits and turns back to Finn, who tosses him a treat.

"You two have been busy." I stand gawking at my perfectly behaved pup.

My heart feels overwhelmed and happy, and I'm attempting to take it all in as the loudspeaker rings out over the crowd. "If you'd please make your way to the stage, where we'll announce the winners of the thirty-second annual Wild Trails."

"Guess we gotta head over there," Alec says.

A hush falls, the family rustling to their feet. Alec's arm is heavy around me, my heart is going a million beats an hour, and I feel something I've never felt before.

I feel rooted.

I CROON, leaning my head into the crook of Alec's neck, letting the heat of him soak into me as the mayor clears her throat and the crowd settles.

"The times are tallied, and we are ready to announce this year's Wild Trails winner."

Alec laces our fingers together, his thumb brushing mine once. I said I didn't care if we won, but my heart is lodged in my throat. Because I do care. Because that prize money will pay off debts and will give me the kind of clean slate I've been clawing toward for years.

"Every year," the mayor continues, "we hold this event to shine a light on our beautiful Alaska, this incredible park, and the local businesses who make this place our home. It's a celebration of grit, community, and this wild land we get to wake up to daily. Unless you're passing through. In which case I say, sucks to be you."

The crowd laughs, but my pulse hammers.

"We had a record-breaking time this year of fifteen hours. The winners of this year's Wild Trails are—" She drags out the pause, and it's working. I squeeze Alec's hand until my knuckles ache.

"Patti and Remi Ko!"

The cheer goes up. My shoulders drop, even as I clap with everyone else. The Ko sisters take the stage, identical grins flashing, and they deserve it. They're Misthaven locals, and they've lived this land, breathed it since birth. They're everything Wild Trails is meant to celebrate.

Still, my chest hollows out. The debt won't vanish. The prize money won't come.

"I'm sorry, Clem," Alec whispers into my hair, the words only for me.

I turn, and the crowd blurs. My gran's clapping, the Hastings crew are whooping, and Finn is trying to teach Yura how to whistle with her fingers. They're happy. They're proud.

I realize I am too.

"It's okay." I swallow. "Sure, it would've been nice to win. To walk away with a check big enough to make everything disappear. But I feel like I've won something else, something I needed more."

Alec tilts his head, eyes searching mine. "What's that?"

"Proof," I say. A breath leaves me like it's been locked up for years. "That I can do what I set my mind to. I didn't just come for the prize money. I came here to see if I could do this, if I could be this version of myself. And I can."

"You can."

I kiss his knuckles. "The debt's still there. It took me years to make it, and it'll take time to pay it off. Slow and steady. One step at a time. But I'll clear it. I don't have to be afraid of that."

His eyes soften, molten and proud all at once. "No, you don't."

I laugh. "I'm richer than I've ever been."

His smile breaks through his disappointment. "Then we'll call this year a win." He squeezes my hand. "And next year? We'll win it all."

I kiss him, fierce and grateful, because I hope there is a next year, and a next after that. Years until our hair turns silver and wrinkles carve our stories into our skin.

"Maybe Mozart can join us," I tease against his mouth.

"If he can resist launching himself out of the kayak every time he sees a fish, maybe."

"A fisherman, like his daddy."

Alec's eyes spark, dark and heated, but then they soften. He cups the side of my face, thumb brushing across my cheekbone like he's memorizing me. "No. Not like his daddy. *Better*. Because he'll have us. He'll know home."

Just like that, the loss doesn't matter. The debt doesn't matter. The future is here, in the press of his hand, the roar of his family behind us, the wild beating of my own heart.

I lean into him, breathing him in. "Then we've already won."

Chapter 52
Alec

It's strange. Seeing my entire family, and now hers too, filling a house that only two months ago was cobwebs and creaking floorboards.

For years, I thought joy was a summit. The burn in my lungs, the sting of wind so harsh it cut, the silence pressing heavy against my ears. I thought that was the point—being alone on top of the world, higher than everyone else, untouched.

But this—this noise, this mess, this warmth—it gives me a high I've never found on any wall of rock or sheet of ice. Turns out, summits don't mean much if you don't have someone to climb back down to.

Control is a stupid illusion, one I told myself made life worth living.

But I'm tired of taking my life for granted. I want to stay up late and hold my girl and pup while watching the stars. I want to share a glass of whiskey with Finn while he reminds me of all our stories together. I want to get to know Yura, Margaret, the people of Misthaven, and let my family in more. *Fear is death on the ice* was useful to me for years, but fear was just an excuse that kept me from taking the scary risk of letting people in. I want to build a life that's loud and messy, even if that means I risk losing people in ways that have nothing to do with the mountain.

I want to live.

I want to be happy.

I want to love my girl more than I ever thought possible.

And the only person holding me back…was myself.

I kiss Clementine's forehead and feel something click into place. It isn't a vow to stop climbing. It's a small, honest truth that I will wake up and choose this. Choose her and us every day.

Out the window, I watch Dante and Cameron race through the shallows, Reese and Daphne shrieking as water splashes up around them. Ezra and Hazel paddle smooth circles across the lake, heads bent close, easy in their rhythm. My brothers have been in love for years, swapping stories about trips and weddings, talking in a language I never thought I'd learn.

But now I get to have that too.

Showing my parents our lodge is nice. Mom cries, of course. She never thought I'd settle. Neither did I, if I'm honest. But the pride on her face, like she can finally breathe knowing I've found something worth coming back down for—that's worth everything.

"I never knew you knew color like this," she says, stroking the cherry wood cabinets and the lace curtains Clementine picked.

"Oh, that's all Clem," I say, pulling her close. She's holding a glass of mulled wine, lips stained red, laughing with my mother. And God, she belongs here.

"You two must come redo our kitchen," Mom says.

"Only if you don't mind a tad bit of flooding," Clem teases.

"It was her damn muffins distracting me." I pinch her side, and she slaps my chest.

"What can I say? Lennox muffins are irresistible," Margaret calls from the barstool, pouring glasses of Bill's favorite whisky.

"You two gonna start a house-flipping show? Who knew Alec could do something other than climb! Rock. Big. Me climb." Frankie crouches under the dining table, trying to sweet-talk Mozart out from beneath it. The dog is gnawing a log like he's carving his own furniture. Better the woodpile than the chair legs—he already whittled one this morning.

"Be careful, Frankie," I warn, "or a tree branch might fall on that shiny new car of yours."

She jerks up, smacks her head on the table, and raises a fist without flinching. "You wouldn't dare, bro."

"Try me." I smirk.

Dad steps in, arms crossed, his grin all mischief. "I'm surprised one of these rooms doesn't have a climbing wall."

"He's actually working on one out back. He already showed me the sketches," Clem says, pride lighting her face.

Dad grins. "You always wanted a wall at the house. Now you're finally getting one, son."

Finn comes in on his crutches, dressed in a button-up shirt and dress slacks. His hair is combed, and his beard is trimmed.

"You're walking!"

"Just for the next five minutes, until Yura makes me sit back down."

"Did you get shorter, bro?" I laugh, giving him a soft hug.

"So, what's next? You really bunkering down here?" Dad asks.

"Iceland next month," I say. "Finishing the docuseries on glacial melt."

"Finn, you going?" Mom asks.

He shakes his head. "Nah. I'm starting an expedition prep program here, like Clem's grandpa did. To help people get ready to climb Denali. I need to hire some real climbers, obviously, 'cause it'll probably be a few years before I can go up." He slings an arm around Yura's blue cotton dress.

"So you'll be doing Iceland alone?" Mom asks me.

"No, Jillian got some experienced climbers to come with me."

"Bet they'll be half as handsome as me." Finn slaps my head, playfully. "And don't worry, Mom, he promised to come back before winter so I can crush him on the slopes this year."

"Okay, maybe we can wait another year before skiing," Yura says, bopping his nose.

Mom's hand finds my cheek. "I love seeing you happy."

I grip her hand, but I'm staring at Clem. "I am. I really am."

"Will you make a speech, Alec?" Margaret motions to the drams of whiskey on the kitchen counter.

"He's not much of a wordsmith." Finn smirks.

"I'd love to." I shove Finn's shoulder. People come in and grab a whiskey.

My people.

"To Bill Lennox, who built this lodge with his hands and left it standing strong enough for us to fill it again. To Margaret, for not coming after me with her gardening shears and for making this place look better than it has any right to. Those ornamental cabbages mean a hell of a lot to me, even if nobody else here gets it."

Clementine's smiling at me, and Margaret's beaming like I just handed her a medal.

"To my siblings—thank you for making me tough and for teaching me that tough doesn't mean unkind. To my parents, who taught me the only three things worth learning: work hard, be decent, and don't be hasty. To Finn—for surviving the stupidest things we tried on K2. I can't wait to see what we get up to in the next twenty-seven years."

Finn lifts his glass, grinning at me.

"To Yura, for making my best friend laugh like I've never

heard him laugh before, and for your physical therapy spread-sheets, which frankly scare me. They rival mine."

Gleams of amusement dance from face to face.

"And finally"—my throat tightens, but I don't care if my voice cracks—"to Clementine. Thank you for not hitting me with a shovel the first day we met, even though you had every right to. Thank you for showing up to every single practice, for your patience and your smartass comments. Thank you for being curious and kind and funny. For turning this house into a home. For turning me into a man who has one. I'd choose you, Clementine, over and over again. I love you. I love all of you."

I lift my glass, and the crowd roars with it.

When I turn, she's already in my arms. I kiss her hard, and the world blurs. My ears are red—I can feel it—but I don't care.

"I love you," I whisper into her mouth. Then, to everyone else and still grinning like an idiot, I say, "Now, I'm stealing away my Wild Trails partner for a proper thank-you."

They all boo, but I flip them a finger and whisk Clementine away.

"I love you too," she says.

"I love you three. I'm serious," I answer, and I am. It's the most serious I've ever been.

The hallway is quiet as we walk to the back of the lodge. "Where are we going?"

"You deserve a place to teach your classes. If you want to teach at the community center, you can. But I thought you needed something of your own. A proper studio."

I push open the door to the old briefing room, Bill's maps and gear long gone, and she stops cold in the doorway.

Floor-to-ceiling mirrors line one wall. A pale barre stretches the length of another, sanded smooth. The floor gleams with polish, the faint scent of lemon oil and sawdust still clinging to the air. The space hums like it's been waiting for her.

Clem covers her mouth with her hand. "Alec…"

"I think I was promised a dance lesson," I say softly, holding out my hand.

Her laugh is a broken thing, halfway between disbelief and wonder. "Now?"

"Yes, Miss Lennox. Now."

I scroll the wheel on my ancient silver iPod. From the speakers, the cello of Gnossienne: No. 1 spills out, slow and velvety. The sound curves around us, filling every inch of the studio.

She steps into my arms, and the world rights itself. My hand at her waist, hers clutching mine, we begin to move. It isn't ballet. It's clumsy, swaying, too much of my boots catching on the floor.

But it's intimate.

Honest.

Ours.

She tilts her head up at me, smiling through tears. "How are you so good at this?"

"Family galas. Parents forced all of us into dance lessons."

"And you never said anything."

"We have a lifetime for me to tell you things."

She lets out a choked laugh, shaking her head. "Good at dancing *and* sappy. Where was this guy all these months?"

I spin her gently, guiding her back into my chest. "Waiting," I murmur, "for someone like you to remind me what life is all about."

Her forehead presses to mine, and for a moment it feels like the whole room is holding its breath.

I shift my grip, careful, steady, and lift her. Higher, until her toes leave the floor. She gasps, laughing, suspended in my arms the way she made me watch in *Dirty Dancing* and on my birthday. I kiss her, and it feels like oxygen after too long without it.

"I could get used to this," she whispers.

"Then get used to it," I tell her. "Come to Christmas in California with me. Bring your gran. Finn and Yura too."

Her brow lifts. "I could ask Mom to drive up from Concord?"

The thought lands in my chest like something heavy and solid, like stone. Like building a world brick by brick. "I'd love to meet her."

"If you think Gran's spicy, just wait until you meet Mom."

"I'd love that," I say again, and I mean it. "And Iceland. Will you come? Not to climb. Just to be on the boat when I come down."

She bites her lip. "Yes. One hundred times yes."

Her laugh rings out, filling the studio. I know I'll carry that sound with me anywhere.

"I love you, Clementine," I tell her. The most certain thing I've ever said. "You're my favorite adventure."

She looks at me the way people look at something they've been searching for. "I love you, Alec Hastings."

We sway across the polished floor, her weight trusting against mine, my hand steady at her back. This is the next summit of my life. The family dinners, the brutal climbs, the mornings with her hair a mess, the nights with Mozart chewing furniture.

Everything I needed was always waiting for me.

I'm not afraid of the climb ahead.

Epilogue
Alec

EVEN AFTER SUMMITING the highest glacier in Iceland, the best thing I've seen in three days is Clementine standing in that small boat, waving like her arms might fall off.

The water gleams around her, all fractured light and color. Deep navy ripples speckled with white ice, flashes of pale turquoise where the glacier lurks just beneath the surface.

She's wrapped in a massive pink puffer coat that swallows her whole, a cream beanie sliding halfway down her forehead. The wind whips her red hair into a wild halo around her face, and her grin—bright and uncontainable—cuts through the gray sky like a flare.

The climb was clean. Perfect, even.

The ice samples are secure, the camera crew is thrilled, and I should be thinking about data logs or tomorrow's debrief. Instead, every step down the glacier, all I could think was, *Three more hours. Two. One.*

Until her.

When the white boat bumps against the glacier's edge, I barely wait for it to steady before climbing aboard. My legs shake, but then Clementine launches herself at me, and I catch her on instinct alone. She hits my chest hard enough that I stagger back into the boat's railing. Her arms lock around my neck, and she makes this sound between a laugh and a sob that does something catastrophic to my composure.

"Three days is too long," she says into my neck. Her breath is warm against my frozen skin. "I'm never letting you do that again."

"Yes, you are." I bury my face in her hair. She smells like woodsmoke and the lavender soap she packed, impossibly soft things in this harsh place. "You'd lose your mind having me brood around you day in and day out."

"That's true." She pulls back just enough to look at me, and her hands come up to frame my face. Her smile falters. Her gloved thumb traces my bottom lip, and I flinch. "But your skin wouldn't be bleeding from the ice burn."

"It's fine."

"It's not fine." She's studying me now, really looking, and I can see the exact moment she catalogs everything wrong. Her fingers ghost over the new cut on my cheekbone, the raw patches where my goggles rubbed, the split in my lip that keeps cracking open. "Your face—"

"Will heal." I catch her wrist, pressing a kiss to her palm through her glove. "Clem, I'm okay."

She makes a frustrated sound and digs through her coat pocket, producing a small tin of lip balm. "Hold still."

"Clementine, I haven't brushed my teeth in three days—"

"I don't care. I like your smell. Also, I'm pretty sure my nostrils froze solid two weeks ago. Can't smell a thing." She's already uncapping the tin, dabbing balm on her finger. "I've been going crazy down here, Alec. Knowing you were up there. So, you're going to shut up and let me take care of you."

There's something fierce in her voice that makes my chest tight. I go still and let her work, her touch featherlight as she traces my bottom lip. The balm stings, but her concentration makes everything else disappear.

"There," she whispers, capping the tin. Then she leans in and kisses me so softly I barely feel it. "A little better."

"Much better," I whisper against her lips and kiss her once more.

Behind us, my team is celebrating, shouting, laughing. Someone's already cracked open a bottle of something. But they might as well be on a different planet.

We take a seat as the boat cuts through the glacial water, and she tucks herself under my arm. The adrenaline is finally wearing off, replaced by bone-deep exhaustion and the kind of contentment that only comes from knowing you're exactly where you're supposed to be.

"I have to be honest." She tilts her head up to look at me, yelling over the wind.

"What's up?"

"I would've appreciated a warning about how boring glacial research is when you're not allowed to touch anything."

"You could have helped with the equipment checks."

"James wouldn't let me near the drills after I asked if I could use one to make snow cones." She grins. "Apparently that's 'not what a hundred-thousand-dollar ice core drill is for.'"

I laugh, wincing when it pulls at my split lip. "I'll need to have a firm talk with James about that."

"I agree." She nods firmly. "I did teach half your research team how to stretch properly—did you know JoJo can't touch her toes? It's tragic." She's ticking things off on her fingers now. "That, and I reorganized the entire camp kitchen, because whoever was in charge of it clearly never learned the alphabet. And I may have convinced Harry to let me use the satellite to call Gran back at the lodge."

"You called Margaret from Iceland?"

"She wanted to know if you were still alive. And also to tell me that Gerri finally nailed her pirouette." Her whole face lights up. "Alec, she *cried*. Gerri actually cried. She said she's been trying to do a real spin since 1987."

I shake my head, grinning. "You've created a monster with those classes."

"I've created a dance troupe." She sits up straighter. "We're calling ourselves the Silver Swans. We're performing at the lodge's New Year's party, and I already warned your mother that it's going to be emotional, because Dorothy has a solo and she's already stress-eating about it."

"My mother knows about this?"

"Your mother wants to join. Actually, your whole family's talking about flying in from California after Christmas." Clementine is fully giggling now.

"I was only gone for three days."

"Three very *long* days." Clem bops my nose. Her laughter catches the wind. She fits so easily into my family—the calls, the updates, the way they all light up when she's on screen. I spent months pushing them away after Finn's accident, and somehow Clementine pulled them right back into me.

"Speaking of your family," she continues, "Brooklyn wants to know if we're coming to Monaco in May. Francesca's racing there, and apparently, we can't miss it."

"Monaco." I let my head fall back against the seat. "In May. That's—"

"I know, it's right after your Patagonia expedition, but Frankie specifically requested we come. She said she needs at least one family member who won't embarrass her in the paddock." Clementine pauses. "I think she meant you, but I'm choosing to believe she meant me."

"She definitely meant you." I hook an arm around her waist, pulling her closer. "But yeah. We'll go. I've never seen her race in person."

"Really?" She twists to look at me. "Your sister is an F1 driver, and you've never watched her race live?"

"The timing never worked out. I was always on an expedition or—" I stop, realizing what I'm saying. "Or I was too focused on the next climb."

Her expression softens. "Well, you're going now. We both are." She settles back against me. "Ezra's supposed to be there too. Did your mom tell you?"

"Ezra?" That surprises me. "I thought he and Hazel were doing the whole wedding planning thing."

"They are. Or they were. Or—I don't know, actually." Clementine frowns. "Your mom mentioned something about Hazel taking a job in Rhode Island? And Ezra maybe staying in California? It was all very vague."

I make a mental note to call my little brother. Ezra and I aren't particularly close. He's always been more interested in being in a pool…while I'm the one hanging off mountains, but still. "That doesn't sound good. I thought you said Harry only let you call your grandma."

"Well, and your mom and sister. They were just checking in on you."

"I'll call them when we get back."

She digs out her phone, icy eyes bright. "Finn sent you something. Said I was supposed to play it the second you got on the boat, but I got distracted by your busted face."

"I swear to god, if Mozart is sleeping in his bed when we get back, I'm gonna be pissed," I joke. Mozart is now over sixty pounds and thinks he's the size of a chihuahua.

"Yura sent me a picture of Finn and him underneath the duvet, snoring."

"Spoiled dog," I mutter, though the truth is, the mutt's grown on me. And Finn's walking again. Hiking around Misthaven Lake without crutches with the dog every morning. That's more than I could've asked for.

Clementine pushes play, and Finn's voice crackles through the speaker. "You did it, you crazy bastard. Knew you would. I'm just sorry for the people who have to look at your ugly mug on camera instead of mine."

I snort. "Jealous."

"But since you went and summited without me, I figured the least I could do was commemorate the occasion. So, I wrote you a song."

"Oh no," I mutter.

What follows is the most off-key, ridiculous ballad about our friendship, complete with rhymes about "ice picks" and "side-kicks" and a truly terrible verse about my "frostbitten dignity." The recording cuts in and out with wind interference, making it even more absurd.

By the end, I'm laughing so hard my ribs hurt.

"It's perfect." I wipe at my eyes.

The boat rounds the bend, and camp comes into view. The research station sits low against the landscape, all weathered wood and small windows, smoke rising from the main cabin, where the team is already celebrating. There's a massive fire, and music drifts across the ice.

"God," I breathe. "A real bed. Real food."

"About that." Clementine's voice has gone sly. "I may have arranged something."

"Arranged what?"

"You'll see."

"Boss." It's James, my lead researcher, grinning. "You look like death."

"Feel like it too."

"The data's clean. Everything uploaded perfectly. You want to go over the—"

"Tomorrow," I say, and the word feels foreign in my mouth. I've never delayed a debrief. "I need sleep. We'll go over everything in the morning."

James's eyebrows climb toward his hairline. "You sure?"

"Yeah." I clap his shoulder. "Great work, everyone."

I don't miss the look that passes between my team members —surprise, maybe a little concern—but I don't care. I'm already walking toward the cabin, toward Clementine, toward something that feels more essential than any summit.

The door swings open before I reach it.

The place doesn't even look like our shabby cabin anymore. The fire's lit, throwing gold across the walls. Candles—actual candles—flicker on the window ledge. There's a hot pot in the kitchen and a tiny table by the fire with two place settings. Real plates, not the usual scratched-up camping ones. Steaks sizzle on a cast iron skillet, roasted potatoes glisten with butter and herbs, vegetables that look impossibly fresh. Next to the table sits a basket filled with chocolate, bananas, and foil.

The usual overflow of my climbing gear and research junk has vanished, replaced by something soft and domestic. Too soft for a place this remote. We're two days from the nearest supply drop, and somehow, she's made it look like home.

"Where the hell did you get candles?" I peel off my jacket and hang it on the hook by the door.

"Can't tell you all my tricks." She tries to wink but ends up scrunching her whole face instead. She's in just a pair of light pink long johns, unbuttoned down to her sternum. Her skin looks unbelievably soft. Her nipples pebble against the fabric. God, I've missed her.

"Clem." I pull her in, resting my cheek against the top of her head. "Have I told you how much I love you?"

"Not enough." Her voice is muffled against my chest before she tips up to kiss me. Then she blinks at me from beneath her thick lashes. "I know you're tired and probably just want to crash, but I thought—I mean, you've been eating freeze-dried food for three days, and since Daisy's doesn't deliver this far—" She stops, biting her lip. "But if you're too tired, I can put everything away."

"No." I hug her again. She squeaks in surprise, and I just hold her. "It's perfect. You're perfect. How did you—"

"You climbed a glacier for three days in sub-zero temperatures. I think I can figure out how to do something special for my man."

"Your man. I love the sound of that," I admit.

Her hands twist around my waist. "I wanted to take care of you the way you always take care of me."

I don't trust my voice, so I just kiss her. She melts into me, and I try to pour everything I can't say into it—gratitude, love, disbelief that this person exists, that she chose me.

When we break apart, I notice that the copper tub that used to be filled with my gear is now full of steaming water, and more candles flicker along the rim.

"You're kidding," I say.

"The water's probably getting cold." She's pulling me toward it, testing the temperature with her hand. "I heated it half an hour ago, if you wanna jump in while I finish dinner."

"You planned this because you wanted to have a show while you prepped dinner, huh?"

"Or maybe it's because I knew you'd smell like Mozart after he runs around in the rain," she jokes. "Now jump in."

"Only if you join me."

"But you're filthy."

"You've never shied away from a little dirt." I flick open another button on her long johns. "Not wearing a bra, my little fox."

"Another gift for you, I guess." She smirks. "Now get in, and maybe if you're good, I'll join you."

I clench my jaw and obey.

Now that the adrenaline's gone, exhaustion hits deep, but there's a thrum of want under it. I strip off my layers, her fingers tracing over nicks and scrapes she's cataloged before. She's seen me naked more times than I can count, but her cheeks still flush, and it makes me want her even more.

I slide into the bath with a groan that sounds indecent, but I don't care. The water bites first, then spreads heat through me, finding every ache and bruise, every place the cold got its teeth into.

"Good?" Clementine asks, settling on the floor beside the tub, her arms folded on the rim. She draws circles on my forearm with her thumb.

"If I died right now, I'd die happy."

She laughs. "Don't die yet. I made dinner."

"Right. Dinner." I let my head fall back. "Give me a minute to remember how to be human."

For a while, we're quiet. The fire pops and crackles, and outside the wind howls against the cabin walls. Everything glows —her skin, the steam, the reflection of the flames in the water.

"Tell me about the climb," she says finally.

"It was good. Clean." I open one eye to look at her.

"You gotta give me more than that. I want to hear everything." She props her chin on her arms.

So, I tell her.

The water goes cold before I'm halfway through, and she ends up bringing the steaks to the edge of the tub.

"We bivouacked halfway up the first day. Slept clipped into the wall with the wind trying to pry us off." I watch her eyes widen a little, like she's trying to imagine it. "You don't really sleep. You just drift. And what made it worse was that Nadra talked in his sleep the entire time." I chuckle, rubbing my forehead.

"That sounds terrifying," Clem says, chewing on a piece of steak, eyes wide.

"It was. But easy. Easier than I expected without Finn. I missed him, but it felt good to be out in nature like that again. And fuck the summit. I mean, you saw how blue the ice is up there." I rub her cheek. "I used to think reaching the summit was the whole point. But coming down to you—" I search for the right word. "It felt better than any peak I've ever reached."

"Alec." She's blinking fast, and I realize her eyes are wet.

"Too sappy?"

"No." She laughs, wiping her face and setting the plate aside. "It's perfect. You're perfect."

"Clementine." I give her a look. "Are you done procrastinating? Are you ready to join me?"

"You're exhausted. Your hands are pruney."

"And I'll be more exhausted if I have to get out of this tub to come get you."

She's already standing, pulling off her long johns. "You're very bossy when you're tired."

"You have no idea."

Water sloshes over the sides as she settles between my legs, her back to my chest.

"We're getting water all over our cabin."

"Who the fuck cares?" I plant a kiss on her shoulder, and she wiggles her warm body against mine with a lazy moan.

"So, Satie, what's next?" she says.

"Not enough that I just got back?"

"I know you," she teases. "I know you're planning the next one already."

She's right about that. "There's a National Geographic campaign in Kilimanjaro."

"You want me there?"

"Clem," I scold.

"Okay, yes." She shifts to kiss me. "Yes, I'll come anywhere with you and make any place a home for us."

"Whatever you want." I brush a strand of hair off her face. "You can buy as many throw pillows as you want."

"Dangerous promise."

"I trust you."

"You really shouldn't." But she's grinning. "I've already got my eye on this vintage Moroccan rug for the great room back home at the lodge. It's ridiculously expensive and completely impractical, but it would look *amazing*."

"Buy the rug."

"What about the adorable teepee dog bed I found on Etsy?"

"How would Mozart live without that?"

"Alec!"

"I'm serious. Buy the rug, get the throw pillows, get our dog whatever he needs or wants, take over the whole damn lodge again." I stroke her hair. "Make it ours. Make it home."

Home. Her. Us. The life we're building in the spaces between expeditions, in lodges and research cabins, at the dance studio and between her classes, and anywhere we can be together.

I press a kiss to her hair and close my eyes.

Tomorrow, we'll fly back to the lodge. Tonight, in this small cabin at the edge of the world, we have everything we need.

Everything.

Acknowledgments

There's a part of us that always feels like we should have it all figured out. But if writing books teaches you anything, it's that clarity is rarely the starting point; it's the result of sitting with the mess, asking the hard questions, and giving yourself room to grow.

When we started writing *Highest Point*, we were both in that in-between space—trying to understand where we were, what we wanted, and how much pressure we were willing to put on ourselves to find those answers. We've never really written from a place of hindsight. Every book we've created has come from exactly where we are in that moment, and this one is no different.

This story was born at a crossroads, of choosing what's next, of navigating the after of a friendship, of letting go of expectations and learning how to hold space for change. That's been personal for us too. Growing up, getting older, knowing each other more deeply…all of that has changed how we show up in our friendship. It's not something we talk about enough: how to prioritize our friendships, how to keep growing together when life wants to pull us apart. But we believe in doing the hard things. In choosing each other. In finding our way back, even after the mess.

Even when it's not easy.

Alec and Finn's friendship holds something sacred. Being known that deeply, for that long, is rare. But being seen for the first time by someone new—like Alec is with Clementine—has its own kind of magic. They're both lost in different ways, and they help each other find the smallest sliver of joy. And sometimes, that's everything!

As always, our stories are full of anxious, overwhelmed heroines and vulnerable, soft-hearted men. That's just what we write. It's who we are. And we're endlessly grateful that you let us tell these stories, that you read them, that you see yourself in them.

To every single one of you—thank you. Thank you for reading, for reviewing, for sharing, for being part of this. These books would still be swirling in our minds without you, tugging at our hearts, waiting to be written. But you gave them a home. You gave us a home. We can't possibly express how much that means, but if we could, we'd give every one of you four gentle head kisses and a warm thank-you whispered straight from our souls.

To our editor, Caroline A., thank you endlessly for hacking through the weeds of our first drafts and finding the flowers hidden in the tangle.

Caroline K., we're so lucky to work with someone as meticulous (and patient) as you. One day (maybe not soon) we promise to finally put our commas where they actually belong.

To our wonderful proofreader, Christine Yates, and our amazing beta team—Brooke, Isabelle, and Nicole—you've been with us through the entire Hastings series, and it's always a joy reading your notes, your jokes, and the ways you help us fall even more in love with these characters.

We love you all, truly.

Playlist

"Mountain at My Gates" by Foals
"Alaska" by Maggie Rogers
"In the Woods Somewhere" by Hozier
"When She Smiles" by Gigi Perez
"Gnossienne: No. 1" by Erik Satie, Alexandre Tharaud
"Dontcha" by The Internet
"Dangerous" by Sleep Token
"Lose My Cool" by Amber Mark
"Wild Again" by The Army, The Navy
"Ain't No Sunshine" by Bill Withers
"I Gave You All" by Mumford & Sons
"Carnival of the Animals" by Camille Saint-Saëns, Yo-Yo Ma, Kathryn Stott

About the Authors

Kels & Denise are authors, best friends, and the definition of the found family trope. The pair bonded over their love for romance and turned all their late-night chats into writing together. Their enjoyment for storytelling morphed into writing impactful love stories.

Stay in touch!

@authorkelsdenisestone

kelsdenisestone.com

Join our newsletter *The Sticky Note*

kelsdenisestone.com/the-sticky-note

Join our Patreon for exclusive content

Also By Kels & Denise Stone

<u>A Cozy Holiday</u>

Standalone Novella

THE HASTINGS SERIES:

Close Knit

Grumpy X Sunshine Romance

On Guard

Bad Boy X Good Girl Romance

Highest Point

Adventure Romance

PERKS & BENEFITS SERIES:

Water Under the Bridge

Workplace Romance

Our Scorching Summer

Friends to Lovers Romance

On Cloud Nine

Fake Dating Romance

Falling for Meadow

Small Town Romance